Praise for SPY IN A LITTLE BLACK DRESS

"SPY IN A LITTLE BLACK DRESS is such a charming and engaging story that I'm hooked. Jackie makes a terrific spy—I'll follow her to Cuba, Paris…anywhere!"

— Ellen Sussman, *New York Times* bestselling
author of *French Lessons*

"Mix spies, gangsters, Cuban revolutionaries, a treasure hunt, and a libidinous young Jack Kennedy, shake but not stir, and you have one potent historical cocktail featuring cub reporter and CIA neophyte Jacqueline Kennedy as the appealing heroine. Let's hope Maxine Kenneth keeps Jackie's adventures coming for many books to come."

— William Dietrich, author of *The Emerald Storm*

"A sexy, suspenseful, and endlessly entertaining novel that combines superior storytelling with impressive research, portraying the era, its iconic heroine, and a fascinating cast of supporting characters in a book that is clever, credible, and utterly irresistible."

— Deborah Davis, author of *Strapless: John Singer Sargent
and the Fall of Madame X*

"In SPY IN A LITTLE BLACK DRESS, Jackie B. is as feisty, fun and fashion-forward as she is fearless."

— J.J. Murphy, author of the Algonquin
Round Table Mysteries

"Pull out your little black Oleg Cassini dress and oversized sunglasses. Turn up the mambo, pour a cool minty mojito, and get ready to accompany sassy (but always chic) secret agent Jackie Bouvier on her adventures to Cold War Cuba. SPY IN A LITTLE BLACK DRESS is an entertaining page-turner about Jackie's spy escapades before she became a Kennedy."

— Susan Elia MacNeal, author of *Mr. Churchill's Secretary*
and *Princess Elizabeth's Spy*

"SPY IN A LITTLE BLACK DRESS features an ingenious conceit, a neat line in cameos, and a string of exotic locales. An inventive spy romp that's fast, playful, and fun."
 —Chris Ewan, author of *The Good Thief's Guide to Venice*

Praise for PARIS TO DIE FOR

"Great fun! Makes you want to buy big sunglasses and fly to Paris."
 —Rita Mae Brown, *New York Times* bestselling author of the Mrs. Murphy mysteries

"JFK loved Ian Fleming's creation of James Bond, so this intriguing novel may not be as far-fetched as you think."
 —Kitty Kelley, *New York Times* bestselling author of *Jackie Oh!*

"A bold book that makes you rethink one of our most beloved twentieth-century American icons."
 —Mark Medoff, Tony Award-winning playwright of *Children of a Lesser God*

"In her last year as an editor, Jacqueline Onassis was actually working on an espionage story that intersected with her own life at key points. I can imagine her paging through PARIS TO DIE FOR with a wicked smile."
 —William Kuhn, author of *Reading Jackie: Her Autobiography in Books*

"PARIS TO DIE FOR is a frothy romp through the City of Love with a determined young Jackie Bouvier. It goes down with a tickle, like a fine champagne."
 —Rebecca Cantrell, award-winning author of *A Game of Lies*

SPY IN A LITTLE BLACK DRESS

Maxine Kenneth

GRAND CENTRAL
PUBLISHING

NEW YORK   BOSTON

Grand Central Publishing
Hachette Book Group
237 Park Avenue
New York, NY 10017

www.HachetteBookGroup.com
Printed in the United States of America
RRD-C

First Edition: October 2012
10 9 8 7 6 5 4 3 2 1

Grand Central Publishing is a division of Hachette Book Group, Inc.
The Grand Central Publishing name and logo is a trademark of Hachette Book Group, Inc.

The Hachette Speakers Bureau provides a wide range of authors for speaking events. To find out more, go to www.hachettespeakersbureau .com or call (866) 376-6591.

The publisher is not responsible for websites (or their content) that are not owned by the publisher.

Library of Congress Cataloging-in-Publication Data
Kenneth, Maxine.
  Spy in a little black dress / Maxine Kenneth.—1st ed.
     p. cm.
  ISBN 978-0-446-56742-8
  1. Women spies—Fiction. 2. Americans—Cuba—Fiction. 3. Cuba—History—1933–1959—Fiction. 4. Castro, Fidel, 1926—Fiction. I. Title.
  PS3611.E667S69 2012
  813'.6—dc23

                                                              2011052225

*Dedicated to the man, who, fifty years ago,
displayed his own profile in courage as he
steered the world away from the path
of nuclear annihilation.*

May 7, 1951. Jacqueline Lee Bouvier, twenty-one years old and about to graduate from college, wrote a letter to Mary Campbell, personnel director of Condé Nast, sadly declining first prize in Vogue *magazine's prestigious Prix de Paris competition. In the letter, on file in the John F. Kennedy Library, Jacqueline states that she cannot accept a position at* Vogue *because she has been offered a "special job on a certain project" with the newly formed Central Intelligence Agency. What happened next has never been revealed . . . until now.*

Everything's legal in Havana.

—Graham Greene, *Our Man in Havana*

SPY IN A LITTLE
BLACK DRESS

PROLOGUE

Granada, Nicaragua, October 13, 1856

Maria Consuela heard the *pop-pop-pop* of musket fire coming from beyond the convent walls and knew that the day of liberation had arrived.

Today the convent gates were thrown wide open, and she and her sister novices ran out into the street, as uncharacteristically giddy as young schoolgirls on holiday, to greet the conquering heroes. There they were, the *norteamericanos*, or the filibusters, as they were known back home in America, supporters of her country's Democratic faction. They wore no uniforms, but instead a rough collection of motley outfits: swallowtail coats and middy jackets, stovepipe hats and cloth caps. Some had bandoliers strapped across their chests; others had leather or burlap ammunition pouches slung over one shoulder. All of them carried their rifles and pistols casually at their sides, raising them occasionally to shoot at the odd Legitimist sniper popping up here and there.

Joining the crowd in support of the liberators was just the excuse Maria Consuela needed to say good-bye to the convent behind whose walls she had lived for so many years, like a prisoner resigned to her fate. She had been forced by circumstance to trade one stifling existence as the dutiful daughter of middle-class parents for another as the young novitiate dedicated to Christ. And now, this liberation of her country was her chance to leave both lives behind and make a fresh start. She would never return to the convent, she promised, even if it meant becoming a *campesino*'s wife and working in the fields from dawn till dusk.

Maria Consuela and the other novices joined the joyous crowd and skipped alongside the filibusters as they marched—strolled, really—through the narrow and twisty streets of Granada, the former Legitimist stronghold. The young women pecked the soldiers daringly on the cheek as a show of thanks for freeing them from the oppressive Legitimist regime and showered them with flowers as a kind of benediction.

One very young soldier caught the flower Maria Consuela boldly threw his way, removed his cap, and put the flower in his hair. His fellow filibusters laughed at him, but he looked at Maria Consuela and winked at her, as though they were sharing a private joke. To Maria Consuela, this soldier, with his thick rimless glasses, looked more like a librarian than a member of a conquering army.

Suddenly, Maria Consuela heard the sound of a single rifle shot coming from above the street and watched as one of the soldiers fell to the ground, his chest exploding in a bright red spray of blood. She had never seen anyone killed before, and it horrified her.

A second rifle shot immediately ensued, and Maria Consuela mistook it for an echo of the first. But when a second soldier collapsed in a shattered heap, she realized just how much danger the crowd was in.

"Sniper," someone called out. And all the soldiers and their well-wishers melted away into the nearest doorways or alleyways, seeking protection from the shooter lying in wait on a rooftop overlooking the street.

Maria Consuela wanted to move to safety too, but found that her legs wouldn't let her. She was frozen in place, paralyzed by fear.

Then a third rifle shot sounded in the street, and a little spray of earth erupted right in front of her. *Something must be wrong,* Maria Consuela thought. The sniper couldn't be such a bad shot that he missed her so completely.

Before she could react, a fourth rifle shot cracked the air, and dirt from the ground spat up to her right.

A fifth, and a clod of dirt sprang up to her left.

Then, with a chill, Maria Consuela realized that the sniper wasn't a bad marksman. He was merely toying with her, using her as a staked goat in order to lure some of the soldiers out of hiding so he could finish them off. He knew that sooner or later someone would come to her aid, and then he would hit his target with deadly accuracy. Unless he got tired of waiting, at which point she was sure to become his next victim.

Maria Consuela cringed, knowing that the next breath she took might well be her last. *Please, God,* she pleaded in the throes of desperation, let me live, *and if you do, I will return to the convent and pledge the rest of my life to extolling your glory.*

But in the interval between the last rifle shot and the one sure to come, a man appeared in the street. He was diminutive in stature and wore a black frock coat with black trousers and a black, flat-brimmed hat that made him look like an undertaker or a fire-and-brimstone preacher. From a holster cinched around his waist, he whipped out a pistol and began calmly and methodically firing it up in the direction the shots had been coming from. Spurts of dust pocked the ground around him as the sniper alternated between returning the gunfire and ducking for cover. But the black-clad little man remained heedless of his own safety and refused to flinch. Instead, he just kept on firing until his pistol was empty and he was forced to reload.

With the echo of the man's last shot still reverberating in the narrow street, Maria Consuela heard a clattering sound from above and watched as the sniper's rifle rolled down the tiled roof and fell to the street. A moment later came the sniper himself. His lifeless body tumbled down the slanted roof and struck the ground within an arm's length of his weapon, landing with a resounding thud. The filibusters and their well-wishers emerged from their hiding places and approached the body to make sure that the sniper was well and truly dead.

Ignoring the dead sniper, the man in black holstered his weapon and approached Maria Consuela.

"Are you all right?" he asked her. His eyes lingered for a moment on her petite form inside her novice's habit, as if trying to assure himself that she hadn't been injured.

Maria Consuela found herself unable to speak, trembling not with fear but out of a profound sense of relief. All she could do was nod, shaking the long, dark curls that stuck out on either side of her wimple. She looked into his eyes and was surprised by their intensity. They were blue and fervent as though lit from within by a holy fire, and his riveting gaze made her feel safe. Something akin to the first stirrings of love quivered inside her, like a cocoon vibrating right before the birth of a butterfly.

"Good," the man in black said as he held out his arm for her to take.

Maria Consuela smiled at this gentlemanly gesture. Arm in arm, she accompanied him through the streets of Granada until they, along with the crowd of soldiers and their well-wishers, arrived at the large and imposing villa that was the former headquarters of the overthrown Legitimist regime.

As she stood next to him, a delegation from the Democratic faction swarmed around the little black-clad man and deluged him with gratitude.

"Oh, thank you, thank you, may God bless you for liberating our country," they said, some with tears streaming down their cheeks.

He accepted their thanks with grace and humility, but Maria Consuela had the distinct impression that he also thought of this acknowledgment as his just due, like Caesar being rightfully rendered unto.

Maria Consuela noticed a man who was holding himself apart from all the others. Hat in hand, he approached the small man in black and introduced himself.

"My name is Domingo Goicuria, and it is my honor to speak to you on behalf of the country of Cuba," he said in a deferential tone, bordering on awe. "I have traveled here to ask you to come to the aid of the Cuban people and free our island from Spanish rule."

It was then that Maria Consuela realized that this man in black, her savior, was the *generalissimo* of the *norteamericano* army of filibusters. Despite his diminutive stature, this American Napoléon had liberated her people and, inadvertently, liberated her as well. His name was William Walker, and he had changed her life forever. On the spot, she abandoned her pledge to return to the convent if she survived the sniper's bullet—a promise clearly made in a moment of foolish weakness. No, now there was no going back. Maria Consuela knew that from this moment on her life would be inextricably bound with this American, who would declare himself the new president of Nicaragua.

PART ONE

THE MEXICAN DRACULA

I

New York City, May 1951

Whether on duty or off, an agent must be aware of his surroundings at all times.

                              —CIA FIELD AGENT MANUAL

I t was a courier run.

Her instructions had been very simple. Go to New York. Pick up a package. Return with the package to Washington, D.C. Spend the day in Manhattan doing tourist things as a cover for her covert activities. But based on past experiences, if there was one thing that Jacqueline Lee Bouvier knew for certain, it was the fact that even the most simple assignment for the CIA could metamorphose into something with complications, ones that could lead to injury or even death. All she had to do was think back on her recently concluded assignment in Paris to recognize how true this was.

As she sat on the passenger train barreling north from Washington, D.C., to New York City, she acknowledged that things were slightly different now. In Paris, she had been a neophyte, completely out of her depth in the world of spies, counterspies, and assassins. Now that she was beginning recruit training at the Farm, the CIA's code name for its spy school at Camp

Peary, she had actual training to draw on. But she still had a
lot to learn and worried that a situation might come up that
she wouldn't be able to handle. At the same time, she had faith
in her natural instincts and native intelligence to get her out of
any scrape that might arise.

Once the train arrived at Pennsylvania Station, Jackie exited
the building on the Seventh Avenue side, admiring the beaux
arts architecture that made it one of the most beautiful railroad
stations she had ever been in, and that included the Gare de
Lyon in Paris. It was a beautiful spring day, and she was wearing a stylish black dress that caught the attention of many a
male passerby on the busy street.

Following directions, Jackie walked up Seventh Avenue and
found herself right in the middle of the Garment District,
where men pushed wheeled racks of clothes through the
streets at breakneck speeds, secretaries ran errands to the stac-
cato tempo of their high heels striking the pavement, and rag
merchants argued volubly right there on the sidewalk with the
intensity of Talmudic scholars. She located the address she was
searching for and entered a building that looked like it had
already been old around the time of the Draft Riot during the
Civil War. Inside, there was a cage elevator, obviously newer
than the building but still looking old and rickety, so Jackie
decided not to risk it and took the stairs instead.

On the third floor, she sought out the office in question,
knocked, and entered. The room held several battered pieces of
office furniture that looked like they might have gone a couple of
rounds with Jack Dempsey. Standing by one desk was a balding,
bulbous-nosed, middle-aged man in an ill-fitting suit. On the
desk in front of him were a pitcher of water and a bottle of seltzer.
As Jackie watched, he poured some water into a glass, then picked
up the bottle of seltzer and spritzed a little into the water, which

he stirred with a spoon. He then held up the glass to her and said, "Would you care for a two cents plain? It's very refreshing." There was the hint of an Eastern European accent to his speech.

"No, thank you," said Jackie, "I never drink seltzer. It gives me gas," wincing at the other half of the nonsensical password.

The man drank from the glass, then put it down. "This is for you," he said, opening a drawer and taking out something that he placed on the desktop for Jackie to see. Francophile that she was, she recognized the object immediately. It was a classic leather Hermès *sac à dépêches* handbag, which the company had been making since the midthirties. Was this the package she had come all this way to retrieve, Jackie wondered to herself. She could hardly believe it.

The man opened the bag to show that it was empty. "Now, please," he said, "put your bag in here."

Jackie had also been instructed to bring with her a small bag or purse. She now placed her bag inside the Hermès bag, glad to see that it fit perfectly.

The man looked intently at her. Jackie wondered if she had done something wrong. "Is there a problem?" she asked.

"Have you ever done any runway work? Because I could always use a new model. We're showing our winter line in a few weeks, and we're short a model or two."

"Sorry," Jackie said, "but I already have a job. I'm a photographer."

"Then maybe you'll come back and take photographs of our show."

"Maybe," Jackie said in as noncommittal a fashion as possible.

She picked up the Hermès bag and said, "Thank you," then headed for the door. As she turned the doorknob, the man called out to her, "Be sure not to lose it."

"I won't," said Jackie as she went through the door. Back on Seventh Avenue, she plotted her next move since her orders stipulated spending the day doing tourist things in the city, making sure to hold the bag firmly under her arm so as not to risk losing it or having it stolen.

She walked over to Fifth Avenue and headed uptown. Her first stop was Charles Scribner's Sons bookstore, where she fulfilled her tourist obligation by spending a brief time browsing. In the fiction section, she came across a mystery novel entitled *Death in the Fifth Position*, by Edgar Box, and smiled to herself. She knew that this was a pseudonym for her cousin Gore Vidal. It seemed that his second novel, *The City and the Pillar*, had scandalized the *New York Times* reviewer Orville Prescott with its frank depiction of a homosexual relationship. Prescott had placed a ban on reviewing any more books by its author. So to get around the critic's embargo and continue to earn money as a writer, cousin Gore had concocted this commercial mystery novel and arranged for it to be published under a pen name. She bought a copy, thinking it would make diverting reading on the train trip back to D.C., and dropped it into the Hermès bag.

Back on Fifth Avenue, she wondered what was inside the bag that made it so important to the CIA. Was there something hidden inside it? Top secret papers, perhaps? Or a large sum of paper money sewed into the lining? Unfortunately, she was in the dark here because she had been briefed for this assignment only on a need-to-know basis.

Suddenly, Jackie felt a slight tingling sensation and glanced casually over her shoulder. A man she had seen in the bookstore was now following her down the street, or so it seemed. He was dressed anonymously in a blue seersucker banker's suit and had an anonymous-looking face to match. But there was something about his manner that told Jackie it might be best to test out some of those evasive maneuvers she had been taught.

Fortunately, she was coming up on Saks Fifth Avenue. According to her training, department stores were excellent places in which to lose a tail. They were crowded with people and had many exits to exploit. Jackie entered the store, spent some time looking in the makeup department on the first floor, then took the elevator to the second floor to look at the new women's fashions, not that she needed to buy anything. She then went to the ladies' room to kill some time, hoping that the man, afraid of being conspicuous, would give up and move on.

After what she thought was a decent amount of time, Jackie left the security of the ladies' room and walked out of Saks, using the exit on Fiftieth Street. Back on Fifth Avenue, she passed St. Patrick's Cathedral, looking occasionally behind her for any sign of the man. She hoped that, if he had truly been following her, she had now lost him.

She headed up to Fifty-Third Street and decided to stop in at the Museum of Modern Art, where she paid her admission and spent her time there viewing a survey exhibition, *Abstract Painting and Sculpture in America*, which featured works by Mark Rothko, Willem de Kooning, Jackson Pollock, and others. Jackie found the paintings both shocking and exciting in their unusual deployment of colors and shapes that forced one to consider art—and life, for that matter—in a new light. But even more shocking was the sight of Mr. Seersucker, as she was now beginning to think of him, pretending to be gazing intently at a Franz Kline. Somehow he had managed to forestall her attempt to lose him at Saks.

With an escalation of that tingling sensation, Jackie looked at her watch while plotting her next move. It was one fifteen. She had enough time to make her way over to Times Square, where she purchased a ticket from a broker and attended a matinee performance of the sold-out musical *Guys and Dolls* at the 46th Street Theatre.

Before the house lights dimmed, Jackie's mind kept turning back to that man. Three times she had seem him in three different locations. This was obviously too much to be a coincidence. What did he want with her? Was he after the Hermès bag? Just thinking about it made her clutch the bag even tighter.

Once the curtain went up, though, she was able to forget momentarily about the anonymous-looking man and lose herself in the musical antics of those characters who sprang to life from the pages of Damon Runyon's short stories: There was hustler Nathan Detroit, scrounging to find a new location for his floating crap game, gambler Sky Masterson hoping to win a wager with Nathan by romancing the Salvation Army sergeant, Sarah Brown, and showgirl Miss Adelaide trying in frustration to get Nathan to the altar. Jackie loved the smooth and handsome Robert Alda as Sky, the earthy Sam Levene as Nathan, the comically winsome Vivian Blaine as Miss Adelaide, and the rousing Stubby Kaye as he led a room full of sinners in "Sit Down, You're Rockin' the Boat." And she thrilled when Sky whisked Sarah off to Havana for a romantic date and plied the straight-laced sergeant with "Cuban milkshakes" until she let her hair down, tipsily sang, "If I Were a Bell," and kissed him. Unfortunately, during the cast's curtain calls, her mood was spoiled when she looked several rows ahead and spotted Mr. Seersucker applauding vigorously along with the rest of the theatre audience.

After the musical was over, Jackie saw that she had more time to kill before she was due back at Pennsylvania Station. As she left the theatre, she looked around and was relieved to see that the anonymous-looking man was nowhere in sight on Forty-Sixth Street. She realized that she had skipped lunch and felt famished. Fortunately, there was a Schrafft's nearby. Jackie entered the restaurant and was surprised to find it so crowded. A hostess informed her that if she wanted to eat dinner, she would have to be seated with another party. Jackie preferred to eat alone, but her stomach insisted on being fed now, so she agreed to share a table.

She was seated with a beautiful young woman whose casual clothing—sweatshirt and black slacks; probably a denizen of Greenwich Village—belied her regal carriage. Despite her bohemian appearance, this young woman was obviously used to having the best of everything, an impression that was confirmed when she opened her mouth to speak and addressed Jackie in a voice that was pure Mainline Philadelphia.

"Hello," the young woman said.

"Hello," Jackie responded. She sat and put her Hermès bag on the edge of the table, where she could keep her eye on it. The woman was reading a book while waiting for her meal to arrive. Jackie glanced at the title and saw it was *The Philadelphia Story* by Philip Barry.

"Let me guess," Jackie said. "Tracy Lord?"

"How did you ever know?" gushed the blonde, putting down the book. "I so identify with her."

"So do I," Jackie concurred. "You look like you could play her."

"Thank you. I'd love to. If they ever revive the play. Or remake the movie."

"I'd be afraid to compete with Katharine Hepburn."

"So would I," the blonde confessed, after a brief hesitation.

"So you're an actress?" Jackie asked.

"How'd you guess?"

"That's a Samuel French edition you're reading," Jackie said, pointing to the printed play script with its distinct yellow cover.

"Guilty," said the actress, laughing. "My secret is out." Jackie noted that she even had the laugh of a true Barry heroine down pat.

"Jackie Bouvier," said Jackie, sticking out her hand.

"Grace Kelly," the actress said, taking it.

The waitress came, and after a brief perusal of the menu, Jackie ordered a toasted cheese sandwich, a salad with green goddess dressing, and an iced tea.

"So how's your career going?" Jackie asked the actress.

"It's going," the actress replied. "I've done some live TV... been directed by Delbert Mann. Oh, and I have a small role in a movie called *Fourteen Hours*."

"That's wonderful," said Jackie.

As she waited for the food to arrive, Jackie looked around and was dismayed to see Mr. Seersucker seated at a table by himself. Her heart sank at the realization that she still had to deal with him. He had lulled her into a false sense of security by not resurfacing until now. Her train of thought was derailed by a question from the actress.

"Is that an Hermès bag?" she asked.

"Yes," Jackie said, adding with a slight twinge of paranoia, "It was a gift from my favorite uncle."

"I'd love to have one of my own."

"Well, maybe one of these days..."

"Yes," the actress agreed, "when I become a famous actress."

They both laughed over that. Their dinners came and they started eating. But Jackie could barely taste her food. All she could think about was her tail, looking so calm and collected several tables away, with a pot of steaming-hot coffee just set down in front of him. She had to figure out a way to lose him once and for all. And as she took another bite of her sandwich, an idea occurred to her.

"Excuse me, Miss Kelly—"

"Call me Grace."

"All right—Grace. I'm Jackie. You see that man over there?" She directed the actress's attention to the man seated several tables from them.

"Yes?"

"He's been following me all over town this afternoon. I'm afraid he might be some kind of masher. Or worse. I have to get away from him. But that will require some assistance. Would you be willing to help me?"

"Of course," said the actress with relish. "We Tracy Lord fans have to stick together."

"Good. Now, this is what I would like you to do."

In a low voice, Jackie briefed the actress on her plan. When she was finished, she held out her hand again.

"It was very nice meeting you, Grace."

"Nice meeting you, Jackie."

"The best of luck with your acting career."

Jackie left the actress some money to pay her bill, then abruptly picked up the Hermès bag, got up from the table, and headed swiftly toward the door. It was past rush hour, and outside there were plenty of available cabs coming down the street with their roof lights on.

As Jackie scooted out the door, Mr. Seersucker stood up quickly, threw some money down on the table, then prepared to follow her.

At the same time, the actress stood up and called out to Jackie, "Oh, miss, you forgot your—"

She then rushed to the door, putting her on an interception course with the man, who was still trying to rise from the table.

As she came level with the table, the actress reached out with her hand and deliberately knocked over the coffeepot, spilling its steaming contents all over the lap of the man's trousers. He let out a scream of pain followed by a series of curses as the scalding-hot liquid soaked through the material of his trousers to his skin, his stream of invective shocking the secretaries and elderly society matrons seated around him.

Instantly he was surrounded by waitresses attempting to blot the stain with napkins taken from nearby tables. Mr. Seersucker tried to extricate himself from their grasp and fight his way through them to the door, but his struggle was in vain.

All this was observed fleetingly by Jackie through the restaurant window as she simultaneously tried to flag down a cab. A yellow Checker stopped for her with a screech of brakes, and Jackie told the driver her destination: "Pennsylvania Station."

As she glanced back through the cab's rear window, she could see the actress looking out through the restaurant window and giving her the high sign. Mission accomplished.

Arriving back at Pennsylvania Station, Jackie had plenty of time to board her train, the Congressional, for her return to D.C. Once on the train, she sat back in her seat and closed her eyes. It had been a long and exhausting day, made stressful by the strange man who had been tailing her. But she had managed to lose him and now here she was, going home with the Hermès bag still in her possession.

The train left the station on time, and through the dusk, Jackie could see the marshlands of New Jersey passing by outside the window. Suddenly, there was the reflection of another person in the glass, and Jackie whipped her head around and was shocked to see the man she thought she had lost now sitting right across from her. In the lap of his trousers was a conspicuous stain.

Mr. Seersucker caught her looking and said, "I hope you'll pay for my dry cleaning, Miss Bouvier."

Jackie's heart plummeted. The man knew who she was. Now she would have to figure out some new scheme to separate herself from him. And she was fresh out of ideas.

The man settled himself in his seat. He must have known what she was thinking. "You can relax, Miss Bouvier," he said. "I'm from the Farm. That was a clever stunt you pulled back at the restaurant. Looks like you passed your first test with flying colors."

II

Washington, D.C., May 1951

I'm as ready as I'll ever be, Jackie told herself as the front door clicked shut like an exclamation point. She drew in the early evening air filled with the fragrance of gardens in bloom and the spice of a new adventure. This was the big night. A date that Jacqueline Lee Bouvier hoped would not live in infamy. She *had* to make a good impression on Jack Kennedy when the Bartletts introduced her at their supper party, which had been arranged for that very purpose.

What Charlie and Martha Bartlett didn't know was that Jackie had met Jack Kennedy once before. As she drove away from Merrywood, her stepfather Hugh Auchincloss's Virginia estate, and headed for the Bartletts' home in Georgetown, Jackie remembered that first random meeting with the young congressman from Massachusetts. She was on a train returning to her junior year at Vassar with a classmate when Jack and his assistant invited themselves into her compartment. Their conversation was all a blur now—mostly flirtatious bantering on Jack's part and tolerant amusement on Jackie's. But what stuck in her mind was Jack Kennedy's indisputable allure. He was matinee-idol handsome, wickedly funny, and fiercely ambitious, yet charmingly shy. Back at Vassar, she had dashed off a letter to a friend, describing what an insistent flirt the congressman had been but admitting that she felt an absolute attraction to him all the same.

Now, as Jackie crossed the Chain Bridge in the 1947 black Mercury convertible given to her by her father, her pulse quickened at the thought of meeting Jack Kennedy again.

Within minutes, she pulled up in front of 3419 Q Street, the typical narrow, brick row house where the Bartletts lived. Jackie had driven with the convertible's top up so her hair wouldn't get mussed, but she didn't bother locking the car. Georgetown, the oldest neighborhood in Washington, D.C., was a safe one. Besides, if the car did get stolen, her mother would be thrilled. She thought that a convertible was unsafe and had been badgering Jackie's stepfather to buy her a Buick sedan. The fact that the convertible had belonged to Black Jack—her mother's philandering ex-husband, who still made her blood boil more than a decade after their divorce—was an even bigger strike against it.

At the front door, Jackie smoothed out the Dior outfit that she'd bought in Paris, took a deep breath, and announced her arrival with the brass knocker.

"Hi, Jackie, we've been waiting for you," Charlie Bartlett said, smiling broadly as he opened the door and gave her a quick peck, appropriate for an old flame who was now a married man with a baby on the way.

"I'm not late, am I?" Jackie asked.

"No, no, you're right on time," Charlie said, squeezing her hand in a way that reminded her of their dates two and a half years ago. Jackie had been an impressionable nineteen-year-old college student then, and he was a twenty-seven-year-old wunderkind journalist who had opened the first Washington bureau for the *Chattanooga Times*, a sister paper of the *New York Times*. Their romance fizzled when Charlie said that he could never give Jackie the exciting high life she coveted, but now he was determined to find a more appropriate suitor for her. Who better than Jack Kennedy, one of Charlie's closest friends and the most eligible bachelor in Washington?

A year had gone by since Charlie had married his perfect mate—Martha Buck, the daughter of a wealthy steel mogul—and now he wanted to help Jackie find the same marital bliss with Jack Kennedy. Little did he know that Allen Dulles, deputy director of the CIA, was even more eager for the two to hit it off.

For a moment, Jackie saw herself back in Dulles's office receiving her assignment, and she again heard his cajoling voice speaking to her about Jack Kennedy. "We're not asking you to marry him," Dulles said. "We would just like you to go out with him a few times and use your considerable beauty and intelligence to persuade him to become a friend of the CIA." Jackie felt a pang of conscience. *What would the Bartletts think if they knew the real reason why I'm here?*

"Let me introduce you to everyone," Charlie said, cutting into Jackie's thoughts and leading her into the living room. Guests were milling around in the small room, which was modestly decorated with a pair of antique armchairs, some inexpensive furniture, and a few nondescript prints on the ivory-colored walls.

Jackie turned to Charlie and gave him an anxious look. "Is he here?" she whispered.

"No, Jack hasn't come yet," Charlie whispered back, "but he's always late."

Martha Bartlett, a visibly pregnant redhead, emerged from the kitchen with a glass of wine in one hand and a cigarette aloft at a jaunty angle in the other.

"Jackie, you look divine," she said, air kissing her on both cheeks, European-style. She turned to her husband. "Charlie, why don't you fix Jackie a drink, and I'll do the introductions."

A quick glance around the room told Jackie that Martha had invited the usual crowd of young, up-and-coming socialite couples who frequented the Clambake Club in Newport and wintered in Palm Beach. The only one who stood out was a beautiful, slim young woman who apparently had come to the party alone.

"And this is Loretta Sumers. She's an accessories editor at *Glamour* magazine and an old Long Island schoolmate of mine," Martha said, introducing Jackie.

"So nice to meet you, Loretta," Jackie said with a tight smile. *Uh-oh, I know who you are. You're the extra woman who's here in case Jack Kennedy doesn't think that I'm his cup of tea.* She couldn't help wondering, cattily, if *Glamour* paid for Loretta to get those fashionable blond highlights in her light brown hair and where Jackie could get hers streaked the same way.

Martha prattled away about how Loretta's family had such fun socializing with the Kennedys every winter in Palm Beach. Jackie listened politely, but when she heard that Loretta's nickname was Hickey, she almost laughed out loud. Then, imagining how Loretta might have come by that moniker and fearing that she would be competing for Jack Kennedy's attention, Jackie fell victim to a sharp stab of self-doubt.

At that moment, the door burst open, and John Fitzgerald Kennedy made his entrance.

He still looks so young, Jackie thought, more like a teenager than a three-term congressman about to be thirty-four in a couple of weeks. He couldn't have weighed more than 150 pounds and had to be at least six feet tall, so he looked as if he were still growing. His haystack of reddish brown hair, toothy smile, and twinkling periwinkle eyes added to the boyish impression. So did the careless way he dressed. *Someone will have to do something about his clothes,* Jackie mused, eyeing the shapeless, too-big sports jacket and unpressed, too-short trousers dangling gracelessly around his ankles. But his overall effect was that of a genial force of nature—a magnetic field of charisma that drew everyone to him irresistibly and captivated them with his charm.

Jack immediately began working the room, inquiring how this person's sailboat did in Nantucket's Figawi race and how that person's trip to Acapulco had gone and when another person's cousin who was serving in the Korean War was coming home. Jackie was amazed at the almost encyclopedic knowledge Jack had about each guest. Even more impressive was his satiric sense of humor and hilarious impersonations of people in the news (everyone from President Truman to a Mafia gangster), which had them all laughing.

Finally, Martha extricated Jackie from her perch on a love seat in a corner, where she'd been observing the scene like a bird-watcher, and brought her over to the life-of-the-party congressman.

"Jack, I'd like you to meet Jacqueline Bouvier," Martha said, tapping him on the shoulder.

"The *lovely* Jacqueline Bouvier," he said, looking at Jackie with interest and flashing his intoxicating smile. "Pleased to meet you, Jacqueline."

"The pleasure is mine," Jackie said, batting her eyelids at him demurely and returning his smile. "Actually, we've met before."

"We have?"

His look of surprise told Jackie that by this time, she had probably disappeared into a faceless crowd of college girls, secretaries, models, actresses, and other assorted females Jack had flirted with instinctively.

"Yes, it was on a train…"

Suddenly, Loretta Sumers was tugging on Jack's sleeve. "Oh, Jack, there's something I need to speak with you about," she said, adding as she glanced at Jackie, "Do you mind?" Without waiting for an answer, Loretta led Jack away. He looked back at Jackie and shrugged, unable to get out from the insistent Hickey's talon-like grasp.

Jackie retreated to her refuge on the love seat, feeling defeated by a score of Loretta, 1; Jackie, 0.

But within moments, Jack was back. With athletic grace, he slipped into the empty seat beside Jackie. "So tell me something about yourself, Jacqueline," he said. Displaying the inquisitiveness that he was known for, he started asking her questions. Where did she go to school? What was her degree in? Had she done any traveling lately? Did she have a job?

Jackie answered all his questions without revealing anything about herself that she didn't want him to know—she had a degree in French literature from George Washington University; yes, she'd just returned from Paris (on a pleasure trip, not a CIA assignment); and she would soon be starting work as the Inquiring Camera Girl for the *Times-Herald*.

This last piece of information seemed to pique Jack's interest. "Really? The *Times-Herald*? Have you been following their coverage of the House Un-American Activities Committee? And of Joe McCarthy in the Senate?"

Jackie wrinkled her nose at Jack's mention of this zealous anti-Communist crusade. The blacklisting of writers, actors, directors, and musicians whose work she loved was unconscionable to her. "I think there's something creepy about a fanatic like Senator McCarthy," she said. "Anyone who works with him has to be a malicious goon who enjoys persecuting the most talented people in the country."

Jack started as if blindsided, then quickly recovered his usual aplomb. "I'll tell my brother Bobby that," he said, his lips curled in an ironic half smile. "Bobby is a staff lawyer for Joe McCarthy's Permanent Subcommittee on Investigations."

"Oh." Jackie gulped and felt her cheeks grow flaming hot. She studied her drink, wishing she could take back her words and drown them there.

Once again, Martha Bartlett saved her, announcing that dinner was being served. "Take your places, everyone," she called out, pointing to the table, which was set with place cards and china.

Naturally, Martha had arranged for Jackie to be seated next to Jack. *This is going to be horrible,* Jackie thought. He probably won't say another word to me all night.

But Jack surprised her. He gave her an admiring look as he pulled out her chair and said with a smile in his voice, "I like a woman who speaks her mind."

Whew! Jackie felt like a death row inmate whose sentence had been commuted, but she didn't know if Jack really meant the comment or was just being polite. *Play it safe,* she warned herself, *and let him do the talking from now on.*

While Jack tore into the chicken casserole that the cook had prepared, Jackie hardly ate. She was intent on following her father's expert mating-game instruction to pay attention to everything a man says. "Fasten your eyes on him like you were staring into the sun," he had told her. But he had also warned her to be inaccessible and mysterious, claiming that once a man possesses a woman, he loses interest in her automatically.

So Jackie hung on every word that Jack said, fixing her large brown eyes on him as if mesmerized, her lips slightly parted, as she responded with an overawed "golly" or "gee" in a whispery, little-girl voice to Jack's monologue. He spoke about what a close-knit family the Kennedys were and how his father had tapped him to fill the empty shoes left by his older brother, Joe, when he had been killed in the war. And although Jackie gave the impression that she found Jack utterly captivating, she remembered what Black Jack had told her about being untouchable. Whenever Jack leaned in too close or put his hand on hers, she politely pulled away.

Jackie's performance was so convincing that everyone else in the room seemed to have disappeared. She needn't have worried about competition from Hickey Sumers (she was the one who looked defeated now) or any other woman there—Jack had eyes only for her. Jackie's intense adulation leavened with a pinch of coquettishness seemed to impel Jack to drop a politician's natural instinct for guarding his privacy. Over dessert and coffee, he confided in Jackie that he was bored with being a congressman and was thinking of challenging Henry Cabot Lodge, the Republican junior senator from Massachusetts, in the coming election.

Jackie wasn't sure how she should respond to this revelation—somehow "golly" and "gee" didn't seem adequate—when Martha stood up from the table and said, "Come on, everyone, it's time for charades."

Oh no, I was doing so well, Jackie thought, when she discovered that she and Jack were on opposing teams. She knew from his history as a war hero and winner of tough political campaigns that Jack was a competitor to be feared. A little tremor of apprehension coursed through her when she imagined making such a complete fool of herself that he might never want to see her again.

"You *didn't,*" she said to Jack when she unfolded the paper he'd handed her and saw the name scribbled on it: Henry Cabot Lodge. Was she a sparring partner for Jack's potential bout with the senator? She felt like slinking off to the powder room, but the teasing grin on Jack's face got her dander up, and an idea came to her that she had to try.

She put her arms out at her sides, began waving them, and mouthed the sounds of clucking. "Chicken," someone on her team shouted. Jackie shook her head and brought her hands toward each other in a shortening motion. "Hen," another team member shouted. Jackie nodded encouragingly, then made a stretching motion. "Henna...henpeck...Henry," someone else called out.

Jackie nodded an emphatic "yes."

Then she depicted a big box with a line down the middle and a knob on each side. "Door," someone shouted. Jackie shook her head. "Closet," someone else called out. Again Jackie shook her head. "Armoire," said another, and they all laughed as Jackie rolled her eyes. Then Charlie Bartlett, who was on her team, shouted, "Cabinet." Jackie nodded and brought her hands together as if squeezing something. And Charlie said, "Cab...cabin..." Jackie nodded hard, and Charlie finally shouted, "Cabot! Henry Cabot Lodge!"

"Oh, yes, thank you!" Jackie said. She wanted to kiss Charlie when she caught the admiring look that Jack gave her. But then she glanced at her watch and gasped. It was nine thirty, almost time for her to be meeting John Husted for a nightcap at the Georgetown Inn. She desperately wanted to break up with John and was hoping that she'd have the courage to do it tonight.

"You're leaving so soon?" Jack asked with disappointment in his voice as Jackie made her round of good-byes.

"I'm sorry, but I have to," she said, softening her insistence with a smile.

As she started walking toward the door, Jackie saw Loretta

Sumers come bounding toward Jack, eager to move in and take her place.

Not on your life, Jackie thought. She turned back to Jack and gave him an inviting look. "If you'd like to walk me to my car, that would be wonderful."

"Of course," Jack said, leaping up from his chair and linking his arm in hers, while a sullen-looking Loretta Sumers was stranded in her tracks.

When they reached Jackie's black Mercury convertible parked in the middle of the block, Jack asked, "Would you like to go someplace for a drink, Jackie?"

He was smiling at her, but he had a predatory look in his silver-blue eyes. It was the same look that Jackie had seen her father give a woman when he was sizing her up to see how fast he could get her into bed.

The womanizer once-over, Jackie thought and looked away. "Uh...I don't know...," she stammered. *Do I have a headache? Do I have to get up early?* As she frantically searched for an excuse, she absentmindedly yanked the car door open.

And to her shock, a body fell half out of the car, like a corpse making its entrance in a mystery melodrama.

It was John Husted!

"Hey, Jacks," he said, to her complete and utter humiliation, "who's your friend?"

Allen Dulles sat behind his desk, puffing on his Kaywoodie, his face expressionless as he listened to Jackie's account of her meeting with Jack Kennedy the night before.

"Everything was going along swimmingly, just as we had planned, when out of the blue, there was my boyfriend," she said, "and I can tell you, Jack Kennedy didn't take it any too kindly." Slumped in a chair across from Dulles, she sounded like a dazed accident victim describing the catastrophe to the police.

Jackie shuddered as she recalled how badly the evening had ended. A rudely awakened Husted explained to her that he was walking along Q Street, saw her car parked there, decided to wait for her in it, and fell asleep. As for Jack, he hadn't bothered to hang around for an explanation. He merely gave Jackie a withering look and slunk off into the night in a mist of bruised ego.

Jackie was beside herself. Leave it to good old dependable John Husted to show up at the most inopportune time and turn such auspicious beginnings into a fiasco. She sighed and looked at Dulles with a pained expression. "If only I had locked the car, that never would have happened."

Dulles nodded. "That's a good lesson learned," he said evenly.

Jackie stiffened, expecting him to reprimand her, but instead, Dulles smiled at her in an avuncular way and said, "Cheer up, Jacqueline. This may turn out to be a bit of serendipity."

"What do you mean?" Jackie asked.

"For a man like Jack Kennedy, nothing is a bigger aphrodisiac than competition," Dulles said with a chuckle. "You'll hear from him again. I guarantee it."

III

Jackie's heart skipped a beat when she picked up the phone and heard a vibrant man's voice with an unmistakable Boston accent say, "Hello, Jacqueline, this is Jack Kennedy. I hope I'm not calling too early, but I wanted to reach you before I got tied up in Congress all day."

What a shrewd judge of character Allen Dulles is, Jackie thought, as she remembered her CIA boss assuring her that she'd hear from Jack again. But the very next day at nine in the morning? From what she'd seen, an indifferent nonchalance was the secret of Jack Kennedy's success as a roué. So Dulles had been right when he predicted that John Husted's appearance out of the blue would ignite a competitive spark in Jack.

"No, you're not calling too early," Jackie reassured him. "In fact, I was just getting ready to take my horse Sagebrush out for a morning ride. The grounds at Merrywood are gorgeous this time of year with everything in bloom."

"Not as gorgeous as the lady on horseback will be, I venture to say."

He wakes up flirting, Jackie thought, but all she said was, "You're very kind."

"Well, I understand that you're quite the horsewoman," Jack said, "but as a Democrat, I'm afraid the donkey is more my speed. Some of my political enemies might say that's because I'm such an ass myself."

"I hardly think that's true," Jackie responded with a chuckle. Jack's self-deprecating humor was a refreshing change from all the braggadocio that she heard at Merrywood, where her step-father's circle of Washington's power brokers frequently gathered to hold forth on their latest accomplishments like talking billboards.

"Actually, I'm allergic to horses, strange as that might seem," Jack said, "so I have a different idea. How would you like to go dancing in the Blue Room at the Shoreham Saturday night?"

"Oh, Jack, I'd love to," Jackie said, forgetting not to sound overeager, as her father had warned her against when a gentleman caller asked her out for a date. But she was genuinely pleased. The Blue Room was the city's swankiest nightclub, drawing stars as big as Judy Garland, and the Shoreham was the most famous hotel in Washington. Senators, congressmen, and diplomats lived there; presidential inaugural balls took place there; and President Truman often came there for his regular poker game. Perle Mesta, Washington's "Hostess with the Mostest," held social gatherings at the Shoreham, and Jackie herself had gone to many a society dance, school prom, debutante's coming-out party, and wedding in its regal ballroom. Jack Kennedy had picked the perfect place for their first night on the town.

It was now a beautiful Friday morning in late spring, cool for that time of year, and Jacqueline Lee Bouvier was enjoying the weather by taking a stroll through the streets of Georgetown. She was glad to have the time off from her training at the Farm. Her mind was stuffed to bursting with all of the information she had learned in Escape and Evasion, Flaps and Seals, and Codes and Ciphers, and her body was stiff from daily bouts of calisthenics and running the obstacle course. With all this behind her for the week, she was looking forward to a civilized lunch with Charlie Bartlett, who had promised to fill her in on the elusive Mr. Kennedy.

Hearing a man nearby speak into an open phone booth with a distinct Boston accent, Jackie turned, thinking it might actually be Jack Kennedy. But when she got a look at the man, she was disappointed to see that the Boston accent belonged to someone else. *That Jack Kennedy,* she thought, giving the devil his due—*so dangerously attractive, he could get under a girl's skin.* But she knew it was her job to get under *his* skin, and she was hoping that Charlie Bartlett would provide her with the insights she needed to do just that.

She loved walking down Wisconsin Avenue in the heart of Georgetown, with its quaint shops and wonderful restaurants, including her favorite, Au Pied de Cochon, which resembled nothing less than a Paris bistro that just so happened to be plunked down in a Washington, D.C., neighborhood. Next to the restaurant was another one of her favorite Georgetown locations, an antiquarian bookstore that was filled with hidden literary treasures. Early for her luncheon date with Charlie, Jackie decided to stop in there for a leisurely browse through the stacks.

The tinkling bell over the doorway announced her arrival to the shop's owner, a tweedy man with owlish glasses and a neatly trimmed Vandyke, who stood behind a counter, removing archaic books from a wooden crate.

"Hello, Miss Bouvier," he said. "What can I do for you today? I just got a very rare first edition of *The Old Curiosity Shop.* It's in excellent condition."

Jackie looked sufficiently impressed, then said, "Sounds like it's too rich for my blood. I'm just a poor working girl. I was wondering, though, if you have any books on Cuba."

Although she was searching for nothing in particular, she thought it might be helpful to pick up a book on Cuba, since this was where her next CIA assignment would be. She knew that there had to be more to that Caribbean island than rum, sugar, the mambo, and Desi Arnaz, that cute Cuban bandleader who had successfully teamed with former MGM beauty Lucille Ball to star in the popular television series *I Love Lucy*.

The owner pointed her to a small section near the back of the shop, and Jackie began to browse the shelves, forgetting all about her recent problems and becoming lost in a place that seemed to have more in common with Dickensian London than with 1950s Washington, D.C. And then, as usually happened while she was immersed in this world of paper and glue and musty smells and dust, one title in particular seemed to rise and float in front of her eyes. This one announced, *A Recent History of Cuba*.

As though under a spell cast by the book, Jackie's hand reached out and plucked it off the shelf. She opened it and laughed to herself. This book had been printed in 1855. Recent, indeed! Although she doubted that there was anything in it relevant enough to add to her current store of knowledge on the subject, Jackie impulsively decided to purchase the book. She took it to the counter, where the owner, acting like a proper English bookshop proprietor, wrapped the book in brown paper and tied it with twine before handing the package to Jackie and taking her money.

Still early for her luncheon date with Charlie, Jackie entered Au Pied de Cochon next door. There she ordered a glass of wine and waited for her friend while examining her new purchase.

Seated at a table where she could watch the great parade of pedestrian traffic pass by, Jackie tore away the brown paper and twine from her parcel. She opened the cover and was surprised to find a bookplate that read PROPERTY OF WASHINGTON COLLEGE. Jackie knew that this was the original name of Washington and Lee University, after the general who provided the initial financial impetus for the institution, George Washington. There was no WITHDRAWN FROM CIRCULATION stamp anywhere on the book, meaning that it had been either illegally removed from the college library or checked out and never returned.

Jackie leafed through the book. The pages were yellowed with age, but the book itself was in surprisingly immaculate condition for one so old. As she looked through it, though, something curious happened. The endpapers at the front of the book popped open and several folded-up pages fluttered out and landed on the table in front of her.

What was this? Jackie put down the book and picked up the pages and unfolded them. They were as yellowed as those in the book, unlined and covered with minuscule handwriting. The author of these pages was obviously intent on writing as much as possible within the confines of the small page.

Jackie quickly looked through them, admiring the writer's neat penmanship. She then started from the beginning and began to read the pages, which she quickly determined were portions of a diary. She turned to the last page, but the name of the diarist appeared to be absent.

The waiter set her glass of wine down in front of her, but Jackie was so caught up in the diary that she didn't notice.

As she skimmed its pages, several individual entries popped out at her:

...February 24th, 1855...a great day. I have joined William Walker's army of filibusters and will soon take part in the invasion of Nicaragua.

...July 13th, 1855...glory hallelujah, we are victorious. We marched through the streets of Granada, greeted by the locals as conquering heroes. One young girl came up and threw a flower at me. I put it in my hair and marched on, warmed by the reception I and my fellow filibusters received...

...[undated]...I have been introduced to Our Lady of the Flower. Her name is Maria Consuela. The introduction was made by the Great Man himself. To my surprise, Maria Consuela, who left the convent on the day of liberation, is now the mistress of William Walker. I guess he mourns no more for the dead fiancée he left behind, buried in their native New Orleans...

...[undated]...the Great Man has become too powerful and his recent rulings have made many powerful enemies back in the U.S. of A., including his chief financial supporter, Cornelius Vanderbilt. I fear that our days in this country are now numbered.

...April 30th, 1857...it is late at night and I find myself a partner in a momentous secret undertaking. Knowing of my friendship with Maria Consuela, the Great Man has charged me with the responsibility of spiriting her out of Nicaragua

and escorting her to safety in Cuba. The Americans will be landing on the morrow with express orders to place Walker under arrest. Under cover of darkness, I will flee with Maria Consuela and the Great Man's treasure to Cuba. I will pray for a moonless night.

…[undated]…we have landed safety in Cuba. I wonder how the Great One is faring back in Granada. Whatever his fate, his treasure is safe here. I will mark its location with a map. Once I have ascertained that Maria Consuela is safe, too, I shall endeavor to return to the U.S. of A., where I hope to resume my career as a professional soldier.

Jackie was surprised to find that there was a small gap in the dates until the unnamed diarist picked up his account again. But there was no time to read them because here was Charlie, on time for their lunch. She put the book and the diary pages away in her pocketbook and rose to greet Charlie. Finding out the unnamed diarist's fate would have to wait.

"One thing you need to know about Jack Kennedy is that as soon as he has a woman, he loses interest," Charlie Bartlett told Jackie over lunch. "The chase is everything to him, the challenge of getting the woman to say yes, and then he's off to the next one. He has a voracious sexual appetite; it's like Chinese food—an hour after a meal, he's hungry again."

Jackie glanced around the room, hoping that no one in the crowd of politicos in conservative suits and dowagers in tasteful outfits had overheard Charlie. She didn't want anyone to know that she was having lunch with him so that he could brief her in preparation for her date with Jack Kennedy. When she expressed concern that they might bump into Jack at the popular Au Pied de Cochon, Charlie had assured her that the congressman always brought his lunch in a brown paper bag to the Cannon House Office Building. "Sometimes, the security guards mistake him for a tourist and try to stop him from going up to his office," Charlie had told her, laughing.

Jackie had to laugh too. "Bringing his lunch in a brown paper bag to the office doesn't sound like much of a ladies' man," she said.

"Well, he's not the kind of ladies' man who romances a woman, takes her out to lunch, sends her flowers, or writes love notes to her. He's a Don Juan type—the kind of rake that women find irresistible. In that respect, he takes after his father." Charlie carefully buttered his chunk of baguette and gave Jackie a questioning look. "You've heard about Joe Kennedy and Gloria Swanson, haven't you?"

Jackie nodded. It seemed that all of Washington knew about Joe Kennedy's scandalous affair with the famous actress, whom he had met years ago when he was a Hollywood producer. Tongues were still wagging about how Joe would bring his mistress into the family home in Hyannis Port and make love to her there while his kids were around and his peripatetic wife, Rose, was shopping in Paris or praying in a shrine in Rome.

"It's odd, but Jack's father always wanted him to be privy to his extramarital affairs," Charlie said, pausing to take a bite of his coq au vin and a swallow of his pinot noir. "Joe would give him an explicit description of every woman he slept with, and when Jack got older, Joe constantly talked about exchanging girls with him."

Jackie picked at her salad niçoise and pretended to be shocked, but her own father had exhibited a similar predilection, drawing her into his lecherous affairs as a confidante when she was a child. Black Jack even told his little daughter how he had slipped away from her mother on their honeymoon while sailing to England on the *Aquitania* and had made love with heiress Doris Duke. Whenever Jackie was alone with him, her father would point out different women and ask her which one she thought he should seduce. *At least Jack Kennedy and I have something in common,* she thought.

"But when it comes to marriage," Charlie informed her, "Jack doesn't want a girl who's an 'experienced voyager,' as he puts it."

Jackie smiled. "You mean he wants a virgin?" she asked, recognizing the "experienced voyager" reference from a collection of Lord Byron's journals and letters. "That's a quaint way of putting it. I didn't know Jack was so literary."

"Oh, he's as avid a reader as you are, Jackie," Charlie said. "He plays it down, but he's as well schooled in the classics as he is in historical and political works. He was very sickly as a child—still has a serious back problem—and was bedridden a lot of the time, so he buried his nose in books."

Another thing we have in common, Jackie thought, remembering how books became her refuge from unpleasantness when she was growing up. To escape from violent brawls between her drunken father and enraged mother, Jackie would retreat to a room with floor-to-ceiling bookcases and read anything that she could get her hands on—Chekhov, George Bernard Shaw, Byron, and *Gone with the Wind*, which she had read three times by the age of eleven. It surprised her that Jack Kennedy had also enjoyed a privileged childhood in many ways, but not the rosy one that most people assumed.

"I wouldn't have guessed Jack was such a lonely bookworm as a boy," she told Charlie. "He seemed so outgoing and self-confident at the party and had such presence. It was amazing."

"He's worked hard to develop that persona, believe me," Charlie said. "When I first met him in Palm Beach right after the war, we were both shy young navy veterans who came from rich Catholic families and were trying to climb the Mount Everest of WASP high society. Jack's looks, charm, and spunk have taken him a long way, but the family carried the stigma of being Irish Catholic 'riffraff.' That's why Rose was so obsessed with neatness and propriety. She made her children pass inspection like the toughest drill sergeant in the army."

Sounds like my mother, Jackie thought. Like Rose, Janet had struggled in vain to gain full acceptance into the higher echelons of the WASP world, even inventing an aristocratic southern lineage for herself to cover the fact that she was the daughter of a rough-hewn businessman. Driven to measure up, Jackie's mother sought perfection in her Porthault sheets, gourmet meals, and ball gowns. And she would not let Jackie out of the house unless every stitch of her clothes was in perfect shape—the same kind of exacting standards that Jack's mother had imposed on him and against which he apparently had rebelled. The more Charlie talked about Jack, the more Jackie thought that she and the congressman might be kindred souls.

One thing that the two of them did not have in common was money. Charlie had previously let it slip that when Jack had turned twenty-one, he had begun to receive income from several trust funds that totaled ten million dollars. "Jackie, that's *a million dollars a year,*" Charlie had said in awe. That was *real* money, as Janet liked to call it, especially impressive compared to Jackie's total inheritance of three thousand dollars from her paternal grandfather and her allowance of fifty dollars a month from her nearly destitute father.

But Jackie didn't want to talk about Jack's money. She was more interested in finding out some specifics about his political leanings. It would be terrible if she committed another faux pas like her outspoken attack on Senator Joe McCarthy, not knowing that Jack's brother Bobby worked with him.

"I'm just wondering, Charlie," she broached the subject, "do you think Jack will care that my stepfather is such a staunch Republican?"

"Oh no, Jack's not a wild-eyed liberal," Charlie said, wiping his lips with his napkin as he finished his meal. "He's a very pragmatic congressman who knows how to work both sides of the aisle. Jack is a new breed of politician, more flexible and open-minded than the stalwarts, and he's not as self-serving as his father. I think Jack really cares about people who are less fortunate, not just in our country, but in other parts of the world too. You know, he'll soon be off to Southeast Asia as part of a seven-week trip around the world. It's not just a pleasure trip. He wants to get a better understanding of the conflicts that are happening in the underdeveloped world."

"That's admirable," Jackie said, genuinely impressed.

"It is, and if you ask me, Jack's sympathies are with the underdog, the new nations that are revolting against the old authoritarian ones." Charlie smiled. "Jack is a rich man's son—a patrician, you might say—but he's a rebel at heart."

Jackie was starting to like the character emerging from Charlie's description more and more. She could identify with Jack's desire to break free of the Old Guard's narrow-mindedness and rigidity—it was the same battle she was waging with her mother. And fresh from her assignment in Paris, where she'd helped a princess save her small country from being carved up by more powerful neighbors, she felt for the underdog too.

Charlie's mention of incipient rebellions against the old totalitarian order gave Jackie an opening to bring up the situation in Cuba. She wondered if Jack knew anything that could help her with her upcoming CIA mission, and she was curious to hear if Jack's sympathy for the downtrodden extended to the plight of the poor there.

She approached the subject casually. "If Jack is so interested in political dissent, why doesn't he visit Cuba?" she asked, after taking the last bite of her salad. "There are always newspaper reports about unrest there, and it's a lot closer than Southeast Asia."

Charlie laughed. "When Jack goes to Cuba, it'll be to see a live sex show or to have a private romp at one of the hotels," he said. He shook his head and rolled his eyes. "Jack hasn't stopped talking about that since a senator friend of his came back raving and offered to go there with him and show him around."

Jackie was sorry she'd asked. Whatever Jack Kennedy did with other women was his business. All she was interested in, as far as the congressman was concerned, was carrying out the task Dulles had assigned her to do: persuade Jack to become a friend of the CIA. But Jack Kennedy was a fascinating man, and she had to admit that she was looking forward to their date Saturday night with the kind of anticipation that could get a girl in trouble if she wasn't careful.

After lunch with Charlie, Jackie saw that the day was still delightfully temperate, so she decided to prolong her visit to Georgetown and take a walk over to the C&O Canal Towpath. She walked down Wisconsin, past the bustling intersection where the avenue met M Street—the epicenter of Georgetown activity. To her right was the campus of Georgetown University, and to her left, in the distance, could be found the White House. When she reached the towpath, she strolled along it until she found a nice empty bench overlooking the Potomac River, one of the best locales in the District to appreciate this beautiful day.

Once again, Jackie took out the book and the diary pages and began to read them where she had left off. Truth to tell, as excited as she had been to hear Charlie expound on the subject of Jack Kennedy, there was something in the back of her mind that kept returning to the unknown diarist and wondering what the rest of his pages would disclose about his fate.

She read on:

...April 15th, 1861...The President has declared war on the South. We will soon take these Johnny Rebs to the woodshed, and wherever we march we expect to leave a carpet of blood-soaked Butternut in our wake...

...September 12th, 1862...we have taken the fight to the enemy. This is where it all began, where John Brown's body lies a-moldering in his grave. Let us pray that his ghost stirs this night to put the fright into the Johnny Reb.

...May 15th, 1864...we have met the enemy and they are—children...in the valley of the Shenandoah...This war has become sickening to me. And yet, we must fight on because our cause is just.

...July 29th, 1864...I have just come from the tunnel, where our sappers have almost finished their labor. A premonition has come to me: When we go into battle on the morrow, I fear that my life will be ended, but whether by rebel ball or bayonet I am yet to know. I have taken precautions and hidden these incriminating diary pages in this book,

*which I have liberated from the Washington College library.
Its title reminded me of Maria Consuela. I am afraid that
being a library thief has been the least of my crimes, which I
expect to pay for when tomorrow's day dawns. The treasure
map I will place elsewhere for safekeeping. May God have
mercy on my immortal soul...*

Jackie turned the page over. With a chill, she saw that it was
blank, an indication that the unnamed diarist's prophecy had
probably come true. She was disappointed to realize that now
she would never know what happened to this nameless Civil
War soldier and Nicaraguan filibuster, whatever that was. And
this William Walker, who was he? He was a historical figure
that she was not familiar with.

Carefully, she folded up the diary pages and put them back
inside the book. She then rewrapped the book and placed it
inside her handbag. Something from those diary entries called
out to her. Cuba and Walker's treasure, and some kind of map
showing the location of the treasure. It was like a half century
of dust and cobwebs had been shaken off and the dead had
come back to life to tap her on the shoulder.

As though a fire had suddenly been lit under her, Jackie
leaped off the bench and ran back up to M Street in search of
a pay phone. She found an empty booth, picked up the phone,
dropped a nickel into the slot, and dialed a familiar number.
When the operator answered and said, "Central Intelligence
Agency," Jackie responded, with a note of urgency in her voice,
"Allen Dulles, please."

IV

Jackie stood above the battle. From her vantage point, she could see the soldiers in blue crouched behind boulders and fallen tree limbs or inside depressions dug into the ground with their entrenching tools. They were poised, muskets raised and pointed at the soldiers in gray as they came charging up the hill with barely any cover to protect them. As she observed the scene, Jackie was only too glad that she was a woman and very unlikely to ever find herself in this kind of predicament.

A voice from behind her left shoulder startled her out of her reverie.

"It's Thursday, July second, the second day of the battle of Gettysburg. About five o'clock in the afternoon. The Twentieth Maine, under the command of Colonel Joshua Lawrence Chamberlain, is taking a stand here at Little Round Top." The speaker pointed to where the men in blue were hunkered down about halfway down the slope of the hill. "And the Confederate forces, the Fifteenth Alabama, under the command of Colonel William C. Oates, are charging up the hill. But instead of defending his position, Colonel Chamberlain orders his men to fix bayonets and counterattacks down the hill. The result is a complete rout of the Johnny Reb."

The narrator of this description was tall and reed thin and

wore a suit that seemed permanently wilted from the heat. Curly haired and bearded, he spoke with a thick Brooklyn accent that seemed foreign in this southern setting. His name was Charles Grimsby, and he was Tulane University's resident expert on William Walker. He was also, judging from the tabletop battlefield set up in his dining room, a Civil War buff.

Here, the entire Battle of Little Round Top was being replayed with cast-lead soldiers placed on an immaculate miniature landscape in which every tree, bush, stream, and rock seemed to have been magically shrunk down to scale and transported from Gettysburg, Pennsylvania, to Professor Grimsby's dining room.

As Grimsby moved around Jackie and began repositioning some soldiers on the field of battle, she thought back on the whirlwind forty-eight hours that had preceded her presence here.

From M Street, after excitedly phoning Dulles to tell him of her discovery of the diary and the map, she had returned to Merrywood, where she made a series of other calls. First, when she found out that Grimsby was the curator of the Walker Collection at Tulane, she phoned him and made an appointment to meet the professor at his home on Sunday.

Then, much as she hated to do it, she called Jack Kennedy and canceled their Saturday night date, pleading a highly infectious virus in a whispery, near-death voice punctuated with a simulated hacking cough. (She prayed that this unplanned thwarting of Jack's notorious libidinous drive would, like the random appearance of John Husted, make Jack only more eager to pursue her.)

On Saturday, through the auspices of the CIA's travel department and with Dulles himself to cut through red tape, Jackie flew to New Orleans and checked into a B and B on stately St. Charles Avenue, across from the Tulane campus and next to Audubon Park.

This morning, Jackie woke up early and, without nearly enough sleep, went to the B and B's high-ceilinged dining room and had a quick but fortifying southern breakfast of biscuits and gravy, hash browns, and the best chicory coffee that she had ever tasted. After that, she took a cab to Professor Grimsby's house, a matchbox affair located on the far side of Magazine Street, the major shopping district for the university's Uptown neighborhood. And here she was, smack in the middle of an uncannily faithful reproduction of a Civil War battle.

The professor picked up a cast-lead soldier in blue and held it up in front of Jackie. "Say hello to Colonel Chamberlain," he said to her. "He commanded the left flank. Most historians would say that Chamberlain's decision to charge downhill and take the battle to the Rebs was the turning point in the Battle of Little Round Top. They would also probably agree that the Battle of Little Round Top was the turning point in the Battle of Gettysburg. And that the Battle of Gettysburg was the turning point in the Civil War, paving the way for the Union victory over the Confederacy two years later. So you might say," Professor Grimsby went on with a slight catch in his throat, "that this man, Joshua Lawrence Chamberlain, not a professional military man but a minister and a history professor at Bowdoin College in Maine—a scholar who defied his school superiors by enlisting in the army—was responsible for the North's ultimate victory in the Civil War."

Carefully, gingerly, with something approaching reverence, Professor Grimsby put the miniature Colonel Chamberlain back in place on the battlefield, surrounded by the Union troops he commanded. Jackie understood that for the professor, history was far from something that had happened a long time in the past. In describing the colonel's heroic action at Gettysburg, it was as though he were talking about an event that had taken place yesterday.

"Did my man fight here?" Jackie asked, trying tactfully to ease the professor back to the reason she had come to see him in the first place.

Professor Grimsby looked down at the diary pages Jackie had sent to him and said, "No, I believe he died elsewhere."

"So you've had time to read the diary?"

"Yes, and thank you for allowing me to see it."

He sat down on a dining room chair and motioned for Jackie to seat herself in the one across from him. She assumed that the professor was a bachelor since what wife would have put up with her eccentric husband transforming their dining room into a Civil War battle scene?

He picked up a pipe from the sideboard, filled the bowl with tobacco, tamped it down, and lit it, puffing on it as he looked over the pages. Thinking about her boss, Allen Dulles, and his beloved Kaywoodie, she wondered what it was about men of a certain age and their pipes.

Once he got the pipe going, the professor continued. "There's not a lot of detail to go on. But there are just enough clues so that not only can I tell you where he died, but I can also furnish you with his name."

Jackie couldn't believe it. This was more than she had expected to hear. "Professor Grimsby, you're amazing," Jackie said with twin notes of admiration and gratitude in her voice.

"Don't thank me," Mr. Grimsby said, pointing to the stacks of official-looking papers making tall piles on the neighboring sideboard. "Thank the U.S. Army for keeping such thorough records."

Jackie waited for the professor to tell her the man's name. But from the way he sat back in his chair, she knew that she was in for a little lecture. Well, if that was the fee he was charging for giving her the information, then it was a small price to pay.

"I started by trying to get a fix on his unit. I based my findings on certain dates in the diary entries. For instance, September 12, 1862: That's the date of the Union attack on Harpers Ferry. That's confirmed by this reference to John Brown's body, since he was the abolitionist who tried to take over the armory there back in 1859. Next comes this date, May 15, 1864, the Battle of New Market. During that battle, the Confederates were so undermanned that they were forced to conscript cadets from the nearby Virginia Military Institute. Beardless fifteen-year-olds were sent into battle that day; can you imagine?" The professor sounded indignant. "That's why your man was horrified that the enemy he faced was children. Finally, this last date, July 29, 1864, corresponds with the eve of the Battle of Petersburg. The Union forces dug a tunnel under the Confederate lines—it's referred to in the diary entry—and blew up the enemy's powder magazines, causing instant slaughter on an unprecedented scale. Since the entries stop there, your man must've died during the attack that followed the explosion."

The professor paused and looked at Jackie. Like the schoolteacher he was, he asked, "Any questions?"

Jackie shook her head no. Grimsby took this as a sign to continue.

"The only unit," he went on, "that fought at all three engagements was the Sixty-Fourth Rhode Island Volunteers. It was very simple then for me to take its casualty list from Petersburg and compare it to the list of volunteers who fought with William Walker as a filibuster."

Jackie interrupted. "Professor, before you go on, could you explain—who was William Walker? And what's a filibuster? I thought that's what Jimmy Stewart did at the end of *Mr. Smith Goes to Washington*."

Grimsby sighed, as though trying to decide how he could condense Walker's life in a way that would be immediately comprehensible to her.

"Let's see. Walker fancied himself an American Napoléon. He tried to set up an independent Republic of Sonora in Mexico in 1853 but got himself kicked out of the country. Then two years later, Cornelius Vanderbilt—the railroad tycoon—hired him to overthrow the government of Nicaragua, which had seized his property there. Walker conquered the country with a band of sixty volunteers known as filibusters. He named himself the new ruler of Nicaragua and changed the name of the country to Walkeragua. But he let the power go to his head and wouldn't release Vanderbilt's property, leaving the tycoon with no choice but to petition the U.S. government to arrest his rogue agent. In 1857, Walker was removed from office. The year 1860 found him back at his old stand, trying to overthrow the legitimate government of Honduras. But he was arrested by U.S. authorities and handed over to the Hondurans, who executed him by firing squad later that same year. He was only thirty-six years old." The professor shook his head. "It's amazing that he managed to cram so much misadventure into such a short life span."

The history lesson at an end, Jackie inquired, "Is there any mention of a young woman named Maria Consuela in your collection?"

"No, but I'm not surprised. The history of Walker in Nicaragua is rather sketchy."

"And what about the man who wrote the diary?"

The professor paused before speaking, like a magician milking the climax of a particularly dazzling illusion. "His name was James Metzger. Not all that much is known about him. He was born in Berlin, Germany, where, as a young man, he apprenticed as a silversmith. Then he and his sister moved to the U.S. and settled down here in New Orleans, where William Walker studied medicine and published a newspaper. The young German was an early convert to his cause.

"Metzger was a bachelor, but his married sister, Harriet Saunders, lived here too. She inherited all his property, including this treasure map, which her descendants eventually bequeathed to our collection here. Unfortunately, we had no contextual resources"—he held up the diary pages—"to know that it was a treasure map."

This was the moment Jackie had been waiting for. She hesitated before asking her next question out of fear that she wouldn't receive the answer she so desperately wanted to hear.

"Professor, is this map still in your collection?"

"Unfortunately not," Grimsby answered gently, like a man breaking bad news to a loved one. "It was stolen from the collection in the early thirties. By Malachi Simon, a supposed scholar who turned out to be a professional map thief."

Jackie could see Grimsby react to the surprised expression on her face.

"There's a lot of money to be made in antique maps," he explained. "Many of them can be worth a fortune."

"And what happened to this Simon? What did he do with the map?"

He shook his head. "I'm sorry to say that I have no idea." He paused and looked wistfully into the middle distance beyond the dining room window. "I wish I had known that Metzger's map was the key to a treasure."

"Why is that?" Jackie asked.

"Because then I would have quit this job and gone to Cuba to search for it. Whatever it was worth then, can you imagine how many times more than that it must be worth today? Hell, do you know how many Civil War soldiers I could have bought with that money? Enough to reproduce the entire Union and Confederate armies, I reckon."

"Do you think anyone has found it by now?" Jackie wondered.

"I doubt it," the professor said. He shook his head and smiled. "If they had, the whole world would have heard about a find like that."

They were waiting for her in her room.

A disappointed Jackie had returned to the B and B. To come all this way and have nothing to show for it rankled her like a toothache. As she walked into the room and turned on the ceiling fan to cool the stifling air, she was shocked to see that she was not alone. There were three men grouped around her bed. They all wore baggy suits that looked like they had been manufactured in the 1940s for the cast of *Guys and Dolls*. One of them was as bald as a roc's egg; another had wiry, receding hair; and the third looked like his mother had cut his hair using a bowl as a guide. They reminded her of the Three Stooges, the low-rent comedy team from the movie shorts.

But what they did next was far from funny. As a single unit, they rushed Jackie, grabbed hold of her, and forced her out of the room, down the stairs, and out the side door of the B and B, where they wouldn't be spotted by any of the other guests. Curly had his hand over Jackie's mouth so she couldn't scream and gave orders to the other two, Moe and Larry, in a language that Jackie identified as German. She assumed that they were not European visitors in search of a young American wife to bring back home. No, these must be Stasi agents, spies for the East German intelligence network. But what they were doing here in New Orleans or wanted with her, she had no clue.

On the side street between the B and B and the western edge of Audubon Park, there was a tan sedan parked at the curb. Jackie knew that the men were planning to hustle her into the car and spirit her off. But to where and to what purpose? She knew if this happened, she would never be seen or heard from again. She had to prevent the men from getting her into the vehicle. But how?

Then two things happened almost simultaneously. The first was the clang of an approaching streetcar. The second was that the man Jackie chose to think of as Larry, being more intent on holding on to her than on watching where he was going, tripped over a section of pavement that had been buckled by an oversized, gnarled tree root growing out of the ground. Jackie had previously noted that this phenomenon was common in New Orleans, where rain and flooding encouraged trees planted along the city's various thoroughfares to shoot right up out of the sidewalk.

As soon as she felt Larry let go of her arm, Jackie immediately went into action and bit down on the hand that was covering her mouth. She was gratified when Curly let out a yelp of surprise and released her. That only left Moe on her other side to deal with. She handled him with one of the deadliest weapons ever designed—a woman's stiletto-heeled shoe. A quick and expertly placed kick to the shin was enough to neutralize Moe momentarily and force him to let go of her.

Jackie made a run for St. Charles Avenue. Unfortunately, these same heels were not made for running, making it difficult for her to race to safety. She saw the streetcar stop in the middle of the street to pick up passengers and decided that this would be the best way to put distance between herself and the three East German spies. Not daring to look behind her to see if they had recovered enough to give chase, she put on a burst of speed, dodging in and out of passing cars, and made it to the streetcar a second before it closed its doors.

Rooting around in her handbag, Jackie handed the driver a dollar bill, waited while he gave her change from his coin belt, then walked swiftly down the center aisle of the streetcar and took a seat in the back so she could look out the rear window to see where the Three Stooges were. Despite the fact that all of its windows were lowered, it felt close and hot inside the confines of the streetcar. As she watched, huffing and puffing from her dash, she saw that the East Germans had gotten into their tan sedan, pulled away from the curb, made a right turn, and were now tailing the streetcar on the right-hand side down St. Charles. *Damn,* Jackie cursed to herself, what was she going to do now?

She suddenly got the impression that she was being stared at. She looked up and saw that every face at the back of the street-car, all of them black, was looking at her. One black woman, wearing a purple dress and clutching a brown paper grocery bag overstuffed with food, leaned over and said, "Sorry, miss, but you don't belong back here." She and the other black passengers looked on nervously, wondering what kind of trouble they might be in for having this young white woman riding back here with them.

Not wanting to cause any trouble, Jackie said, "I'm sorry. Excuse me." Feeling chastened for reasons that she didn't totally comprehend and had no time to examine in depth, she got up and moved forward to the "whites only" section of the street-car, where she took a seat at the right-hand window in order to keep track of the tan sedan as it unnervingly kept pace with the streetcar. Burying her face in her hand, Jackie had no idea how she was going to get shut of these three East German spies.

Her breathing finally back to normal, Jackie decided to stay on the streetcar as long as possible. She saw that the vehicle was headed in the direction of downtown. As it passed Lee Circle, she knew the time was nearing for her to make her move. She would wait until the pedestrian traffic was as thick as possible, then jump off the streetcar with the intention of losing herself in the crowd. Unfortunately, the volume of people she hoped to see never materialized, and then a view of the twin gleaming white spires of the St. Louis Cathedral in the near distance told her that the streetcar was rapidly approaching the French Quarter and the end of its route. She looked out the side window and was dismayed to see the tan sedan still keeping pace in light traffic, pulling even with the front of the streetcar.

At the next stop, Poydras Street, Jackie abruptly rose and bolted off the streetcar, using its middle doors to exit and hoping that the men in the tan sedan wouldn't notice her among the black passengers disembarking. She looked around to get her bearings. Like the good spy trainee that she was, she had spent time on the plane familiarizing herself with a map of New Orleans and the layout of the city, so she knew that the Mississippi River was on her right and the French Quarter on her left.

Jackie headed down the first street that she came to, not looking to see if the tan sedan was following her. She walked down the street as briskly as possible but found her way blocked by a funeral procession stretching from sidewalk to sidewalk. At the head of the procession was a coffin on a horse-drawn cart. Following the horse-drawn cart was a dense assembly of slow-walking black mourners. And behind them came a brass band, its members swaying as they walked and performing a funeral dirge that seemed to set the mournful pace of the procession. *Damn,* Jackie thought, there was no possible way she could interrupt this funeral and make her way through the crowd.

For the first time, she looked back and saw that the Three Stooges had ditched their car and were coming after her on foot. They shambled forward in a way that wouldn't call attention to themselves or make their intentions known to any police officers who might be in the vicinity. Jackie took advantage of their restrained gait to quicken her pace until she found herself at the very edge of the procession, with no way to broach the wall of mourners.

Suddenly, the brass band switched musical gears, and the funeral dirge was transformed into a sprightly version of "When the Saints Go Marching In." At the same time, the mourners broke rank and the previously impermeable crowd suddenly became porous, allowing Jackie to intermingle with the throng. Parasols and handkerchiefs sprouted as the mourners began to dance around in time to the music, an ecstatic combination of joy mingled with grief. Jackie tried to blend in with the mourners by joining in their cakewalk. She saw an elderly black woman, wearing her Sunday best, who was having trouble opening her parasol and asked, "Would you like me to help?"

"Yes," said the woman, who surrendered her parasol to Jackie. Jackie had no trouble opening it and held it over herself and the elderly woman, using it to shield her features from the Three Stooges, who were gaining on the procession. She saw that they were having trouble pushing their way through the high-spirited crowd of gyrating mourners as they danced down the street.

Sashaying arm in arm with the elderly woman, Jackie walked her to the leading edge of the procession, which was approaching the intersection at Canal Street.

"Thank you," Jackie said to the woman, handing the parasol back to her.

"You're welcome," the puzzled woman said in return, but by this time Jackie was gone, breaking for Canal Street.

There was a brick wall at the corner—the edge of the aboveground cemetery the mourners were approaching—and Jackie hoped that it would block her from view as she sought to lose the Three Stooges once and for all.

She found herself headed back toward the Mississippi River, with the St. Louis Cathedral now on her left. She ran past shop after shop selling pralines, souvenirs, antiques, and daiquiris, and turned onto Decatur Street, barely having the time to note that she was passing that jewel-like, vest-pocket park known as Jackson Square on her left.

Coming up was some kind of restaurant that seemed to be doing land-office business based on the crowd lined up outside, where a street musician was entertaining the tourists with his own accordion version of "When the Saints," which seemed to be the unofficial theme song of New Orleans.

Heedless of the calls from those waiting on line, Jackie defied the crowd and entered the restaurant. Normally, she would never think of doing such an impolite thing as cutting a line, but this was an emergency. She was running for her life, and there was no time to offer any apologies for her actions.

Past the front door, the restaurant featured an outdoor terrace with a giant green awning. It was here that Jackie went to try to hide herself from the Three Stooges. As she looked around, she saw that the diners' clothes were sprinkled with white sugar. The sugar was coming from the beignets that were to be seen on every table. Jackie realized that this must be the Café du Monde, which, for many, was the center of New Orleans society, an egalitarian institution open twenty-four hours a day, where everyone—rich, poor, white, black, native, and tourist—came to enjoy beignets and café au lait. It was considered a badge of honor to leave the café with one's clothes covered with powdered sugar from the deep fried doughnuts.

The only guest who didn't seem to be covered in sugar was a young man in a white suit holding court at a table of young male acolytes in one corner of the terrace. The young man looked somehow familiar to her, and after jogging her memory, Jackie realized that he was the young playwright Tennessee Williams, whose productions *The Glass Menagerie* and *A Streetcar Named Desire*—the latter set in his native New Orleans—had caused such a big fuss on Broadway. He closely resembled his newspaper photographs. He was also, she knew, a friend of her novelist cousin, Gore Vidal.

But before Jackie even had the chance to consider going over and introducing herself, the Three Stooges burst onto the terrace in search of her, and she was forced to slip out through the side entrance, where she found herself back on Decatur Street.

She looked around and tried to figure out where to go next. She could either cross the street to Jackson Square and try to lose them there or take the set of steps to the left that led to the levee overlooking the Mississippi River. Jackie decided on the latter course of action and took the steps as fast as her legs would carry her. She glanced down and saw the Three Stooges just exiting the Café du Monde and looking around to see where she had gone.

Arriving at the levee, the first thing Jackie saw was an antique steamboat at the dock, the *Natchez*, looking for all the world like something out of *The Adventures of Huckleberry*

Finn. It was obviously a tourist attraction, and Jackie bought herself a ticket at the booth on the levee and joined the rest of the tourists as they boarded the boat. She went from deck to deck, looking for someplace to hide, and was lucky to find a ladies' room, which she entered and locked behind her, not planning on coming out until enough time had passed to feel safe.

A short while later, she heard the sound of twin steam whistles and guessed this was the signal telling the visitors to the attraction that it was time to disembark. This, however, was followed by a jolting movement that threw Jackie forward. Then came a powerful vibration from below, and Jackie knew that this came from the steamboat's twin paddlewheels slowly beginning to turn. To her chagrin, she realized that this was no stationary tourist attraction. This was a working steamboat taking tourists on a cruise up and down the Mighty Mississip.

Opening the door slowly, Jackie cautiously peeked her head out and saw the levee, Jackson Square, and the St. Louis Cathedral gliding slowly past them. She also saw, standing among the passengers who thronged the railings to look out, the Three Stooges. Before she could duck back into the relative safety of the ladies' room, she was spotted by Curly, who pointed her out to his fellow Stooges.

Without thinking, Jackie went up the nearest stairway until she arrived at the top deck, right abaft the wheelhouse and the twin smokestacks. The companionway leading to the rear deck was blocked by a roped-off sign that read NO ADMITTANCE / CONSTRUCTION UNDER WAY / DANGER. Jackie ignored the sign, hopped over the rope, and found herself entirely alone on the top deck of the steamboat.

She heard three sets of footsteps from the stairway and knew, with a sinking feeling, that the three East German spies were on their way. And now here they were, clambering over the rope one at a time and heading right for her. They walked slowly as though not to spook their prey, and they had all the time in the world to deal with her. Jackie backpedaled as far as she could and found herself up against the boat's stern railing, with something pushing against her back—a life preserver. She looked briefly over her shoulder and saw a tugboat trailing the *Natchez* in the distance. As the men continued their inexorable approach, she knew what she had to do.

"Don't come any closer," she shouted to the Three Stooges, her voice quavering with fright. "Stay right there or I'll jump."

But the three East German spies just kept on coming. They either didn't believe Jackie or didn't speak English well enough to understand what she was saying.

"I mean it. I'm going to jump," Jackie warned them in a voice that rang out with fear.

Just in case they didn't understand English, Jackie hiked up her skirt and put one leg over the railing.

Unfortunately, that did nothing to dissuade the implacable men, who moved slowly, inexorably forward.

Jackie knew that she had no choice. Planting one foot on the outermost part of the deck, she then eased her other leg over the railing so that she was now perched with nothing standing between her and the river below. She looked down and saw the steamboat's white, boiling wake. Before the sight of it could turn her nauseous, Jackie raised her eyes and looked at the Three Stooges as they approached. Their faces telegraphed their desire to do her grave harm.

And so, with a deep gulp of breath and praying for the best possible outcome, Jackie grabbed the life preserver and leaped off the boat, down into the roiling, dark waters of the Mississippi.

V

Havana, Cuba, March 1952

*B*uenas noches," Miguel greeted Gabriela Ortiz in a voice that sounded like truck tires crunching thick gravel. The owner of La Europa had a prizefighter's barrel chest and hands like boxing gloves, and the jacket of his expensive-looking linen suit was open enough for Gabriela to see a gun tucked in the waistband.

Gabriela's hands shook like maracas while she told Miguel how pleased she was to meet him. When he asked her to dance for him, she performed a few well-practiced ballet steps, and he cut her off quickly with a wave of his hand.

"*¡Basta!*" Miguel said, "you'll do fine for the chorus." He told her the pay, and Gabriela couldn't conceal her disappointment at how low it was.

"If you want to make more money," Miguel said, "you can give private dances to customers. And to make a *lot* more money, there are rooms upstairs. Of course, I get a percentage of everything you earn."

Gabriela gasped when she realized what he was talking about: *prostitution.* That was out of the question. She was determined to stay a virgin until she met someone she loved, and Gabriela was in no hurry to get married. She'd seen how marrying at seventeen had shattered her mother's dream of becoming a ballerina, and it was not going to happen to her.

"Look, you don't have to sleep with the men you give private dances to," Miguel said. "Just sit on their laps with your bra off and tease them—rub your body against them, breathe in their ear—and they'll pay you." He looked at her closely. "You could probably charge a hundred pesos a song. The rich businessmen who come here like a young, innocent-looking girl like you. You're who they dream of when they're in bed with their wives."

A hundred pesos a song? That was tempting, but the thought of sitting on strange men's laps and rubbing her naked breasts against them repulsed her.

"I just want to be in the show," she said.

Miguel shrugged. "We're short a girl, so you can go on in the chorus tomorrow night. It'll be two hours of rehearsal a day and one show a night."

That sounded heavenly to Gabriela. La Europa was a far cry from the magnificent clubs like the Tropicana or the Sans Souci, but she was immensely grateful to have *any* job as a dancer. As she walked out of the dingy club into the sunlight, she felt that the long, dark night of her soul that had begun eight years ago was finally beginning to lift.

On the way back to her apartment, Gabriela couldn't help thinking about how long and dark that ordeal had been. It had started when she was a nine-year-old girl riding a bus to the Home for Children Without Parents and Family, as the Americans called it. The bus was filled with other United Fruit Company workers' children who had been orphaned by the sugar cane fire that destroyed hundreds of acres of the planta- tion. Before that, Gabriela's childhood had been a happy one. Her father had a good job as a stoker for the company railway line, and her mother, who could not have more children after Gabriela was born, brought in extra money teaching dance at a school.

The rumor was that someone had deliberately burned the cane to protest how the workers were being exploited, even if innocent lives had to be lost putting out the blaze. The fire had left Gabriela feeling like an only child in the most desolate sense of the word. She had no idea of her ancestry—all of her relatives had died or moved far away long ago. And now her parents were gone. Most of her possessions were gone too, but not the half of a silver locket with strange markings engraved inside that her mother had given her as she lay dying from her burns. Gabriela had no idea what had happened to the other half, but she loved the remaining piece with all her heart. She wore it on a chain around her neck and swore that she would never take it off.

Gabriela felt a pang of that old desolation as she recalled how day after day of her years in the orphanage had dragged by in the same bleak routine of classroom lessons, household chores, and dining hall meals. She didn't know how she would have survived if Sister Evelina hadn't found Gabriela holed up in the kitchen one night, dancing around in the darkened room while she listened to a classical music station on the Haitian cook's radio. After that, whenever she could steal time from running the orphanage, the kindly nun had sat down at the rickety piano and played melodies from the classics while Gabriela danced to her heart's content.

At seventeen, Gabriela had left the orphanage and struck out on her own. Her plan was to enroll in ballet school after making enough money as a showgirl at the Tropicana, the Sans Souci, or some other elegant place known for putting on fabulous nightclub extravaganzas. But after a long string of humiliating auditions, Gabriela was at her wit's end. She was almost out of money. She didn't want to become a maid or a dishwasher— she'd had enough of those chores to last a lifetime—or worse, a waif on the street. And God help her, she would rather jump off her balcony than go back to the orphanage. But how could she stay in Havana with no job and no money?

That's when Luis, the sixtyish native *habanero* who was the desk clerk in her building, came to Gabriela's rescue. "I know the man who owns La Europa," he told her yesterday when she came home crying from her last audition. "Miguel, the owner, is a tough *hombre*, but he has a lot of connections. Everyone hangs out at his place—gamblers, gangsters, spies, rebels, gun-runners, drug smugglers, and even movie stars and presidents when they're looking for something different. I'll call and tell him you'll be coming to see him tomorrow. Here's the address."

Movie stars and *presidents* had sounded good enough to Gabriela to make her overlook the scary part. She took the slip of paper with the address scribbled on it and said with a big smile, "*Gracias*, Luis. You've saved my life."

Her first night as a chorus girl was a rite of passage. After the rehearsal in street clothes, Gabriela walked into the dressing room crowded with women in varying stages of undress. They scarcely looked at her, but Inez, the heavyset wardrobe lady, waddled over to her and surveyed her with a quick glance.

"Get undressed and put this on," Inez said, grabbing a bright orange costume covered with sequins and feathers. She handed Gabriela a G-string, fishnet stockings, and a rhinestone-studded bra to wear under her gown. To compensate for Gabriela's lack of height, Inez gave her a headdress that looked a mile high atop her upswept mass of dark curls and put lifts in her dance shoes.

Gabriela almost froze when she heard the danzón music start, but she quickly joined the chorus line and took a position upstage. The beat of the music was so infectious that she abandoned herself to it, losing all inhibition and sense of where she was, and moved with the same torrid flamboyance as the rest of the chorus line.

As the youngest girl working at La Europa as a regular, Gabriela grew accustomed to being treated like a little sister by the other dancers, but she did not have much in common with them. Most nights, after the show, Gabriela liked to sit at the bar before going home. She didn't drink, but she enjoyed chatting with the bartender, Diego, a wiry young man in his twenties who was working his way through the University of Havana.

Diego provided a storehouse of information about the shady characters who frequented La Europa and the illegal activities they conducted hand in hand with local government officials, who grew rich from a cut of the profits. Gabriela listened, fascinated, as Diego spun dark tales of kickbacks, fraudulent government contracts, and the skimming of public funds. It was a pattern of corruption that fostered a whole underworld of cocaine peddlers, black market gunrunners, and gamblers who ran illicit cockfights and the daily bolita numbers racket. In hushed tones, the bartender also spoke of military strongmen who spied on rival political groups, often assassinating their leaders in the dead of night, and of revolutionaries who had infiltrated the army and were planning acts of sabotage.

It gave Gabriela goose bumps when she looked around the room and recognized the big shots and gangsters whose faces she had seen in the newspaper. Here they sat at tables in La Europa, smoking Montecristo cigars and drinking the mojitos and daiquiris that Diego had prepared.

"That's Batista over there," Diego told Gabriela one night, nodding toward the strikingly handsome man in a white linen suit who was seated in a roped-off section. Gabriela remembered her father telling her about Batista when Arturo was a stoker and Batista a brakeman for the United Fruit railway. "They teased him for being a pretty boy and called him 'El Mulatto Lindo,'" Arturo had said, "but I thought he would grow up to be president some day."

Her father had been right. Batista *used to be* president, but then he retired to Florida to marry Marta Fernández Miranda, his beautiful young mistress—"so romantic," Gabriela's mother had said. But three years ago, Batista had come back to Cuba to become a senator.

True to form, Diego had inside information. "Batista really wants to be president again," he told Gabriela, "but he might lose if he runs for election next year, so he's got to get rid of President Prío before that. I bet that's what he's sitting there plotting with his aides right now."

"Aides" seemed like a polite word for the sinister-looking henchmen surrounding Batista in the booth. "The man next to him in the soldier's uniform looks mean," Gabriela said. "Who is he?"

"Oh, that's Guillermo Sanchez. He's a major in the secret police, and he *is* mean. He murdered a lot of people for Batista, and he even stuck one man's head on a long pole and mounted it in front of his house."

Gabriela shivered when she heard this, and the next night, another tremor ran through her when she spotted Guillermo Sanchez sitting by himself at a table near the stage. During the show, she caught him staring at her, and she quickly looked away.

"Seems like you have a fan," the other showgirls teased Gabriela when Sanchez started coming to the club all the time. It was clear that Gabriela was the one who had captured his fancy because he seldom took his eyes off her during the show.

But Sanchez never approached her for a private dance. He kept his distance, Gabriela assumed, because Miguel had told him that she didn't do private dances and being unattainable made her all the more attractive to him.

When she hadn't seen Sanchez at La Europa for a couple of weeks, Gabriela thought that he had grown tired of watching her perform. Then, in the early morning hours of March 10, 1952, the *golpe* happened—the military coup d'état that Diego had suspected Batista of plotting with his henchmen.

A few nights after President Prío had fled Cuba, Guillermo Sanchez was back at La Europa, celebrating the coup with some other army officers as they downed one drink after another. Their loud laughter and raucous shouts caught Gabriela's attention while she was sitting at the bar after the show. She looked in their direction and was alarmed to see Sanchez staring back at her like a hungry cougar waiting to pounce. He raised his hand, pointed to her, and signaled to Miguel, who was standing at the bar.

Before she knew what was happening, Miguel had yanked Gabriela off her stool and was leading her to a room upstairs.

"Miguel, let me go!" she cried as she tried to wriggle out from his iron grasp, but he held on to her firmly.

"Shhh, don't make any trouble," he told her. "Just do what the major wants, and everything will be fine. Otherwise, heads will roll."

Gabriela remembered what Diego had told her about the head of a Sanchez victim on a pole, and her heart froze with terror.

"She's all yours," Miguel said to the major when he saw Sanchez lumbering toward them, obviously drunk. He handed Sanchez a key, then turned on his heel and left.

Sanchez opened the door and roughly pushed Gabriela

inside. Then he locked the door, pocketed the key, and turned toward her. When he began ripping off her clothes, Gabriela felt a scream rising in her throat. She clutched at the half of a silver locket around her neck and silently prayed to her mother in heaven to help her.

Carmela must have heard her prayer because, at that moment, Sanchez stumbled on the worn carpet and fell backward against a table. While he pawed at the air, trying to regain his balance, Gabriela picked up a lamp and brought it down on Sanchez's head with all her might.

"You little *puta*," he mumbled as he sank to the floor and passed out.

Gabriela didn't care that he had called her a prostitute. All she wanted was to get the key out of his pocket without rousing him. She kneeled down beside Sanchez's prone body and, shuddering at the sight of the gun strapped around his waist, slipped the key out of his pocket as delicately as if she were threading a needle. He stirred, and Gabriela leaped to her feet when she saw Sanchez's hand reach blindly for his gun.

Without looking back, Gabriela bolted for the door and was out in the hallway—and ran smack into Diego. *Oh, no,* she thought, *he's come to make me go back in that room and let that horrible, drunken murderer and rapist have his way with me.*

But Diego took her arm and said, "Come with me, Gabriela. I know a way to get out of here without anyone seeing us."

Flooded with relief, Gabriela clung to him as he flew down a back stairway to the street. Once outside and at a safe distance from La Europa, Gabriela put her arms around Diego and hugged him, wetting his cheek with her tears.

"*Gracias*, Diego," she said. Then she stood back and looked at him, puzzled. "But I thought you worked for Miguel. How come you helped me get away?"

"I work for Miguel only as a cover," Diego said with a little smile. "I'm a spy for a new rebel movement. Our leader hates everything Batista stands for—the corruption, the goon squads, the social injustice, the raping of innocent women like you. As a bartender at La Europa, I overhear a lot of secret information that can help get rid of Batista and free the Cuban people from oppression."

Gabriela felt strangely moved by this disclosure. She couldn't explain it, but when she smashed the lamp over Guillermo Sanchez's head, something had exploded inside her, and she knew that her days as an innocent showgirl had come to an end.

VI

Washington, D.C., May 1952

It was shocking to see. There he was, the trusted valet for the British ambassador to Turkey, and he was using his position to pass on top secret documents to the enemy. And he wasn't acting alone; he was receiving help from a beautiful refugee Polish countess he had designs on. His idea was to take the money he accrued as a spy, quit his job as a valet, and retire to Rio de Janeiro, where he and the countess would live comfortably for the rest of their lives.

To make matters worse, the traitorous valet was being portrayed by the suave British actor James Mason.

Jackie sat back in her seat and tried to concentrate on the movie, *5 Fingers*, which began with a statement that the events depicted in the film were based on a true story. As she watched, she tried to evaluate the movie based on her own experiences as a neophyte spy for the CIA, paying careful attention to the valet's tradecraft and comparing it to what she had learned as a trainee at the Farm.

Jackie looked at her watch in the dim light cast by the projector beam overhead. It was almost three o'clock. She wasn't used to going to the movies during the day. And she wasn't really here to watch the movie. Yesterday, when she had returned to her car in the parking lot of the *Times-Herald*, she saw that someone had dropped an envelope on the front seat. She opened it and withdrew a single piece of notepaper. Printed in large block letters, the note read:

TOMORROW
3 PM
UPTOWN THEATRE
BALCONY
ROW 3/SEAT 7

She knew that the Uptown Theatre was located on Connecticut Avenue past Dupont Circle in Cleveland Park, a neighborhood where inexpensive housing made it possible for underpaid congressional aides and other young professionals to pool their resources and rent houses together. So early this afternoon, she'd arrived at the Uptown, not knowing why she was here or whom she was supposed to meet. She found the designated seat in the balcony, which was deserted, and sat through the coming attractions, the newsreel, the travelogue, and the cartoon before the actual movie got under way.

As she waited for three o'clock to arrive, Jackie thought back on her recent conversation with Allen Dulles at the Pickle Factory, the CIA's own term for its temporary headquarters in Foggy Bottom. As usual, it took place in his office. The only unusual aspect of the meeting was the fact that his assistant, Tod Henshaw, was not also present.

Dulles began by once again asking Jackie to go over the particulars of her visit to New Orleans, which was now almost one year in the past. During that time, Jackie had continued her training at the Farm, had gone to work as the Inquiring

Camera Girl for the *Times-Herald*, and had seen her assignment to Cuba scrapped over what Dulles had termed "the continuing and uncertain political turmoil" in that country.

"During World War Two," Dulles explained to Jackie, "the Abwehr, German military intelligence, employed a listening post in New Orleans so they could receive reports on when convoys departed the port. They operated out of one of those stately old mansions right on St. Charles Avenue, not far from where you stayed, actually. After the war was over, Stasi, the East German intelligence service, took over the listening post and ran it for their new masters, the Russians. We knew about the listening post and decided to let them keep it going, just on the off chance we could use it to feed them false information. I guess, when they got wind of your arrival and saw you visit the professor, they got curious and decided to find out what you were doing in town."

Dulles cleared his throat, an indication to Jackie that he was about to switch conversational gears. "And what about your collateral assignment?"

"Jack Kennedy? I'm sorry to say that I had to break a date with him in order to go to New Orleans."

"Having Jack Kennedy on our side could be even more of a plus than we first thought. I'm sure you know that he has formally announced his candidacy for the Senate. With a crackerjack campaign manager like his brother Bobby, the odds are good that he'll defeat Henry Cabot Lodge in November and become a national force." Dulles pursed his lips. "You probably haven't heard from him because he's been so busy with his campaign, so you'll have to use your ingenuity to get his attention again."

"I'll do it," Jackie said, having no idea how she would, but confident that something would occur to her in due time.

"Now, about Cuba," Dulles went on. "I'm sure you know that our old friend Fulgencio Batista is back in power. Eighty days before the national elections, he staged a coup and took over the reins of power again. He may be a dictator, but he's our dictator because he leaves our business interests there alone and because we don't want anyone else coming in who might favor the Communists. If the island goes Red, it could cause all sorts of problems for us, especially being only ninety miles away from the U.S. coast."

Jackie nodded in agreement. During her research, she had learned that Cuba, if it fell into Soviet hands, could be used as a staging post for an invasion of the U.S. Or worse, with these new rockets in development by both the U.S. and the U.S.S.R., Cuba could be used as a launchpad to hurl nuclear-tipped missiles at cities up and down the eastern seaboard, a truly frightening prospect, especially if Washington, D.C., was the chief target. And this was a possibility that she knew the CIA and the State Department were taking all possible steps to prevent.

Dulles continued, "Your trip to Cuba is back on. But this time your assignment is a completely different one."

Jackie looked surprised. She had figured that the Cuban mission was dead in the water.

"Batista's takeover has angered many Cubans, as you can imagine. There are several groups in opposition to him, actively plotting his ouster. One such group is led by an attorney. He was running for office in the last election, but Batista's coup put an end to his political career. So he has gathered a handful of followers and is hiding out in the Sierra Maestra, the mountains of Oriente Province. That's where he was raised. His family are wealthy landowners there. We want you to go to Cuba and meet with this lawyer. Find out what his intentions are should he ever come to power. Is he a friend of the U.S.? Or does he lean more to the left?" Dulles paused. "The far left."

He looked at Jackie and smiled, a facial expression that Jackie had not often seen him indulge in.

"The funny thing is, this lawyer once had a promising career as a baseball player. He was scouted as an excellent left-handed pitching prospect with a mean curveball. He even came here, to the States, for a tryout with the Senators. But he just didn't have the stuff, as the sportswriters say. That's why he ultimately decided to become a lawyer instead."

"And what is the name of this southpaw?" Jackie asked.

"Fidel Castro."

Jackie filed the name away for future reference. "And who is going to take me to meet him at his mountain hideout?"

"Your Cuban contact is a young man named Emiliano Martínez. He was a law school classmate of Fidel Castro's and a fellow student activist. They were both recruited by the Ortodoxo, the Cuban People's Party. It had a strong following among student groups at the University of Havana who were hoping to become the country's future leaders."

Another idealistic young politico in the Jack Kennedy mold, Jackie thought. *Sounds promising.*

"And will I be going undercover, like the last time?" she wanted to know. The memory of her cover story in Paris was a sore spot with Jackie, since it seemed that everyone she met there was able to see through it in about two seconds.

"In a limited way. But I have someone else who will brief you on that part of your assignment. Because it also concerns your visit to New Orleans."

That could mean only one thing. Jackie asked, "Walker's treasure?"

Dulles put up his hands. He obviously didn't want to give too much away.

"Patience, Jackie. The man who will brief you is somewhat unconventional and will get in touch with you in his own way and his own time. His name is Robert Maheu. He's a former FBI agent. He now works as a freelance security consultant. And we sometimes make use of his—how shall we say—unusual abilities."

And with that, Jackie had found herself dismissed.

Now, here she was, at the Uptown Theatre, watching *5 Fingers* and waiting for this Robert Maheu to show up, as he was obviously the one who had left that unorthodox invitation in her car yesterday.

At three o'clock on the dot, Jackie's patience was finally rewarded. A man came down the aisle and sat in the seat next to her. Jackie looked around at the empty balcony. It seemed that they had the place all to themselves. In his right hand, he held a briefcase, in his left a bag of popcorn. She wondered if the popcorn was just for the sake of verisimilitude or whether he really planned to snack on it during their meeting. He seated himself, put the briefcase down on the floor, then offered the bag of popcorn to Jackie.

Jackie looked at him and said, "No, thank you." Jackie loved going to the movies, but she drew the line at eating fattening snacks from the concession stand.

"Okay, then, more for me," the man responded and shoveled a handful of popcorn kernels into his mouth. Jackie tried to get a good look at him, but it was difficult in the darkness of the theatre. She did get a sense, though, that he was a man who felt at home in both darkness and shadow.

"Oh, I'm Robert Maheu," the man said. He held out his

hand for Jackie to take, then thought better of it. He produced a handkerchief, used it to wipe the butter off his hand, then offered his hand again to Jackie.

Taking his hand, she said, "I'm Jackie—"

But Maheu cut her off. "Yes, I know who you are. Thanks for meeting me here. I know this is an unusual location."

Jackie nodded in appreciation of his understatement.

Maheu glanced up at the screen. Jackie had lost track of the narrative, but it looked like James Mason was navigating the back alleys of Ankara in order to lose a Nazi tail.

"How do you like the movie so far?" Maheu asked.

Jackie tried not to look exasperated. Surely Maheu hadn't asked to meet her here to discuss the cinematic merits of *5 Fingers*. She turned to him and said, "I'm afraid I'm finding it difficult to concentrate."

"You know what I find so interesting about this movie?" Maheu asked, and charged on before she could even respond to his question.

"James Mason's character is a spy for the Nazis. But he doesn't do so out of any political or ideological commitment. He does it because he wants to make money and become a man of leisure. I think that's kind of interesting, don't you? Especially in light of the reason I've asked you to meet me here."

Finally, Jackie thought, then broke in before Maheu could have the chance to continue. "Does it have something to do with Walker's treasure?"

"I'm coming to that," Maheu said, as though the question was impertinent on Jackie's part.

He put aside the paper bag of popcorn, now empty, and picked up the briefcase and put it on his lap.

While fiddling with the combination lock on the brief-case—Jackie had no idea how he could see the numbers in such dim light—Maheu said, "Your boss, Mr. Dulles, asked me to do a little investigating on your account. Apparently, you were doing some research and took things as far as you could go. I have my own…special…resources, so he thought he'd let me take a crack at it."

Having opened the briefcase, Maheu reached in, removing a spiral-bound reporter's notepad and riffling through it until he found the page he wanted. He looked at it, causing Jackie to wonder if the man had eyes like an owl's that could pierce the darkness.

After conferring with the notebook, Maheu looked up and said, "This Malachi Simon was a real character. He would pretend to be a scholar, complete with forged credentials from Oxford or Cambridge, and talk his way into university libraries and private collections, where he would then razor map illustrations out of ancient texts to sell on the open market for inflated sums.

"I traced the map he stole from the Walker Collection at Tulane to a man named Enrico Salazzo. He was a Hollywood set decorator in the thirties. I talked to some of his relatives—he's dead now—and they knew nothing about any map. So I guessed that was a dead end."

Jackie couldn't keep the disappointment from showing on her face.

Maheu continued. "But I had a hunch. I went to Universal Studios, where he worked, and talked to some of the people in the art department there. I found this one old geezer who remembered working with him. He said that this Salazzo was a real practical joker. Said he liked to work an anachronistic prop into every movie he worked on. Something small so the audience wouldn't notice unless they looked real close. But people are usually too busy watching the movie to pay that careful attention. And if they are, that means something's wrong with the movie."

He laughed, then caught himself and cut it off so as not to draw any unwanted attention to himself. Since the balcony was still empty, Jackie thought that this was a bit of unnecessary paranoia on Maheu's part.

"So that got me to thinking," Maheu went on. "With the help of the old geezer, I went through the property logs for the movies Salazzo worked on. And there were a lot of them, I can tell you. Looked at them till my eyes glazed over."

Jackie wanted to tell him that her eyes were about to glaze over if he didn't get to the point soon. But she was too polite to say anything and just let him tell the story in his own way.

"Have you ever heard of the Mexican *Dracula*?" Maheu asked Jackie, abruptly changing the subject.

Really, Jackie thought, *how many detours can this man make in one conversation?* She tried to hide her growing frustration and shook her head. "I barely know about the regular *Dracula*. Bites necks, drinks blood—isn't that right?"

"In a nutshell," Maheu agreed. "Well, at any rate, it turns out that there are two different versions of *Dracula*. The one with Bela Lugosi that everyone knows, made in 1931. And one that was done at night, on the exact same sets, with a different director and a Mexican cast. The studio decided to do it that way rather than show the American version dubbed or with subtitles in Spanish. The movie's actually supposed to be better than the American version. The Mexican lead actress is sexier, and the movie is supposed to be scarier."

Jackie tried to figure out a way to signal to Maheu that he was really getting off the beaten path here. But before she could, he found his way again.

"Well, at any rate, I found out that Salazzo worked on the

Mexican *Dracula*. And do you know what the property log for the movie shows?"

Before Jackie could answer, Maheu infuriatingly went on.

"It shows that Salazzo inserted Metzger's treasure map on a wall in Dracula's castle."

This time, Jackie broke in before Maheu could cut her off.

"Then all we have to do is watch the movie, and we'll see the treasure map?" She felt incredibly elated.

"Yeah, I thought of that too. Only one problem, though." He paused for dramatic effect. "The reel that shows the map on the wall is missing. For some reason, the negative disappeared a long time ago, and it's not in any of the surviving prints still in circulation."

Coming hot on the heels of her relief, Jackie's disappointment made her feel like a marionette being jerked up and down at the hands of a sadistic puppeteer.

Maheu just sat there as though another thought had crossed his mind. Taking advantage of his momentary pause, Jackie plunged right in and said, "Mr. Maheu, there's one thing I don't understand. What does any of this have to do with my assignment in Cuba? What's my cover story supposed to be?"

"I'm coming to that," he said in an aggrieved voice, as though unhappy at having his silent contemplation interrupted.

The screen turned momentarily bright, and in the sudden illumination, Jackie could see Maheu's notepad open in his hand. The page she saw had three words on it:

THE THORNDYKE FUND

And they were underlined three times as though to denote their importance.

Jackie wondered what the Thorndyke Fund was and why

it should be of such seeming importance to Maheu. And what was it doing in the same notepad that contained all his Walker sleuthing? She decided to add the name to her mental filing cabinet, which was expanding daily due to all the new demands of her CIA training.

Maheu closed his notepad with one flip of his hand, put it away in an inside coat pocket, and reached into his briefcase, from which he produced a movie flyer.

"You're going as yourself, a reporter from the *Times-Herald*, to cover a cultural event in Havana. It's already been cleared with your boss. So you don't have to worry about having to memorize a new legend." Jackie remembered that "legend" was CIA lingo for a false identity.

"And what is this event?"

Maheu held up the flyer for Jackie to see. Even in the shadowy light she could read what it said:

ONE NIGHT ONLY
THE "MEXICAN" *DRACULA*
THE LOST VERSION
EL TEATRO DE CINEMA
PRESENTED BY
EL PRESIDENTE
FULGENCIO BATISTA

"They found the film?" Jackie asked in amazement.

"Yes, they found a complete answer print in the vault of some old movie exhibitor in Havana. Batista is declaring it a 'cinematic miracle' and is hosting the movie to show that he's the new steward of Hispanic culture. It's a publicity stunt to take some of the sting out of his coup. What a con man." He shook his head in rueful admiration, then paused and said, "That's some coincidence, eh, about the movie being found?"

You can say that again, Jackie said to herself.

To Maheu, she said, "So do you think he'll get away with it?"

"Who, Batista"—he turned to the screen—"or James Mason?"

Jackie didn't answer, but turned her attention back to the movie. James Mason was stealthily removing top secret documents from the ambassador's safe and using a camera to copy them. *You're lucky,* Jackie thought. Mason had only another hour to find out his fate. The problem with real life was that it usually took a lot longer to find out one's own.

VII

Havana, Cuba, May 1952

They took her right off the street.

Jackie was walking back to her hotel on the spacious Paseo del Prado, wearing a lightweight raincoat over her summer dress as protection against the light mist coming off the Malecón, which bordered Havana Bay.

As she walked along the esplanade, she noted with continual openmouthed wonder that while Paris was blue, Rome was ochre, and Madrid was umber, Havana was colored unlike any other city she had ever seen. Everywhere you looked, building lintels and pediments and friezes and frescoes were tricked out in pleasing pastel hues—blue, green, yellow, red—making it the most festive-looking city she had visited.

No sooner had she made this observation than a big gray sedan pulled up next to her with an urgent squeal of brakes. She looked over to see what was happening, but before she could react, two men burst out of the back of the car and rushed over to the curb, effectively blocking her from flight. Then they grabbed her by both arms and forced her into the back of the vehicle, which took off with another squeal of the tires. Unfortunately, this was a quiet time of day, and there were no food vendors, pedestrians, or tourists on the boulevard to come to her aid or raise the call for help. From first squeal to last, it couldn't have taken thirty seconds for the two men to hustle her off the street and into the sedan.

"Hey," Jackie protested to the men, "what do you think you're—"

But before she could get the last word out of her mouth, the man to her left pushed a piece of cloth into it while the man to her right slid another piece of cloth down over her eyes, effectively blinding her. Then, together, they pushed her down on the floor of the car, and each kept a knee on her to make sure she stayed there, where she couldn't be seen by any passersby.

She recognized these men. They were the same East German spies who had caused her to cut short her intelligence-gathering assignment in New Orleans last year. The trio that she had dubbed Moe, Larry, and Curly. Moe was to her left, Larry to her right, and she assumed that must be bald-headed Curly behind the wheel.

Fortunately, her CIA training immediately kicked in. The first thing to do under the circumstances was to try to remain calm. It was always better to make decisions with a rational mind than it was to act out of blind panic, "blind" being the operative word here, as she remained unable to see where the Three Stooges were taking her.

With her face pushed down in the rear rubber floor mat, unable to look at her watch, she tried to keep track of the time the best way she knew how—by counting her heartbeats. This was a little trick her E and E (Escape and Evasion) instructor had taught the class. The human heart beats approximately sixty times a minute, he'd told them, so use your heartbeat as a clock to keep track of the time. Waiting until her heart rate had returned to normal, she placed her right forefinger on the pulse in her left wrist and tried to count her heartbeats as best she could, reckoning that it took the cab approximately 12,600 heartbeats, or three and a half hours, to reach its destination. It took all her concentration to keep track, but counting also distracted Jackie from thinking about what lay in store for her once they reached their destination.

Jackie had also been instructed to be aware of her surroundings. If you were in a position where you couldn't see, her teacher had told her, use your ears to keep track of where you were being taken. During the drive, Jackie could hear the heavy city traffic give way to a more occasional vehicular sound and could feel the road beneath the tires go from the usual smooth running of asphalt to the bounce of unpaved roads, with the accompanying pings of pebbles bouncing up against the sides of the car. Which led her to surmise that she was somewhere in the country.

So now she was in possession of two rough facts about where she was being taken, good to know should she be fortunate enough to extricate herself from this situation.

Finally, the sedan came to a halt, the rear doors opened, and Jackie was ushered out of the vehicle and into a building of some kind. From nearby, she thought she could hear the sound of ocean waves crashing and smell the tang of salt air—another important clue to her unknown location.

The blindfold and the gag were removed, much to Jackie's relief. It took several minutes for her eyesight to come back into focus and adjust to the dim light in the room. It was coming from a bare bulb hanging from the low ceiling.

Larry held Jackie's handbag. He opened it up and dumped its contents out on the floor. Moe knelt down and sifted through the detritus of Jackie's daily life—lipstick, keys, handkerchief, address book, old movie and theatre stubs—apparently looking for anything that she might use as a weapon or escape device. He came up with a nail file and took it, along with her hotel key. As he rose, he pocketed the potential weapons and left the rest of Jackie's things, along with the handbag, lying on the floor. Then he and Larry left the room. She heard a metallic clicking sound from outside and assumed that she had been locked in.

Looking around, Jackie quickly inventoried the furnishings of the room, which appeared to be some kind of empty storage space. It didn't take long, because the only piece of furniture in it was a rickety wooden chair. Jackie sat down on it. One leg was slightly shorter than the other three, making the chair rock like a ship at sea.

From this vantage point, Jackie saw that the door was metal and thick and, most dismaying, without a doorknob or handle. The walls were made of rough poured concrete, and there were no windows or vents to make even the merest hope of escape possible. She tried to get comfortable in the chair and figure out her options. Unfortunately, there were none that she could think of. She would just have to wait for the Stooges to return and take it from there.

She didn't have long to wait.

After what could only have been a half hour or so—Jackie had stopped counting her heartbeats when they arrived at this unknown destination—Moe and Larry entered the room and stood on either side of her. They motioned for her to rise; then each took hold of one arm and led her out of the room, down a dimly lit hallway, and into another room, the central feature of which was a shallow, funnel-like depression set in the floor. It was blocked at the bottom by what appeared to be a round hatch. Jackie wondered where the hatch led and whether it could prove viable as an escape route.

For some reason, the room smelled like a butcher shop, although there was no raw meat to be seen anywhere around.

Moe and Larry pushed her down in a chair that, like the one in the other room, likewise had one shorter leg (Jackie wondered if they came from the same set). The two Stooges stood over her, waiting for something to happen or someone else to join them.

After another half hour, during which the two Stooges stood silent and did nothing but occasionally glower down at her, the door opened and Curly entered. At the sight of her, he rubbed his hands together vigorously, as though eagerly anticipating what was to come. He turned to face Jackie and addressed her in English that came filtered through a thick East German accent.

"Hello, Miss Bouvier," he said. "So nice to see you again. I trust that you enjoyed your visit to New Orleans."

Jackie tried to keep from acknowledging in any way that this was her correct name. Based on her training, she knew that everything that had happened so far had been done with one purpose in mind—to keep her off balance and lower her resistance. Just knowing this helped her resolve to stay strong and not give in to these men. But at the same time, a small voice at the back of her brain kept repeating the words that her fellow agent Jacques had spoken to her when relating the story of his friend, Henri, tortured at the hands of the Gestapo during World War II: "Henri ended up talking. Sooner or later, everybody does."

Instantly, Jackie banished that thought from her mind. Instead, she chose to focus on her success during last year's special assignment in Paris. If she could survive those incidents and live to tell the tale, then she could withstand whatever the Three Stooges intended for her.

Curly said, "So your name is Jacqueline Lee Bouvier, yes?"

Jackie refused to answer either yes or no, although it did bother her that he knew her name.

"And you work for the CIA, yes?"

Jackie worked hard to keep her face blank, not giving away anything that would confirm her status as a CIA undercover agent.

Curly stood in front of her, waiting patiently for her to answer. It was his patience that Jackie found so unnerving. She might have been more comfortable had he done something tangible to show his anger. She decided that playing mute was her best course of action in this situation.

Undaunted, he continued his questioning. "And what, Miss Bouvier, is your current assignment for the CIA?"

Once again, Jackie had to try her best to keep from reacting. It was getting more difficult with each passing question. Curly seemed to know so much about her. At the CIA, she was just a small cog in a very large machine. So why had they kidnapped her in particular? What information did they hope to get from her? And most important of all, what did they plan to do with her once they had this information?

Curly turned away from Jackie and addressed Moe and Larry in their native language. Moe went over to the wall, picked up a long gaff that was hanging there, and used it to reach down and pry open the hatch at the bottom of the funnel. The room was instantly assailed by a fetid and primordial smell, from which everyone recoiled. Then, upon further instructions from their boss, Larry and Moe grabbed Jackie by either arm and dragged her over to the edge of the funnel, where they forced her to look down.

The area below the base of the funnel was dark, but Jackie thought that she could detect movement down there. She heard

a slithering, swishing sound multiplied many times and punctuated by some kind of ominous snapping sound. Jackie got
the impression of scaly skin and prognathous jaws. And when
she finally was able to pierce the darkness, she saw that the room
below this one was a pit filled with crocodiles, all of them now
snarling up at her with a look of hungry appraisal on their reptil-
ian faces.

With a chill in the pit of her stomach, Jackie realized that
it was feeding time at the zoo and the Three Stooges intended
to serve her up as the entrée du jour unless she gave them the
information they wanted.

Jackie tried to wrestle herself out of Moe and Larry's grasp to
put a little distance between herself and the edge of the funnel.
But the floor here was slippery and gave no traction to Jackie's
high-heeled shoes. She found herself slipping off the rim. Moe
and Larry held on as long as they could, then let her go so as
not to be dragged into the pit along with her.

Jackie slowly slid down the incline toward the hole below.
She grabbed on to the rim of the funnel and momentarily
arrested her slide, but her fingers could find no solid purchase
there. She looked up at Moe and Larry and croaked out, "Help
me. Please."

Moe and Larry looked to Curly, who was suddenly by their
side. "Not unless you tell us what you're doing here in Havana,"
he called down to Jackie in a surprisingly reasonable tone of
voice. "Does it have anything to do with William Walker's
treasure?"

Jackie couldn't believe it. Walker's treasure. She should
have known that's what they were after. Somehow they knew
about it. It also explained why they had been after her in New
Orleans. But little good that information was doing her now.

Moe retrieved the gaff and held it at the ready, waiting to hook Jackie and pull her back up should Curly give the word.

Her fingers slipped a little bit more, and she knew it was only a matter of seconds before she slid down the funnel into the crocodile pit and was torn to pieces by those ravenous creatures. It would be so easy to save herself. All she had to do was answer Curly's questions. But that was unthinkable, given the pledge she had made to the CIA and her country. Her life was literally going down the drain.

And as she slid slowly, inexorably, down the slick incline of the funnel, with the Three Stooges waiting impassively above her and the hungry crocodiles waiting impatiently below, Jacqueline Lee Bouvier asked herself, *For God's sake, how did I get myself into this mess?*

PART TWO

EL TEATRO DE CINEMA

VIII

Feeling like Alice tumbling down the rabbit hole, Jackie plummeted through the opening at the bottom of the funnel and fell, luckily, only a short distance. She landed with a thud on the muddy floor of the crocodile pit and had the wind momentarily knocked out of her. Trying to convince her lungs to breathe once again, she scanned her new environment and found to her horror that she was at the epicenter of about twenty hungry crocodiles, their scaly hides glistening wetly in the murky light of the pit. One of the beasts was practically face-to-face with her, his breath so foul that it caused Jackie to flinch and her eyes to water. Fortunately, the crocodiles had been totally shocked by her sudden arrival and were holding off from eating her until they had sized up how much of a danger she presented. So, even as they surrounded her, these lumbering beasts maintained a slight, cautious distance from Jackie.

Slowly rising to her unsteady feet, struggling at the same time to gather her wits, Jackie tried hard not to panic. Fear would have been a normal reaction for anyone in this predicament had it not also run counter to her newly honed survival skills as a CIA-trained espionage agent, which, admittedly, hadn't prepared her for this eventuality. *Steady, Jackie,* she told herself, *you can get out of this. All you have to do is apply your brain*. And then, having said this, she felt something stirring in the back of her memory that she knew she must work quickly to retrieve.

It was a memory only several months old, so she didn't have to work all that hard to recover it. Her family was gathered in the living room watching a show on the new cabinet-model DuMont television. Going upstairs to get ready for a date, she passed the set and stopped to see what they found so engrossing. But what show was it? And how could it be applicable to what she was facing now? As the crocodiles continued to circle menacingly, Jackie racked her brain to remember what her family had been watching that night. And then it came to her.

A dapper-looking man in a safari jacket. Marlin Perkins. Yes, Marlin Perkins, the famous zoologist and host of *Zoo Parade*, broadcast on NBC from Chicago's Lincoln Park Zoo. And there he was standing next to a crocodile, the creature looking slightly more docile than the ones sizing her up here, and talking about the peculiarities of the species.

Jackie remembered him looking into the camera and saying, "Crocodiles are fast moving but slow-witted. They will eat almost anything but will back off from any creature that is larger than they are."

Jackie had her answer. But how to put it into effect?

Slowly, not wanting to make any sudden moves that would alarm these improbably patient crocodiles, Jackie reached down with both hands and gathered up the material at the back of her raincoat until she was holding on to its hem. Then, just as slowly, Jackie raised her arms to their fullest extension, until she had the raincoat high over her head, like a cape that the wind had blown upward. Once again careful to make no abrupt moves, she slowly turned in place, facing the crocodiles while simultaneously letting out a growling sound that she hoped approximated the warning of a jungle predator and would, along with her enlarged silhouette, have the desired effect on these salivating creatures. Jackie figured that the extended cape added another two feet to her already five-foot, nine-inch frame.

For several moments, nothing happened. The crocodiles continued to assess her as their next entrée. Undeterred, Jackie continued to growl and revolve slowly in place, like an actor performing in the round. Her arms were beginning to tire, but she still held the raincoat, maintaining her outsized silhouette. Just when she thought that damned Marlin Perkins didn't know what he was talking about, she was rewarded with the sight of one crocodile backing off slightly. To her relief, the others seemed to follow this crocodile's lead, leaving her with some much-needed breathing room.

Jackie heaved a sigh of relief. Even though the pit was in near darkness, she thought that she could see the outline of a door at the opposite end. She began to move in that direction, keeping her arms up just to make sure that the threatening crocodiles would maintain their distance from her. As she moved at a stately pace, worthy of Queen Elizabeth, Jackie saw the beasts begin to turn with her as they followed her escape route to the door. Perhaps they were feeling emboldened and were revising their original opinion of her threat potential.

The closer she got to the door, the more the crocodiles once again began to close in on her. Jackie didn't know if she could make it to the door in time to prevent herself from being torn to pieces. And when she did arrive at the door, then what? Suppose it was locked from the outside, a sure way to keep these crocodiles from getting loose. But she put that thought out of her head, deciding that the only proper course of action was just to put one foot in front of the other and literally take things one step at a time.

Her arms tiring, Jackie momentarily lost her grip on her raincoat, which fell once again to its original shape closer to her body. Deflated to normal size, Jackie watched as the crocodiles, with boldness renewed, began to close in for the kill. One snapped its mighty jaws at her and took a big bite out of the back of her raincoat. Following suit, another tried a taste of the garment but found it wanting and spat it out. A third was about to take a sample of her actual flesh when—

A beam of light stabbed into the room. Their prehistoric reptile eyes sensitive to the light, the crocodiles were momentarily distracted from their meal. A thankful Jackie looked up and saw that the beam of light was coming from the door, which was slowly opening. And the more it opened, the more daylight streamed into the pit, ceaselessly flooding it with illumination and causing the crocodiles to retreat to the dark recesses at the back, leaving Jackie alone, praise be to all the saints.

When the door opened all the way, Jackie saw the outline of a woman framed in the doorway and heard her say, "Señorita Bouvier?"

Jackie was surprised to hear herself addressed by this strange woman in this unusual place. So it took her a moment or two to collect herself and say, "Yes."

In Cuban-accented English, the woman said, "Please come with me."

She held out her hand to Jackie and motioned for her to move with all possible haste through the door.

Jackie didn't need a second invitation. Outside the pit, she found herself in a fenced-in crocodile pen. Fortunately, it was empty, except for the woman. She led Jackie toward an old, rattletrap pickup truck on the far side of the pen. The woman, a strikingly beautiful blonde, wore dungarees and a loose-fitting chambray shirt, but beneath them Jackie could detect a well-developed female form.

Before they could even arrive at the truck, the Three Stooges rounded the side of the building that housed the crocodile pit and were even now racing across the pen to get to Jackie. They must have waited for a few minutes before daring to find out what condition the crocodiles had left their hostage in. As they ran, Moe, Larry, and Curly all pulled out pistols and brandished them in the direction of the fleeing pair.

As Jackie watched, the woman reached into one pocket of her dungarees and withdrew a hard-looking ball. With a quick side-arm movement, she flung the ball in the direction of the Three Stooges. The well-aimed sphere hit Moe in the right shoulder, spinning him around like a top and knocking him to the ground as a large moan of pain passed through his lips. Forgetting all about the fleeing Jackie, Larry and Curly went to the aid of their fallen comrade.

The woman climbed over the fence, then held out her hand and helped Jackie clamber over it. Once on the far side of the pen, the woman made for the truck and got in on the driver's side of the cab. Jackie jumped in on the passenger side. She looked through the window and saw that Moe was sitting up and rubbing his right arm, which hung loosely at his side. Larry and Curly rose and, pistols in hand, began firing at the truck before it could leave. Jackie cringed as one bullet spanged into the right front fender below her and another shattered the driving mirror next to her.

Unfortunately, the truck was slow to start, and the woman had to grind down on the gears a few times before the vehicle finally lurched forward and began to roll away. Its springs were gone, and the truck bounced up and down as the woman pressed on the accelerator. A few more shots came from the remaining Stooges, but they fell short of their mark. Jackie quickly looked out the rear window and saw Larry, Moe, and Curly as they receded into the distance. Moe was obviously in no condition to give chase.

The truck was now flying down a dirt road. The woman was careful to make sure that she drove over every dip, rut, and pothole in the road, or at least that's the way it seemed to Jackie as she jounced up and down in her seat. After a while, the road leveled out and the ride became slightly smoother.

Jackie turned to the driver and said, "Thank you."

The woman turned and said, "You're welcome." She stuck out her hand and said, "Rosario."

Jackie took it and said her name.

"Yes, I already know who you are, Señorita Bouvier."

"Call me Jackie. Anyone who saves my life is entitled to call me by my first name."

"*Sí*, Jackie."

They drove in silence for a few minutes, the hot air wafting through the truck's open windows. Jackie swiped a stray wisp of hair from in front of her eyes and said, "Is this what you do, Rosario, cruise around the countryside rescuing damsels in distress?"

"No, Señorita Jackie, I've been following you ever since you arrived."

This brought Jackie up short. She had no idea that she had picked up a tail at the airport, much to her chagrin. She had been taught at the Farm to know better.

Rosario explained, "I work for Emiliano, and he wanted me to keep an eye on you until he could meet with you. To make sure you stayed out of trouble until your meeting. So I was nearby when those three men kidnapped you off the street. I was unable to get to you in time, but I followed you to the crocodile farm and waited for my chance to help you."

Jackie looked at Rosario and said with gratitude, "I guess that makes you my guardian angel."

Behind the wheel, Rosario blushed.

Jackie could smell the salt air. So her senses hadn't deceived her before. She looked out the side window and, through the lushly growing mangrove plants bordering the country road, she could see the ocean in the near distance.

Jackie looked back at Rosario and asked, "What do you call this place?

"Bahía de Cochinos," Rosario responded.

"And what does that mean in English?"

Rosario looked over at Jackie and said, "Bay of Pigs."

Rosario drove her back to the city. On the way, she didn't have much to say. She seemed to be a woman of few words—in English or Spanish. Nevertheless, Jackie found her presence extremely comforting. She seemed to give off a sense that all would be well and remain well as long as she was around.

Leaning her head against the doorframe as they drove past vast, shaded fields where tobacco was grown and harvested, Jackie tried to relax and couldn't help thinking about everything that had happened since her arrival in Havana. It seemed to rival last year's Paris assignment for the alacrity with which events had spun out of control. Hours after arriving in Paris, she was having dinner at Maxim's with a handsome Russian spy planning to defect to the U.S., went to meet him the following night at his rented garret, found him dead, was chased by his killer, spent one danger-filled week on the run trying to find out why the Russian had been killed, and in the bargain, helped an exiled princess return to her homeland. Of course, it didn't hurt that her partner for this mission was a dashing young French photographer with whom she had fallen foolishly in love.

And now, here she was, only hours after landing at the Havana airport and checking into her hotel, kidnapped off the street while taking a walk, and almost eaten by crocodiles before being rescued by this strange Cuban woman. If this was any indication of what lay in store for the rest of her assignment, then Jackie was not so sure that she wanted to go through with it.

"So, Rosario," Jackie inquired in an attempt to get out of her own head, if only for the moment. "What was that thing you hit Moe with?"

Rosario looked uncomprehendingly at Jackie.

"Sorry, the man with the bowl haircut. I call him Moe because he reminds me of one of the Three Stooges. You know the Three Stooges?"

Rosario had a confused look on her face, then said, "*Sí, sí,* Los Tres Chiflados."

"Yes, what did you hit him with?"

With one hand on the steering wheel, Rosario reached into her right dungaree pocket with the other, taking out another one of those black spheres and handing it to Jackie. It was small and hard and looked like it could be deadly in the right hands, such as Rosario's.

"What is this?" she asked Rosario.

"A pelota," she explained. "You use it in jai alai."

"Ah, you play jai alai?" That explained her sidearm maneuver and the way she was able to strike Moe so expertly. Jackie hadn't known there were any female jai alai players.

Rosario didn't answer for a moment, then said, "A friend

taught me. He used to play jai alai. But he had a little problem with gambling so he had to quit."

Jackie had read, in a classified Justice Department report provided by Robert Maheu, that jai alai was under the thumb of the Italian American criminal organization known as La Cosa Nostra, which literally translated into "Our Thing." Mobsters such as Meyer Lansky and Charles "Lucky" Luciano controlled the nightclubs, the gambling, and other sports activities in Havana too. So if Rosario said that her friend had a little gambling problem, and mobsters like those were involved, it was no wonder that he had taken himself out of the game.

"And you work for the revolution?"

With surprising vehemence, Rosario said, "Batista, *no*; Castro, *sí*."

Jackie smiled at that.

"You think that this Castro will make a good leader?"

"*Sí*. He is *muy* smart, *muy simpático*. He has the welfare of the *campesino* and the working man at heart."

Jackie nodded in appreciation. "And do you have any sense of his political leanings?"

Rosario thought before answering. "I know that he despises Batista and all the corruption he stands for. He wants to replace his despotic rule with a more democratic form of government. And that is good enough for me."

Jackie was impressed. Despite her taciturn manner, Rosario appeared to be a well-spoken and dedicated revolutionary.

By this time, they were back in the city. Rosario was driving the truck through the old part of town, Habana Vieja, and stopped in front of a crumbling white, five-story structure. Jackie looked at her questioningly.

"Your hotel," she said simply.

"This isn't my hotel," Jackie protested.

"It is now," Rosario said.

Jackie waited patiently for her to explain.

"Those three men," she went on, "back at the crocodile farm, they are sure to know where you are staying. So you must stay someplace else."

Jackie looked up at the building. She imagined that the place was overrun by bedbugs and that the water in the taps must run brown from rust. She shuddered at the thought of staying there and tried to challenge Rosario's choice by saying, "Here?"

"*Sí.*"

"But what about my bags? My clothes."

"Don't worry. I will go to your hotel. And once I see that the coast is clear, I will get your things and bring them here to you."

Jackie shuddered once again at the thought of what was in store for her once she crossed the threshold of this hotel. Rosario must have detected her lack of enthusiasm for the choice of accommodations.

"Don't worry," she said, "it won't be so bad. And it will probably only be for one night. I'm sure Emiliano will pick out another place for the rest of your stay that will be safe from prying eyes.

"He wants to meet with you tonight. I can't reveal the location now. But I will come at eight and take you to him. In fact, I will be back earlier with your clothes so you have enough time to change."

"And how shall I dress for this meeting with Emiliano?"

Rosario thought about it, then answered, "Have you ever danced the mambo?"

Jackie shook her head and said, "Not really." She would have to go through her luggage and see if she had packed anything appropriate in which to dance the mambo. A dance that she didn't know but that she would have to pick up on the fly, which seemed to be the way almost everything on one of these espionage assignments came to her.

With a sigh, Jackie got out of the truck and walked up the steps to the hotel entrance. All of a sudden, she felt tired from the events of the past few hours, and badly in need of a nap, and knew that nothing, not even bedbugs or a sagging mattress, was going to keep her from her much needed date with oblivion. She just hoped that if she dreamed, it wouldn't be of crocodiles.

IX

What is Fernando Lamas doing riding around with Rosario in that old pickup truck? Jackie wondered when Rosario showed up at her fleabag hotel to drop off her clothes. She had been waiting for Rosario outside, and the tall, lean Hispanic man emerging from the passenger side of the truck looked exactly like the Latin lover whose dark, wavy hair, caramel-colored skin, and gleaming white teeth had made him a sensation in Hollywood.

But this handsome young man walking toward her was unsmiling and carried himself stiffly, a serious-minded individual apparently, who had no use for glamour.

"This is Emiliano Martinez," Rosario told Jackie, nodding toward the man walking beside her, carrying Jackie's suitcase.

Her Cuban contact, but why had he come here?

"Pleased to meet you, Emiliano," Jackie said. "Has there been a change in plans? I thought Rosario was going to bring me to meet you at a club somewhere at eight o'clock tonight."

"She was, but I had some spare time before Javier, our Cuban emissary, will be at the club, and I thought you might enjoy a little sightseeing in our beautiful city," Emiliano said in textbook English with scarcely a hint of a Cuban accent.

Beautiful city? Jackie almost laughed out loud as she looked askance at the dilapidated hotel behind her, and Emiliano quickly added, "I'm afraid your temporary lodgings haven't given you a fair impression of Habana Vieja, and I'd like to correct that, if I might."

"That's very thoughtful of you," Jackie said with a warm smile, grateful to have someone show her something of the town other than a crocodile pit. "Just give me a few moments to change, and I'll be right down."

"Excellent," Emiliano said, handing Jackie her suitcase. "I'll wait for you out here. Rosario has to leave."

Wear something to dance the mambo in if we're going to a club later, Jackie told herself as she searched through the clothes in her suitcase. *This'll do,* she thought, pulling out a sultry but still elegant off-the-shoulder Coco Chanel black cocktail dress with a cinch waistline and a curve-hugging skirt. It seemed perfect for dancing the night away in Havana, although, judging by Emiliano's straitlaced demeanor, she doubted that she'd get to do much dancing.

Rosario had already left when Jackie rejoined Emiliano in front of the hotel.

"Are you ready to see the town, Miss Bouvier?" Emiliano asked, sounding like a trolley car conductor, completely indifferent to how she looked in her Coco Chanel. God, *he's as stiff as a starched collar,* Jackie thought. Jacques would have ooh-la-la-ed, and Jack Kennedy would have given her his womanizer once-over and a basket of compliments.

"Yes, I'm ready, and please call me Jacqueline," she said, well aware that suggesting "Jackie" was asking too much.

Walking down the maze of narrow streets, lined on both sides with boutiques, small art galleries, and cafés and bars, Jackie was glad to have Emiliano as a guide in this historic part of town. He was an amazing font of information, pointing out landmarks with a relish that was a testament to his obvious, deep-seated love of the city.

"That's El Floridita, the most famous bar in Havana," Emiliano told her when they passed a café on the corner of Calle Obispo and Calle Monserrate. "It's known as the 'Cradle of the Daiquiri.'"

"Isn't that a favorite hangout of Hemingway's?" Jackie asked, recalling what she'd read in *Life* magazine about how Ernest Hemingway had spent last year in Cuba working on a novella that the magazine would be featuring in a few months.

"Yes, El Floridita is a favorite of his," Emiliano said. "Some day there will probably be a life-sized replica of Hemingway propped up in his usual seat."

Closer to the seafront, Emiliano led Jackie through the ancient city, which was filled with impressive castles, churches, and civic buildings constructed in baroque and neoclassic styles, replete with myriad columns and ornate stonework.

Everywhere she turned, there was something remarkable to see. "That's the Catedral de San Cristóbal, known as 'music set in stone,'" Emiliano said, pointing to a beautiful, asymmetrical church. "The remains of Christopher Columbus were once housed there." About each museum, concert hall, monument, and historic building, Emiliano imparted some tidbit that Jackie found fascinating. *He should be a professor,* she thought, *not a lawyer and a political activist.*

As they reached the waterfront, Emiliano explained that the array of imposing walls and fortresses had been erected to protect the city from the constant siege of corsairs and pirates. Jackie could imagine pirate ships turning back in trepidation from the massive Castillo del Morro guarding the entrance to Havana Bay and the intimidating La Cabaña fortress with its eighteenth-century walls.

Soon Jackie and Emiliano found themselves joining the parade of tourists and locals strolling along the Malecón, the seaside avenue that was the throbbing pulse of the historic walled city. Jackie wished that she had her camera with her to photograph the charming view. On one side, the blue waves of the Caribbean splashed against the craggy rocks of the seawall, and on the other, the golden sheen of the setting sun burnished the beautiful old pastel-colored buildings.

"Emiliano, this is so lovely," Jackie said. "I can't thank you enough for showing Old Havana to me."

Instinctively, she grasped his hand and pressed it. It was an innocent gesture, but it seemed to embarrass him.

"I think we'd better be going," Emiliano said, withdrawing his hand and glancing at his watch. "We don't want to be late for our meeting."

Don't feel insulted. He's just shy, Jackie told herself. Emiliano reminded her of some of the scholarship students she had met at college—the ones called "grinds"—who restrained their social lives and were awkward around girls because their education was paramount to them. But they didn't look like Emiliano. His torrid handsomeness was at odds with his bookish reserve, an incongruity that Jackie found amusing.

On the walk back to catch a taxi, Jackie took a stab at learning more about her reticent escort without seeming to pry. "I like your name," she said. "Emiliano Martinez has a nice ring to it. Were you named after anyone special?"

"Yes, my parents named me after Emiliano Zapata." He looked at Jackie with an arched eyebrow. "Do you know who he is?"

"Of course I do," Jackie said. "He led the Mexican Revolution against the Díaz dictatorship and the landowners who stole the peasants' farms from them."

Emiliano looked impressed. He had no idea that Jackie knew about Zapata, not from any history book, but from a press kit that the entertainment editor at the *Times-Herald* had shown her for a new Elia Kazan movie coming out soon called *Viva Zapata!* and starring Marlon Brando. There were pictures of a fierce-looking Brando with a thick black mustache overhanging his lip and a sombrero tied under his chin with the tag line: "Roaring Story of Mexico's Tiger on a White Horse!"

Jackie cast a sidelong glance at Zapata's namesake walking beside her, the scholarly young man dressed in summer slacks and a simple white sports shirt, and suppressed a giggle at the thought of him as a tiger on horseback.

"My parents were poor farmers like the Mexican peasants," Emiliano explained, "and they wanted their son to grow up to be like Zapata and fight for the oppressed in Cuba."

Traffic on the six-lane Malecón was flowing heavily, but Emiliano managed to hail a taxi. "La Europa," he told the driver once he and Jackie were inside.

Looking out the open window, Jackie drew in her breath at the sight of a majestic hotel rising on a hill a stone's throw from the sea.

Emiliano followed her gaze. "That's the Hotel Nacional," he told her. "Beautiful, isn't it? A lot of famous people have stayed there and still do, everyone from Winston Churchill to Errol Flynn. And well-known American gangsters too, like Meyer Lansky and Lucky Luciano."

"Didn't Frank Sinatra and Ava Gardner stay at the Nacional on their honeymoon last year?" Jackie asked. She remembered seeing an item about that in the gossip columns that she perused daily to keep current with celebrities for her Inquiring Camera Girl column.

"Where else would they stay?" Emiliano rejoined, a note of

bitterness in his voice. "Frank Sinatra has a suite there, and so does Luciano. The Mob—a perfect name for your country's organization of Italian American gangsters—controls the big hotels, nightclubs, and casinos in Havana."

Yes, I know that, Jackie thought, but she kept listening.

"The Mob backed Sinatra's singing career when he was starting out, and in return, Sinatra became a cash courier for them. Five years ago, he landed at Havana airport carrying a suitcase stuffed with two million dollars in cash, profits from the Mob's criminal activities in the States. He went to the Nacional with two gangster friends and delivered the cash to Luciano to pour into the Mob's activities here."

Jackie was shocked. All she knew about Sinatra was that he had a voice like a dream and wasn't a bad actor either.

"What has happened to Cuba is sinful," Emiliano said, the bitterness in his voice more pronounced. "Our beautiful island—the 'Pearl of the Antilles'—has been corrupted by crime and greed. On the surface, it's all bright lights and glitter, but there's an undercurrent of violence. We Cubans want our nation back. The guidebooks describe Havana as 'a volatile mix of Monte Carlo, Casablanca, and the ancient city of Cádiz all rolled into one.' Well, that volatile mix is going to explode some day."

Jackie didn't know what part of town the taxi had driven them to, but it was off the beaten path. Except for the neon sign that said LA EUROPA over the doorway, the club might have been a large private home out in the suburbs somewhere. It reminded Jackie of pictures she had seen of Prohibition-era speakeasies in the States—a faintly scandalous-looking place for seekers of forbidden pleasures and celebrities who didn't want to be gawked at by tourists.

Before they went in, Emiliano briefed Jackie on how to conduct herself. "We're going to sit at the bar and wait for our Fidel Castro contact to come. If they ask you why you're there, say that you write a newspaper column on entertainment. You love dancing, and you wanted to see the show."

Well, I love ballet—that much is true, Jackie thought.

As soon as Jackie followed Emiliano into the club, her nostrils were assailed by a pungent odor that reminded her of the stables at Merrywood. She assumed it was from the thick clouds of cigarette smoke swirling around the room and thought the smell was even worse than the acrid aroma of the Gauloises that she'd tried in Paris.

Emiliano pulled out a seat for Jackie at the bar, told the bartender to make her a mojito, and looked around the room. "Our friend isn't here," he said to Jackie. "Enjoy your drink while I go look for him."

This is good, Jackie said to herself as she took the first few sips of her mojito. *I wonder what's in it?*

"Delicious drink, isn't it?" the man seated next to her said, as if reading her mind.

Jackie turned her head to see an impeccably dressed gentleman in what looked to be a bespoke Savile Row suit with a silk handkerchief nestled in the breast pocket—attire that seemed as out of place in a club like La Europa as a tuxedo at a clambake.

"Why, yes, it is delicious," Jackie said. "Do you know what's in it?"

"White rum, sugar cane juice, lime juice, sparkling water, and mint," the man said, sounding like an expert mixologist. "The mint is called yerba buena, a spearmint that's very popular on the island. People in the know say that La Europa's mojitos are even better than the ones at La Bodeguita." The man smiled suggestively. "And you get a lot more than drinks here, if you know what I mean."

Jackie was afraid that this strange man was trying to pick her up, but he quickly put her at her ease. "I would love to chat more with you, but I'm afraid I must be going, Miss...?"

"Bouvier. Jacqueline Bouvier. And you are?"

"Arthur Phillips," he said. "I'm here from the States seeking investment opportunities for my company, and I'm having dinner with a prospect who's probably waiting for me by now."

The man fished a bill out of his wallet and laid it on the counter. "This is for you, Diego," he said to the bartender, an intense-looking young man busy fixing drinks. Then Phillips withdrew a business card and handed it to Jackie. "It was a pleasure meeting you, Miss Bouvier. I hope our paths cross again sometime."

As Arthur Phillips took his leave, Jackie glanced at the card he had given her. Printed on it in bold letters, she saw the name THE THORNDYKE FUND.

That's funny, Jackie thought. Those were the same three words that she had seen on Robert Maheu's notepad. What was the Thorndyke Fund? Why was Maheu so interested in it? And what kinds of investments were involved?

Any questions that she had about the Thorndyke Fund flew out of Jackie's head when she looked up from the card and saw the man sitting on the stool next to the one vacated by Arthur Phillips.

The high forehead, the bushy white beard and mustache, the brute masculinity of an aging lion king tamed by advancing years. It had to be. It *was*. Ernest Hemingway. In the flesh.

Without missing a beat, Jackie slid into the seat next to him, leaned in close, and said, "Mr. Hemingway? I'm Jacqueline Bouvier of the *Washington Times-Herald*, and I'm so thrilled to meet you." Her voice came out in a vibrato like the voice of Babykin, the talking doll popular back home, and she was afraid that Hemingway would ignore her.

But he didn't. He downed the rest of his mojito and turned toward her with a flushed face and bleary eyes. "And what brings a lovely young thing like you to La Europa?" he asked. "Did the newspaper send you?"

He sounded wary, and Jackie remembered that his last book, *Across the River and into the Trees*, had been published two years ago to bad reviews. *He probably thinks I'm a critic out to do him in*, Jackie surmised, so she quickly said, "Oh no, I'm here on vacation. And I must tell you that I love *all* your work"—she deliberately stressed the "all"—"and can't wait to read your next one, Mr. Hemingway."

"Call me Papa," he said, his eyes crinkling in a smile. "My new book is called *The Old Man and the Sea*. It's the story of a four-day battle between an old, experienced fisherman and a giant marlin far out in the Gulf Stream. I wrote the first draft in eight weeks in my home in Finca Vigía here."

"Eight weeks! That's amazing!"

"Well, it's a short book," Hemingway said modestly, "and the idea had been brewing for years." He signaled to Diego to make him another mojito. "I've spent a lot of time fishing for marlin off the coast of Cuba on my boat, *Pilar*, and I turned that struggle into an allegory about the battles we go through in life."

"It sounds wonderful," Jackie exclaimed.

Diego set down a new drink for him, and Hemingway took a hefty swig of it. "I don't know what the critics will say about it," he ventured, "but it's the best I can write ever for all of my life."

"I bet you'll win the Pulitzer Prize for it," Jackie said.

The band struck up a mambo, and Jackie turned her head toward the dance floor, watching it fill up with couples.

"Would you like to dance?" she heard Hemingway say.

Would I! Jackie felt a little thrill rush through her, but when she turned back to Hemingway, she saw that his question had been addressed to someone else—the heavily made-up, scantily clad Hispanic woman, obviously a prostitute, sitting on the other side of him.

Red faced, Jackie slipped off her stool, looked around, and spotted Emiliano standing at the end of the bar. She didn't know how long he had been there, but she was glad to see him.

"I looked everywhere and couldn't find Javier," Emiliano told Jackie when she rushed over to him, "but I see you like celebrities, so I've asked my friend Diego to introduce you to one."

Hoping that she wouldn't get another brush-off, Jackie followed Diego, a tray of drinks held high in his hand, weaving through the dance floor, which was crowded with couples vigorously shaking their hips in time to the mambo's catchy beat. Finally, they came to a roped-off area that Jackie assumed was reserved for big shots. Diego undid the rope and motioned Jackie inside.

Jackie gasped when she saw who was sitting in the first booth, along with three sinister-looking men.

"Mr. Sinatra, I'd like you to meet Jacqueline Bouvier. She's a columnist for the *Washington Times-Herald*," Diego said as he set down the drinks on their table.

Face-to-face with the idol of every teenaged girl in America, "The Voice" himself, Jackie thought that she would swoon like one of his legion of adoring bobby-soxers, but she held her ground with a frozen smile on her face.

Sinatra gave her a long look. "A columnist, eh?" he said,

narrowing his eyes. "Well, you're a helluva lot better-looking than Walter Winchell, I can tell you that."

"Thank you, Mr. Sinatra," Jackie murmured, batting her eyelashes out of sheer nervousness.

Sinatra patted the empty space beside him on the banquet. "Have a seat," he said to Jackie. "We'll buy you a drink. I could use some good press."

His thuggish-looking companions guffawed at that, while Diego took his cue and left, reaffixing the rope behind him.

Too excited to speak, her heart thumping a mambo of its own, Jackie sat down next to Sinatra. Up close, she was surprised to see that he looked gaunt and tired. There were lines around the famous mouth, hollows under the high cheekbones, and a worried look in the riveting blue eyes. He seemed edgy, a coiled spring of tense energy.

"Let me introduce you to everyone," he said to Jackie. "The guy with all the bottle caps on his chest is Colonel Guillermo Sanchez," Sinatra said, pointing to a hatchet-faced man in a khaki military uniform with a jacket full of medals. "He's a hotshot in the secret police, and President Batista just gave him a promotion."

Jackie didn't want to think about what Sanchez did to merit that reward. And she didn't like the way he leered at her either.

"That's my pal Sam Giancana," Sinatra said, nodding at the thin-lipped, shady character sitting next to Sanchez. Sam Giancana, Jackie knew, was a name synonymous with "Mafia hitman." "He's very popular in Chicago—paints the town red," Sinatra added with a crooked smile.

Giancana caught the joke and laughed. He had a cackle like an ice cream headache—the maniacal ha-ha-ha-ha of a bloodless psychopath, Jackie thought, looking away from Giancana's cold, dead eyes peering at her from behind horn-rimmed glasses. Frank Sinatra did indeed have ties to the Mob, as Emiliano had said. The CIA's secret report of Giancana's string of murders, love affairs, and financial interests read like a sensational crime novel.

Jackie was surprised when Sinatra introduced the henchman sitting next to Giancana as the "Mambo King."

For some reason, that brought another burst of maniacal laughter from Giancana. Jackie's skin was beginning to crawl. As thrilled as she was to be rubbing elbows with Frank Sinatra, this was not the kind of company she wanted to keep.

"What are you drinking?" Sinatra asked her.

"A mojito," Jackie tossed off, hoping to sound sophisticated.

"Here, take this one," Sinatra said, passing her one of the drinks Diego had brought. "That's Ava's favorite drink in Havana too. She just left for Africa to make a movie there with Clark Gable called *Mogambo*. Some new young actress from Philadelphia is in it too. I think her name is Grace Kelly."

Grace Kelly, the girl from Schrafft's. I hope this is her big break, Jackie thought, smiling inwardly as she remembered their coffee-spilling gambit in the restaurant. To Sinatra, she said, "Africa—that sounds exciting." She tried to sound impressed, but it was disconcerting to know that when the cat was away, the mice would play, even when the cat was the gorgeous Ava Gardner. "Will you be joining her there?"

Sinatra frowned. "My show is opening at the Club Parisién next week, so I'll be stuck in Havana for a while. Africa would be great, but I gotta keep up with Nat King Cole and Tony Bennett, and the movie offers aren't rolling in right now."

Suddenly, Jackie had a suggestion for Sinatra that she thought would cheer him up.

"You know, I just finished reading *From Here to Eternity*, and I think you'd be perfect for Private Maggio in the movie."

A light came on in Sinatra's eyes. "Say, that's a great idea," he said. "Maggio, the little Italian guy who has a lotta guts but no luck. Why didn't I think of that? I'll get on Harry Cohn at Columbia right away." He looked at Jackie with new appreciation. "You're a smart girl. Classy too. What are you doing after the show?"

Jackie knew that Sinatra had only one thing in mind, and she wasn't interested. Besides, Guillermo and Giancana were deep in conversation—she caught the words "Castro" and "poison" in the same sentence—and that made her exceedingly nervous.

"I'm with someone, and I really must be getting back to him," Jackie said, rising from the table, "but thank you so much for the drink, and good luck getting the part of Private Maggio."

Emiliano looked worried when Jackie caught up with him at the bar. "Javier still hasn't come," he said, "but maybe he'll show up during the show. It'll be starting soon. I reserved a table for us."

"Good. Maybe I'll get to see the Mambo King perform. He was sitting with Sam Giancana and Sinatra. Is he like Pérez Prado?"

"Oh, he's not a musician," Emiliano said. "They call him that because he likes to use his machine gun to make his victims dance before he kills them."

"How awful!" Jackie exclaimed. She shuddered and shook her head to rid it of the grotesque image.

Seated at an intimate table for two in the darkened room, munching on the tasty paella that Emiliano had ordered, Jackie heard the band launch into an opening number. She sat up expectantly as a line of curvaceous showgirls in low-cut, flashy, sequined gowns took the stage. Jackie thought that their towering Carmen Miranda–style headdresses looked as if a crate of fruit salad had fallen on their heads, but she admired their dancing. It was scandalously exciting, especially to the men ogling them ringside—one of them, Guillermo Sanchez, Jackie could recognize by the stage lights glancing off the rows of medals on his chest.

When the show was over, people started filing out of the room. Soon, except for some showgirls at the bar or deep in one-on-one conversation with male customers scattered about, Jackie and Emiliano were the only patrons left. And still, there was no sight of Fidel's contact anywhere.

"I guess we'd better leave," Emiliano said with a sigh. "It doesn't look as if he'll be coming."

But someone else was arriving, walking through the door and into the nearly empty room, directly in Jackie's line of vision. *Oh God, not him,* Jackie wailed to herself. But it was— *Jack Kennedy*—no mistake about it this time.

Catching up again with the senatorial candidate was high on Jackie's to-do list, but certainly not in Havana—that would raise too many questions. It didn't surprise her that Jack was here—the U.S. had vital interests in Cuba, and Jack also had a keen interest in Havana's showgirls, according to Charlie Bartlett—but why did he have to come here now?

When Jack turned his head in her direction, Jackie suddenly sprang up and said to Emiliano, "I've got to go to the ladies' room. I'll be right back."

Jackie didn't know where the ladies' room was, but she headed in the opposite direction from the bar. *There's got to be someplace I can hide,* she thought as she made her way along a wall, *but where?* Ah, perfect: a room with a curtain hanging in front of it—probably a dressing room of some sort.

Jackie pushed aside the curtain and almost screamed. There,

seated on a man's lap, was a gyrating seminude showgirl, her gown lying on the floor, her naked breasts brushing back and forth across the man's face.

Without making a sound, Jackie closed the curtain and kept searching for a hideout. A stairway. *That must lead to the ladies' room,* she thought, and raced up the steps. She came to a hallway, but none of the rooms on either side had a sign on the door.

She heard the sound of laughter coming from the bottom of the stairs and turned to see Jack Kennedy, a showgirl on his arm, about to start up the steps. *Oh God, now what am I going to do?* Jackie asked herself, quickly turning away. Having seen what was behind the curtain that she had opened, she was unwilling to try any of the doors.

Jackie stood in the hall, frozen to the spot, knowing that in a matter of moments, Jack Kennedy would be *this close.* Frantically, she looked around, searching for something to hide behind, but saw nothing. But then, beside a large door at the far end of the hall, Jackie spotted her salvation: a telephone on the wall and a phone book on a stand beneath it. She ran to the phone, hurriedly thumbed through the book until she found the number for La Europa—an office number that was different from the one on the hall phone—and dialed it with trembling fingers.

"*Hola,*" a gruff man's voice said.

Disguising her voice, which she needn't have done since it was trembling so hard, and in passable Spanish, Jackie said, "This is United States congressman John F. Kennedy's personal secretary. Please have him come to your office immediately. I have an urgent message for him."

"*Un momento,*" the man said.

Jackie waited, and when she finally had the courage to turn

around, at the bottom of the stairs she saw a burly-looking man leading Jack Kennedy away from the showgirl.

With a sigh of relief, Jackie hung up the phone and quickly rejoined Emiliano, who was standing at the bar. "Is it all right if we leave now?" she asked. "I'm afraid I'm not feeling well. I think I just need some air. I'll wait outside while you call a cab."

"Of course," Emiliano said, looking concerned. "You look as if you've just seen a ghost."

X

So tell me, what did you think of La Europa?" Emiliano asked Jackie over lunch at Café Rodney, the Tropicana's charmingly bohemian restaurant.

"It's a strange place," she said after a long moment. "You never know who you'll bump into there."

Not wishing to elaborate any further on the chance encounters of the night before, Jackie sipped her mojito, savoring the way the citrus and mint flavors enhanced the kick of the rum—*I could get addicted to these,* she thought—and quickly changed the subject. "The Nacional is absolutely magnificent, Emiliano. It was so good of you to arrange for me to stay there."

"Deputy Director Dulles is the one you should be thanking. I was only the messenger. When I told Mr. Dulles about the unfortunate experience that happened to you on your first day here, he was very sorry to hear it. He wanted to make it up to you, so he chose a world-class hotel that has airtight security. You know, Winston Churchill and his wife stayed there after the war. It's a luxurious place, but it's also very safe."

"I hadn't counted on such a treat," Jackie said, remembering her delighted surprise when Emiliano told the cabdriver outside La Europa to take them to the Nacional. She couldn't believe how short the cab ride was from the sleazy club to the legendary hotel in Vedado. It was like going from the Bowery to Park Avenue in the blink of an eye.

Glorious, Jackie had murmured to herself as she stepped out of the taxi and admired the breathtakingly lush tropical setting of tall royal palms, giant fruit trees, and cascading fountains. It was also apparent to Jackie that with so many eye-catching sights to behold and so many famous people around, Dulles had assumed that a nobody like Jacqueline Bouvier was likely to go unnoticed. Why would anyone be looking at her when they could be ogling big-name stars like Gary Cooper, Rita Hayworth, or John Wayne?

"Don't worry about your suitcase," Emiliano had told her before she checked into the hotel. "I already arranged for it to be sent up to your room."

Once again, Jackie had been impressed with how considerate Emiliano was. *He's going to make some woman a good husband one day,* she'd thought, *if he ever warms up a bit.*

Standing in line at the reception desk, Jackie began tapping her foot impatiently as she waited behind a woman giving the clerk a litany of instructions in a thick European accent. A bellhop stood by with the woman's truckload of Louis Vuitton luggage, looking as if he had turned to marble. Finally, the tall, urbane-looking man at the woman's side prodded her arm.

"Zsa Zsa darling, I'd rather not spend the entire night in the lobby, if you don't mind. Let's get on with it, shall we?" the man said in a smooth, upper-class British accent. Jackie had thought he looked familiar, but now he was immediately recognizable. *George Sanders!* Addison DeWitt, the acerbic theatre critic in *All About Eve,* an Academy Award–winning role come to life. And the woman ahead of Jackie was his famous movie-star wife, one of the glamorous Hungarian-born Gabor sisters. When Zsa Zsa turned to her husband and nodded, Jackie was so dazzled by the perfection of her heart-shaped face and porcelain skin that her impatience gave way to awe.

"I heard from Fidel's contact, and he apologized profusely for not showing up," Emiliano was saying when their lunch arrived. "I asked him what happened, and all he would say was that he had run into some trouble with the secret police. But he promised to meet with us tomorrow and swore that he would be there. So that gives us this whole day to ourselves."

"Well, you couldn't have picked a better place for lunch," Jackie said.

The Tropicana, surrounded by colorful tropical foliage, was every bit as spectacular as the Nacional. Jackie had been struck by the beauty of the Nymphs Fountain at the entrance to the casino and the lovely ballerina sculpture in front of the outdoor nightclub adjoining the casino, the world-famous Paradise Under the Stars.

Jackie's guidebook had raved about the club's spectacular shows featuring a cast of more than a hundred dancers and musicians, the dancers performing on aerial walkways around the treetops. She could see why the Tropicana was known as a mecca for tourists, international celebrities, beautiful women, and well-heeled gangsters.

And now, incredibly, here she sat, having lunch with Emiliano in Café Rodney, named after Roderico Neyra, the famous choreographer known in Cuban song and dance circles simply as Rodney. Born a leper and raised in a leper colony, according to Emiliano—was there anything this man didn't know?—Rodney had launched his career with a burlesque show at the Shanghai, one of Havana's most notorious strip clubs. From there, he worked as head choreographer at the elegant Sans Souci, staging lavish, talk-of-the-town, Afro-Caribbean shows for shock value and fun, until the nearby Tropicana had lured him away.

"This is delicious," Jackie said, after her first mouthful of *enchilado de camarones*, a flavorful dish of shrimp, tomatoes, green bell pepper, onion, and garlic. "Back home we call this shrimp Creole, but this is an even tastier version."

"I'm glad you like it," Emiliano said. "After lunch, is there anything in particular that you'd like to do?"

"I haven't really thought about it," Jackie said. "We could walk around the grounds, but I'd rather not go into the casino. I'm not much of a gambler." *When your job pays $42.50 a week, there's not a whole lot to play with,* she said to herself.

"I don't like it either, but I'm afraid gambling has become Cuba's national pastime. There's the official national lottery— the legal one—and then there's the bolita, the black market numbers game where Martin Fox made all his money before he bought the Tropicana."

"He must be making a lot more with the casino here," Jackie said, remembering the line of shiny black Cadillacs and long white limousines bringing patrons to the casino last night when her cab pulled up in front of the hotel.

"Oh, yes, a casino is a license to print money. The big ones rake in millions of pesos a day, and the gangsters and the crooks like Batista line their pockets with money from them." Jackie could see a flash of anger in Emiliano's eyes. "There's something wrong when the people running things live like kings, and five hundred thousand *campesinos* live in miserable shacks, working four months in a year and starving the rest. The rich landowners live high off the hog while a hundred thousand poor farmers like my parents are feudal serfs who have to pay for using a small plot of land by giving up a share of its produce. Do you think that's right?"

"No, of course not," Jackie said, shaking her head, overwhelmed by the sheer magnitude of the numbers he had reeled

off. "It's terribly unfair for people who do an honest day's work
to be victimized so badly by a corrupt system. I feel sorry for
them. Your heart would have to be made of stone if you didn't."

The anger faded from Emiliano's eyes. "Forgive me for lec-
turing to you," he said, looking slightly embarrassed. "I didn't
mean to spoil your lunch. We should talk about something
more pleasant." He thought for a moment. "I've seen some of
your writing, and I have to say that I was quite impressed."

"You mean my Inquiring Camera Girl articles?" Jackie asked,
surprised. Emiliano seemed much too serious to appreciate light-
hearted copy like that.

"No, the piece that you wrote for the Grand Prix contest."

"Where on earth did you see that?"

"Deputy Director Dulles mentioned that you won the *Vogue*
contest when he gave me some background on you. I wanted to
see what you wrote, so I went to the library and got hold of the
copy of the magazine that printed your winning essay in it."

A true scholar, Jackie thought, flattered by Emiliano's interest in her work but also somewhat uneasy at being snooped on
in a way.

"And you liked what I wrote?"

"Very much. You're an accomplished writer, Jacqueline, but
I was wondering," Emiliano said, sounding curious, "why did
you pick Charles Baudelaire and Oscar Wilde as literary subjects you wish you had known? They were rather decadent,
weren't they?"

Jackie laughed. "Yes, they were decadent, but that's not why
I chose them." She didn't want to tell Emiliano that she was
drawn to Baudelaire and Wilde, both rich men's sons who
lived beyond their means and died in poverty, because they
reminded her of her father's plight. So she said, "I admired
them because even though they wrote about the seamy side

of life from firsthand experience, they were still idealists who
believed in a better world. They brought about reform in their
own way, not by leading a rebellion, but by using their words
to accomplish what activists had been trying to do for years."

Emiliano nodded. "Yes, sometimes, the pen is mightier than
the sword, as they say. But I'm afraid there are other times
when you need both the pen *and* the sword. And for Cuba,
we've come to the point where words alone are not enough."

"It's sad to think that violence is the only answer," Jackie
said. She took another bite of her shrimp dish, gathering her
thoughts before she went on. "I've done some background reading myself...on Fidel Castro...and there are people who say
that although he's an eloquent orator and very smart, with a lot
of talent as a leader, he's too fond of guns, too reckless. Do you
think that's true?"

Emiliano shook his head. "No, not really. That may have
been true when we were freshmen in law school and gangsterismo was very popular. Young men, even educated ones like us,
wanted to show how tough we were. You know, like imitating
John Wayne in your country, which was rather foolish, I suppose." He smiled in a self-deprecating way. "Fidel was like that,
so he carried a fifteen-shot Browning pistol on his person all
the time and got into fights with rival gangs. But in his senior
year, he gave an impassioned speech against *gangsterismo* at the
university before a group of administrators and students, and
he hasn't changed his position since then."

Emiliano pointed his fork at Jackie like a defending counsel
stressing a point in a closing argument to a jury. "Believe me, if
there was a peaceful way to depose Batista, Fidel would be all
for it. But when a dictator seizes power with a military junta
and holds on to power by squashing protest with a murderous
secret police force, a bloodless revolution is a vain hope."

Much as she hated violence, Jackie was swayed by Emiliano's discourse on Cuba's dire straits. "You're an eloquent speaker yourself, Emiliano," she said. "You must be very effective in the courtroom." Now it was her turn to be curious. "If you don't mind my asking, how could poor farmers like your parents afford to send you to law school?"

"They couldn't afford to," Emiliano said simply. He pursed his lips. "Before I explain, let me give you some idea of how hard it was for my parents just to survive, let alone support a family. My father came to Cuba fresh off the boat from Spain in the early 1900s, with no prospects and no way of making a living. He met my mother, and they fell in love. He wanted to get married and start a family. But how, when he had no money? Then along came Major Walter Reed, the U.S. Army doctor. You've heard of him, I'm sure?

"Of course," Jackie said quickly. "He was the one who conquered yellow fever. They even named a hospital after him. It's in Washington, D.C."

"Well, actually it was a Cuban doctor, Carlos Finley, who first had the idea that the germ that caused yellow fever was transmitted by mosquitoes," Emiliano informed her. "Finley gave Reed a batch of mosquito eggs so he could grow them to adulthood and test out his theory. Volunteers were paid to see if they contracted the disease when they were bitten by the grown mosquitoes. Some of the men were drawn from the U.S. Army's own ranks. Others were new immigrants from Spain. My father was one of the five Cuban volunteers on the first team. He knew there was every chance that he could contract the disease and die. But he wanted to help the doctor find a cure for this terrible scourge, and he said that if he couldn't have my mother, life would not be worth living anyhow." Emiliano's eyes glowed with a look of filial affection and pride. "Obviously, my father survived, but you can imagine how desperate and deeply in love he was to take such a courageous step."

"I can," Jackie said softly as she felt a sudden wave of tenderness for Emiliano. She reached out and touched his cheek, wanting him to know how much she appreciated the poignancy of his father's courage.

Emiliano blushed, but a smile played around his lips, and Jackie knew that her gesture was not lost on him. "Now, do you want to tell me how you could afford to go to law school?" she asked.

"I worked my way through as a cigar reader."

A cigar reader? Was that like reading tea leaves? Emiliano didn't seem like the fortune-teller type. Jackie looked blank.

"I should have said a cigar-*factory* reader," Emiliano corrected himself. "We have a long-standing tradition in Cuba of hiring people we call *torcedores*, or lectors, as you would say, to help our cigar-factory workers pass the time by reading to them while they roll the tobacco leaves into cigars. The lectors sit in the front of the factory room and read aloud all day long. They start out with the newspaper in the morning, and after that, it could be anything the workers might like—self-improvement books, magazines, modern novels, or classics."

"That's a wonderful idea, but doesn't that distract them?"

"No, actually, it improves their concentration by keeping them from getting bored, and they're not allowed to look at the reader or talk to their workmates because quotas have to be met. So instead of distracting the workers, the reading helps them keep on rolling cigars at top speed while it entertains and informs them."

"Whoever thought of that was brilliant."

"Ironically, the idea was originally developed for prisons. Nicolás Azcárate—he was an activist and intellectual back in the 1860s—proposed reading to people locked up in jail as part of their rehabilitation. And the link to the cigar industry came about since many prisoners rolled cigars to earn wages."

"I can see the parallel," Jackie said, nodding. "In a way, the tobacco workers are like prisoners too, only they're locked up all day in cigar factories instead of jails."

"Exactly," Emiliano said, beaming at Jackie like a school-teacher who has just gotten the right answer from a student called on in class.

I wish he would smile more, Jackie thought. *He's so gorgeous when he does.*

But Emiliano quickly returned to his pedantic mode. "Most cigar workers have never read a book in their lives," he said. "Many of them can't even write their own names. The reading gives them their only access to literature and useful informa-tion about the outside world." He smiled again, crookedly this time. "What the factory owners didn't count on is that reading increases efficiency, but it also encourages revolutionary ideas. The cigar workers are probably the best-informed sector in the labor force right now, and we think they'll be vital in the fight for independence."

Jackie tried to imagine what she would read to the cigar workers if she were a lector. "There are so many books to choose from, I wouldn't know where to begin," she pondered.

"The workers have their favorites," Emiliano said. "Dumas's *The Count of Monte Cristo* has been popular for a long time. In fact, the book was read to them so often that they named the Montecristo cigar after it."

"I was wondering where the cigar got that name," Jackie said. "My stepfather smokes that brand."

"Another favorite classic of the workers is Shakespeare's

Romeo and Juliet. That's where the name of the Romeo y Julieta cigar comes from."

"Who knew cigars had such a rich cultural history?" Jackie said, laughing.

Emiliano's eyes snapped as if a sudden idea had come to him. "Would you like to see the cigar factory where I worked as a lector? It's in the Vedado, the University of Havana neighborhood. I can take us there in my car, and you can see an actual reading for yourself."

"Oh, I'd love that," Jackie said. "Let's do it."

Emiliano's car was an old, bilious green Chevrolet, déclassé for the Tropicana, but not nearly so embarrassing as the rattletrap truck that had brought him to her when they first met.

"I like this neighborhood," Jackie said when they entered the barrio of El Vedado. It was a pleasant downtown district with lots of exclusive-looking shops and businesses, a large public square, and an abundance of dance clubs and cabarets common to a university town. And of course, there was a movie theatre with the name YARA in bold letters on the front. It was not nearly as impressive as El Teatro de Cinema in Habana Vieja, but it looked large for a local theatre.

"Many film festivals are held in that movie house," Emiliano said, pointing to the Yara, "and the round building in front is the Coppelia ice cream café, where the students like to congregate."

When they came to a large building on the corner of Figuras Street—the H. UPMANN BUILDING, the sign said—Emiliano drove around to the back and parked on the lot.

"Upmann? That sounds German," Jackie said as they walked toward the entrance.

"Yes, the company was founded by German immigrants.

Two brothers who were bankers and cigar aficionados. They were always sending cigars back to their friends in Europe and finally decided to open their own factory, but it has Cuban owners now." Before they went inside, Emiliano said, "You know, it doesn't surprise me that your stepfather smokes Montecristos. Handmade Cuban cigars are very popular with the Washington crowd."

Suddenly, Jackie remembered Jack Kennedy lighting up a cigar after dinner at the Bartletts and telling her that it had been made in Cuba. *Oh great, all I need is to find him lurking inside this factory,* she thought, *the way he showed up at La Europa.*

But inside, there was nothing except row upon row upon row of long wooden tables with workers seated on benches, side by side, eyes down, their hands busily flying. Seamlessly, one after another, the workers rolled leaves of tobacco into cylinders and clipped the ends as they listened to a matronly woman lector reading the *Gaceta Oficial* newspaper into a microphone from her perch on a chair on a high wooden platform. Except for the thick, tangy smell of tobacco that permeated the air, the room was like a huge study hall with exceptionally well-behaved students.

It was so hot and humid in the factory that Jackie had to fan her face with her hand. "They can't have air-conditioning in here," Emiliano explained, "because it would dry out the tobacco leaves."

Jackie followed Emiliano to the front of the room, where he found a chair for her. Then she watched him withdraw what appeared to be a well-worn book from a stack of reading material, climb the steps of the platform, and greet the lector with a friendly smile. She smiled back, obviously happy to see him, exchanged a few words with him, and nodded.

Jackie assumed that Emiliano had selected a book for the lector to read. But to her surprise, the lector rose from her chair and descended the steps, and Emiliano took her place.

I hope he won't lull the workers to sleep, Jackie thought nervously, but she sat up in her chair when Emiliano raised the book in his hand and announced the title into the microphone in a resonant voice that was like a call to arms: *"Los Miserables."*

Great choice, Jackie thought. Victor Hugo's masterpiece was one of her all-time favorites. She had actually devoured all nineteen hundred pages of it in French, mesmerized by the brilliance of the ideas and the emotional pull of characters like Jean Valjean, sentenced to nineteen years of hard labor in prison for stealing a loaf of bread, and Fantine, a poverty-stricken mother reduced to prostitution to pay for her daughter's care. *Les Misérables* was so familiar to her, and French was so similar to Spanish, that Jackie was confident that she would grasp what Emiliano was about to read.

Before he began reading, Emiliano gave a short introductory speech about the book's themes of struggle and redemption in France culminating in the July Revolution of 1830 and the student-led uprising of 1832. The similarity between France at that time and present-day Cuba was implicit.

" 'Chapter Twelve. The Future Latent in the People,' " Emiliano said in Spanish. Then he launched into the reading in a vibrant voice, more animated than his normal conversational tone, but it wasn't until he was almost midway into the passage that he caught fire:

" 'There exist these immense numbers of unknown beings... rabble, multitude, populace. These are words and quickly uttered. But so be it. What does it matter? What is it to me if they do go barefoot! They do not know how to read; so much the worse. Would you abandon them for that? Would you turn their distress into a malediction? Cannot light penetrate these masses? Let us return to that cry: Light! And let us obstinately persist therein! Light! Light! Who knows whether these opacities will not become transparent? Are not revolutions transfigurations?' "

Jackie saw that the workers kept their eyes on their fingers, but she could feel excitement coursing through the room like an electrical current as Emiliano went on, becoming even more intense and passionate, his voice rising to a powerful crescendo:

" 'Sow enthusiasm, tear green boughs from the oaks. Make a whirlwind of the idea. This crowd may be rendered sublime. Let us learn how to make use of that vast conflagration of principles and virtues, which sparkles, bursts forth, and quivers at certain hours. These bare feet, these bare arms, these rags, this ignorance, this abjectness, this darkness may be employed in the conquest of the ideal. Gaze past the people, and you will perceive truth. Let that vile sand which you trample underfoot be cast into the furnace. Let it melt and seethe there. It will become a splendid crystal, and it is thanks to that, Galileo and Newton will discover stars.' "

Jackie's eyes were moist when Emiliano closed the book and began to come down from the platform. Around her, the workers' eyes were still fastened on their fingers busily rolling cigars, but she could tell from the expressions on their faces that Emiliano's reading had touched their hearts as much as it had touched hers.

For the first time, Jackie had seen the fiery soul hidden behind Emiliano's wall of reserve. No, he was not a tiger on horseback, but he was, she had discovered, a figure even more intriguing and magnetic to her—a sleeping tiger. And she wanted to be there when that tiger came to the fore again.

Jackie rose from her seat and was walking toward Emiliano

to congratulate him on his performance when she felt a slight tug on her sleeve. She turned, and a small, thin Hispanic man who looked like a *campesino* wordlessly handed her a note and quickly walked away, disappearing through a side door. Jackie glanced at the slip of paper and read:

TOMORROW
THE DANCE ACADEMY
3 PM

When Jackie reached Emiliano, she smiled broadly at him and told him how wonderful she thought his reading had been. "I was thrilled by it, and so was everyone else."

Then she showed him the note that the strange man had slipped into her hand. "Do you know what this is about?"

"Yes, the Dance Academy is where the rebels hold their meetings," Emiliano said.

The Dance Academy? *That sounds promising,* Jackie thought. *Maybe I'll finally get to do the mambo after all.*

XI

It was just like a Hollywood movie premiere, Jackie thought. Not that she had ever been to one, but she had seen them in the newsreels, like the one for *Gone with the Wind*. And the Teatro de Cinema was an architectural marvel to rival Grauman's Chinese Theatre on Hollywood Boulevard, looking for all the world like a Moorish castle in Castile, complete with turrets and archways and parapets along which shrubbery grew in great abundance. The theatre had just been restored to its former glory, and this was its inaugural presentation. Its marquee proudly read:

THE "MEXICAN" DRACULA
THE LOST VERSION

Klieg lights outside the theatre stabbed up into the night sky, announcing that something big was taking place. So did the red carpet leading to the theatre's entrance, where limousines were pulling up at regular intervals and depositing luminaries. A tuxedo-clad announcer, his hair brilliantined to a high shine, accosted the celebrities and thrust a huge microphone into their faces for them to sound off on Radio Havana.

Both sides of the roped-off red carpet were swarming with

fans hoping to catch a sighting of their favorite personality. They were held at bay by members of the secret police working as crowd control. Knowing that there would be so many police around, Jackie had convinced Emiliano that she would be perfectly safe without him as her bodyguard. She wanted a night out on her own, a chance to experience the event as just another starstruck moviegoer in the crowd of avid fans. And they were more avid than any Jackie had ever seen before. Every time a new limousine pulled up to disgorge its passengers, the fans greeted them with a roar that crescendoed to a frenzy before subsiding, but only until the arrival of the next limo.

Circulating through the crowd was a company of actors dressed as Count Dracula, his main victim, Eva Seward, and his nemesis, Professor Van Helsing. Among the excited onlookers stood Jackie, swaying back and forth with the throng of fans as they attempted to catch a glimpse of Hollywood stars Desi Arnaz and Cesar Romero, who had both flown down to Havana just to attend the premiere. Playing the dutiful journalist, Jackie was checking out the scene outside the Teatro de Cinema before entering the theatre herself. She was wearing a simple black sleeveless dress designed for her by Mini Rhea, the Georgetown dressmaker who had become her own personal High Lama of style.

From this vantage point in the crowd, she spotted Frank Sinatra and Sam Giancana, who both appeared with gum-chewing blond showgirls on their arms. They walked in to shouts of "Frank! Frank!" and "This way! This way!" as press photographers in the crowd attempted to capture this historic moment in Cuban cultural history for posterity.

As Jackie watched the parade of celebrities stroll down the red carpet, she became aware of a man standing near her. Unlike the other members of the mob, he didn't call out to any of the passing celebrities, didn't even seem to acknowledge them or rubberneck to stare at them. Instead, he seemed, at least to Jackie, to be biding his time.

And now here came Fulgencio Batista himself, as effulgent as a peacock in his full military regalia, and accompanied by an equally full phalanx of bodyguards. He waved to the crowd as he quickly entered the theatre. There was applause for the less than popular El Presidente, as who in the crowd would be foolhardy enough to boo him and risk getting beaten up by the secret police?

Once again, Jackie was aware of the man near her, whose interest seemed to have perked up somewhat with the appearance of Batista. His eyes followed El Presidente as the leader and his retinue walked down the red carpet and into the theatre. Jackie also noticed that the man, who was dressed in coveralls and carrying a metal toolbox, seemed to have come straight from his job to be a part of the crowd outside the Teatro de Cinema.

More applause came from the crowd, and Jackie looked to see who was coming down the red carpet next. After a few more celebrities unknown to Jackie strutted into the theatre, in snuck Papa, the only movie guest not to be found in appropriate evening attire. With his sneakers, wrinkled cotton chinos, Windbreaker, and long-billed baseball cap, he looked like he was dressed to step onto the deck of his fishing boat, *Pilar*.

But the loudest applause was reserved for Carlos Villarías, the movie's Count Dracula, and Lupita Tovar, who, according to the program Jackie held in her hand, played Eva Seward. Both of them greeted their fans with exaggerated courtesy, as though they hadn't received this kind of attention in a long, long time, which was probably the case. Jackie had read that Lupita Tovar's husband, Paul Kohner, was the producer at

Universal who'd thought up the idea of filming a Spanish-language version of *Dracula* as a vehicle for his sexy young wife. Despite the passage of years, she was still an incredibly beautiful woman.

Jackie looked around but was surprised to find that the man in the coveralls was nowhere to be seen. He seemed to have vanished entirely. But by now, the last celebrity had entered the theatre, so, dismissing the man from her mind, Jackie detached herself from the crowd, walked down the red carpet herself (and knew enough Spanish to understand the fans who asked, "Who is she?"), showed her ticket to the usher at the entrance, and was waved through into the theatre.

Which turned out to be as elaborate an affair on the inside as it was on the outside. The Moorish castle theme of the theatre's exterior was continued here with a large Diego Rivera-type mural that wrapped around three walls of the auditorium and illustrated scenes from Spanish history, from El Cid's noble defense of Valencia, through Christopher Columbus's discovery of the New World, to the first settlements founded on the islands of Hispaniola and Cuba.

Jackie looked at her ticket stub and found her seat, which was located about ten rows back from the screen. Seating herself, she tried to find where Batista was sitting, and found him with his retinue in one of the boxes on the right-hand side of the auditorium.

Seated several rows ahead of her she could see Sinatra, Giancana, and their "dates" for the evening. The men were busy talking to each other and barely spoke a word to their window dressing. Nearby, Hemingway made himself comfortable and put his feet up on the back of the lone empty seat in front of him.

The two *Dracula* stars, Jackie saw, had a box to themselves on the left-hand side of the screen and couldn't seem to wait for the movie to begin.

Just then, the houselights went down, and Jackie settled herself in her seat. She took out a reporter's notepad, a pen, and a miniature flashlight and prepared to take notes during the movie when Metzger's treasure map appeared in the film. If Maheu was right, she would have to wait until the third reel. For that reason, she would have to be aware of the reel changes, always designated by four dots that appeared consecutively at the upper right-hand corner of the screen to warn the projectionist that the projectors needed to be switched.

The movie began with the familiar Universal art deco logo of the airplane flying around the globe. Then the titles announced

CARL LAEMMLE
presenta
"DRACULA"

The audience burst into spontaneous applause.

The movie opened with a group of tourists being taken by carriage through the Carpathian Mountains. They were informed that this was *Walpurgisnacht*, when the dead walked, and that they must be sure not to leave the safety of the inn where they were staying. It was rather funny to watch as one tourist, a frightened young woman wearing owlish glasses, kept getting rocked right into the arms of a male fellow traveler.

As she watched the movie, the memory of the man in the coveralls kept coming back to Jackie. Something about him didn't seem quite right. The way he didn't fit in with the rest of the crowd. And the way his attention perked up only when Batista made his entrance. And then there was the matter of his toolbox, which could have concealed any manner of things besides tools. Like a weapon, for instance. Or even worse, a bomb.

More scenes continued to unspool. Count Dracula creepily arising from his mist-filled coffin, greeted by three seductively beautiful lady vampires. The English lawyer, Renfield, arriving at Castle Dracula and giving the count the deed to Carfax Abbey. Jackie found herself torn between watching the movie for any sign of Metzger's treasure map and concern about that man in coveralls and what possible mischief he might be up to at this very minute.

Jackie watched with growing discomfort as Renfield spent his first night at Castle Dracula, where the count looked on as his three lady vampires feasted on the English lawyer. Then, from out of the corner of her eye, Jackie caught sight of some movement from the edge of the auditorium to her right. There he was, the man with the coveralls. Only now he was wearing a Dracula cape over them to disguise his appearance. Now, for sure, Jackie knew that something wasn't right. She looked around for someone she could warn about this. But the nearest police were guarding Batista in his box and there was no time to get to them.

Not wanting to waste another second, Jackie quickly stuffed her notepad, pen, and flashlight back into her purse, jumped up out of her seat, and started down the row to the aisle.

"*Perdóname, perdóname*," she said to those also seated on the row, whose viewing pleasure she was disturbing.

Once out in the aisle, she turned to see where the man in the Dracula cape had gone. To her right, she saw a sudden shadow flitting up the arched stairway leading to the projection booth, ironically, to Jackie's eye, imitating the movie's gothic, shadow-filled mise-en-scène. Without a moment's hesitation, she went up the stairs and found the door to the projection room. Again, without hesitating, she tried to open it, but the door was locked. Either locked or blocked—she wasn't sure. So she tried again. And again nothing happened. She tried a third time, now putting the force of her body behind her attempt to open the door. It gave slightly, and Jackie pushed her shoulder up against the door and tried to force it open. It gave a little more, and a little more, and finally she was able to open up a big enough wedge for her to squeeze through.

Immediately upon entering the room, Jackie almost tripped over the door's obstruction. It was the projectionist, and he was lying unconscious on the floor.

Looking up, Jackie's instincts told her to move her head to the right, preventing something from smashing into it from the left. That something was an empty film can, and it had been flung at her by the man in the Dracula cape. He was now crouched down over his toolbox, which lay in the middle of the floor. To Jackie's horror, she could see that the toolbox was packed to the rim with sticks of dynamite. Why, there must have been enough sticks there to blow up the entire theatre. He obviously wanted to assassinate Batista and didn't care how many innocent people went up along with El Presidente.

The man in the Dracula cape unrolled a length of fuse from the toolbox and was about to light it with a cigarette lighter when he was jumped by Jackie, who couldn't think of any other way to stop him. It was very close quarters inside the booth, which was crammed with three giant movie projectors and tables piled high with cans of thirty-five-millimeter film. There was also a chair for the projectionist to sit on between reel changes. And it was this chair that Jackie met with now as the man in the Dracula cape threw her off him and sent her hurtling across the room.

She hit her head, losing consciousness momentarily. When she came to, she saw, through hazy vision, the man in the Dracula cape leaving the room. She leaped across the floor and made a grab for him, but all she could latch on to was the cape, which came away in her hands. She let it fall to the floor and heard the clatter of footsteps as the man made his escape down the stairway, leaving her and the unconscious man alone in the room.

Jackie quickly looked at the toolbox. The quick-acting fuse was almost at the end of its run. The dynamite would ignite in about ten seconds if Jackie didn't do something about it—and fast. She shook her head to clear her vision, then spit on two of her fingers and rubbed the fuse right ahead of where the spark was sputtering. Jackie felt a brief hot stinging in her fingers as the spark went out. She collapsed on the floor, realizing how narrowly disaster had been averted.

But a smell in the room told her subliminally that the threat was not yet over. Because when Jackie had thrown herself at the man in the Dracula cape, she had sent his cigarette lighter flying. It must have landed in an open can of highly flammable nitrate film stock, which, to her shock, she now saw was on fire. In his rush to retrieve the lighter and ignite the fuse, the man in the Dracula cape had obviously ignored the incendiary potential of this situation.

Jackie looked around for something to put out the blaze but saw no fire extinguisher, no bucket of sand or water, nothing. Apparently some short cuts had been taken in the restoration of the Teatro de Cinema to get it ready in time for its opening, clearly in violation of the city's fire codes.

Before her eyes, the entire projection room began to go up in flames. Jackie ran over to the nearest projection port and shouted out, "Fire! Help! Fire!" hoping that she could be heard above the movie's dialogue. "Fire! Help! Fire!"

Turning back to the room, she knew that she had two things to do. The first was to look for reel three of *Dracula*. There was no way she was going to leave without it.

She looked over at the projectionist and saw that he was just coming to, rubbing the back of his head. Good, because that was the second thing she had to do—get him out of here.

"Are you all right?" Jackie asked him in her Berlitz crash-course Spanish.

The man looked too confused to respond.

Despite this, Jackie continued, "Reel three—I need it. Do you know where it is?"

The room began to fill with smoke. The fire was spread-ing. Jackie knew that they had only a few moments before they would have to abandon this room or risk getting burned to death.

"Reel three—where is it?" Jackie demanded of the projec-tionist again.

This time he seemed to understand what she was saying. He nodded and went over to a table that was piled high with cans of film. On their sides, they were all labeled DRACULA and numbered. Unfortunately, they were out of sequential order. But the projectionist was able to find one and handed it to Jackie. She looked at it with difficulty through the growing smoke and saw that it was labeled REEL 3.

Holding the film can firmly in her hand, Jackie said, "You better get out of here," to the projectionist and pushed him in the direction of the door. He was starting to cough from the smoke. So was Jackie, who saw the Dracula cape lying on the floor and used it to cover her mouth and nose.

By now, the booth was thick with smoke, and the flames were consuming the nitrate film stock with the avidity of a starving beggar eating his first meal in a week. Coughing and sputtering, her eyes smarting from the smoke, Jackie made her way to the door, where she spotted a messenger bag used to transport film cans hanging from the inside doorknob. Removing it from where it was hanging, she put reel three in the messenger bag, looped its strap around her neck, and fled the projection booth.

Suddenly she remembered—the dynamite. The flames could set it off at any minute. Jackie ran back inside, risking the smoke and flames, and felt around until she stumbled across the explosives, which she tucked inside the messenger bag along with the reel of film.

She went down the stairway to the main floor. People were swarming out the emergency exits on both sides of the auditorium as well as the doors leading to the lobby. Ushers and the actors dressed as Dracula, Eva Seward, and Van Helsing had been pressed into service to make sure the evacuation of the theatre was an orderly one.

Jackie looked up and saw that the box Batista had been sitting in was empty. She wasn't surprised at that. Instead of remaining in place and setting a calming example for the others, he had probably been the first one out of the theatre after she sounded the alarm. If he had been the captain of the *Titanic*, his watch cry might have been, "Women and children last."

Jackie glanced over at the screen. Improbably, the movie was still playing. Only now it looked like Castle Dracula was going up in flames, thanks to the fire that continued to fill the confines of the projection booth. When was the fire department going to get here?

Jackie decided to leave through the lobby, which seemed to have the least crowded exits. The lobby itself was also starting to fill with smoke. Through its doors, the boulevard in front of the theatre was visible, and Jackie was dismayed to see three familiar figures waiting there: Moe, Larry, and Curly. Moe had his right arm in a sling, a painful reminder of Rosario's pelota-hurling ability. As she watched, Moe stayed in place while Larry went to the right and Curly to the left so they could each watch one side of the theatre for her exit. How had they known she was at this movie premiere? The answer didn't matter for now, because she had to get past them if she didn't want a repeat visit to the crocodile farm.

Jackie retreated back into the auditorium, the flames now spreading beyond the projection booth. She needed some sort of disguise. Still clutching the Dracula cape over her mouth and nose, Jackie suddenly realized that she had one ready to hand. She draped the oversized cape over her shoulders and drew it firmly around her. She saw that it not only covered her entire body, but also came up high enough to shield almost her whole face. It also did double duty in hiding the messenger bag hanging down from her neck.

The auditorium was emptying out, and it appeared that the actors were no longer needed. As a group, they made their way to the back of the auditorium to leave through the lobby exits. When the mob of Draculas passed by her, Jackie simply joined them, mixing in as they left the theatre.

Outside on the boulevard, fire trucks were just now beginning to pull up. Firemen jumped out and began attaching their hoses to the nearest fire hydrants. Smoke was billowing out of the theatre, and the firemen would have to act fast if they wanted to save it before it was in need of another restoration.

Moe was standing there on the sidewalk, his eyes darting keenly from one crowd of moviegoers to another as they dispersed to make way for the firemen and their equipment. Jackie did her best to blend in with her fellow Draculas. The way the individual crowds had formed, it was impossible, though, for her to avoid passing Moe at close range.

As she came level with him, she drew up the collar of the cape as high as it could go. Jackie avoided meeting his eyes as she walked past Moe in the company of the other Draculas. Her mouth dry, her heart beating at a Souza tempo, she walked by him on his right, the side with the sling, and prayed that he wouldn't notice her. Moe looked right at her, and for one fleeting moment, Jackie thought that the game was over. But his eyes instantly dismissed her before moving on to the next caped Dracula in the pack.

Once they were down the boulevard and out of Moe's sight, Jackie separated from the parade of Draculas. She looked back and saw the crisscrossed sprays of the fire hoses as the firemen worked quickly to save El Teatro de Cinema from complete destruction.

On her own, Jackie walked another two blocks before hailing a cab. She gave the driver her destination, then collapsed in the backseat, suddenly exhausted from her ordeal. Her body ached in several places where she had impacted with the chair, and she knew she would have some ugly bruises to show for it by morning. In the meantime, she did have the all-important third reel in her possession. Hugging the messenger bag to her bosom beneath the Dracula cape, she realized that she was going to need a place to screen the footage. Surely the resourceful Emiliano would know of a screening room somewhere in the city where she could watch the reel and find Metzger's treasure map.

Which reminded her—Emiliano, her handsome but supremely reserved Cuban contact. It was a pleasant diversion to wonder what would happen the next time they encountered each other.

And other than that, Mrs. Lincoln, how was your evening at the theatre?"

Jackie couldn't believe it. Here was Emiliano, making a joke, after hearing about her close call the previous evening at El Teatro de Cinema. It was so unlike him that she laughed twice over—once because the joke was so apt, and once because Emiliano's sudden exhibition of a sense of humor was so delightfully unexpected.

She had been glad to pick up this morning's paper, *Prensa Libre*, and read—in her rudimentary Spanish—that the fire at El Teatro de Cinema had been extinguished in time, so, surprisingly, only minimal and readily repairable damage had been done. She was not surprised, however, to see that there was no mention of an attempt to blow up the cinema and assassinate El Presidente. With the newspapers under such close governmental scrutiny, Jackie hadn't thought that any news of Batista's narrow escape would ever see the light of day. After all, why put the idea in some fanatic's head or encourage others to try their hand at putting an end to El Presidente's latest political incarnation?

"I'm sorry that I underestimated the threat and allowed you to go to the theatre by yourself," Emiliano said in a sudden shift from the jovial to his usual sober self. In some ways, Jackie thought, Emiliano reminded her of Jacques, able to turn on a dime and go from one emotional state to a diametrically opposite one. With Jacques, it had been carefree Jacques versus secret agent Jacques. With Emiliano, it was serious Emiliano versus, well, a slightly more relaxed version of Emiliano that disappeared almost as quickly as it appeared, causing Jackie to wonder whether this fleeting manifestation was just a hopeful fantasy on her part.

Whatever the case, Emiliano was here now and was taking her to the much-anticipated rendezvous with Fidel Castro. On the way, he once again acted as her tour guide to this glamorous city of polo players, race-car drivers, and international playboys. Jackie welcomed this opportunity to have him fill her in on some of the historic locations, places where musicians had fashioned their melodies and poets had crafted their rhymes. To Jackie, much of Havana was turning out to be a dream city composed of the myriad romantic longings of its citizens, all set to an Afro-Caribbean beat that set the pulse racing and the toes tapping.

After breakfast, Emiliano had picked her up in a cab— Jackie assumed that his old Chevrolet might have conked out. He had the driver take them to the Vedado again, explaining that he wanted to show Jackie something more plush than a cigar factory on this return visit. Now she could see that this northwest part of the city was home to luxe shops and posh restaurants, as well as many office towers and apartment houses, making Havana the rival of any major city in either hemisphere when it came to luxurious living.

They were now walking through a beautiful outdoor flower market, a veritable Eden plunked down right in the middle of this urban landscape. It was crowded with tourists taking pictures and sailors from many nations buying tokens of affection for the young women who escorted them, many of whom looked to be of dubious propriety. The market vendors offered a profusion of mariposa, heliotrope, and yellow morning glory, among other tropical breeds—a riot of colors that was difficult for the eye to take in at one time and a variety of scents that was intoxicating. In her colorful, flower-print summer dress and matching ballet flats, Jackie felt that she blended right in with her surroundings.

"Such beautiful flowers," Jackie marveled as she looked around in awe.

"Would you like me to buy you one for your hair?" Emiliano asked her with a shy smile.

Jackie felt like blushing, not for her part, but for Emiliano's. She could well imagine how difficult this intimate gesture was for him.

"I'd like that very much," Jackie said.

They stopped at the next vendor, where Emiliano asked Jackie to pick out a flower that she liked.

"This is beautiful," Jackie said, pointing to a precious-looking white butterfly jasmine.

Emiliano smiled. "That's the official flower of Cuba," he told her.

After a brief but brisk session of haggling with the vendor, Emiliano purchased the flower, then handed it to Jackie to fix in her hair with a bobby pin. She took out a makeup mirror and gave it to Emiliano to hold while she manipulated the jasmine in place until he pronounced it, "Perfect."

"Thank you," Jackie said simply, and Emiliano nodded in response as they walked on.

After a few blocks, Emiliano stopped and said, "I just want you to know one thing about the man you are going to meet."

Jackie looked up at him.

"He is no political dilettante. No mere dabbler in causes," he continued. "Four days after the coup—ten days before your government officially recognized Batista—Fidel stood up in one of Cuba's highest civil courts and denounced El Presidente. He even asked for a public trial for him. That is the man you are going to meet."

Jackie looked at Emiliano. He sounded almost as passionate as he had when he was reading that stirring exhortation from *Les Misérables* to the cigar-factory workers. It was the same kind of passion that had animated Rosario during their conversation in the pickup truck. She wondered about this Fidel Castro, and what it was about this man that brought out such strong emotions in others. Well, she would soon find out.

Once past the flower market, Emiliano guided her beyond the spacious thoroughfares of the Vedado to a series of streets that ran in a slightly narrower fashion. Once again, he stopped to tell Jackie something important.

"This place where we are headed is very close to the local police precinct. It is also not far from the headquarters of the Service of Military Intelligence. The Colonel Sanchez you met the other night is a member of this secret service. The interrogation cells there are stained red with the blood of many innocent victims. So you see, Fidel and the members of the resistance are operating right under the very nose of the lion."

Abruptly, he started walking again. It took Jackie a moment or two to take in the information that Emiliano had just imparted. He was now a little way ahead, and she ran to catch up with him, clutching her camera bag, which she had taken along as part of her cover as a journalist. Inside it, along with the trusty Speed Graphic—a parting gift from Jacques before he took off for Balazistan—was the thirty-five-millimeter film reel of *Dracula*. Given the key it held, there was no way that she was going to let it out of her sight. It sat in the messenger bag she had taken last night, which in turn was nestled inside of her capacious camera bag.

Finally, they arrived at their destination: a wide building of pink-washed stone. A sign next to the door read

DANCE ACADEMY
THIRD FLOOR

And next to it was an arrow pointing upward.

"Here we are," said Emiliano as he opened the door for Jackie and led her up a winding set of stairs. As they climbed, an arresting female voice floated down to them. Although the voice sounded young, it sang of a sadness that could come only from years of experience with love and loss. On the second-floor landing, Jackie was able to see into the rehearsal room where the voice came from. She was surprised to see an exotically beautiful young woman who sang from somewhere deep in her soul.

"That's the most beautiful voice I've ever heard," Jackie remarked to Emiliano. "Who is she?"

"Her name is Celia Cruz. She sings with a local band, but she's going to be world famous one of these days. You mark my words."

After listening, entranced, for a minute more, Jackie and Emiliano resumed their climb, and the singer's voice was quickly replaced by the pulsating sound of mambo music coming from the next flight up.

The stairway ended at a room that appeared to take up the entire third floor. It was long and narrow and high ceilinged, with three large windows at either end that bounced sunlight off the whitewashed walls, making the room seem extra-bright.

The parquet floor, buffed to a high gloss, was difficult to see because of the dozens of couples dancing on it. At the far end of the room—the front, actually—the dance master and dance mistress mamboed together as an example for their pupils to emulate, for this was indeed the Dance Academy that had been advertised on the first-floor sign. Two more dancers—one male, the other female—circulated through the room, showing individual couples what they could do to improve their dance steps.

Jackie looked around for a band, but there was none to be seen. Instead, the music was provided by a large antique Victrola standing in one corner of the room, its megaphone-like horn broadcasting the mambo beat.

Emiliano gave Jackie a moment to take in the room, then said, "Would you like to dance?"

Jackie tried hard to cover her surprise at the invitation. Stuffed-shirt Emiliano was asking her to dance with him?

As though he had read her mind, Emiliano added, "This is just for the purpose of cover, of course."

"Of course," echoed Jackie with a small smile. She put her camera bag down on one of the many chairs that lined the long walls of the ballroom, then fitted herself neatly into Emiliano's arms—which felt enjoyably muscular through the thin sleeves of his linen sports jacket—as he led her across the dance floor. To her surprise, he was an excellent dancer, although with just a hint of the stiffness that she saw now as his courtly deference to the opposite sex. In some ways, Emiliano seemed like a man from a different century entirely. She had no trouble envisioning him as Don Quixote de la Mancha paying gentle court to his Dulcinea.

As they danced in time with the mambo music, Jackie noticed something curious happening. One by one, couples

melted off and drifted in the vicinity of a doorway in one corner of the ballroom that seemed to lead up to the third floor
of the building. As the remaining dancers widened their steps
and spread out to hide the gaps in their ranks, Jackie's practiced eye could gauge that about half the couples in the ballroom were no longer to be seen. Where had they gone, and to
what purpose? she wondered.

She didn't have to wait too long for an answer. With one
practiced movement, Emiliano had led Jackie so they were now
positioned with easy access to the doorway. He stopped dancing, and Jackie felt a pang of disappointment. It was romantic
being held in his arms and, for a brief moment, forgetting that
there was an ulterior reason for her being here, in this room,
with him.

Emiliano motioned for her to go through the doorway, but
Jackie stopped to retrieve her camera bag before following him
up the stairs. In case things went wrong—and Jackie had to
admit to herself that in situations such as this, that was a likely
possibility—she didn't want to be far from her camera bag and
the film reel it concealed.

The room that Emiliano led Jackie into was almost as large
as the ballroom below. Unlike the room on the third floor,
though, this one was as dark as the other one was light. Its windows were shuttered, and there didn't seem to be any exit other
than the one they had just come through. One end of the room
was piled high with ballroom chairs, some of which had been
taken down to accommodate those assembled here. They had
grouped themselves in a semicircle around a speaker who wore
a white muslin dress. It took a moment for Jackie to recognize
her as Rosario, the blond-haired beauty who had rescued her
from the Three Stooges at the crocodile farm.

Emiliano sat in a chair at the back of the semicircle and

patted the one next to him for Jackie to take. But Jackie held up one finger—indicating to him to wait "one minute"—and sidled over to the nearest window, where she opened the shuttered blinds and looked out. She saw that there was a fire escape leading down to the alley below. This was standard CIA protocol she had been taught at the Farm. Never enter a room without taking note of all possible points of egress. In an emergency, just such foreknowledge could save your life.

Jackie went to check out the other set of windows but found her arm captured by Emiliano, who silently urged her to take a seat—and at once. Jackie did so with a slight shrug of the shoulders to indicate that she was doing so under minimal protest. She sat there and listened as Rosario, standing at the front of the group, read off a list of offenses that El Presidente had committed since seizing office earlier in the year.

As Rosario continued, Jackie took the opportunity to examine those seated around her. They all seemed to be her age, in their early to mid-twenties. But judging by how varied they were in their demeanor and mode of dress, Jackie saw that they were a diverse group of men and women—workers and college graduates, *campesinos* and poets, professional men and laborers, as evidenced by the musculature beneath their shirts and the calluses on their hands. Yet there was another thing that they had in common, Jackie noted, other than their youth. It was the shining light in their eyes, the pure fervor of the revolutionary convinced that his cause is just. It was a source that, if tapped by the right individual, had the potential to change the world.

When she was finished, Rosario's place was taken by a man dressed in a tan suit. Before he launched into his speech, he removed his jacket and handed it to a man seated in the first row. The speaker was handsome in an unassuming way and had an unassuming manner to match. He was neatly barbered, with a small mustache and a head of thick dark hair. He spoke in a soft voice and was somewhat halting in his manner. *Hardly a galvanizing speaker,* was Jackie's first impression of the man.

But then something curious happened. The man continued to speak in his soft voice. And the people seated around him leaned forward to catch his every word. This seemed to spur on the man, who slowly raised his voice and addressed his audience with increased passion.

Jackie looked around and saw from the rapt looks on their faces that everyone in the room was mesmerized by this man's words. He grew more ardent with each passing moment. Although she had only a basic grasp of what he was saying, the fervent way he spoke needed no translation. She found herself at risk of being carried off by the soaring power of his voice.

And then all the little hairs on her arms rose to attention as, with a thrill, Jackie realized that the speaker was the very man she had come to Cuba to meet—Fidel Castro. Very soon now, she was going to be able to fulfill one-half of her mission: speaking to him and finding out what his intentions were should he ever manage to overthrow El Presidente and become the new— and hopefully more democratic-minded—leader of Cuba.

But before that could happen, the windows at the other end of the room—the ones left unexamined by Jackie—burst open, allowing shafts of sunlight to spear the darkness, followed by men who were even now catapulting into the room behind the beams of illumination. Some were dressed in uniform. Others wore rumpled dark suits. All had guns drawn or rifles raised, and they were being led by the man Jackie recognized as Colonel Sanchez. Apparently, this member of the secret service had finally caught on to the fact that the rebel headquarters in the city lay only a stone's throw from his own command center.

There was a mass scraping of chairs as the revolutionaries rose and bolted for the doorway, hoping to get downstairs and outside the building before this flying squad from the Service of Military Intelligence could round them up. Jackie watched as two men from the front row grabbed Fidel by both arms and dragged him toward the exit. But the doorway was a narrow one, and there was a bottleneck as all the rebels tried to flee the room at the same time. Jackie's natural instinct was to follow them down the stairs. But instead, she held back and put a hand on Emiliano's arm, silently urging him to follow her lead.

Between the shafts of sunlight, there were still deep pockets of shadow, and it was into one of these shadows that Jackie now dissolved, with Emiliano instinctively at her side. She followed the pocket to the wall against which all the remaining ballroom chairs had been piled, found the slight gap between the wall and the chairs, and slipped into it. After Jackie's slight tugging on his sleeve, Emiliano did too.

Trying to control her heavy breathing and rapid heartbeat, Jackie looked out through the chairs and watched horror-struck as Rosario, the last rebel out of the room, was nabbed by Colonel Sanchez, who seemed to wear a look of vindication on his face. There was something unusual about that moment of capture, but Jackie had no time to think about it now, as she was too busy trying to plot their escape from this room.

She waited until Sanchez and Rosario started down the stairs in the wake of the other members of Sanchez's flying squad. Then Jackie put one finger on her lips as a signal to Emiliano to step as quietly as possible, and they emerged from behind the relative security of the chairs. She needn't have worried about making any noise, however, because sounds of absolute chaos came from the ballroom below as terror was unleashed on the remaining dancers.

Jackie walked quickly over to the windows that she had checked out upon first entering the room. The shutter was easy to raise. Jackie lifted one, then stepped through the window onto the fire escape, first stopping to make sure that her camera bag was secure. She motioned for Emiliano to step over the sill and join her. The fire escape creaked and vibrated and shook in place. Jackie guessed that it was now only rust that was holding the structure to the wall. Best to get off it as quickly as possible. She pointed downward, then started down the rickety iron ladder to the landing directly below.

As she clambered down the rusted ladder, she began to replay in her mind the end of the scene that she had just witnessed. There was Rosario trying to flee from the flying squad. She was the last through the doorway and would have made it had not Colonel Sanchez seized hold of her from behind. He grabbed her around the waist and flung her around, spinning her so fast that her blond hair, obviously a wig, flew off her head to reveal a thick mane of dark brown, curly hair. Now, why would someone with hair like that want to disguise it?

XIII

They were on the run.

Once down the rickety fire escape, Jackie and Emiliano exited the alley opening to the street, hoping they were far enough from the building's entrance to escape being spotted by any members of the flying squad who had been positioned there. The scene in the street was absolute pandemonium as the rebels caught by Colonel Sanchez's men were placed in army trucks parked at the curb. People had come out to rubberneck and were being held back by police officers supporting the flying squad with crowd control. Jackie could only hope that some of the rebels had managed to take advantage of this crowd and blend in with the gawkers as Sanchez's men herded the ones already captured into the rear of the waiting trucks.

In one of the vehicles, she spotted Rosario, noticeable now by her long, dark brown curls. She looked frightened, as anyone would have been under the circumstances. Jackie's heart went out to her, and she wished that there was something she could do for her. Maybe later. Maybe then she could find some way to save the life of the brave young woman who had done the same for her.

Jackie motioned to Emiliano that they should go back and exit the alley from the other end. But before they could, there was a cry from one of the police officers holding back the crowd.

"Look! There are two more," he shouted, then took a whistle out of his breast pocket and began to blow on it. This attracted several members of the flying squad, who took off after Jackie and Emiliano as they ran back down the alley and out the other side.

Jackie had no idea where they were, so she let Emiliano take the lead. Fortunately, he did know where he was going and led the flying-squad members on a breathless chase through the back alleys of the Vedado. At several points, Jackie could have sworn that they had lost their pursuers and were safe. But just as soon as she thought they could stop running, the flying-squad members would find them and the chase would be on again. She wished now that she had worn something else, because she felt like she could be spotted a mile off in her colorful flower-print summer dress. The only place where it could have provided proper camouflage was back at the flower market.

They were now running through an area adjacent to the Vedado, one where elegant restaurants had given way to fly-ridden food stalls, and office buildings had been replaced by block-long factories and warehouses. By now, it was late in the afternoon, and many of these businesses had shut down operations for the day.

They heard footsteps behind them, coming at a fast pace. The long, featureless street they were on afforded no cover, and they were walking briskly past a brick wall.

"Jacqueline, this way," Emiliano said, making a stirrup out of his hands for her to put her foot in, then boosting her up and over the wall. On the other side of it, Jackie climbed down into what she saw was a parking lot filled with large trucks. There appeared to be no one around. A moment later, she was joined by Emiliano. They kept silent and heard the sounds of the footsteps running past them on the other side of the wall.

"That was quick thinking," said Jackie. She couldn't hide that she was exhausted from the long chase.

"We need transportation," Emiliano suggested. "They'll never suspect us if we're in one of these trucks."

They explored the lot and went from truck to truck until they found one that had its key in the ignition.

"*Gracias a Dios,*" Emiliano said, looking up at the heavens.

In the back of the truck, he found two sets of coveralls and two caps. He handed one of each to Jackie and said, "Here, put this on."

Jackie looked questioningly at him.

"For camouflage," Emiliano explained, "in case we hit any roadblocks."

Jackie and Emiliano put on the coveralls over their clothes. Jackie pushed all of her hair under the cap so she wouldn't be recognized as a woman.

"How do I look?" she asked Emiliano.

Emiliano looked her up and down and said, "I think there's only one thing missing to complete your disguise."

As Jackie looked on, Emiliano disappeared under the truck. When he reappeared, his right hand was thick with axle grease. Before she could stop him, Emiliano had taken several swipes at her face with his right hand, smearing it with the grease. He stood back and assessed his handiwork.

"Perfect," he exclaimed.

Was it her imagination or was Emiliano somehow enjoying this? Well, if so, two could certainly play at this game.

Emiliano was all set to get into the truck when Jackie stopped him by saying, "What about your disguise? Shouldn't it be as complete as mine?"

Before Emiliano could stop her, Jackie rubbed her right hand against his, transferring some of the axle grease to her fingers. She then used her fingers to paint Emiliano's cheeks and forehead with the grease, making her feel like a Comanche maiden putting war paint on her brave for a ritual dance. She stood back to examine her artistic creation.

"Perfect," Jackie proclaimed.

A chagrined Emiliano said, "Can we get in the truck now?"

Jackie found a rag in the back pocket of her coveralls. She used it to remove the axle grease from her fingers. She then passed the rag to Emiliano, who did the same.

The two of them got into the truck cab, and Emiliano slowly pulled the vehicle out of the parking lot.

Several blocks away, they encountered a roadblock quickly thrown up to catch them or anyone else who had escaped from the Dance Academy. Traffic moved slowly as each vehicle approaching the checkpoint was stopped so the guards could check out those inside. Jackie felt her heart begin to beat at an accelerated rate.

Emiliano must have known what she was feeling because he said, "Easy, Jacqueline. They are looking for a man and a woman, not two grease-stained workmen in a truck. Try to remain calm. Don't do anything to attract their attention and we'll get through this."

A grateful Jackie looked over at Emiliano, who appeared as serene as a Buddhist monk at meditation. She would use him as an example and try to put herself in the same frame of mind. It wasn't easy, especially knowing what would probably happen to them if they were stopped and arrested. But Jackie did her best to control her heart rate and steady her breathing.

The line of cars moved slowly. But finally, it was their turn. Emiliano pulled up at the checkpoint and stopped the truck. A guard stood on either running board and looked into the cab, barely glancing at either Jackie or Emiliano.

The guard on Emiliano's side brusquely asked him to open the rear door of the truck. Emiliano got out of the truck and went around to the back with the guard, leaving Jackie alone with the other guard. Instead of refusing to make eye contact, which she knew would make her seem suspicious, Jackie bravely looked the second guard right in the eye and gave him a tired-looking smile, just an average worker going home at the end of a very long day.

After what seemed like an eternity, Emiliano returned to the truck and got back in the driver's seat. The guard waved them on; then he and the other guard went to inspect the next vehicle in line.

Once they were far enough away from the roadblock, both Jackie and Emiliano gave out a loud sigh of relief.

"That was a close one," Emiliano said, taking off his cap and blotting the sweat on his forehead with the same greasy rag. Apparently, his Buddha-like calm had been a facade displayed for her benefit.

"We pulled it off," said Jackie with a note of triumph in her voice. She felt incredibly grateful to Emiliano and, surprisingly, very close to him in that moment.

After he had been driving awhile, Jackie noticed that they were headed away from what she thought was the direction of her hotel and toward the outskirts of the city.

"Aren't you taking me back to the Nacional?" she asked, a note of concern in her voice.

"No, this city has become too hot for us."

"Where are we going, then?"

He turned to Jackie and fixed her with an intense look.

"You still want to meet him, don't you?"

Jackie nodded vigorously. "Of course I do. But didn't Sanchez capture him?"

"I'm sure Fidel got away. Like *el gato*, he has nine lives. And
I didn't see him in any of the trucks with the others. So have
you ever heard of the expression 'If the mountain won't come
to Muhammad, Muhammad must go to the mountain'?"

"Yes, and where will we find this mountain?"

"In the Sierra Maestra of Oriente Province. Fidel's home."
He paused for effect. "And mine as well."

"But what about Sanchez? Won't he order his men to follow
us?"

Emiliano glanced at the road before turning to Jackie.

"Where we're going, the country is so mountainous and his
men so spread out that there's very little chance of us encountering them. Or them encountering us, for that matter."

Oh, well, Jackie thought, settling back in her seat and kick-
ing at the food wrappers gathered at her feet. She should have
gotten used to this by now, having to flee for her life and leaving all her clothing back at some hotel. But this time, there
would be no one to bring her suitcase to her, and she found
herself beset by the age-old question that haunts every woman,
no matter what her circumstances: *What am I going to wear?*

XIV

They drove out of the city headed east through Matanzas Province. It was dusk, and Emiliano steered the truck with the sun sinking behind them and the darkness falling ahead. Leaving Havana, they had encountered no further roadblocks, which meant that either they had gotten out of the city in the proverbial nick of time or Colonel Sanchez had decided not to throw up any more. As he drove, Emiliano turned on the headlights to cut through the gloom and switched on the dashboard radio, tuned to an English-language station in the Florida Keys. Instantly, the truck cab was filled with the swooning voice of Kay Starr singing "Wheel of Fortune."

After they had been on the road awhile, Emiliano pointed south and said to Jackie, "Over there's the Bay of Pigs. That's where Gabriela rescued you from the crocodile farm."

Jackie had no idea who Emiliano was talking about. "Gabriela?" she said. "Don't you mean Rosario?"

"Oh, I'm sorry. You know her as Rosario. That's her underground name. She joined Fidel's group after Sanchez tried to rape her and she had to coldcock him to escape. Gabriela is her real name."

Jackie remembered the look on Sanchez's face as Rosario's—make that Gabriela's—blond wig came off, and she shuddered with disgust at the thought of that pig getting his hands on her again.

She turned to Emiliano. "We have to get her out of his clutches," she said in a voice strained with emotion.

"Fidel knows the situation. We'll leave it up to him to decide what to do."

Emiliano's cool-as-you-please statement was infuriating to Jackie. Her mind was plagued by the sickening image of Gabriela being sexually assaulted by Sanchez.

"How can you be so damned casual about this?"

"I'm afraid it's the only way I can be." He glanced over at her as he drove. "Look, Jacqueline, the minute Gabriela joined the rebels, she became a soldier in our army. She knew what the stakes were, the chance she was taking. Now she's been taken prisoner. That's part of the fortunes of war. And we'll do everything we can to free her. But we can't let that deflect us from our higher cause—freedom for the entire nation of Cuba."

"So you think one person's life is less important than your main goal?"

Without a moment's hesitation, Emiliano said, "Yes."

Jackie turned away from him. If this was what the rebels believed, then maybe she already knew which side of the political spectrum Fidel would ultimately fall on.

They drove in silence for a while. It was an awkward silence filled with unspoken reproach, and Jackie could tell that Emiliano knew from her tightly sealed lips how much his curt response had rankled her.

There was a new song on the radio. Louis Armstrong was singing "A Kiss to Build a Dream On." Satchmo's soothing voice seemed to have a conciliatory effect on Jackie. And when she looked at Emiliano, she saw that his mood was mellowing too.

Finally, he looked over at her and said, "Do you want to tell me what's so important about that reel of film?"

"What reel of film?" Jackie asked, playing innocent.

"The one in your camera bag."

"You looked through my camera bag?" Jackie bristled at the very idea of Emiliano having had the temerity to examine her things.

"Hardly," he said, sounding defensive. He hiked his thumb toward the area behind the seats, where Jackie had tossed her bag. Improbably, the reel of film was peeking up through its opening.

Looking sheepish, Jackie said, "Oh, *that* film reel."

"Yes. A souvenir from El Teatro de Cinema, I take it."

Jackie cleared her throat. "This is actually classified information."

"Well, you can tell me, if you like. Deputy Director Dulles has assigned me Cosmic clearance."

Jackie thought about it, mentally weighing the pros and cons of confiding to Emiliano what the film reel contained. Finally, she turned to him and said, "Okay. I'll tell you." She then went into the entire saga of Walker's treasure, beginning with her purchase of the antiquated book on Cuba and her accidental discovery of Metzger's diary and ending with Maheu's revelation that the key to the treasure's location could be found in the reel of film. She turned to Emiliano and saw an odd look on his face.

"What?" she asked him.

"From the way you speak about him, I think that on some level you identify with him, this nineteenth-century soldier of fortune."

Jackie pondered that and said, "I don't know if I identify

with him, exactly. But I'm struck by his story. Here he was, an idealistic young man, signing up as a filibuster to help Walker free Nicaragua, only to find that Walker was totally corrupt and probably crazy in the bargain. Then he returns to the U.S., where he fights for the North in the Civil War, but ends up wondering if any just cause is worth the price you pay in blood."

Her fervor took even Jackie by surprise. "You see, Emiliano, that's why I don't believe violence is the necessary response to any political problem."

Emiliano looked over at her and nodded. "I understand your position perfectly. And I think you understand mine. So, at least for now, can we just agree to disagree?"

Jackie nodded in return. "A truce," she said.

"A truce," he agreed.

The town was a small collection of whitewashed buildings radiating from a dusty central square with a rusted fountain that had stopped dispensing water many years ago. One of the buildings turned out to be a hotel, and Jackie and Emiliano decided to take a room there. Because he didn't want to let her out of his sight, Emiliano insisted that they pass themselves off to the desk clerk, a small man with a big mustache, as husband and wife.

But once in the room, the first thing Emiliano did was take a blanket off one of the twin beds and use a clothesline he found in one of the dresser drawers to rig up a curtain to divide the room in two to give Jackie her privacy. Jackie smiled inwardly at Emiliano's constant deference to decorum.

"You make me feel just like Claudette Colbert in *It Happened One Night*," Jackie said, referring to Clark Gable's similar solution to sharing a room with his unmarried traveling companion.

"Well, if you're expecting me to act like Clark Gable and take off my shirt, you'll be disappointed," Emiliano said. Jackie was surprised. Here was Emiliano displaying a hide-and-seek sense of humor again, as well as his familiarity with a romantic comedy. And beyond that, revealing that maybe he was more shy about sharing a room with her than she was about sharing a room with him. It was an odd turnabout of gender roles, but Jackie found Emiliano's modesty completely endearing.

The hotel had no dining room, but they found a cantina nearby that was still open. Jackie thought that it was the equivalent of the twenty-four-hour diners back home. The place was rustic, with a menu to match. Jackie and Emiliano both ordered arroz con pollo and fried plantains, a dinner that turned out to be rather tasty. Afterward, they returned to their hotel room, where they retired to their beds on either side of the makeshift curtain.

Jackie closed her eyes but found that sleep just wouldn't come, partly because a chain of events kept playing out in her mind. First, there were the events of the day, then the events of the last few days after her arrival at the airport, and then the events of the past year—starting with the discovery of the diary—that had led to her being here, in this hotel room, in a small nameless Cuban town in the province of Matanzas, with this stand-in for Fernando Lamas. And that, she had to admit to herself, was the other reason she was finding it so hard to fall asleep: having the gorgeously handsome man lying on the other side of the curtain.

After what seemed like several hours of tossing and turning, Jackie gave up all thoughts of sleep. In a small voice, she called out, "Emiliano?"

At first there was no response. Then, from the other side of the curtain, came, "Yes?"

"Are you awake?"

"Yes."

"Oh, you can't sleep either?"

"Well, frankly, all your tossing and turning is keeping me awake."

"Sorry," Jackie said contritely. "Well, since we're both up, would you like to talk?"

Before he could answer, Jackie drew back the curtain, hoping the sight of her would encourage Emiliano to say yes.

"I guess so," Emiliano said, sitting up in bed. His shirt was off, but unlike Clark Gable, he was wearing a sleeveless undershirt. Even so, the sight of his muscular biceps and chest rippling beneath the shirt made Jackie's eyes widen. "What would you like to talk about?"

Jackie thought about it. "Why don't you tell me a story?"

"What kind of story?"

"Oh, I don't know." Then a thought occurred to her: "Why don't you tell me about your childhood? You said you were from Oriente, and so was Fidel Castro. Did you grow up together?"

"We played together as boys even though my father was a poor *campesino* and Fidel's father owned a sugar plantation. But you see, Fidel wasn't raised at home. He spent most of his childhood in foster homes and private Catholic boarding schools."

"How sad," Jackie said. "Why was that?"

Emiliano seem reluctant to go on, but he finally said, "Well, it's common knowledge in Cuba that Fidel was born out of wedlock to a household servant of Angel Castro's when Angel was married to another woman. He didn't divorce her to marry

Fidel's mother until Fidel was fifteen. All the other children made fun of Fidel for that. But I didn't. I liked him because he was such a smart student and a good athlete. We both played on the baseball team at El Colegio de Belén, a Jesuit school in Havana. I was an outfielder, and Fidel was a pitcher. A very good one, I might add."

"Yes, Mr. Dulles told me about that," Jackie said. "So you were both athletes. Were you both always interested in politics too?"

"Yes. History was my favorite subject in school. Maybe being named after Zapata had something to do with that. And Fidel's biggest heroes were political figures." Emiliano smiled. "Do you know what his most prized possession was as a boy?"

"No, what?"

"A letter from U.S. president Franklin D. Roosevelt, thanking Fidel for the letter that he wrote to him when he was fourteen years old."

Jackie was incredulous. "Fidel wrote a letter to President Roosevelt when he was fourteen?"

Emiliano smiled again. "Yes, but he said he was twelve in the letter. I guess he thought that sounded more impressive."

Jackie smiled too. "Here I thought only women lied about their age," she said. "What did he write in the letter?"

"He was learning English, and he addressed the letter to 'My good friend Roosevelt' and told him how happy he was that Roosevelt got reelected. Then he wrote, 'If you like, give me a ten dollar bill green American, because never, I have not seen a ten dollars bill.'"

Jackie laughed. "I don't suppose he got the ten dollars, did he?"

"No, but he got a very nice form letter that he still has to this day."

"That's a cute story," Jackie said. "A history buff and a Roosevelt fan. I can see how you both wound up in law school. That must have made your parents very proud."

"It did. I was the first one in my family to even go to college." Emiliano's voice dropped to a low tone, almost as if he was speaking to himself, but his eyes were fixed on Jackie's, and she could see sadness pooling in them. "I wish my father had lived to see me graduate from law school," he said softly. "That was his dream. But the life of a farmer is a hard one. My father worked ten hours a day in the broiling sun just to put food on the table, hardly eating anything himself most of the time. He died when I was in my junior year of college. My mother was devastated. He was the love of her life, just as she was his."

"Oh, Emiliano, I'm so sorry," Jackie said. She squeezed his hand, half expecting him to extricate it from hers the way he had the first time she had reached for it, but he didn't seem to want to let it go. Overcome with feeling for him, Jackie inched her face closer to his until their lips were almost touching. It felt strange to know that he was waiting for her to make the next move, and yet it excited her to be the one in control for a change. She brushed his lips lightly with hers, testing him. When he didn't draw back, she threw caution to the wind and kissed him full on the lips, drawing her arms around him as their mouths opened, and the kiss went on and on.

Finally, they pulled apart, gasping for air. Emiliano had such a stricken look on his face that Jackie began to laugh. "Emiliano, it's all right," she said. "We're allowed to show affection for each other if we feel it. We're only human."

Emiliano shook his head. "Yes, we're only human, but in circumstances like these"—he pulled the sheet around him and glanced at the narrow space between their beds—"perhaps it would be best if we to try to be superhuman."

Jackie had to laugh again. "Yes, I guess you're right," she said, pulling her own sheet around herself. "This is a pretty slippery slope we're on here."

Now it was Emiliano's hand that reached for Jackie's and held it just long enough for a warm feeling to suffuse her inside before he gently pulled it away. She took that tender gesture as a plea for understanding that Emiliano was withdrawing from her not because he didn't find her attractive, but because he did—dangerously so.

"Well, I hope my little bedtime story will help you be able to fall asleep now," Emiliano said with a hint of irony in his voice.

"Yes, I think I do feel sleepy now," Jackie said, covering a yawn with her hand. Actually, she felt a kind of dreamy contentment at achieving a breakthrough with Emiliano, brief as it was.

"Good."

He drew the makeshift curtain across the space between the two beds, and from the other side of it, she could hear him say, "Good night, Jacqueline."

"Good night, Emiliano," Jackie said, settling herself down in bed again. But she knew that, with the feel of his strong hand in hers and that delicious kiss lingering in her mind, it would be hours longer before she could shut her eyes and enjoy the welcome release of sleep.

XV

They were traveling east along the spine of the island, the Escambray Mountain Range.

Emiliano suggested that they stick to the back roads, just in case Colonel Sanchez had roadblocks set up on the highways to catch them. On a map she found in the truck's glove box, Jackie saw that taking the back roads meant driving either through the jungle or along the side of the mountain range.

Driving through the jungle, they encountered roads so overgrown with vines and creepers that passage became next to impossible. While Jackie drove the truck, Emiliano stood on the front bumper, holding on to a metal pole that had been soldered upright to be used as a handhold. In his free hand, he employed a machete that he had found in the back of the truck to scythe through the dense overgrowth blocking the vehicle. The squawking of parrots in the distance created a rude counterpoint to the hacking sounds made by Emiliano's machete. It was hard work, especially when you factored in the heat and the mosquitoes, which were a constant source of aggravation. Jackie couldn't believe how improbably her situation with Emiliano had changed. It was like entering a movie theatre to watch *It Happened One Night* and have it turn into *The African Queen*.

They continued to wear the coveralls they had found in the truck, which seemed better suited to the terrain than their own clothes, now neatly folded and stashed in Jackie's capacious camera bag.

As they drove east, they made conversation to pass the time and continued to exchange life histories. Emiliano learned what it was like for Jackie to have grown up with a much loved but philandering father and a controlling mother whose only aim in life was to see her daughter married well. As she spoke of this, she caught Emiliano smiling.

"What?" she asked him.

Emiliano said, "As a lector, I sometimes read from *Orgullo y Prejuicio* or *Sentido y Sensibilidad*. I was just thinking that you could have been the heroine of a novel by Señorita Austen."

Jackie blushed, unable to hide from Emiliano that his comment had touched a hidden nerve.

As they continued east, Jackie learned what it was like for Emiliano to have grown up poor, his present success due to his loving parents' support and the helpful intervention of the United Fruit executive who saw something in the young Emiliano that made him want to help the boy.

And now that the cat was out of the bag, they talked about Walker's treasure and debated what it might consist of—gold bars, priceless jewelry, or maybe even the gold doubloons and pieces of eight of pirate legend.

Sometimes they wouldn't talk at all, but just rolled along in companionable silence and stared out the window, gazing upon the incredible scenery passing by: the seemingly endless green fields of sugar cane, the deeper jade green of the jungle, and the sheer walls of the mountains.

The radio, still tuned to that Key West station, provided continuous musical accompaniment. It was now broadcasting

Hank Williams's roistering "Jambalaya," a pleasant distraction from the scenery, which had become wildly vertiginous as the truck traversed a switchback road that clung tenuously to the side of a mountain. The roadway was only two lanes wide here, and there was no guardrail anywhere along its length to keep them from hurtling out into the abyss should the driver lose control of the vehicle.

All of a sudden, Emiliano, who was now back behind the wheel, slammed on the brakes, forcing the truck to slew crazily to the left and bringing its left rear tire, spitting gravel, perilously close to the edge of the precipice.

"Emiliano, what is it?" Jackie asked, a rising note of panic in her voice.

Instead of answering, Emiliano opened the cab door, jumped out, and walked forward several feet along the roadway. He was quickly joined by Jackie, who wanted to see for herself what the problem was.

They stood at the edge of a crater that took up almost the entire roadway. Something had gouged a huge chunk out of the road's surface. It was easy to see that the hole was wide enough and deep enough to prevent the truck from continuing forward.

"What happened here?" Jackie asked.

"I don't know," Emiliano said. "Maybe a torrential rainstorm washed away some of the road. Or maybe a slight earth tremor caused this section to collapse."

"How are we going to get around it?"

"We can't go forward; that hole's too deep and too wide. There isn't enough room here to turn the truck around and go back the way we came. And I don't see us driving backward until we find someplace wide enough to turn the truck around. That could be miles back down the road."

"So what are we going to do?"

"I guess we're stuck here, unless you want to hike the rest of the way to Oriente Province."

Jackie made a face and looked down at her ballet flats. "Unfortunately, I left my hiking shoes at home."

Emiliano looked up in frustration. Jackie followed his line of vision.

Directly above the crater, about fifteen feet up the side of the mountain, was a shelflike outcropping. It seemed to be holding in place a tumble of rocks that had somehow shaken loose from the mountain above them. The accumulation of rocks had been prevented from falling farther down the slope by this small ledge.

Hearing a sound from down the mountain, Jackie went over to the edge of the road and looked over it. Below on the switchback, headed in their direction but still some distance away, was a jeep climbing the mountain road. It held four soldiers, and Jackie could see a machine gun mounted on a post at the rear of the vehicle.

"Emiliano," she called with urgency in her voice.

Emiliano joined her and looked down. He saw the jeep and said, "Could be Sanchez's men. Or just a random road patrol. Either way, if they stop us, we're dead meat. We have to figure a way to get over that crater before they get here."

As Jackie watched, Emiliano looked over at the crater in the roadway, then up to the suspended rock fall, then back down again. He did this, looking down, then up, several more times. Something was obviously going on in his mind.

"Emiliano," she prompted him. As though shaken out of his trance, he looked at her.

"It's odd," he said, "but there seem to be enough fallen rocks up there to fill this hole in the roadway. If only we had some way of removing that shelf. If we could just blow it up, all those loose rocks would come tumbling down the slope and fill up this crater." He sighed, then continued, "Where's a stick of dynamite when you really need one?"

Jackie could see that Emiliano was unprepared to have his rhetorical question answered in so prompt a fashion. "Wait here," she said, and ran back to the truck. When she returned to him, she was holding the messenger bag. As Emiliano looked on, Jackie reached into it and withdrew a single stick of dynamite. Emiliano's jaw literally dropped open.

"Jesus, Mary, and Joseph, Jacqueline, what else do you have in there? A bazooka? A battering ram? A nuclear warhead, maybe? Where did you get that?"

"From the Teatro de Cinema. I took the dynamite to keep the fire from setting it off. I guess I forgot that I had it with me," she explained with a note of chagrin in her voice.

"You forgot?" Emiliano asked in disbelief.

"Well, we've been on the run, and I've had so many more important things to think about. Besides, I had no idea where to ditch them."

"Them? You have more than this one?"

"Oh, yes, I have a whole bundle of them. Do you want more?"

"No, I think one will suffice." He shook his head as though unable to believe that his companion of the last few days had been walking around with enough dynamite to blow them to pieces, and yet hadn't thought to warn him of that distinct possibility.

Her face red with embarrassment, Jackie handed him the stick of dynamite and watched while Emiliano looked it over. She saw him frown.

"Is there a problem?"

"Yes," said Emiliano, continuing to examine the dynamite stick in his hand. "See this fuse? It's very short. There is no way I could light it and get back down the slope before it set off the dynamite."

They checked the other dynamite sticks and saw that all the fuses were of the same length. Emiliano looked visibly deflated. It had been such a good plan. And now it seemed like all that hope was in danger of being quashed. Jackie tried hard not to appear equally crestfallen.

"If only there was some way we could extend the fuse," Emiliano said, succinctly defining the problem.

Jackie felt the weight of the messenger bag in her hand and a thought occurred to her. She reached into the messenger bag and, like a magician conjuring a rabbit from a hat, produced reel three of *Dracula*. "I was told that this movie was made on nitrate film stock. That's extremely flammable. If we could—"

Emiliano saw where she was headed and rushed to fill in the rest. "Just take several feet of film and use it to extend the fuse, I could light the dynamite and be down the slope before it exploded. Jacqueline, you are a genius."

Emiliano was so obviously overjoyed at Jackie for coming up with a solution that he embraced her, squeezed her tight, and spun her around.

"Jacqueline, I could kiss you," he said with one of his uncustomary outbursts of emotion, perhaps abetted by the fact that they would soon have company to deal with.

"Why don't you?" Jackie blurted out before she could stop herself.

Emiliano accepted the invitation and kissed Jackie full on the lips. It was the first time he had kissed her since that night in the inn, and she was reminded all over again that no matter how infrequently he used them, Emiliano definitely knew what to do with his lips when it came to kissing a woman and leaving her yearning for more. Unfortunately, thoughts of the jeep coming up behind forced them to cut this romantic interlude short.

As soon as Emiliano broke off the kiss and the scenery around her stopped spinning, Jackie opened the film can and took out the reel of film, which she handed to Emiliano. He unspooled several feet and held up the film to look at it. It appeared to be blank.

"Good," he pronounced. "I think this is what they call the leader, so we can take some film without damaging the actual movie."

That was Emiliano, Jackie thought, the cautious lawyer, always scrupulously tending to details.

From his pocket, Emiliano produced a pocketknife and opened the blade. He continued to unspool the reel of film until he judged that he had enough, then used the knife blade to cut off a large section of leader from the rest of the reel. He then gave the reel to Jackie; she put it back in its can and placed it in the messenger bag.

By this time, Emiliano had started up the slope. Jackie followed, and Emiliano held out his hand to steady her as she climbed up after him. It was a somewhat steep ascent, made more awkward by the loose stones beneath them that constantly threatened to undermine their balance.

Finally, after some careful tacking back and forth up the slope, they arrived at the ledge holding the pile of rocks in place. Emiliano bent down and examined the underside of the shelf, checking for the exact right place to plant the dynamite stick.

"This one stick ought to do the job if we place it right here," Emiliano said as he wedged the dynamite in place beneath the ledge.

"You look like you've done this before," Jackie observed.

"I did. I picked up a rudimentary education in explosives when I worked in the mines."

"When was that?"

"When I was in law school."

"I thought you said you worked your way through law school as a lector."

"I worked in the nickel mines too. In the summers. Law school was very expensive."

As she watched, Emiliano spliced the end of the fuse onto one end of the leader by taking the fuse and threading it through the first set of sprocket holes on either side of the film. He tugged on it gently and the two pieces held firmly together.

"There, that should do it," Emiliano said, closing his knife and pocketing it.

They went back down the slope, being careful not to slip and fall. Once back on the roadway, they returned to the truck, which Emiliano drove back about fifty feet, judging it to be a safe distance outside the blast radius of the explosion.

"I guess we're ready," Emiliano said to Jackie. He reached into another pocket, took out a monogrammed silver cigarette lighter, and flicked it open, but nothing happened. He flicked it several more times, but with the same results.

"Must be out of fuel," he said. He searched his pockets but came up empty. "Damn," he said, "I'm all out of matches too. You?" Jackie shook her head at Emiliano.

"I guess this isn't my day," he said and took out his frustration on the truck by banging on a fender.

"I know," Jackie said, looking inside the truck. "The cigarette lighter." She pushed in on the lighter on the dashboard, waited for it to pop, then took it out and held it up to Emiliano. "That's excellent," he said to her. He took the lighter from her, its end glowing cherry red.

"Okay," he told her. "Now, stay in the cab. No matter what happens, don't come out. Not until you see me or hear from me. Got that?"

Jackie nodded to show that she understood.

"Good."

Cigarette lighter glowing in his hand, Emiliano started up the road, then stopped and returned to the truck. He took out the monogrammed silver lighter and handed it to Jackie.

"It was a graduation gift. Please hold on to it, and you can give it back to me later."

"Good luck," said Jackie, feeling the inadequacy of the words to convey what she really felt. She had known him only a couple of days, and yet she found her thoughts constantly turning to him. She knew what emotional bellwether that signified. Emiliano started back up the roadway and began climbing up the slope until he was lost from sight.

Disobeying Emiliano's orders, Jackie got out of the truck cab and walked over to the edge of the roadway. Looking down, she could see the jeep. It was still several switchbacks behind, but it would catch up to them in the next several minutes. So even if Emiliano's plan did work, there was still the tiny matter of having a jeep filled with soldiers and a machine gun on their tail. There was no way they could hope to lose them on this narrow mountain road. She hoped that Emiliano also had some plan in mind to deal with them, because she had run out of ideas, like a car whose fuel gauge was now on empty.

Jackie returned to the truck cab. She thought about all the things that could go wrong. Emiliano sliding down the slope and breaking a leg, or worse. Emiliano underestimating the timing on the fuse and being blown to smithereens by the dynamite. Emiliano not making it back to the roadway in time and having his body pelted by a hail of shrapnel.

Instead, she tried to think positive thoughts and visualize just what was happening as she sat there. She saw Emiliano climbing carefully up the slope until he arrived at the ledge. She saw him straighten out the film leader, then hold the glowing red end of the cigarette lighter against its free end. She saw the film begin to spark as it caught fire, and the flame run down to the dynamite stick's fuse, which accepted the fire like the handoff of the torch in a marathon race. She saw Emiliano, at the same time, running back down the slope and searching for cover before the dynamite exploded.

KA-BOOM!

Jackie was jerked upright in her seat as she heard the dynamite explode up the slope. A second later the shockwave from the explosion reached the truck and shook the cab. At the same time, the truck was pelted with shards of rock that the explosion had sent hurtling through the air in all directions. It was like a hailstorm of stones that must have lasted only thirty seconds. But Jackie was concerned to see that there was no sign of Emiliano through the smoke and dust that now shrouded the truck.

She stuck her head out the cab window and called out. "Emiliano? Emiliano!" But there was no answer.

She hopped out of the truck and ran through the dust cloud. Three-quarters of the way to the crater, she practically tripped over something in the middle of the roadway. It was Emiliano lying motionless on the ground.

"Emiliano," Jackie called out to him as she knelt by his side to assess his condition. His eyes were closed, but his chest was heaving up and down, obviously as a result of the run down the slope and away from the explosion. Thank God for that. Very gently, she lifted a comma of hair off his forehead and could see he was bleeding from a slight cut where a piece of flying rock had obviously nicked the skin. Her tender touch must have done the trick because Emiliano opened his eyes.

"Jacqueline," he said simply and smiled up at her. To Jackie, it was the best smile she had ever seen, and she could feel her heart expanding inside her chest, knowing that Emiliano was alive.

"Are you okay?"

He nodded at her and gave her a small smile to show that he was all right.

"Piece of pie," Emiliano said.

"Piece of cake," Jackie said, smiling down at him.

Ever mindful of the jeep that could catch up with them at any minute, she asked, "Can you get up?"

"I think so."

With Jackie's help, he levered himself to a sitting position, then slowly rose to his feet.

He and Jackie both looked ahead. To their immense relief, their plan had worked. The scree from above had rolled down the slope after the explosion had obliterated the shelf of rock and had neatly filled up the crater in the roadway, enough at least for the truck to drive over.

"We did it!" exclaimed Emiliano.

"We did it!" echoed Jackie.

"We make quite a team, don't we?"

"We certainly do." Jackie beamed.

Letting him use her body as support, Jackie led Emiliano back to the truck. It was good feeling his weight against her, good to support him as she now knew he would support her in any crisis to come. At the same time, she knew that she had to hurry because that damned jeep could arrive at any second.

She opened the passenger door and helped him inside. "I guess I better drive for a while," she said, and was happy to see that Emiliano didn't try to challenge her. They looked back and saw the jeep in the near distance and coming up fast. Obviously, they were driving quickly now to investigate the source of the explosion.

"Emiliano, what are we going to do?"

Instead of answering, Emiliano reached into the messenger bag, pulled out another dynamite stick, and lit its fuse with the still hot cigarette lighter. Then, hissing dynamite stick in hand, he jumped down from the truck cab to the ground.

"Wait here," he shouted back to Jackie. "I'll be right back."

As she watched, Emiliano ran forward and jammed the dynamite stick in the narrow stretch of ground between the edge of the crater and the outer edge of the roadway. He then came running back to the truck, got in, slammed the door shut and shouted, "Let's go."

In the rearview mirror, Jackie could see the jeep swiftly rounding the last bend and gaining on them. She put the truck in gear and jammed her foot down on the accelerator. Instantly, she could feel the loose stones that had filled up the hole in the roadway crunch beneath the weight of the truck's heavy-duty tires. She passed the dynamite stick wedged in the ground and saw its fuse sputtering away.

Seconds after the rear end of the truck passed over the crater, the dynamite stick blew. Through the side-view mirror, Jackie could see that the explosion had blown away that narrow stretch of ground and created a V-shaped crack at the outer edge of the roadway, a downward-sloping channel that allowed all of the rocks to come pouring out of the crater and down the lower side of the mountain, like water draining out of a burst dam.

Still looking in the side-view mirror, she watched as the jeep came to a screeching halt on the far side of the crater, which, empty of the scree, was now as big a hole as it had been before the first explosion. Unfortunately, the driver put on his brakes much too late and, as Jackie looked on openmouthed, the jeep skidded forward and drove right into the crater, disappearing from sight like a tasty morsel swallowed up by a giant stone maw.

"Emiliano, you're brilliant," Jackie told him as she continued to put distance between them and the now vanished jeep.

"And you are an incredible driver, like Juan Manuel Fangio at the 1951 Spanish Grand Prix."

She wanted to lean over and kiss him but thought it was more prudent to keep her eyes forward and on the road. Despite the long and potentially dangerous journey still ahead, it felt like nothing could stop them now.

XVI

A h, luxury at long last," Jackie said to herself as she settled back in the Pullman compartment's comfortable seat next to Emiliano, who looked equally relaxed. The compartment was a luxurious combination of leather, wood, and brass, everything glossed with a patina of age but very well maintained, like an elderly dowager who insisted on taking good care of herself. It was easily the most civilized place they had been in since leaving Havana for their cross-country trek.

It had been a rough twenty-four hours, beginning when the truck decided to break down in the middle of nowhere. The engine had overheated to the point where it had completely seized up and stopped running. Emiliano twisted open the radiator cap and saw that the reservoir was empty of water. A close examination of the grill showed that the radiator had been punctured by one of the stones thrown off by the explosion, causing all the water to drain slowly and imperceptibly out of it.

All seemed lost until Emiliano looked at the map and determined that they were not all that far from a village that also functioned as a stop on the railroad line that ran between Havana and Santiago de Cuba on the southern coast of Oriente Province, not far from their ultimate destination, the Sierra Maestra. All they had to do was find a way to the village.

"But won't we be conspicuous on a train?" Jackie asked Emiliano.

"If anything, they're looking for two people in a truck, so the train is the last way they'll be expecting us to travel. Besides, it's about time we ditched this truck anyhow. If that jeep had a radio on board, Sanchez's men are sure to be on the lookout for it."

Jackie seemed satisfied with Emiliano's explanation. Together, they pushed the abandoned truck into the undergrowth, where it wouldn't be spotted from the road, and hiked the short distance to the highway leading to the village.

After two hours of walking by the side of this lonely stretch of road with their thumbs outstretched, they were rewarded by the sight of a truck stopping for them. The good news was that the driver was headed for the same destination and said they could ride in the open back of the truck. The bad news was that the truck was transporting goats to market. Jackie and Emiliano were forced to spend an uncomfortable two hours sitting amidst a dozen or so goats. Their combined smell was close to unbearable. Jackie tried to hold her nose for the seemingly endless ride to the village but found that after a while, it was best to just give in to the smell and try to ignore it.

After arriving at the village and thanking the driver for his kindness, Jackie and Emiliano went to the train station and found out that they had three hours until the next train to Santiago de Cuba arrived. This gave them enough time to go to the village's only inn and get themselves a room. On the way, they passed two soldiers on horseback, but the men showed no interest in the two ripe-smelling vagabonds. At the inn, they removed their coveralls, now dirty, torn and stiff with sweat from their overland trek, bathed, scrubbing off the odor of goat, and put on their own clothes again so they would look presentable for the train ride and not attract any undue attention.

Returning to the station, Emiliano paid for a Pullman compartment, explaining to Jackie that though he usually abhorred such wasteful luxury, he thought a private compartment was necessary in this case to insulate them from any prying eyes. The train itself was reputed to be the most luxurious one in all of Cuba, this island's version of the Orient Express, The Flying Scotsman, or Le Train Bleu. Now, sitting in their luxe compartment, Jackie and Emiliano stared out the window and couldn't wait for the train to leave the station.

"What's holding us up?" she asked.

Emiliano shrugged and pointed to a peculiar-looking train car on the tracks next to them. It was completely covered with armor plating, with slits in its metal sides in place of windows. The car looked like a giant sardine can on wheels, but with a completely ominous aspect to it, as though unspeakable things could be happening inside.

Emiliano shivered involuntarily, causing Jackie to ask, "What's the matter?"

"I know that car. It's Colonel Sanchez's private armored train car. That's how he usually travels around the country. I guess it's an accurate reflection of how well liked he is by the people."

Jackie smiled at that but wanted to know, "What's it doing here?"

"I have a very bad feeling that we're about to find out."

As they watched, a touring car with its top up bumped over the tracks and stopped alongside the armored train car. Three people disembarked. One of them was Colonel Sanchez, descending from the vehicle with all the ceremonial pomp of a petty tyrant, which, come to think of it, he was. The other two were women. They were both dressed head to toe in black and wore black veils over their faces. They looked like mourners on the way to a funeral.

Now it was Jackie's turn to shudder involuntarily. "The 'sisters Death and Night,'" she murmured.

"Walt Whitman. *Leaves of Grass*," Emiliano said. "How appropriate."

"Who are those women?" Jackie asked, almost afraid to look at them.

"I've heard of them, but I didn't know they were real. I thought they were only a rumor. Or the kind of fairy tale used to frighten young children. They are Sanchez's handpicked female agents. He uses them to infiltrate revolutionary groups such as Fidel's. They are smart. And beautiful. And entirely deadly."

"But why the veils?"

"So their identities will remain hidden in public."

Through the compartment window, she and Emiliano watched as Sanchez and the sisters Death and Night, walking in lockstep, entered the armored train car. Finally, their locomotive began to pull out of the station, then stopped, and Jackie and Emiliano could feel a slight vibration from the rear of the train.

"That was the armored car being hooked on. So their destination is obviously Oriente," Emiliano said.

"And what's in Oriente?"

"We are. Or rather, we will be." After a thoughtful pause, he added, "I think Sanchez must know about the treasure. That's why he's after us."

"Suppose he decides to inspect the train?"

"Doubtful. He thinks we're in a truck headed east. And he

feels safe in that armored car, so that's where he'll stay until the train arrives at Santiago de Cuba." Emiliano pursed his lips. "And if he knows about the treasure, then I'm sure others do too. Walker's treasure and Metzger's map must be the worst-kept secrets on this island."

"What do you mean?"

"I have a feeling they're not going to be the only ones on this train coming after us. We're going to have to be careful. Stay in this compartment as much as possible until we reach Santiago de Cuba."

Several hours later, in darkness, the train passed over from Camagüey into Oriente.

They spent the night in separate berths. Emiliano took the upper and, ever the gentleman, offered the lower one to Jackie. Jackie was both relieved and disappointed to find that Emiliano made no attempt to steal into her berth in the middle of the night. They were exhausted from their journey to the village and were desperately in need of sleep.

The next morning, Jackie awoke to a growling stomach. In the upper berth, Emiliano was still sleeping, snoring mildly, which made her smile. The train had pulled into a station, and through the compartment window, she could see a vendor on the platform. Knowing that eating in the dining car was out of the question, she impulsively decided to go out and buy some breakfast food for herself and Emiliano.

Outside the train, the air was still relatively cool from the night before, but with just a hint of the daytime heat to come. Jackie approached the vendor and ordered two tostadas and two *cafés con leche*.

While the vendor was wrapping the tostadas, Jackie looked

up the platform and was shocked to see someone she recognized—the Mambo King, Sam Giancana's murderous henchman. He was flanked by two men who looked like they might have been participants in the St. Valentine's Day Massacre. Wearing sharkskin suits, all three seemed out of their element in this out-of-the-way train station. Hoping against vain hope that the gangster hadn't caught sight of her, she quickly turned her head in the opposite direction, where she found another surprise waiting for her.

Down the platform, Larry, Moe, and Curly were stretching their legs. Before she could turn away again, Larry caught sight of Jackie and nudged his two compatriots.

Jackie quickly paid the vendor, gathered up the food, and fled back into the Pullman car, where Emiliano was just waking up. He looked at Jackie inquisitively. "What is it, Jacqueline?"

She put down the food, took a deep breath, and told Emiliano that the East German spies had seen her on the train platform. "Oh, Emiliano, I'm so sorry," she said with a measure of self-reproach in her tone. "If only I hadn't left the train. I should have known better."

Emiliano put a hand on her shoulder. "That's all right, Jacqueline. You didn't realize. And I guess it's better to know we have traveling companions."

"But how did they manage to find us here?"

"It's just bad luck that we all ended up taking the same train."

Jackie frowned, and Emiliano continued to rub her shoulder. She didn't want him to stop. But eventually, he removed his hand and said, "I guess we'd better have our breakfast before our food gets cold."

As they ate, they listened for any sound in the outside corridor that might announce the presence of a band of intruders. The fact that the Three Stooges were riding in the next car back and the Mambo King and his men in the next car up made it difficult for Jackie and Emiliano to find any room in which to maneuver. But they knew that something had to happen before the train reached the next station, Santiago de Cuba, the last stop on the railroad.

Just as they were finishing up their tostadas, there was a knock at the compartment door. Jackie looked at Emiliano, who put a finger over his mouth to tell her to keep quiet. Perhaps if they didn't respond, whoever was knocking would eventually tire and go away. There was a second knock at the door, this one more adamant.

Then a voice spoke from the corridor with a blunt Chicago accent. "We know yer in there. So open up before we make this door look like Swiss cheese."

Emiliano shrugged. Jackie realized that they didn't have any choice either. There was nowhere to hide from a fusillade of bullets. So in the end, she watched as he took a deep breath and opened the door.

"So we meet again, lady," the Mambo King said as he and his two gunsels pushed into the compartment. It was now as crowded as the stateroom scene from *A Night at the Opera*. But unlike the Marx Brothers, there was nothing funny about the three guns the Mambo King and his henchmen had trained on them. Jackie guessed that the Mambo King had left his trademark machine gun back in his own compartment because it was too unwieldy to use here.

Jackie and Emiliano were ordered to sit on the couch. The three men stood opposite them. The Mambo King gave a slight tilt of his head, and his two comrades began to examine the compartment.

"If you tell us what you're looking for," Emiliano interrupted, "we might be able to save you some time."

The Mambo King tilted his head in the opposite direction,
and the two men froze in place.

"The treasure map," the Mambo King said succinctly.
"Hand it over, and we'll let ya live."

Emiliano was all set to speak when Jackie interrupted him.
"All right, I'll get it," she said. She stood up and went to the
door leading to the adjoining bathroom. The two men tried to
stop her, but the Mambo King waved them off.

"Let 'er go," he told them. "What's she gonna do, pack a
powder puff?"

The two henchmen let out a raucous laugh, a very unpleasant sound to Jackie's ears. She slid past them, entered the bathroom, and started to close the door, but one of them prevented
her. Jackie looked at the Mambo King.

"I'd like some privacy, please."

The Mambo King shrugged. "Sure. Go ahead. I'll give ya
one minute."

The last thing Jackie saw as she shut the door was the look
of concern on Emiliano's face. Poor dear, he had no idea what
she planned to do.

There it was, resting on the shelf under the mirror in the
bathroom—her camera bag. There had been no room for it in
the compartment. Jackie opened it quickly and got to work.
She figured that she had only forty-five seconds left, more than
enough time to work up the nerve to do what she was about
to do.

When the door to the bathroom opened again, the Mambo
King and his two gunsels looked unprepared for the sight that
greeted them. There stood Jackie, a dynamite stick in one hand
and Emiliano's monogrammed silver lighter in the other. The

three gangsters had no idea that the lighter was out of fuel, but Jackie prayed that she could bluff them without actually having to use it. She glanced at Emiliano and could see that he was as surprised as the three intruders.

"Nobody move," Jackie said, "or I light this thing, and we'll all be blown to kingdom come." To illustrate her point, she moved the lighter closer to the fuse of the dynamite stick, her finger set to flick it on at a moment's notice. "Now, drop your weapons."

"Who's gonna make us?" the Mambo King asked with a show of bravado.

"My little friend here, Mr. Dynamite Stick. He can be very persuasive," Jackie said in her best rat-a-tat gun moll imitation, hoping the tremor in her voice wouldn't betray her. She moved the lighter closer to the fuse, her finger looking ready to conjure up a flame at any second. To her disappointment, the Mambo King and his underlings acted as if they still needed a more convincing argument.

"She's bluffing, boss," one of the gunsels said.

"Oh, you think so," said Jackie, pushing the dynamite stick right into his face. "Try me, and you might soon be singing a different tune—with a heavenly choir."

The gangster backed up until he was against the couch. But no one was listening to Jackie's orders. She knew that she had to step things up a notch or her bluff would soon be spotted for the fake-out it was.

"Don't mess with me, boys. I guess Lucky Luciano never told you about me. He calls me the Black Widow. Whenever he wants a lady killer, I'm his girl."

Jackie had plucked Luciano's name out of her brain like a lucky ace from a deck of cards. From what she'd read about the exiled New York City crime boss in the report from Robert

Maheu, she figured that the last thing these Chicago thugs wanted was to get into a gangland war with him. She stared intently into the eyes of the Mambo King and was relieved to see that he was the first to blink. The three gangsters looked from one to another in growing consternation. Maybe this crazy dame was on the level.

"So ditch the rods," Jackie ordered, warming to her new role as a mob assassin. "Put 'em down and your hands up!"

This time, her words seemed to have the desired effect. The Mambo King gave the slightest of nods to his accomplices. Very slowly, all three men bent down and placed their weapons on the floor, then just as slowly rose and raised their hands in surrender.

Without being prompted, Emiliano retrieved the guns from the floor, pocketing two of them but taking the third and holding it on the three gangsters.

"Okay, you two—get in the bathroom. Now!" Jackie commanded the Mambo King's accomplices. Reluctant to take orders from a woman, even if she was holding a dynamite stick in her hand, they looked at their boss.

"Listen to the lady," he said.

One by one, they filed into the small room, but not before Jackie removed her things. She could see that the space was a tight fit.

"Now it's your turn," she said to the Mambo King. He fixed her with a look that could have curdled milk and followed his two accomplices into the crowded room. Now it was an even tighter fit in there, and the Mambo King looked less than pleased with his new accommodations. Very quickly, Emiliano began to close the door. The Mambo King stuck his head out, his eyes radiating pure hatred at Jackie, and said, "Lady, you'll pay for this."

"Just put it on my tab," Jackie said with perfect nonchalance and nodded at Emiliano, who pushed the door closed, forcing the Mambo King to withdraw his head like a turtle going back into its shell.

Emiliano took out his penknife and used its blade to jam the lock and keep the three mobsters incarcerated until the conductor could free them. Then he gave Jackie a grateful look. "That was fast thinking, Jacqueline."

"Good thing I still had your lighter." She handed it back to Emiliano, who already had his hands full with the pocketknife and the gun. "Let's get out of here," he said.

As they went out into the corridor, Emiliano turned to Jackie and said, "Where did you ever learn to talk like that?"

"Watching old James Cagney and George Raft movies on *The Late Show.*"

For what they planned to do next, Emiliano went to the conductor and bribed the railroad man into lending him his spare uniform. More money changed hands, and the conductor gave up the number of the compartment where the Three Stooges were lodged. Jackie and Emiliano figured that if the bluff worked once, it might work a second time. So they walked back one car and went down the corridor until they found the Pullman compartment with the right number. Inside, they could hear the Three Stooges talking in German to one another. Probably scheming how they were going to accost Jackie in her compartment.

Gun in hand, Emiliano looked at Jackie and asked if she was ready. Dynamite stick in hand, Jackie nodded. Emiliano knocked on the compartment door.

"Who is it?" one of the Stooges asked.

"*Es el conductor del tren,*" Emiliano replied, followed by "Please open the door." The door opened slightly, and Jackie could see that whoever was on the other side was giving Emiliano the once-over to make sure that he was really the conductor.

The door opened wider, and Emiliano, gun drawn, forced his way into the compartment, with Jackie right on his heels. The Stooges were as surprised as the Mambo King had been at the sight of the dynamite stick in Jackie's hand. Less than fifteen minutes later, the fugitive couple reemerged from the compartment, having perfected their drill.

They quickly walked down the corridor toward the back of the car. Emiliano removed the conductor's uniform, which he was wearing over his own clothes, neatly folded it, and placed it on a metal shelf. Then he led Jackie through the door and out onto the rear platform of the Pullman car. Right behind it was Colonel Sanchez's forbidding-looking armored car, the last car on the train. A brisk breeze blew Jackie's hair all over the place, and she was having a difficult time keeping it out of her face. Emiliano said, "We have to get off the train before it reaches Santiago de Cuba. Someone might have arranged a reception committee for us there. I know there's a curve coming up, which will force the train to slow. That's when we'll make our move."

"Define 'move.'"

"We'll have to jump."

"Jump?" Jackie asked, her voice rising to a note of terror.

"Don't worry about it. I've done it before."

"You have?"

"Plenty of times. When I was a student, I couldn't afford the price of a train ticket. So I rode the rails like a hobo."

"You're kidding."

"*Es verdad*," Emiliano said simply.

It was merely another facet of Emiliano's life to add to the complex picture of him Jackie was putting together—and continuously revising—in her head.

"We had to watch out for the railroad bulls, patrolling the yards and the trains to keep hobos out. In fact, that's how Colonel Sanchez started out, as one of those railroad bulls. He had a reputation for being the most sadistic of the lot. But when he found out that being a secret policeman paid better than being a railroad bull, he decided to change professions.

"And that's why I'm going to take so much pleasure in doing what I'm about to do. I'll be right back."

And as Jackie looked helplessly on, Emiliano very carefully climbed over the railing at the rear edge of the platform and stepped down so that he was now standing on the metal tongue that ended in the knuckle coupler connecting this Pullman car to the colonel's armored car. Jackie was scared out of her wits.

A giant metal pin held the coupler's two halves together. With her heart in her mouth, Jackie looked on as Emiliano very carefully removed the pin in order to decouple the two cars. There was a sudden jerk as he lifted the pin free, and he almost lost his balance as the two halves of the knuckle coupler separated. But with the unexpected grace of Nijinsky, Emiliano maintained his balance, executed a neat about-face, and climbed back over the railing, almost as though he had done this kind of thing before.

Jackie watched as the distance between the two disconnected cars slowly increased with each passing second. Pretty soon, the armored car would coast to a stop, and Colonel Sanchez would find himself stuck in the middle of nowhere, with the engineer of the train being none the wiser that he had lost one of his cars.

Standing once more beside her, Emiliano said, "Too bad we won't be around to see the look on Sanchez's face when he realizes what has happened."

Jackie realized that, in the space of one hour, she and Emiliano had neutralized all three groups that had been on their trail—not bad for two people who had been outnumbered and outgunned.

Suddenly, the train surged forward and Jackie was flung backward over the railing. She let out a shriek of fright that coincided with a blast from the engine's steam whistle. At the last possible second, she grabbed on to the bottom of the railing with one hand and stopped herself from falling onto the track, but she was now upside down and she couldn't lift herself up, her legs having become entangled in the railing's vertical bars. With her body stretched out over the tracks and her face only inches from the wooden railroad ties, she could count each one as they passed right before her face and feared that this was going to be the end of her.

"Emiliano," she cried out in a weak voice, afraid that the slightest movement would cause her to lose her grip on the railing.

"Don't panic, Jacqueline," Emiliano called down to her, "I'll get you."

She looked up and could see him leaning down in order to grab hold of her wrist through the gaps in the railing.

Jackie tried to convince herself that her situation wasn't all that dire. After all, she had been in worse predicaments, such as hanging 228 feet above the ground from the top of Notre Dame's south bell tower. Hanging off the end of a train was nothing compared to that. At the same time, as she continued to hold on, the wind whipping her hair every which way, she had to admit that Notre Dame hadn't been barreling along at sixty miles an hour when she had been dangling from its towering pinnacle.

Finally, Emiliano gripped Jackie's wrist with both of his hands though the bars and very slowly and carefully pulled her up to safety. As soon as he'd hauled her over the railing, she collapsed in his arms, and he held her head against his chest, where she could feel his heart beating rapidly. At least she wasn't the only one.

They stayed that way for a little while, until they could feel the train begin to slow down. Breaking their embrace and looking around the corner of the car, they could see the bend in the tracks in the near distance.

Emiliano let go of her and said, "This is it. I want you to jump first. The verge here is grassy and soft. Try to roll as you land and you'll be okay."

Jackie looked up at Emiliano with absolute trust. "Okay."

"Get ready. Bend your knees when you jump." When the bend appeared ahead, the train slowed until it seemed like it was going less than thirty miles an hour.

"Now," Emiliano said and gave Jackie a firm push. It was only a short distance to the grass verge. She hit the ground with her hands and knees and tumbled down a shallow slope before coming to a stop. Emiliano had been right. The grass was a soft carpet beneath her. She sat up and was seized by a momentary wave of dizziness. Fortunately, that subsided rather quickly, but it prevented her from moving out of the way as Emiliano came plummeting into her vicinity. He barreled right into her and grabbed hold of her. The two of them rolled the rest of the way down the shallow slope.

When they finally reached the bottom, Emiliano was on top of Jackie with his arms tight around her. This was the most intimate they had ever been. Their faces were so close together, their lips practically touching, that kissing seemed the most normal thing to do under the circumstances. The kiss seemed to last a long time, but Jackie was ultimately forced to wriggle out from under Emiliano because something was jabbing her in the ribs. It was her camera bag, which Emiliano had taken with him. Instinctively, she looked inside to make sure that her trusty Speed Graphic and the Mexican *Dracula* reel had made it through the fall intact, along with the bundle of dynamite sticks. To her great relief, they had.

Emiliano rose to his feet and held out his hand, helping Jackie to her feet. He led them in a direction south of the railroad line. Jackie walked on slightly unsteady legs, but whether it was from the kiss or the jump from the train she would have been hard-pressed to say.

XVII

I hope that isn't a mirage, Jackie thought as a magnificent mansion appeared in the distance, shimmering in the sunlight that slanted down on its red-tiled roof. "Is that where we're going?" she asked Emiliano.

"That's it," he said. "Walter Mitchell's estate."

Jackie brushed thick tendrils of sweat-matted hair away from her eyes and let out a long breath. "It looks like a palace. Do all United Fruit Company executives live in homes like that?"

"No, they all have big, beautiful houses on La Avenida, but Mitchell's is at the end of those and larger and grander because he's so high up in the company. Wait until we get closer. You'll see what I mean."

"At this point, I'd settle for a cot in a tent somewhere. Anything to get out of this broiling sun and away from these damn mosquitoes." Jackie smacked at her arm, where a new insect bite had just left a swelling, itchy, red welt to add to the others dotting her arms and legs.

After their hair-raising jump from the train, Jackie had been trekking with Emiliano through the dense brush of the Oriente countryside for what seemed like days. Her legs felt leaden, her feet were bleeding, her throat was parched, and her stomach growled with hunger pangs. She was grateful that Emiliano

had become increasingly protective of her, often slipping an
arm under her elbow to prevent her from stumbling over a rock
or covering her head with his hand to shield her from an overhanging tree branch. The tenderness of his touch told Jackie
that Emiliano was not just being a gentleman anymore; he was
exhibiting genuine caring. A tide of circumstances—the assignment they shared, their travels together, and the dangers they
had faced—had propelled them into a closeness that was now
inching toward intimacy.

Jackie's feelings for Emiliano deepened when they passed
a shantytown where the cane cutters lived in mud huts that
looked like a colony of large ant hills, and he told her that he
had grown up there.

"You mean you and your family lived in one of those
shacks?" she asked, her incredulity mixed with compassion.
"They're so small, and they have no windows."

He nodded. "Yes, the area is called a *batey*, and we lived in
a one-room dirt *bohío* with no windows, no plumbing, and no
electricity either. The only light came through the open doorway and cracks in the walls. We slept in hammocks and cooked
our meals outdoors, and my parents had to carry water in buck-
ets from a spigot at the edge of the cane fields." He said it without a trace of self-pity or bitterness, simply as a fact of life.

Jackie looked at the scrawny children running around in the
batey, without clothes on their backs or shoes on their feet, and
couldn't imagine Emiliano as one of them. Tears gathered in
her eyes as she turned to him. "What a terrible childhood," she
said softly.

"No, actually, it wasn't," he told her. "My parents gave me
unconditional love, and it was enough to sustain me through
all the surface deprivation." He pointed ahead to Walter
Mitchell's mansion, growing ever closer. "And don't forget,

I had a benefactor. Mr. Mitchell was very generous to me. It was because of him that I was able to go to expensive boarding schools and the University of Havana."

Jackie was intrigued. "How did he happen to take such a liking to you?"

"He was grateful to me because I got his son, Ricky, out of some trouble."

"Oh? What kind of trouble?"

"The American kids weren't supposed to go near the *batey*, but Ricky was adventurous and liked to play with the Cuban boys. Then one day, some rough boys ganged up on him and tried to steal his clothes. I broke the fight up and brought Ricky back home. He was beaten up, but it could have been a lot worse."

Jackie looked at him and smiled. "Your heart was always in the right place, wasn't it? I'm proud of you."

"Anyone else would have done the same thing. Ricky didn't deserve that."

"So the Mitchells repaid you by providing for your education?"

"Yes, and Ricky and I became pals. His parents thought I was a good influence on him, like a big brother. They always welcomed me into their home. Ricky and his sister, Stephanie, are away at college in the States now, so the Mitchells miss having young people around. They'll give us a warm welcome, I'm sure." Emiliano glanced at Jackie's precious camera bag, which he was now carrying for her. "And when no one's looking, we'll sneak into their screening room with your reel of the Mexican *Dracula* and see if we can find Metzger's treasure map."

"I can't wait."

At this point, they had reached the palm-tree-lined approach to Walter Mitchell's estate near the sea wall. As Emiliano had said, the estate stood in singular glory apart from the other beautiful homes on La Avenida, the gated managers' row. Jackie inhaled the fragrant bougainvillea in the arbor and stared at the stately arcades and columns of the sprawling mansion surrounded by profuse gardens. It looked like Merrywood transplanted in a tropical setting.

Emiliano pulled Jackie aside before they reached the guard at the front gate and said in a low voice that only she could hear, "Now, remember, Walter Mitchell is a close friend of Batista's. He has no inkling of my involvement with the rebels, so you must never breathe a word of it or say anything favorable about Fidel Castro. I'll make up some story about who you are and why we're here in such a sorry state."

"Got it," Jackie said.

The private guard, a sleepy-eyed, middle-aged man in a pale green uniform, gave Jackie a wary look but recognized Emiliano and nodded at him. "*Buenos días*, Señor Martinez," he said, and opened the gate for them.

Jackie eyed the Olympic-sized turquoise pool on the grounds enviously, wishing that she could tear off her damp, grimy clothes and dive in, but she quelled that urge as she followed Emiliano to the front door. After several loud raps of the brass knocker, the door opened, and there stood a stout, pale, motherly-looking woman with graying hair piled high on her head in a towering beehive and a wide smile on her face.

"Emiliano, how nice to see you," the woman said, holding her hands out to him. "Do come in." She eyed Jackie with a look of curiosity tinged with sympathy, as if to say, *Who is this poor, bedraggled creature?*

"I hope we're not disturbing you with this surprise visit, Mrs. Mitchell," Emiliano said in a contrite tone, "but my friend and

I had a car accident on the road, and we had nowhere else to turn."

"A car accident? Oh, you poor dears," Mrs. Mitchell clucked. "Of course you're not disturbing me, Emiliano." She glanced at Jackie. "And who is your beautiful friend?"

Jackie smiled, grateful for the "beautiful," as she thought how her mother would have disowned her on the spot had she seen Jackie out in public looking so god-awful, no matter how calamitous the reason.

"This is Jacqueline Bouvier," Emiliano said. "She's an American journalist on a tour of Cuba. A mutual friend asked me to show Jacqueline Oriente Province. I was happy to be her guide, but unexpectedly, my car had some kind of mechanical failure. It happened so quickly that we went off the road and crashed into a tree. Luckily, we weren't hurt, but we had to continue on foot until we got here."

"How awful," Mrs. Mitchell exclaimed with a little shudder. Then her face brightened, and she returned to being a cordial hostess. "Well, thank heavens you weren't injured. Make yourselves at home," she said as she led her guests into the breathtakingly spacious, lavishly furnished living room, an architectural triumph with a stunning parquet floor, marble columns, and vaulted windows. "I'll have Esmerelda fix you something to eat and drink, and then you can rest up and spend the rest of the day here doing whatever you like."

"That's so kind of you, Mrs. Mitchell," Jackie said. "I can't tell you how much I appreciate your hospitality."

"My pleasure, dear." Mrs. Mitchell beamed at Jackie and Emiliano as if she had some good news. "Actually, you two couldn't have picked a better time for a visit. Tonight, we're having a dinner dance for Ambassador Beaulac, and of course you're invited to join us. Mr. Mitchell is at the club now, but I know he would insist on it if he were here."

Jackie gulped. "That's such an honor, but..." She glanced down at her filthy, torn cotton dress, and her voice trailed off.

"Oh, don't worry about what to wear," Mrs. Mitchell said quickly. "You can borrow something from the clothes my children left behind when they went off to college. They're living in dungarees now." The wistful note in her voice reminded Jackie of Emiliano's description of the Mitchells as lonely parents who missed having their children at home. "A dinner jacket of Ricky's should fit you perfectly, Emiliano." She looked at Jackie with an appraising eye. "You're about the same size as my daughter, Stephanie, so help yourself to a gown of hers for tonight and feel free to borrow whatever else you need for the daytime."

Mrs. Mitchell left Jackie and Emiliano comfortably ensconced on a plush, hibiscus red sofa and went off to tell the cook to fix them something to eat.

It didn't take long for a white-jacketed butler to appear with a tray laden with omelets, breads, assorted fruits, pastries, and a steaming pot of coffee. "*Ven acá, por favor,*" he said, and escorted them out to a table on the patio, shaded by a portico and overlooking the exquisite gardens.

Suddenly, the thought of poor Gabriela being held hostage by Sanchez and suffering unspeakable indignities at his brutal hands came back to haunt Jackie. "Emiliano, what about Gabriela?" she asked, her voice trembling. "Do you think Fidel will have her rescued?"

Emiliano reached for her hand and held it. "Yes, I do," he said with conviction. "Fidel is not going to rest easy with so many of our people captured. He'll figure out a way to get them back."

Jackie felt reassured. From the little she'd seen of Castro, he had impressed her as someone who could achieve whatever he set out to do.

"Good," she said, and dropped the subject.

Jackie thought she would want to take a nap after breakfast, but the jolt she received from the thick, high-voltage Cuban coffee gave her a second wind and the urge to enjoy these beautiful environs. "That pool looked so inviting," she said to Emiliano as the butler cleared the table. "Why don't we change into swimsuits, loll around for a while, and take a dip?"

Emiliano nodded. "Yes, I would like that. We could use some relaxation."

Jackie jumped up, not even waiting for Emiliano to perform his usual gentlemanly custom of helping her out of her chair. "Good; then I'll meet you at the pool."

A uniformed housekeeper directed Jackie up the winding, mosaic tile staircase to Stephanie's bedroom, one of many on the second floor. The embroidered silk bedspread, French mirrors, lace curtains, and hand-painted antique furniture provided a décor fit for a princess. Jackie had to admit, with a twinge of remorse, that it put her bedroom at Merrywood to shame.

After a fast shower, Jackie found a bathing suit in a bureau drawer and slipped it on, breathing a sigh of relief that she was indeed about the same size as Mrs. Mitchell's daughter.

"Waiting long?" Jackie asked when she met Emiliano at the pool.

"No, I just got here myself."

Jackie couldn't take her eyes off him. In bathing trunks, a state of undress that she had never expected to see him in, Emiliano revealed the broad shoulders, muscular torso, and flat, hard stomach of a male model or a professional athlete.

"Beautiful" was not a word that Jackie normally applied to a man, but after they'd rested a while, and Emiliano dove into the pool and began to swim, "beautiful" was the only word she could think of. He was all sinewy grace, tan arms rotating through the water with smooth, even strokes that had a hypnotic effect. Soon, Jackie leaped up from her chaise and joined him. Over and over again, they did laps together from one end of the pool to the other, moving side by side in perfect rhythm, attuned to each other like twin creatures of the sea. It was, Jackie thought, incredibly sexy.

"You're a good swimmer, Jacqueline," Emiliano said when they were toweling off. "Is that your favorite sport?"

"No, horseback riding is. I've been riding and competing in shows since I was a little girl. I've won trophies, but that's just the icing on the cake for me. I'm passionate about riding for the pure pleasure of it, the feeling it gives me of running free."

Emiliano's eyes crinkled in a smile. "That sounds like you have the makings of a rebel, Jacqueline."

Jackie smiled back. She liked this playful side of Emiliano, which he had rarely shown her before. It made her feel more attractive to him and more willing to share who she really was. "Yes, I do have a rebellious streak, but not in a political sense," she said. "I have a sense of adventure, a curiosity about the world, and I refuse to be tied down by all the rules and regulations of someone in my social position. When I'm out riding, I feel as if I'm leaving all that behind."

"You're fortunate to have an escape like that," Emiliano said with a touch of envy in his voice. He dropped his towel on the chaise and gave her a questioning look. "How would you like to go riding now? The Mitchells have horses, and they're probably bored being cooped up in the stable without Ricky and Stephanie here to take them out."

"Oh, what a great idea," Jackie said. "I'd love to." Something in her did a little cartwheel. She was still feeling the after-effects of swimming in a kind of sensuous aquatic dance with Emiliano. *If he's as sexy a horseback rider as he is a swimmer, this is going to be good.*

It was better than good. They started slowly, trotting at a leisurely pace, then advanced to a medium trot, and once they were out in the countryside, went full speed ahead in a thundering gallop. Jackie's heart was racing as fast as her horse's hooves. At Merrywood, she usually went riding alone, but now, having a partner to keep up an exhilarating pace and even prod her faster and faster filled her with a glorious sensation. With Emiliano at her side, the feeling of liberation that riding always gave Jackie was magnified tenfold.

When it looked as if they were approaching a town, Emiliano turned his head to her and shouted, "Are you ready to go back?"

"Yes," Jackie called out at the top of her lungs, wanting to make sure Emiliano heard her over the loud stomping of the horses' hooves. Although she felt as though she could have ridden forever with Emiliano, disappearing into the sunset like Roy Rogers and Dale Evans in *The Cowboy and the Señorita*, she was sweating profusely and in need of another shower. Besides, if Emiliano had been testing her to see if she could keep up with him on this ride, she had passed the test with flying colors. Now it was time to discover what else might bring them even closer.

It was lunchtime when they arrived at the estate, and Emiliano had an idea. "After we freshen up, why don't we go on a picnic?"

"A picnic? Oh, I'd love that. I couldn't think of a better place to have one." It sounded so romantic, Jackie thought, as if Emiliano was actually starting to court her.

When they set off on their picnic, Emiliano had another

surprise for Jackie. Instead of taking her somewhere on the grounds, he led her to a cove where a gleaming white yacht was docked, gently rocking in the water.

"Mrs. Mitchell said we could take their boat to Saetía for a couple of hours," he said, "and have our picnic there. It's a beautiful island with a private beach. United Fruit Company owns the property, and Cubans aren't allowed to go there without the company's permission." He jiggled the cooler he was carrying. "I have something to drink in here, and if you like fish, I can catch some and cook it on the outdoor grill. All the equipment I need is on the boat."

"Sounds wonderful," Jackie said. A New England clambake, Cuban-style.

Wearing her oversized sunglasses and a kerchief around her hair, Jackie sat on the deck of the beautifully appointed yacht and watched Emiliano steer the craft through the clear turquoise water. When they approached the island, she admired his skill as he maneuvered through an opening in the reef, entered the bay, and docked.

"This is like paradise," Jackie said when she saw the iridescent pink sand of the beach sparkling like champagne, and beyond that, the tropical fruit trees laden with mangoes, papayas, avocados, and huge flowers bursting with color.

"I won't be long," Emiliano said as he left Jackie at a picnic table in a secluded spot and went off to join some boys fishing from the reef.

"We're in luck," Emiliano said when he returned. "I caught us two beautiful red snappers."

"Great," Jackie said, turning her eyes away as Emiliano went to work cutting and filleting the fish with the precision of a surgeon. She busied herself setting out the picnic dinnerware they'd taken from the boat and opening a bottle of the vintage wine that Emiliano had brought in the cooler.

"Dinner is served, *señorita*," Emiliano said as he set down two plates of beautifully grilled fish accompanied by slices of some avocados that he had plucked from a tree.

"Oh, Emiliano, this is delicious," Jackie said, biting into the succulent snapper with the taste of the sea still on it. Even more delicious than the fish was her delight at being waited on by this latter-day Robinson Crusoe, who combined manly strength and resourcefulness with old-fashioned chivalry. She felt that they were like two castaways on a remote, idyllic island, sharing a private world of their own.

After their meal, they sat down on a blanket that Emiliano had spread on the ground. Woozy from the sun and the wine, Jackie stretched out with her head in Emiliano's lap. Dreamily, she thought of how his awkward tentativeness toward her at first had gradually evolved into open affection and a strong bond throbbing with sexual tension. They had even gotten to the point where he felt comfortable calling her Jackie.

Gazing at the lush beauty of their surroundings, she wondered how Emiliano could give up access to all of this by joining forces with the rebels. When she asked him that, he said, "The Mitchells have been very good to me, but I'm still an outsider. As a Cuban, there's a line I can never cross with them and an equality that I can never hope to achieve. Yes, they let me visit their estate and take their boat here on occasion, but that's an anomaly. It's only because I happened to be in the right place at the right time, or the wrong time for Ricky, that I'm not barred from La Avenida like all the other Cubans."

He looked down at Jackie and sighed. "I don't think you can understand what it's like to be dependent on the kindness of a family that isn't your own, knowing that whatever they're giving you can be snatched away at any time."

"Oh, but that's where you're wrong, Emiliano," Jackie said. She explained how tenuous her financial situation was as the stepdaughter of Hugh Auchincloss, whose five direct descendants were the only ones legally allowed to have the family trust funds.

"So you see, as the 'poor little rich girl,' I have more in common with you than you think," she concluded. The sight of the primitive dirt shacks in the *batey* came back to haunt her, and she quickly added, "But of course, I could never compare my circumstances to yours." She reached up and stroked his cheek. "Honestly, Emiliano, even with help from the Mitchells, it's amazing how far you've come. It seems to me that you could reach the heights if you wanted to."

When he was quiet, Jackie said, "Maybe I shouldn't bring this up, but I'm worried about you. What will happen to you if this revolution doesn't succeed? I just hope you're not throwing your future away."

He shook his head. "But I don't want a rosy future if it means toadying up to imperialists who have taken over my country," he asserted. "The Mitchells are good people, but they're *company* people. They have no problem exploiting slave labor for United Fruit, I'm sorry to say." He took a gentler tone, as if he was trying to enlighten her. "You see, Jackie, that's the difference between Batista and me. He was born in a dirt shack the same as I was and grew up always having the iron gate of managers' row shut in his face. That made him want to gain the acceptance of the ruling class. So when he came to power, he groveled for them, accepted their bribes, and did their bidding while he kept his own people crushed underfoot. But I'm like Fidel Castro. I don't want to curry favor with the overlords.

I want them to leave. They're not my heroes; my people are. When I read those passages from *Los Miserables* to the cigar-factory workers, I meant every word of them as if I had written them myself."

"I know that, Emiliano," Jackie murmured. She remembered how moved she had been listening to him read, and now those same sentiments welled up in her again and filled her heart to overflowing. She knew, suddenly, that she loved him, that she wanted to be one with him, if not forever, at least right here, right now. She was humbled by his passionate idealism, so pure and strong that he was willing to forgo everything and give his life for it. He was everything she admired in a man—intelligent, brave, loyal, and true. The setting was so perfect, the moment so right, that what she sensed was about to happen seemed inevitable.

She sat up, and they both moved toward each other at the same time. She looped her arms around his neck, and he held her in his arms while their lips pressed together and their mouths opened in long, deep, probing kisses that flooded her with pleasure. She pressed her body against his as the heat between them mounted and she felt herself being carried away on waves of passion relentlessly rolling out to a point of no return. With a low moan, she melted in his arms, beyond thought or caring.

Suddenly, Jackie felt Emiliano draw back from her and snap his head away. "*¡Jesucristo!*" he muttered angrily.

Her eyes blinked open, and she saw him leap up and yank a large branch from a tree. "What is it?" she asked, terrified that he had seen a snake. Her body began to tremble uncontrollably. Then she heard the noisy chugging...chugging...chugging sound of the boat's motor starting up in the bay.

"It's those kids who were fishing on the reef. They're taking the yacht," Emiliano cried, brandishing the tree limb like a club and shouting "*¡Vete! ¡Vete!*" as he ran toward the bay.

Jackie jumped up and ran after him. She stood on the beach and watched, ready to help Emiliano if he needed her. But luckily, the boat was still anchored, and the three boys, who looked like Cuban *guajiros* who had snuck onto the island illegally, jumped into the water and began swimming away when they saw Emiliano coming after them. They were probably pranksters, Jackie thought, who had just wanted to take the boat for a joyride. A rueful sigh escaped her. Little did they know that the joke had been on her.

XVIII

D ressed in Stephanie Mitchell's exquisite white chiffon gown was like being swathed in Queen Anne's lace, Jackie thought, but she felt like an imposter. Wearing someone else's dress was only half the problem. The other, more troublesome part, was keeping up the pretext Emiliano had concocted to explain their unexpected presence at the estate. Mrs. Mitchell had accepted their story of a car accident on blind faith, but what if her husband or one of the guests started probing for details? Jackie would have to employ her imagination and dissemble convincingly or the ruse would blow up in their faces. But deception, she had discovered, was a sine qua non for this CIA job, and she was surprised at her growing proficiency in it. She just hoped this talent wouldn't carry over into her personal life.

Emiliano, too, was becoming quite adept at skullduggery. When Jackie went upstairs to get dressed, he asked her to give him the pouch with the *Dracula* reel in it so he could hide it in the screening room. "It's too big to fit in an evening purse, so I'll stow it away until we're ready to see what's on it," he told her, looking around to be sure that he could not be overheard by anyone. "After dinner, when the dance starts, no one will notice if we disappear from the crowded ballroom."

The cocktail hour was in full swing when Jackie entered the party. Her eyes swept over the crowd of elegantly dressed men and women, mostly middle-aged American industrialists and their wives, interspersed with a sprinkling of upper-class Cubans. A squadron of butlers in white jackets and black bow ties circulated among them, bearing trays of drinks and hors d'oeuvres. Emiliano was nowhere in sight, and Jackie assumed that he was in the screening room, surreptitiously finding a hiding place for the reel.

Unable to shake the feeling that she was a gate crasher, Jackie hung back uncertainly on the fringe of the crowd, nursing a glass of champagne and nibbling on flaky, cheese-filled *pastelitos* and caviar on toast points offered on passing trays. What was keeping Emiliano? she wondered. She hoped he hadn't been caught in the act.

Finally, Mrs. Mitchell, her ample figure concealed in a voluminous red gown and a jaunty gardenia nestled in her hair, sailed up to Jackie and took her by the arm. "Jacqueline, dear, I almost thought you were my daughter in that dress," she gushed. "Let me introduce you to some of our guests."

With whirlwind speed, Mrs. Mitchell presented Jackie as a visiting American journalist to one guest after another and didn't give her time, thankfully, to exchange more than a few words of innocuous small talk with each one. The names all went by in a blur.

It was only when Mrs. Mitchell introduced her to a short, slim, dark-haired American man who was walking toward them with the studied ease and aplomb of a performer that Jackie experienced a shock of recognition. "Jacqueline, this is George Raft," Mrs. Mitchell said. "George is famous for all the Hollywood movies he's starred in, and now he's a part owner of the Capri casino and one of Havana's most popular men-about-town."

"What a thrill it is to meet you," Jackie said in a girlish voice. As a film buff, she knew of George Raft's star-making gangster role in *Scarface* and a string of subsequent movies he'd made with Humphrey Bogart, Gary Cooper, and Marlene Dietrich. Incongruously, she remembered reading somewhere that George Raft had turned down the lead role in *Casablanca* because he didn't want to work with "some unknown Swedish broad named Ingrid Bergman."

Humphrey Bogart must be forever in your debt, Jackie said to herself as George Raft nodded a polite smile at her and continued on his way, and Mrs. Mitchell led her to the next guest.

"Arthur, I'd like you to meet Jacqueline Bouvier," she said, tugging on the sleeve of an impeccably dressed man who was standing by himself and seemed deep in thought. When the man turned to look at Jackie, she immediately recognized him as Arthur Phillips, the same gentleman who had given her an impromptu lesson on the mojito when she was seated next to him at the bar in La Europa.

"I believe we've met before," Jackie said. "It's so nice to see you again."

"Yes, and you as well," he said, giving Jackie a bland smile.

"I'll leave you two to chat," Mrs. Mitchell said, seizing this opportunity to circulate among her other guests now that Jackie had found someone she knew.

Jackie smiled at Arthur Phillips as she recalled the business card that he had given her. "You're with the Thorndyke Fund, aren't you?" she asked, spouting a name that had stuck in her mind because she had also seen it in Robert Maheu's notebook.

"I am indeed," Arthur Phillips said. He looked pleased that

she had remembered. "Did I tell you that I'm seeking business opportunities in Cuba?"

That sounded familiar. "Yes, I believe you did."

"Well, I suppose that's why I was invited to this event," he said as though he knew Jackie was wondering what he was doing here. "Mr. Mitchell is a friend, but he's also a big proponent of economic development in this country. He thought it would be a good idea for me to meet Ambassador Beaulac and make some other contacts that could prove very profitable for everyone involved." He chuckled as if at a private joke. "It's always good to be well connected, you know."

"That's true," Jackie said, glancing around at the moneyed crowd of distinguished-looking men in European-tailored suits and bejeweled women in fashionable designer gowns. "What kind of business opportunities are you seeking?"

He waved his hand dismissively. "Oh, you know, the usual kind. Everything and anything, really. The field is wide open."

It struck Jackie that Arthur Phillips was being purposely vague and evasive in a way that suggested duplicity. Something seemed off-kilter, and she wondered what he was really doing in Havana and why she kept bumping into him in places as wildly different as La Europa and the Mitchell estate.

At that moment, the lights dimmed, signaling that dinner was about to be served, and Jackie bade Arthur Phillips goodbye and went off to find Emiliano. She spotted him standing near the entrance to the dining room, waving to her and looking heart-throbbingly dashing in Ricky's tuxedo.

"Dewar's White Label scotch is our official whiskey," she heard a man say as she made her way toward Emiliano. "A man by the name of Joseph Kennedy runs the Dewar's franchise in the States, and he's a good friend of mine."

That caught Jackie's attention. It seemed that no matter

where she went in Havana, she couldn't escape the Kennedys. First the son, and now the father in absentia. When she looked back, she found that the speaker was the strapping, ruddy-faced host of the event himself, Walter Mitchell, who had met her earlier that day and welcomed her into his home as gregariously as his wife had.

"What took you so long?" she asked Emiliano when she caught up with him.

"The door was locked," he said in a low voice. "I had to get a housekeeper to open it for me so I could leave a present for the Mitchells there. She wouldn't go away until I gave her back the key."

"Did she lock the door again?"

He nodded, looking crestfallen.

"No problem," Jackie said. She patted her upswept hair. "That's what bobby pins are for."

When they entered the dining room, Jackie was awestruck. The crystal chandeliers that sparkled like mammoth nests of diamonds, the luxurious drapes, and a massive table with carved cabriole legs seemed like something out of Versailles. At the head of the table, flanked on either side by the Mitchells, sat Ambassador Beaulac. Although suave and statesmanlike, His Excellency reminded Jackie of Basil Rathbone's Sherlock Holmes. The resemblance was striking. He had the same long, thin face and nose and expressive eyes that seemed to be taking everything in. All he needed was a deerstalker cap and an Inverness cape to complete the picture.

Jackie and Emiliano found their place cards and took their seats. The dinner was a triumph: plump, juicy oysters as large as plums; tender, perfectly cooked venison; caramelized plantains that tasted like candy; and an elaborate, multilayer cake lathered with a sinfully rich icing. Wine flowed like a heavy

rain, goblets magically refilling thanks to the omnipresent butlers, even before the last few drops were gone.

Compared to the meal, the conversation that swirled around
Jackie was a deep disappointment. The women talked about
nothing except their difficulties adapting to life in a tropical
climate and their complaints about the help. It seemed that
each of the women had a staff of at least six servants, including
a butler, cook, housekeeper, gardener, laundress, and chauf-
feur, and not one was anything to rave about. Jackie tried to
listen attentively and clucked sympathetically at times, but it
all flew in one ear and out the other without making the slightest impression other than mild annoyance. It was like listening
to a Greek chorus chanting a sad song out of tune.

"Even with the fans going full blast, your makeup runs as
soon as you put it on."

"The commissary charges a fortune for tomatoes, but my
family has had all the avocados we can stand."

"The laundress shrinks everything she washes, and the cook
burns everything she makes."

"The farms here are so unsanitary, I'm afraid we'll all get
ptomaine."

The men's conversation didn't seem any more scintillating,
but then Jackie caught something with political overtones that
made her sit up and take notice.

"Batista is a great friend of ours," Mr. Mitchell's booming
voice proclaimed. "We pay him once a year, and we get off
scot-free on taxes and tariffs. Never have to worry about labor
laws and unions either. Can't beat a deal like that."

"Yes, but Fidel Castro and his rebels could ruin everything
if Batista doesn't squash them," Jackie heard another man say.
"He's got the workers all riled up, and that could spell big
trouble."

"Rest assured, Castro won't amount to anything," Ambassador Beaulac responded in a cultured tone. "He's just some gun-toting hooligan hiding out in the hills after he made a public nuisance of himself when Batista became president again."

Hooligan hiding out in the hills. Nice alliteration, Jackie thought. Then she heard Mr. Mitchell say something that really gave her a start.

"Well, if Castro and his gang become too much trouble, we can ask Allen Dulles to do something about it. You know, a CIA undercover operation of some kind. Allen is a friend of mine, and he's on our company's board."

Dulles, a United Fruit Company man? Imagine that. Jackie glanced sideways to see Emiliano's reaction. His face was expressionless. She was sure that he had heard the comment, given Mr. Mitchell's stentorian voice, but was keeping his emotions under wraps. Arthur Phillips, on the other hand, was staring intently at Mr. Mitchell with an odd look on his face. Jackie couldn't tell what his expression meant, but it made her more curious than ever about the enigmatic Mr. Phillips, and increasingly suspicious about what he was up to.

The sounds of an orchestra starting to play trickled into the room.

"Time for some dancing," Mrs. Mitchell called out.

Like schoolchildren obeying the teacher, the guests rose from their seats and began filing into the ballroom.

"Oh, my goodness, did you see that?" Jackie asked Emiliano when they passed the bandleader, who was waving his baton with one arm while in his other arm he held a Chihuahua.

Emiliano laughed. "Don't you know who he is? That's Xavier Cugat, and the Chihuahua is his trademark."

"Cugat, of course," Jackie said as she looked back and recognized the famous Hispanic bandleader with the arched eyebrows, smiley eyes, and pencil-thin mustache. "I've seen him in movies, and I saw him once in person when he was leading the band at New York's Waldorf-Astoria Hotel, but he didn't have a dog with him then." Her glance traveled to the curvaceous singer with the sultry voice and long, dark curls cascading down to her shoulders. "And he wasn't married to Abbe Lane then either."

"Would you like to dance?" Emiliano asked as the floor began filling up with company executives and their wives, who looked like Arthur Murray graduates eager to put their lessons into practice.

"I was hoping you'd ask me," Jackie said with a smile, longing to be in Emiliano's arms again. She remembered being pleasantly surprised at what a good dancer Emiliano was the first time she mamboed with him at the Dance Academy, before Colonel Sanchez's raid sent everyone fleeing for their lives. That seemed like a hundred years ago, and tonight, in this beautiful place with this beautiful man, she felt perfectly safe.

The way Emiliano moved rhythmically in time to the beat and smoothly brushed his body against hers made Jackie feel that she could have danced with him until the sun came up. But when the song ended, he glanced at his watch and said, "We'd better leave now, Jackie, while the dance floor is still crowded."

Jackie sighed. "Okay, let's go."

When they arrived at the screening room, in a secluded part of the mansion, Emiliano tried the crystal doorknob and found that it wouldn't budge. "Just making sure," he said.

"Why do you think Mr. Mitchell keeps the room locked?" Jackie asked.

Emiliano shrugged. "Who knows? My guess is that he

brings his men friends here for private screenings of racy movies like the live sex acts at the Shanghai Theatre. He wouldn't
want his wife barging in on them, would he?"

"No, I think she'd be appalled."

"But that's not our worry. Right now we have to get the door
open." Emiliano turned to Jackie with a wave of his arm like
a master of ceremonies presenting the star of the show. "And
now, Señorita Houdini and her magic bobby pin."

Jackie was ready. She slipped the bobby pin into the keyhole,
maneuvered it around a bit until she heard a little click, turned
the knob, and opened the door. It amused her to think that if
all else failed, she could have a future as a safecracker.

Emiliano retrieved the reel from its hiding place under a
thick sofa cushion, set up the projector, and turned out the
lights.

Jackie took a seat and peered at the screen, determined to
find Metzger's treasure map on a wall in Dracula's castle, even
if it took all night. She tried not to be distracted by Carlos Villarías's dreadful acting. His exaggerated walk and gestures were
almost ludicrous. She was too young to have seen the original
Dracula, with Bela Lugosi as the count, but she imagined that
Lugosi had to be a more convincing vampire than this clown-
ish Mexican imitation. She shook her head, forcing herself to
stop thinking about the acting and concentrate on the scenery.

"This looks like a bedroom in the castle, right?" Emiliano
asked.

"Yes, it's the bedroom where Dracula put a lawyer named
Renfield up for the night. That's Renfield lying on the bed
after he's been attacked by Dracula and his wives." Jackie sat
up sharply. "Wait. Can you stop the reel and go back a little? I
think I saw something on the wall above the bed."

Emiliano rewound the reel and stopped it at the point where

the object on the wall could be seen. "It looks like a picture of a crocodile," he said.

Jackie shuddered and let out a sigh. She'd had enough of crocodiles in Havana to last her for the rest of her life. "Oh well, keep on going."

In the next scene, Renfield, now a crazed slave to Dracula, was aboard a schooner bound for England, with Dracula hidden in a coffin. Jackie frowned. "I don't see how we're going to get back to the castle on this reel," she said. "In fact, if the movie follows Bram Stoker's book, the rest of it is all going to take place in London."

"Do you want me to start over again?"

"Yes, please." A thought suddenly occurred to Jackie, and she smacked her forehead with her hand. "How can we be so dumb? That picture of the crocodile? Cuba is shaped like a crocodile, isn't it? I have a hunch that's the treasure map we're looking for."

Once again, Emiliano rewound the reel and let it unspool to the spot in the bedroom with the picture on the wall.

Jackie jumped up and got so close to the screen that her nose was practically touching it. "I was right, Emiliano!" she cried. "It's a map of Cuba. If you get close enough, you can see the names of the provinces." She pointed to different places. "La Habana…Matanzas…Granma…Holguín…Camagüey…" She stood on her tiptoes, straining to see. "It looks like there's an *X* on the very tip of La Habana, right in the center. That's where Walker's treasure must be buried."

"Let me take a look." Emiliano drew closer to the screen and peered at the *X* on the map. "It's on the southern coast of Oriente Province, somewhere between Santiago de Cuba and Guantánamo Bay."

"The *X* has some writing under it. Can you see what it says?" Emiliano squinted and read aloud:

LEPROSARIA
CAMPO SANTO
57
AD

"Campo Santo?" Jackie repeated, picking up a nearby pen and pad of paper and scribbling down the legend from the map. "That means 'cemetery,' right? And 'Leprosaria,' that sounds like—"

Suddenly, the door flew open and the lights went on in a blinding glare, catching Jackie and Emiliano red-handed. Jackie quickly ripped off the piece of paper from the pad, turned her back momentarily, and shoved it down her cleavage.

"What are you doing in here?" Mr. Mitchell demanded, his face flushed with anger. Two other men in tuxedoes were with him, looking discomfited and ready to turn on their heels.

"I...I'm so sorry, sir," Emiliano stammered. His apology spilled out in a headlong stream of words. "I just wanted to show Miss Bouvier a film that would help her with her work. We only used the projector. We didn't touch anything else."

Jackie noticed that all the while he was speaking, Emiliano was carefully removing the reel and slipping it into its pouch.

Mr. Mitchell opened his mouth to respond, but before he could say a word, a band of masked men in green fatigues burst into the room like a thunderclap, brandishing guns.

Jackie gaped at them, too shocked and terrified even to scream. Emiliano dropped the pouch to the floor and put a protective arm around her, but the two men in tuxedoes fled.

"This is outrageous," Mr. Mitchell huffed. He looked truculent but backed away from the gun pointed at him.

The men in fatigues grabbed Jackie and Emiliano roughly by the arm. Pressing guns in their hostages' backs, the kidnappers marched them out of the mansion and into a jeep that was waiting in the driveway. Jackie looked for the guard at the gate and saw that his mouth was taped and his wrists were bound with cords.

"Where are we going? What do you want with us?" Jackie asked querulously, but she was quickly silenced by a hand over her mouth. The driver waited for blindfolds to be tied over Jackie's and Emiliano's eyes and then took off with a loud crunch of tires.

In a cold sweat, Jackie sat with her arms pressed against her chest to quiet the uproarious pounding of her heart. This abduction was eerily reminiscent of being taken off the street by the East German spies and made Jackie wonder if she was fated for yet another mano a mano encounter with a pit of live crocodiles. *No, not that again, please,* a voice inside her pleaded. But what if it was something worse? She couldn't imagine what that might be, but not being able to imagine the unknown made it all the more horrific and terrifying. And now she was frightened not only for herself, but for Emiliano too.

Jackie could tell from the bouncing of the tires and the turning and twisting of the jeep that they were on a narrow, winding road in the rocky countryside. When her ears began to pop and it became harder to breathe, she knew that they were ascending higher and higher above sea level.

Finally, the jeep came to a stop, and everyone climbed out. When their blindfolds were removed, Emiliano looked around and said, "We're in the Sierra Maestra."

Jackie saw tents pitched everywhere and figured that this

was some kind of camp. The sound of footsteps approaching from behind made her stiffen in fear. Rooted to the spot, she turned her head sideways and saw a man's hand pointing a gun at Emiliano's back.

"Oh no," Jackie gasped, terrified that Emiliano was about to be shot to death.

But then, inexplicably, the man lowered the gun and burst into laughter.

Emiliano whirled around to face the man and was suddenly seized with laughter too.

"What's so funny?" Jackie asked, at a loss to understand why Emiliano and this threatening gunslinger were cackling like fraternity brothers enjoying a hilarious practical joke. She turned around to look at the man…and was dumbstruck.

It couldn't be, but it was. She would recognize him anywhere.

Fidel Castro.

PART THREE

OUR WOMAN IN HAVANA

XIX

Jackie could not fathom what kind of sick joke this was. Why on earth did Fidel Castro have his close friend and an innocent woman abducted at gunpoint to this godforsaken rebel camp in the mountains? As she looked around at the men and women in fatigues stomping around the rugged terrain in mud-caked army boots or sleeping in hammocks slung between trees, Jackie was certain of only one thing: She was overdressed. She felt like a peacock in a henhouse. The organza evening gown, so elegant at the Mitchells' gala dinner party, now seemed ridiculous, and the whole, crazy ruse infuriating. But when she saw tuxedo-clad Emiliano, who looked as absurd as she did, wiping his eyes from laughing so hard, Jackie's anger dissipated, and she had to laugh too.

Fidel Castro beamed a smile at her that made her insides turn to taffy. "Ah, Señorita Bouvier, I trust that you have forgiven me for bringing you here in such an unseemly fashion," he said in flawless English. Apparently, his fluency in the language had improved greatly since he had dashed off a schoolboy's letter to the White House. Castro also cut a much more dashing figure tonight than he had when Jackie had first seen him at the Dance Academy. His tight-fitting army T-shirt and paratrooper fatigue pants showed off his tall, strapping physique, and his mass of wavy black hair and finely trimmed mustache set off his ruggedly handsome features. Up here in his heavily forested domain, he looked like a Cuban Robin Hood.

Jackie managed to find her voice. "'Unseemly' is hardly the word for it, Señor Castro. Terrifying is more like it." She wanted answers, but seeing the rifle in his hand and knowing his reputation for hotheadedness, she was careful not to provoke him by sounding accusatory. "I'm sure you must have had a good reason for bringing us here like that."

"A very good reason, Señorita Bouvier." Castro turned serious. "I needed to inform the two of you about an urgent matter, but I couldn't let it appear that you were coming here of your own volition. Mr. Mitchell is a good friend of President Batista's, and it would be very bad for Emiliano if his benefactor knew that he was associated with me."

"She already knows we have to keep that a secret," Emiliano said with a trace of impatience in his voice. "So what is this urgent matter that you need to tell us about, Fidel?"

Suddenly, Castro's jovial manner returned. "I'll come to that, *amigo*. First, I'm sure you and Señorita Bouvier would like to change into something more comfortable. And then I'd like to show you what we've been doing here."

Jackie wondered if the matter that had prompted Castro to kidnap them was not really all that urgent or if he was simply giving them time to recuperate from their harrowing journey before springing some bombshell revelation on them.

"This way, *por favor*," he said as he motioned for Jackie to slip off her high heels and led them across the craggy, brush-covered grounds. As she looked out over the vista, even in the moonlight, Jackie could see that this was made-to-order guerrilla territory, virtually impenetrable. An advancing column of vehicles would have a hard time navigating the sharply curving ranges that dropped off into steep valleys at every turn, and a foot soldier's one false step would send him plummeting to his death. But for Jackie, it was an alluring locale. The mountain air was invigorating, and the sound of numerous insects was a pleasant chorale. Even the stray goat chomping on a midnight snack looked quaintly bucolic.

"Here we are," Castro said, inviting them into a sizable thatched-roof cottage. Jackie was surprised at how comfortable it looked compared to the other rebels' tents and hammocks that she had seen in the camp. If she and Emiliano had to stay overnight, she was hoping it would be here. Sleeping out in the open, where voracious mosquitoes or other predators, animal or human, might prey on them, did not appeal to her.

Castro offered Emiliano a cigar, and while the men sat at a table smoking, Jackie went into a room to change into fatigues and boots that Castro had given her. She felt terrible that she could not return Stephanie Mitchell's exquisite gown to her parents, but that seemed impossible under the circumstances. Slipping into the army clothes that, amazingly, didn't fit her too badly, Jackie had a disturbing thought. She wondered whether she was destined to spend the rest of her life wearing hand-me-downs while her own designer wardrobe moldered away in a closet in Merrywood.

When she came out of the room, Jackie saw that Castro and Emiliano had been joined by a third man, and the three of them were standing together. The newcomer appeared to be about five years younger than Castro and a head shorter. He was Hispanic but had almond-shaped eyes that made him look Chinese.

"Señorita Bouvier, this is my brother Raúl," Castro said, surprising Jackie with this introduction because the family resemblance between the two was so slight.

"So nice to meet you, Raúl," Jackie said. She gave him a friendly smile, but the young man, apparently shy and no match for his older brother in the charisma department, mumbled, "*Buenas noches, señorita,*" and looked down at this feet. Then he said something to Castro in Spanish and hurried out the door.

Emiliano went off to change his clothes, and now Jackie was left alone with Castro.

"Have a seat," he said, motioning to one of the barrels that served as dining room chairs around the rough-hewn table. "May I offer you something to drink?"

It amused Jackie that Castro seemed determined to play the gracious host, even in these makeshift surroundings and with some mysterious pressing matter waiting in the wings, but she went along with it.

"Yes, I could use a drink, if you don't mind," she said. She couldn't resist adding, "Being abducted at gunpoint leaves one's mouth rather dry."

Castro ignored the jibe and went on fixing drinks. *At least he didn't get mad,* Jackie thought, nervously eyeing his rifle, which was now resting against a wall.

"This should help," he said, offering her a glass filled with an orange liquid. "It's a fruit juice called *prú*. We make it ourselves."

Jackie took a sip and recognized the sweet-tangy taste of mangoes. "I like this," she said. "It's very refreshing." Actually, she would have preferred a healthy shot of the pungent rum that Castro was drinking, but she didn't want to ask for it and appear rude.

Castro sat down at the table across from her, puffing on his cigar. Normally, Jackie hated the smell of cigar smoke, but like the earthy aroma at the cigar factory, this was not unpleasant.

She waited for him to speak, but he just sat there, puffing

quietly on his cigar and staring at her. He seemed to be biding his time, mulling over something to say until Emiliano came back and Castro could divulge his big secret to them. The awkward silence made Jackie turn her head away from him, and her eye fell on a color photograph nailed to the wall. It was a picture of Castro and his bride on their wedding day. Jackie was struck by how American looking his beautiful, blond-haired bride was and how her bridal gown might have come straight out of the pages of *Vogue*. It certainly didn't look like something stitched together by a poor Cuban seamstress or snatched off the rack in a local department store.

Deciding to break the ice with small talk, Jackie said, "Your wife is very pretty. What's her name?"

"Mirta Diaz-Balart. And she is beautiful. One of the most beautiful women at the University of Havana, where I met her. She was a philosophy student."

"The name Diaz-Balart sounds familiar to me," Jackie said, furrowing her brow as she tried to remember where she had heard it. "I think someone with that name was at the Mitchells' party."

"You're right, Jacqueline. Mirta's father, Señor Rafael Diaz-Balart, was at the party," Emiliano said as he rejoined them, Ricky's stylish tuxedo having been replaced by baggy camouflage fatigues. "Mrs. Mitchell probably introduced him to you. He's the main lawyer for the United Fruit Company and an ally of Batista's."

That's strange, Jackie thought. She knew how much Castro hated the United Fruit Company for exploiting his country and its *campesinos*, yet his own father-in-law was a key player in helping the American company avoid Cuban labor laws and taxes by paying off Batista. She tried to hide her puzzlement, but Castro caught it.

"The Castros and the Diaz-Balarts were like the Capulets and Montagues in *Romeo and Juliet*," he said with a small smile. "They were two powerful families who lived a half hour apart from each other and were completely at odds, but the parents couldn't stop their children from falling in love with each other and, in our case, getting married. Mirta's father was politically connected but not wealthy, and my father made a lot of money as a landowner, but he was a *guajiro* from the countryside."

Jackie was beginning to get the picture. Castro had married a society girl, but he would never be accepted by that class, nor did he want to be. Like Emiliano, he had grown up as an outsider, and now both men wanted to obliterate those class distinctions once and for all. She wondered how poor Mirta was holding up under all of this.

"How long have you been married?" she asked Castro.

"Four years," he said, taking a long pull on his cigar and blowing out a stream of smoke.

"And what a honeymoon they had," Emiliano interjected, looking at Jackie and rolling his eyes. "Fidel's father paid for them to stay at the Waldorf-Astoria in New York for a couple of weeks and at a luxurious hotel in Miami where the shah of Iran stayed. Not only that—his father gave Fidel money to buy a Lincoln Continental so he could drive his bride from New York to Miami in style."

Jackie did a quick computation in her head and figured that the cost of the honeymoon and the car had to come to about twenty thousand dollars. Not bad for a *guajiro*. "That was very generous of your father," she said to Fidel. Thinking of herself, she added, "A life of privilege can be addictive. I admire you for being able give it all up and fight for what you believe in."

Castro smiled. "Knowing my middle-class childhood, no one would have predicted that I would turn out to be a revolutionary. My circumstances as the son of a landowner and my education in religious schools attended by the sons of the rich would have made it logical for me to be indifferent to the hardships of others. Living in Cuba, where all films and publications were 'made in the USA,' was another reason that I should have been a reactionary." He gave his pointed remark a chance to sink in like a well-aimed dart, and then smoothly continued, "But I defied all the odds when I entered the university. Out of the thousands of students, I became one of only thirty who were anti-imperialist. At age twenty, I joined the fight to overthrow the Trujillo dictatorship in the Dominican Republic, which your government tacitly supported, and wound up swimming nine miles through shark-infested waters to get back to Cuba."

Jackie ignored the anti-imperialist barbs and said, "That was very heroic." She was reminded of the stories she'd heard about Jack Kennedy swimming off an island in the Pacific to get help after his PT boat was hit by a Japanese destroyer.

Now Castro seemed to have found his niche talking about his favorite subject—himself. "Seven months after that, I joined thousands of Latin American activists in Bogotá, Colombia, for a conference to come up with a unified statement against U.S. imperialism. That ended in an explosive three-day riot. When the police came after the students who were active in it, the Cuban embassy gave me refuge, and I was flown home to Havana aboard a Cuban aircraft with a shipment of bulls."

Jackie laughed out loud as she remembered hitchhiking a ride with Emiliano in a truck full of goats, but she desperately wanted to change the subject to something other than American imperialism. Looking around the room for something else they could talk about until Castro was ready to tell them why he had summoned them, her eyes traveled back to his wedding photograph. Not far from it was another picture of Castro and his wife in street clothes, posing with a cute toddler in front of them.

"Is that your son?" she asked Fidel.

"Yes, that's my little Fidelito," he said, beaming. "He's three years old now. He and my wife are at our apartment in Marianao." He sounded almost apologetic. "My wife is very supportive of me and is separated from her family because she doesn't think Batista should have come back. But Mirta doesn't want to get involved in politics. She would rather devote herself to being a mother and homemaker and let me do what I was born to do."

Jackie sensed a red flag in a marriage where a husband's immersion in politics has separated his wife from her family and even from the husband himself, but she said nothing. *When is he going to tell us why he brought us here?*

But Castro seemed stuck in the past and eager for Jackie to understand what made him so passionate about political activism. "Even in my grade school years, I spent most of my time standing up to authority. Whenever I disagreed with something the teacher said to me, I would swear at her and immediately leave school, running as fast as I could. One day, I was racing down the rear corridor, took a leap, and landed on a board from a guava-jelly box with a nail in it. My mouth was open, and the nail stuck in my tongue. When I got home, my mother said to me, 'God punished you for swearing at the teacher.' I thought that was true, but it didn't stop me from becoming a rebel."

Jackie cringed at the bizarre image of young Castro impaling his tongue on a nail, but his mother's reaction to it made her laugh.

Her laughter at his story encouraged Castro to go on. "From grade school, I went to a school run by a Catholic order that believed in strict discipline, and I was always getting slapped. I was arguing with a kid one day when we were playing ball, and the priest came up behind me and hit me on the head. I turned on him, threw a piece of bread at his head, and started to hit him with my fists and bite him. I didn't hurt the priest much, but that event became legendary at the school."

"I can understand why," Jackie said dryly, thinking that Castro's mother must have had her hands full with such an unruly little son. "Were you that rough on your teachers in college?"

"No, things got better when I left Oriente and went to preparatory school in Havana. It was a Jesuit school with wonderful teachers who encouraged me in sports and public speaking. I thank those priests for instilling in me a thirst for knowledge and a sense of social justice that changed my life."

Emiliano, who had been listening quietly all this time, suddenly chimed in. He looked at Jackie and sounded as if he wanted to set the record straight for her. "You'll hear some people say that Fidel Castro is only out for revenge against Batista for thwarting his political ambitions, but that's not true. I can tell you that even at an earlier age, my friend here always said that the worst sin a person could commit was to tolerate injustice and that violence was justified, even necessary, to combat violent repression."

Castro nodded. "Yes, violence is the only thing Batista will listen to now, and we're getting ready to be heard. Let me show you something," he said, rising from the table.

Jackie and Emiliano followed him to the room where they had changed their clothes. Castro pulled back a curtain that was serving as a closet door and said, "Look at this."

Jackie gasped. A stockpile of weapons of every type imaginable, at least to Jackie, rose almost to the ceiling.

Emiliano let out a low whistle. "That's quite a collection you have here, Fidel. Rifles...tear-gas shotguns...machine guns... fifteen-shot Browning pistols...," he enumerated as his eyes roved over the collection. "Where did you get all this?"

"Some we got from retired Rural Guardsmen, some were stolen from police precincts, some were left over from our *gangsterismo* days, some we bought from gun smugglers, and the rest we got any way we could," Castro said with a note of pride. "The point is that we are preparing for the day when we can come down from the mountains and launch an attack that will wake up the Cuban people and set off a nationwide revolution. We are deadly serious about this rebellion and prepared to sacrifice our lives for it. Every day, more and more insurgents are joining us, but we can't afford to lose a single one that we now have, which is why I brought the two of you here. We're facing a crisis that only you can resolve."

Jackie drew her breath in sharply. *At last, we're finally getting to the bottom of this ruse.*

Eagerly, she walked back to the other room with Castro and Emiliano and sat down at the table.

It took a moment for Castro to prepare himself to deliver the news. Finally, with his eyes focused squarely on Jackie, he said, "I'm afraid that my attempt to rescue Gabriela and the others captured in the raid at the Dance Academy failed. The rescue team fled for their lives and came back with the news that all of the captives are being held for ransom by Colonel Sanchez. One of his spies is a movie aficionado. He found out from the projectionist at the Teatro de Cinema that you stole a reel of film, and he reported to Sanchez that it has a map of Cuba hidden in it. Sanchez figured that it must be a treasure map. He knows you're hunting for that treasure, and he wants it in exchange for the hostages' freedom. You have forty-eight hours to hand it over to him. Otherwise, they will all be executed."

Jackie gasped and clutched her throat. *Executed.* The very word sent shivers coursing up and down her spine. She couldn't bear to think of such a cruel and undeserved death being visited upon Gabriela, her own brave angel of mercy, and the other passionate revolutionaries who had flocked to Fidel Castro as their only hope of deliverance from tyranny.

Emiliano, pale and visibly shaken, spoke up. "We think we know where the treasure is," he told Castro. "At least we have some idea of where it might be. According to a map we found, it's probably right here in Oriente Province, on the southern coast somewhere between Santiago de Cuba and Guantánamo Bay." He drummed his fingers on the table and shot an urgent look at Jackie. "But we only have forty-eight hours to find it. We'd better get moving."

Jackie was bone tired and would have liked nothing more than to catch a few hours of sleep, but with the clock relentlessly ticking down the minutes to their deadline, she shook off her fatigue. "I'm ready," she said.

On the one hand, she wished that Castro had not taken so much time letting them unwind, but on the other hand, she appreciated learning about his personal history and plans for the future. Now Jackie's mission to find the treasure went far beyond her own emotional reasons, strong as they were; they had a context in the larger, all-encompassing scheme of things for the Cuban nation.

When she returned to the States and reported to Dulles, she would be able to tell him that Fidel Castro was a force to be reckoned with. Contrary to Ambassador Beaulac's disparagement of him as some hooligan in the hills who wouldn't amount to anything, Jackie would let Dulles know that Castro was determined to free his people at all costs and was gathering the resources to do it. She would also warn him that unless things changed, American business interests in Cuba could be in jeopardy. The Cuban people were fed up with Batista's corruption holding sway over them hand in hand with American imperialism (Castro's word, not hers). Castro was a champion of human rights, but he was also rash and impulsive and something of an egomaniac. The situation was a powder keg ready to explode.

Jackie was getting ready to leave when Castro stopped her. "There's something I want you to see," he said as he picked up a copy of *Bohemia* magazine from the table, opened it to a page, and handed it to her.

It was an article about Castro's public protest of Batista's coup, accompanied by a photograph of him addressing a crowd. He pointed out some lines with his finger. "Why would anyone say something like that?" he asked her, his voice rising in indignation.

Jackie quickly scanned the lines, a quote from a U.S. observer of the rally whose assessment of Castro echoed the one made by Ambassador Beulac. The observer, a well-regarded political commentator, described Castro as "a young Cuban of wealthy background who, in a prolonged rebellion against the extravagances of his youth, has gravitated toward gangsterism and politically naive rabble-rousing that will probably not gain much headway."

When Jackie looked at the photograph of twenty-seven-year-old Castro, she was struck by how much younger he appeared than his years. It occurred to her that it wouldn't be hard for someone who didn't know him to think that this was an overgrown kid who was playacting at being the leader of a national revolution.

Castro's eyes searched Jackie's face. "You're an American journalist," he said. "You know how your people form their opinions. What do I have to do to be taken more seriously in your country?"

"Grow a beard," she said.

XX

They left the camp in a jeep borrowed from Fidel's extremely limited motor pool. By the time they got to the abandoned leprosarium, it was dusk, which they hoped would give them just enough time before it turned full dark to explore the grounds, locate the cemetery, and find the grave that they thought might hold the treasure.

To Jackie, the treasure had started out as a kind of puzzle, an academic exercise of wading through the bargain basement of history to arrive at the truth. But after the meeting with Fidel, the game had gone from the merely abstract to the frighteningly concrete. Now people would die unless Jackie and Emiliano managed to locate the treasure in time and used it to barter for the safety of the captured rebels whose fates Colonel Sanchez was holding in his murderous hands.

After debating the meaning of the legend printed on the map, Jackie and Emiliano had decided that the *leprosaria* must be a reference to a leper colony, the *campo santo* to a cemetery within the colony, and the 57 AD to the date on a particular gravestone. Fortunately, as indicated on the map, there was only one leper colony along this section of Oriente Province's southern coast.

The abandoned leprosarium was difficult to find at first

because it had been reclaimed by nature long ago. The remains of the buildings were overgrown with vegetation so thick that it almost completely camouflaged the structures from view. Finally, after having driven past it three times, Emiliano spotted the entrance, recognizing that it wasn't a natural rock formation at all, but something built by man that had surrendered itself to nature.

On the ground, partly obscured by jungle vines, was a fallen sign that read:

LA LEPROSARIA DE SAN JUDAS TADEO

Jackie looked at Emiliano. "San Judas Tadeo?"

"Yes. You perhaps know him better as St. Jude."

Jackie smiled to herself. There were worse things you could name a leper colony after, she supposed, than Jude, the patron saint of lost causes. On impulse, she offered up a silent prayer to him that their mission here wouldn't prove to be an equally lost cause.

Beyond the front gate, the grounds were impassable by vehicle so Emiliano parked the jeep directly outside. Moving to the back of the jeep, he picked up a rucksack containing everything they thought they might need to locate the treasure. Then he and Jackie passed under the gate and made their way through the undergrowth in search of the graveyard.

Emiliano said, "You have to hand it to your man, Metzger. Whatever this treasure is, he hid it where no one would ever dream to look for it. Think of two places people naturally try to avoid. Cemeteries and leper colonies. And he managed to hide Walker's treasure in a cemetery inside a leper colony. It's genius, really."

"It is," Jackie agreed. She wondered what this place was like when Metzger had arrived here with Maria Consuela and the buildings were whole and populated by lepers and their nurses. His diary was a total blank for this part of his life. Did Metzger and Maria Consuela work here serving the leper community, he out of his sense of idealism untarnished by his service under the corrupt William Walker, and she out of the values instilled in her as a young novitiate? Or was Metzger afraid that the forces opposed to Walker would come to Cuba looking for Maria Consuela and cleverly thought that the safest place for her would be inside the walls of a leper colony?

In the near darkness, it was easy to let one's imagination run riot and catch fleeting glimpses of the ghosts of those who had suffered and died here almost one hundred years ago. Perhaps Jackie was walking in the very footsteps taken by Metzger and Maria Consuela back in 1857.

"Do you have any ideas for finding the right grave?" Emiliano asked, breaking into Jackie's momentary reverie.

"The 57 AD on the map must be the year when Metzger and Maria Consuela landed here from Nicaragua—1857," Jackie said, having brought her intelligence to bear on this very subject. "So I imagine he hid the treasure in a fake grave with that date on the headstone to make it easy to find. I expect the name on the headstone to be made up, so we should probably look for one with the last name of Walker or Metzger. After all, he wanted to make sure that someone would eventually make his way here and find the treasure."

Emiliano nodded. "That makes a lot of sense."

The overgrown grounds of the leprosarium and the growing dark made walking through the compound slow going. Emiliano gallantly held on to Jackie's arm to make sure that she wouldn't slip and fall.

They passed the crumbling, vine-choked remains of several large structures, probably buildings for administration or clinical facilities, as well as individual huts that must have been home to many of the lepers not immediately in need of medical treatment. There was also a small white clapboard building with a steeple on top, obviously a church.

"Let's look over there," Emiliano said. "Wherever you see a church, you usually find a graveyard nearby."

Rounding the corner of the decaying clapboard structure, they did, indeed, come across a graveyard behind the church. It held about thirty tombstones laid out in a haphazard fashion. As they entered the cemetery, dusk gave way to darkness. Emiliano reached into his rucksack, removed two flashlights, and handed one to Jackie.

"We'll make better time if we split up," he said. "Just give a shout if you find something you think is it."

"Will do," Jackie responded and walked to the headstone farthest from the center of the graveyard. She couldn't recall ever having been in a cemetery after dark before and didn't like the feeling. As a child, though, she had never been particularly superstitious and thought that now was not a good time to allow her imagination to go haywire. And a cemetery in the middle of an abandoned leprosarium—it was just too much to think about, *really*! So she purged all such broody thoughts from her head.

She looked up and could see Emiliano's flashlight beam at the opposite end of the graveyard and felt instantly relieved. All she wanted to do was find the right tombstone, locate the treasure, and get out of this godforsaken place as quickly as possible.

The jungle had made relatively few inroads here, as though instinctively respecting the sanctity of this last resting place of the lepers. Jackie raked her flashlight over all the headstones in her section of the cemetery but so far had yet to come across a date or name or combination of the two that cried out to her— *this is it; this is where the treasure is!* The combined effects of wind and rain over time had begun to erode the legends chiseled on the headstones, making many of them difficult to read. She quickly grew disappointed and began to worry that she had read the treasure map all wrong. Maybe her entire premise was faulty and Metzger had done nothing more than accidentally set his descendants up for a wild goose chase.

But just as she reached the end of her section and began to despair that they would never find what they were searching for, Emiliano called out, "Jackie, please come here."

Jackie pointed the flashlight in Emiliano's direction and quickly joined him in front of a large tombstone.

"I think this might be it," he said to her. He aimed his flashlight at the headstone and Jackie did the same. It read:

HERE LIES HIDALGO WALTER
1824–1857
A MAN'S LIFE IS SHORT
MAY HIS LEGACY BE LONG

"The only problem is the name. It's not one we're looking for," Emiliano said.

"No," Jackie said, looking at the headstone, "but 1824 is the year of Walker's birth. It could be a coincidence, but I don't think so. Besides, doesn't Hidalgo Walter seem like a fake name? Hidalgo could be a hidden reference to Maria Consuela's Hispanic heritage and Walter to Metzger's German origins."

"Yes, and Walter is one letter away from Walker, and the name means 'army leader' in German."

Jackie gave Emiliano a quizzical look.

"I've had some German clients, so I'm slightly familiar with the language."

Shaking her head in further amazement at Emiliano's many hidden accomplishments, Jackie said, "Well, I examined all of my headstones and didn't find a thing, so let's give this one a try."

Emiliano shucked off the rucksack and removed a shovel from it. While Jackie trained her flashlight on the grave, Emiliano was all set to dig, then stopped himself and put down the shovel. He stood over the grave, looking solemn, and made the sign of the cross, then picked up the shovel and began digging.

As Jackie looked on, Emiliano expertly wielded the shovel, and a mound of dirt quickly grew into a small hill beside the grave. After a while, he stepped down into the hole to continue his digging.

"Let me guess," Jackie said. "You also worked your way through law school as a gravedigger."

"Night watchman," Emiliano admitted, "but I sometimes had to pitch in with a shovel. But only for one semester. I thought I'd be able to get a lot of work done in such quiet surroundings, but who knew the dead need so much looking after?"

Jackie laughed at Emiliano's idea of graveyard humor. She was immediately silenced as he said, "I think my shovel just struck something solid."

Jackie moved closer to the edge of the grave and pointed her flashlight into the hole. Emiliano was standing to one side and carefully brushing away the dirt from the top of what appeared to be a wooden lid. He moved more dirt aside, and from the shape of the lid, it was obvious to Jackie that Emiliano was standing on top of a coffin.

"Should I open it?" he asked Jackie.

"It's the only way we'll find out for sure."

Emiliano used the tip of the shovel to pry up one corner of the coffin lid. The wood was visibly rotting, and the nail heads that held the lid down were rusting, so it took little effort to force the coffin into giving up its secrets.

Jackie waited with bated breath to see what the coffin held. Emiliano pushed the lid to one side so that they could get a better look at its contents. She shined the flashlight on the coffin's interior and caught a glimpse of ivory and deep blue. What she saw caused Jackie to drop the flashlight in horror.

The ivory was the color of human bones picked clean by the effects of time, and the deep blue belonged to the shards of what was once the clothing in which Hidalgo Walter had been buried.

Jackie was so sickened at the sight of the desecration that she turned away from the grave. The flashlight beam skittered across the ground between headstones. She was frozen in place, unable to retrieve it. She stood there wondering about the life and death of the peculiarly named Hidalgo Walter and hoped that, wherever his spirit now resided, he took no offense at having his final resting place disturbed.

Several minutes later, Jackie was joined by Emiliano as he climbed out of the hole, having first reaffixed the lid to the coffin as best he could. He picked up the flashlight and handed it to her. "I guess it was the wrong grave after all," he said simply, then went to work refilling the hole with the dirt piled up next to it.

When he was finished, they stood over the grave. Jackie looked down and said, "Rest in peace, Hidalgo Walter."

Emiliano returned the shovel to the rucksack and placed the bag back on his shoulder. Silently, after checking the remaining graves and drawing a blank, he and Jackie followed their steps back across the abandoned grounds of the leprosarium and through the gate to the jeep. They remained silent until Emiliano started the jeep's ignition and turned on the headlights.

"I was so sure it would be here," Jackie said, almost in tears.

"You have nothing to feel bad about, Jacqueline," Emiliano said in a vain attempt to mollify her. "You did the best you could with the information you had. Professional treasure hunters spend years searching for the objects of their obsessions. I guess it was unrealistic to think you would find what you were looking for on your very first attempt."

"But professional treasure hunters don't have the lives of others depending on them."

He put his hand over hers in a comforting gesture. "I know. We will just have to think of some other way to rescue them. Maybe when we go back to the camp, Fidel will have some ideas."

As they drove away, Jackie turned back for a final look and caught one last glimpse of the sign over the gate. The name San Judas Tadeo seemed to be mocking her. Feeling chastised by the patron saint of lost causes, she quickly faced forward again as the jeep raced through the night.

They were hungry and stopped for something to eat at a small cantina that was about to close, but the cook took pity on them and stayed open long enough to feed them. "Cantina" was too grand a word for what was basically just an open-air kitchen with a scattering of rough wooden tables and chairs inside a small courtyard. The cook wore a grease-stained apron, but his cooking smelled delicious, and it wasn't long before he placed two overflowing bowls of *ropa vieja* on the table in front of Jackie and Emiliano, who dug in with the true gusto of those whose recent labor had caused them to work up an appetite.

As they ate, the cook remained at their table and tried to make polite conversation in Spanish.

"And what brings you to these parts, if you don't mind my asking?"

Jackie thought about what to say before finally settling on an approximation of the truth. "We came here to explore the remains of that old leper colony."

"Which one?" asked the cook.

His question took both Jackie and Emiliano by surprise and caused them to pause in midbite.

Jackie felt both a sudden resumption of hope and a fear that it would only be ripped away again, so she paused for an unconscionably long time before asking, "Why, is there more than one leper colony around here?"

The cook wiped his hands on his apron before answering. It seemed to take forever for him to get his words out.

"Of course there is more than one leper colony around here. There is the one you just came from, the leprosarium, and then there is the one at Fort Mengues."

"Fort Mengues?" Emiliano asked, joining the conversation for the first time.

"Yes. It's a small coastal fortress overlooking an inlet not too far from here. Used to protect against pirates and smugglers. It was called the leper colony because of its location, so far from civilization. Being sent to serve there was considered a kind of punishment."

"Let me guess," Emiliano said to the cook, "you used to be in the army."

"I was a mess chef. That's where I learned how to cook."

"If this is an example of the food you served, then your men were well fed."

"*Gracias.*"

"And is there a cemetery there?" Jackie interrupted, hoping against hope that the cook would supply the answer she so desperately needed to hear.

The cook looked thoughtful. "Yes, I believe there is."

"And is this fort also abandoned?" asked Emiliano.

"Yes, since there's no more need to be on watch for pirates."

Emiliano turned to Jackie and gave her a look of relief, which she fully returned.

"I think we had the wrong leper colony," he said to her in what could have been the understatement of the year.

Jackie couldn't help but look up, apologize to St. Jude for ever doubting him, then give silent thanks to him for coming through for them in the end.

XXI

They found the second cemetery just as dawn was breaking. It was nestled halfway between the beach and the coastal fortification guarding the pirate inlet, just where the cook had told them it would be. Even though it had been left derelict for many years, Fort Mengues had been so solidly constructed that it could have been occupied today with only the slightest need for repair or restoration. Wreathed in the last of the morning mist, looking both substantial and ethereal, it reminded Jackie of Fort Zinderneuf, the Foreign Legion post manned by dead men in *Beau Geste*.

"We're not too far from Guantánamo Bay," said Emiliano.

"The U.S. Navy has a base there, right?" Jackie asked.

"Right. It was ceded by Spain at the end of the Spanish-American War and originally used as a coaling station for American ships."

"But navy ships don't run on coal now, do they?"

"No, but your country likes having a presence in this part of the world," Emiliano responded pointedly.

They saw that the cemetery was a fenced-in plot of land sloping down to a beach rimming a small cove. In days of old, this must have been perfect for pirates embarking on raiding parties or smugglers picking up or dropping off embargoed merchandise.

Emiliano parked the jeep on the far side of the cemetery from the fort, and he and Jackie got out. It was shaping up to be a beautiful day. The pink and gold sunrise was glorious, and there was an offshore breeze that felt refreshing, while at the same time leaving Jackie's hair thankfully in peace.

Jackie saw a smudge near the horizon. "What's that?" she asked.

Emiliano looked where Jackie was pointing. "That's a small island, close enough to be considered Cuban property. But I'm not even sure it has a name."

Emiliano toted the rucksack as he and Jackie approached the cemetery. It wasn't until they entered the graveyard that their optimistic mood was instantly transformed. To their shock, they were greeted by about one hundred wooden crosses planted in neat, orderly rows. As they got closer, they could see that none of the crosses had any inscriptions on them. These were the nameless dead.

Emiliano put his hand to his head as though dazed. "Unmarked graves. They must belong to shipwrecked bodies washed ashore without identification. The soldiers manning the battery above us would have considered it their duty to give them a good Christian burial. But without dates or names, we'll never be able to figure out which is the right one. There's just no way we can dig up all the graves."

He slumped against the fence as though crushed by the enormity of the task. Jackie felt the same weight pressing down on her so hard that she could barely breathe. Somehow she managed to croak out, "This is so damned unfair. Just when we think we've gotten somewhere, it turns out we're really nowhere at all."

"It's called running a Red Queen's race."

Jackie fixed Emiliano with a brave smile. "Leave it to you to quote Lewis Carroll at a moment like this."

"He's not a bad example, you know. He taught mathematics, and *Alice in Wonderland* is really an essay in logic disguised as a book for children."

"You think we need to apply logic to this problem?"

"It's all we have left."

"Spoken like a true lawyer." With a sigh, Jackie reached into a pocket and removed the note she had scribbled to herself, ensuring that she remembered the words printed on the map. Once again she examined the puzzle left behind by James Metzger:

LEPROSARIA

CAMPO SANTO

57

AD

"Okay," she said, "this is a leper colony of sorts, so we're obviously in the right place. And this is the cemetery attached to the leper colony, so we've got that right too."

She looked up at Emiliano. "Agreed so far?"

"Agreed."

"Now let's look at this date again—fifty-seven, the year when Metzger and Maria Consuela arrived here in Cuba." She stopped and thought. "But wait. What if it isn't a date?"

"But it has to be," Emiliano pointed out. "Look at the AD underneath it."

"You know, that's always bothered me. They obviously didn't land in fifty-seven BC. So why bother to put the AD there at all?"

As though in answer to her own question, Jackie said breathlessly, "But wait a minute. What if AD doesn't stand for 'anno Domini,' the year of our Lord? What if it means something else entirely?"

"Like what?" Emiliano asked, sounding as if his renewed sense of hope was catching fire from hers.

"I don't know. Let me think." She looked up from the piece of paper to the orderly rows of graves facing them. There was something about those rows, their regularity, that seemed familiar to her, but at the same time their meaning remained frustratingly out of her reach. She thought about the basic cryptography course she had taken at the Farm. She had been shown a one-time pad used for enciphering and deciphering messages, really just a piece of paper made up of printed rows of empty boxes waiting to be filled in with transposed letters. For some reason that made her think about playing Scrabble at home with her family. And then it hit her.

"Across and down," she said.

"What?" asked Emiliano.

"AD stands for 'across and down,'" said Jackie with rising enthusiasm in her voice. "Like the rows of graves here. They're orderly, regimented, like a Scrabble board or a crossword puzzle. I bet the grave we're looking for is the one where row five across meets row seven down."

Emiliano looked at Jackie with amazement. "I think you're right," he said. "If he were here, Lewis Carroll would be very proud of you."

"Well, let's hope that when we dig up the grave, it leads to more than just a rabbit hole."

It took about an hour for Emiliano to dig down into the grave found at the intersection of the fifth row across and the seventh row down. This one had a wooden cross that seemed no different from the others. But he and Jackie were probably now only minutes from discovering whether her hunch was right and the grave would give up Walker's treasure instead of just another coffin or, more probably, a decomposing corpse in the remains of a shroud. Jackie hoped that they wouldn't be forced to defile any more graves. Seeing the disinterred bones of Hidalgo Walter had been chastening enough for one lifetime.

Once again, Jackie and Emiliano heard the sound of the shovel striking something hard, and once again, Emiliano shoveled the dirt out of the way until what was underneath was laid bare.

Jackie mouthed a silent "Thank God" when she saw that it wasn't the lid of a coffin. Instead, it appeared to be the slightly rounded top of a chest. *A treasure chest,* she wondered to herself. With the melody for "gold doubloons and pieces of eight" playing in her head, Jackie tried to restrain herself until Emiliano had put down the shovel, then used both his hands to lift up the chest and push it up over the rim of the grave. Jackie knelt to inspect it and saw that the chest was made of dark wood held together with brass fixtures. A sea chest most probably.

Not wanting to begin until Emiliano was by her side, Jackie couldn't wait to find out just what was inside the chest, which she had been chasing down ever since those endpapers had popped open at Au Pied de Cochon and Metzger's diary pages came spilling out. It had been a very long, emotionally fraught, and physically exhausting journey, and now it looked like it was about to end. She couldn't help but recall the Robert Louis Stevenson quote, "To travel hopefully is a better thing than to arrive." Well, given what was now at stake, Jackie needed the reassurance that this arrival would be as hopeful as the road to getting here had been.

A single click broke into her thoughts. She knew that sound—a gun's hammer being cocked—and it seemed to stop her heart for a beat or two. When she turned around to find where it came from, she could feel her stomach lurch with a roiling sense of fear. For there they stood arrayed once more before her: the Three Stooges. Two of them had guns drawn, while the third, Moe, was still rendered hors de combat by the sling he wore. Instead of a gun, he carried a menacing look on his face.

So it was basically two against two, Jackie thought, assessing the situation. Those were great odds if she and Emiliano had anything to fight back with. Unfortunately, they had left the only weapon Fidel would part with, a vintage Springfield-Lee rifle that looked like it hadn't been fired since the Spanish-American War, in the back of the jeep, where it would do nobody any good at all.

Just then, Emiliano pulled himself out of the grave and immediately caught sight of the Three Stooges. He instinctively followed Jackie's lead and put his hands up in the air. The sea chest rested between them. Jackie knew that there was no way she could hide its presence from the East Germans, who had obviously deciphered the secret of the treasure map or somehow lucked onto their trail and had come here to take Walker's treasure.

Curly motioned with his gun, and Jackie and Emiliano picked up the chest by its side handles and walked in the direction the Stooge's gun was pointing—to the fort. Moe ran ahead and swung open the gate. A hastily abandoned cooking fire near one interior wall told Jackie that the battery must have recently been used as accommodations for some dispossessed *campesinos*.

With the Three Stooges walking behind them, Jackie and Emiliano entered the fort. It was basically a hollow square with defensive parapets on the three landward sides and a battery of cannons, now rusting, on the rampart facing the seaward side. The walls, at least twelve feet high and equally thick, held the barracks for the men, the mess hall, and the armory. Stone steps led up the walls to the parapets that ran around the top of the structure.

The dirt parade ground beneath their feet had been beaten into a hard surface by the thousands of boots that had been drilled up and down, back and forth, in this square. It was in the middle of this parade ground that Jackie and Emiliano stopped and put down the sea chest. Curly motioned with his gun for the two of them to step aside. Then, while Larry trained his gun on Jackie and Emiliano, the bald Stooge and Moe moved in to examine the chest.

They heard a shuffling sound from above them and looked up. Jackie and Emiliano did too. One man stood on each of the three landward parapets. It was difficult to see them clearly because they had the early morning sun behind them. But it could clearly be seen that each held a submachine gun in his hands. Even before she heard the voice, Jackie knew who these three men were.

"Drop those guns and raise yer hands." That Chicago-accented voice could belong to only one person Jackie had met recently—the Mambo King. It looked like the Three Stooges weren't the only ones to figure out where Jackie and Emiliano had been headed.

As she looked up, the mobster and his two gunsels walked down the stone steps, their machine guns trained at the small grouping surrounding the treasure chest. When they reached the ground, they took up positions around Jackie, Emiliano, and the Three Stooges, who had obeyed the Mambo King and were standing, weaponless, with their hands up in the air. They looked totally out of their depth here. It was almost enough to make Jackie feel sorry for them. Almost.

While one henchman collected their guns from the ground,

the Mambo King and his other henchmen approached Jackie and Emiliano.

"Well, look who we got here," the Mambo King said to his cohorts. "It's the Black Widow herself. How's your stinger, lady?" he said to Jackie in what she found to be a most insinuating and insulting tone of voice. She guessed this was what came of associating mainly with strippers, gun molls, and other women of low calling. She resolved to keep quiet so as not to provoke the anger of the notorious Mambo King and prompt him into displaying his penchant for machine-gun mayhem.

He pushed his face right into Jackie's. But if he expected her to flinch, then he must have been disappointed, because Jackie refused to back down. She had his number and knew that the only way to deal with this adult version of a schoolyard bully was to meet force with equal force. Finally, when it became obvious that he was wasting his time, the Mambo King withdrew his face from hers and said, "So what didja find here?"

"I don't know yet," Jackie said. "With all these interruptions, I haven't had the chance to find out."

"Well, what're ya waitin' for? Open the freakin' thing!" the Mambo King ordered. As an added inducement, he swung the machine gun's muzzle in Jackie's direction.

She knelt down in front of the sea chest. There was an ancient hasp lock preventing the lid of the chest from being opened. Fortunately, these old locks were comparatively primitive affairs, easy to open, according to her Picks and Locks instructor at the Farm. Jackie took a bobby pin out of her hair—still the secret-agent gal's best friend—bent it open, and carefully used one end to probe the opening of the antique lock. A few deft manipulations with the bobby pin and the locking mechanism popped open. The Mambo King and his men looked on with amazed eyes, as though remarking to one another, *Maybe this dame really does have moxie.*

While one henchman kept his gun trained on the Three Stooges, the Mambo King and the other henchman looked on as Jackie, holding her breath, opened the lid of the sea chest. Emiliano leaned down too, so he could see what it held.

"What is that crap?" the Mambo King asked before the others had the chance to react.

Jackie reached into the chest, which seemed to be filled mainly with books—old, yellowing, crumbling tomes—and removed them.

"These are called books," Jackie answered sharply.

"Why, you—I oughta—" An angry Mambo King reversed his machine gun and was about to use its butt end to strike Jackie for her impertinent remark, but Emiliano interposed himself between the two of them.

"I wouldn't do that if I were you," he said.

"And I wouldn't crowd me if I was you," the Mambo King said.

Having momentarily deflected the Mambo King's anger away from Jackie, Emiliano wisely backed off.

At the bottom of the chest, there was a large vellum envelope with red sealing wax over its flap. Very carefully, Jackie removed the envelope from the sea chest and held it in her hand. What could be inside it? A will? A treaty of some kind? A map? *Oh, please,* Jackie prayed to herself, *please don't let it be another map.*

"Well, don't just sit there; open it," the Mambo King commanded. Jackie looked up at Emiliano, who nodded his approval.

Taking another deep breath—if she kept this up she would surely start hyperventilating and accidentally lose consciousness—Jackie broke the seal on the flap and opened the envelope. It contained only two items—a piece of foolscap and, inexplicably, one half of a silver locket. She looked at the paper, some kind of document, then bypassed the Mambo King and handed it directly to Emiliano. The Mambo King gave her his most fearsome look.

"It's in Spanish," Jackie explained. "And he's a lawyer."

Emiliano spent several minutes perusing the document while Jackie, the Mambo King, and the forgotten Stooges and his henchmen looked on. The air was pregnant with a feeling of anticipation. Finally, Emiliano looked up from the document. But his reaction was an unusual one: He started to laugh.

And he kept on laughing. Unfortunately, he chose not to share the source of his humor with anyone, which also served to provoke the Mambo King's mounting ire. He swung his machine gun in Emiliano's direction and said, "What's so freakin' funny?"

Emiliano looked at the gangster as though seeing him for the very first time.

Without a word, he passed the document back to Jackie, once more bypassing the Mambo King, who didn't appreciate being ignored in this fashion. She looked it over and started laughing too. Jackie knew enough Spanish to understand that the document attested that, on September 3, 1857, a baby girl had been born to William Walker and Maria Consuela Garcia in the province of Santiago de Cuba, the original name for Oriente Province. The name of the baby girl was Josefina Luisa Walker. And the birth certificate was witnessed by one James Metzger.

At last Jackie understood the true meaning of Metzger's words from his diary. Walker's treasure had not been a literal one. No gold or jewels were involved. No, his treasure, according to the poetically inclined Metzger, was the child that a pregnant Maria Consuela was carrying in her belly and transporting from Nicaragua to Cuba. It was all there in the diary entries. All one had to do was read between the lines and Metzger's meaning became clear. You could easily chalk up this misunderstanding to the man's nineteenth-century sense of circumspection and rectitude.

"What does that thing say?" the Mambo King demanded.

"It says there is no treasure," Jackie told him.

"No treasure," roared the Mambo King. "What do you mean, no treasure? That's impossible."

"It's not only possible; it's true," Jackie countered. As proof, she lifted up the sea chest and upended it. Of course, nothing fell out of it save for some clods of dirt and a few stray scraps of yellowed book paper. At the sight of this, the Mambo King's face turned red, then purple. He looked like he was about to have a stroke. Or explode. He walked off several feet, raised his machine gun, and fired off a one-armed burst into the air. Jackie instinctively winced at the incessant chattering sound made by the weapon.

"No damned treasure," he roared.

Jackie could well understand his anger. If she were the Mambo King, she wouldn't know how to offer this bad news to his boss, Sam Giancana, either. She had been in his company only once, but he looked like the type who would be more than happy to kill the messenger for the unhappy news he delivered.

"Just one thing I don't understand," Emiliano said, interrupting the Mambo King's tirade. "Why did Metzger go to all this trouble to bury a birth certificate?"

"I was just thinking the same thing," Jackie said. "I imagine that Walker made many powerful enemies. Cornelius Vanderbilt, for instance. Maybe Metzger figured that Walker's ene-mies would try to strike out at him through his child. So, loyal soldier that he was, he decided to keep the birth of Walker's daughter a secret from the world. But he left clues in his diary so that future generations would know the truth."

"What are you two jabberin' about?" asked the Mambo King, looking from Jackie to Emiliano, then back again, his machine gun once again trained on them.

"It doesn't matter," Jackie said as matter-of-factly as possible. "There's no treasure here, and that's that." She tucked the letter and the silver half locket back inside the envelope, then placed the envelope in one of her pockets.

"*Es verdad,*" added Emiliano.

"Sorry, Pancho, but I don't speak the language," the Mambo King said, thrusting his machine gun in Emiliano's direction.

"The name's not Pancho; it's Emiliano. But that's only for my friends. And you're no friend of mine."

"I could kill you, you know," the Mambo King said menac-ingly. "Your companion too," he said, indicating Jackie, who shrank back from the threat.

"Yes, but you won't," countered Emiliano. "I know it, and you know it. And do you know why you won't kill us?"

"Why?"

"Because we're not worth it, are we?"

The Mambo King looked momentarily stumped, then said, "That never stopped me before."

"This time's different, though," Emiliano went on. "Too many powerful people know we're here. Colonel Sanchez will have you clapped in irons in the Presidio Modelo before you can board the next boat or plane off this island." Jackie knew that Emiliano was referring to the notorious prison located on the Isla de Pinos, which, with its hellish living conditions and dreaded solitary confinement cells, could give Devil's Island a run for the money.

"So that's why you're going to let us live," he continued. "Because you've already calculated the odds, and they're not in your favor."

"You should go work at a casino, you know that?"

"I worked my way through law school as a croupier at the casino in the Hotel Nacional. So I know a thing or two about trying to beat the house."

Jackie looked at Emiliano in surprise. Another part-time career he hadn't told her about.

"Okay, croupier, you got me. I'm going to let you live. Her too," he said, swinging his machine gun in Jackie's direction. "But if I ever see either of you again, you're gonna wish I had killed you *this* time. Because next time…"

But the Mambo King had run out of either grisly metaphors or patience, because he just let that last threat sputter out to nothing, like a wet firecracker on a damp Fourth of July evening. With a look of disgust, the Mambo King said to his gunsels, "Let's blow this joint."

And without another word or a look back, the gunsels followed the Mambo King across the parade ground and out the front gate of the fort, dropping the Three Stooges' weapons on the ground as they went. Jackie and Emiliano and the Three Stooges, slowly lowering their hands and recovering their weapons, watched them go. Jackie and Emiliano gave each other a look that said, *What now?*

Suddenly, there was a stutter of machine-gun fire from outside the walls, causing everyone inside the fort to flinch. The sounds bounced around the battery's interior, magnifying the racket and making it seem like a small battle was taking place outside. Jackie turned to Emiliano and said with a rising note of fear in her voice, "What was that?"

"I don't know, but it sounded like someone declared war."

He and Jackie watched as Larry, Moe, and Curly, with guns drawn and battle-ready looks on their faces, quick-stepped through the gate and promptly disappeared from view.

"I don't think that was very wise of them," Emiliano said.

Several seconds later, the truth of his words seemed to be borne out by a second round of machine-gun fire.

Jackie turned to Emiliano. "What do we do?"

"I don't know, but I'm beginning to regret leaving that rifle in the jeep."

Jackie put her arms around Emiliano as though afraid of what the next few minutes would bring. Emiliano put his arms around her as though to say that no matter what happened, he would do his best to protect her.

From outside the fort came the sounds of footsteps marching nearer. Jackie and Emiliano turned as one to face this new threat together. Three figures stood framed in the open gateway of the fort: one man and two women. All three carried machine guns with smoke coming out of the muzzles. They walked into the fort in lockstep, and Jackie and Emiliano could see that they were Colonel Sanchez and the sisters Death and Night, the latter two with veils firmly in place to prevent identification. If they had looked intimidating from the train compartment window, they now seemed positively terrifying close up. All three were pointing their smoking machine guns right at them.

The colonel looked at Jackie and Emiliano and said, "I am Colonel Guillermo Sanchez of the Servicio de Inteligencia Militar. Now, where is this treasure I have heard so much about?"

XXII

Colonel Sanchez and the sisters Death and Night planted themselves between Jackie and Emiliano and the gate, making any escape impossible. Then a straining of gears sounded as a canvas-covered, two-and-a-half-ton army truck roared through the entrance and came to a screeching halt in the middle of the parade ground. Instead of a tailgate, the back of the truck bed was covered by a metal grill, through which Jackie could just make out some cowering figures.

She turned from the truck to the colonel and said, "Very clever."

"I'm sorry," said Sanchez, playing dumb, a role infinitely aided by his brutish looks.

"You figured out the location of the treasure from the movie reel we left behind at the Mitchells', then leaked the information to the East Germans and the mobsters. That way, you could lure them here and take care of them all at the same time, far from any prying eyes back in Havana."

Jackie envisioned the killing ground outside the fort, littered now with six dead bodies. The mobsters had gone unknowingly to their deaths, but the Three Stooges, like their namesakes, had failed to use good sense and had fallen into the colonel's trap.

Colonel Sanchez looked at Jackie with new awareness. "You are a very smart woman, Miss Bouvier. Perhaps I underestimated you."

"It wouldn't be the first time," said Jackie under her breath.

Emiliano smiled at Jackie's comment. Without a moment's hesitation, Colonel Sanchez reversed his submachine gun and slammed its butt end into Emiliano's stomach, driving the lawyer down to his knees. Emiliano clutched his stomach and looked up at the colonel, waiting for an explanation.

"You think I don't know who decoupled my train car. Left me stranded in the middle of nowhere. You think that was a funny joke?"

"Not especially," said Emiliano, grimacing in pain and rising to his full height again. The colonel reversed his submachine gun once again so that its muzzle was now pointing at Emiliano and Jackie. No one could mistake the fact that he was deadly with either end of the weapon.

The colonel spat out orders to the driver of the truck. The man quickly got out of the cab and unlocked the grill. He made a motion to the figures inside the back of the truck, and twelve bedraggled prisoners clambered out, their arms and legs obviously stiff from being in such close confinement for so long. Among them, Jackie could make out a dark-haired beauty who looked familiar. Even shorn of her blond wig, she was obviously Rosario, whose real name she now knew was Gabriela. Jackie looked at her and felt an immediate pang, identifying with the young woman and all she had gone through.

"So let me get this straight," the colonel said to Jackie and Emiliano. "There is no treasure. No gold bars. No antique coins. No jewels. No agreements making Cuba a sovereign nation. Nothing."

"*Nada,*" responded Emiliano.

"That is too bad, because you heard what I said would happen if the treasure was not turned over to me. I said that these twelve prisoners would be executed."

Jackie tried hard not to look over at the truck but couldn't resist a peek at the prisoners, who all had justifiably terrified looks in their eyes.

Sanchez shouted out more orders to the driver. The man had the prisoners line up with their backs against one wall of the fortress. They stood facing the sisters Death and Night, who walked over to them with their machine guns drawn.

Jackie felt her knees go weak and her heart begin to hammer as she realized that she was about to witness a mass execution. She wanted to scream, but no sound came out.

"You can't do this," Emiliano stated firmly.

"Why not?" asked the colonel. "I can do anything I like."

"That doesn't make it right," Emiliano said, speaking to the colonel as though he were arguing a brief against execution before a hanging judge.

"Right doesn't have anything to do with this. I made you an offer. You reneged on it. It was a simple contract. As an *abogado*, you should understand this."

"As a human being, you should understand that some things are beyond a person's control."

"Then that is your second mistake—mistaking me for a human being."

The sisters Death and Night moved several steps to the side and took up positions to the right and left of the line of prisoners, who faced their executioners with a variety of looks on their faces—sadness, anger, terror, despair. Jackie was glad to see that Gabriela looked defiant. Jackie suddenly flashed on Gabriela coming to her aid at the crocodile farm and knew that she couldn't let her die. Couldn't let any of them die. There had to be something she could do. And in fact, there was...

Colonel Sanchez addressed the prisoners. "You have one minute to say your prayers and make your peace with God." The colonel took out a pocket watch and looked at its sweep-second hand.

For Jackie, that minute seemed to last an eternity, but she was grateful that it gave her more time to work out her plan. When it was over, the colonel looked up from his watch and said, "On the count of three, my agents will fire. *Uno...*"

Jackie looked at the prisoners. Some of them began to cry. Still others begged for their lives. She knew that the time had come to do something.

"*...dos...*"

Before Sanchez could say *tres*, Jackie shouted out, "Colonel Sanchez."

The colonel looked at Jackie, annoyed to be stopped in mid-count.

"Yes, *señorita*, what is it?" he asked with false patience.

"Take me."

"What?" he asked, not fully understanding what she was saying.

But Emiliano did understand what Jackie meant and cried out, "Jackie, no!" He grabbed her by the arms, as though ready to shake sense into her if he had to. "I can't let you do it."

"You have to."

More insistently, he said, "You can't do this."

"I have to," Jackie said with equal insistence.

Jackie broke free of his embrace and put her hands on Emiliano's arms as though to communicate the strength of her words to him. "I'm sorry, but it's the only way."

Turning back to the colonel, she said, "Take me instead of

the hostages. Let them go and I will be your prisoner. You can ransom me to my government and claim a prize as large as the one you expected to find here. Maybe even more if you deliver me in one piece."

Colonel Sanchez turned to Jackie to digest the meaning of her words. As they began to sink in, a big smile spread across his ugly face, making him seem—if it were possible—even more evil than he already looked.

"Well, that is very noble of you, *señorita*. Very noble. And you think one *gringa* equals twelve of my people?"

"No, not at all. But there aren't twelve of my people here. Only me. And to my government, I am more than worth my weight in gold. The price may be inflated, but you shouldn't complain since you are going to receive full value. If you let Emiliano go too, he will make sure to carry your message back to the American embassy."

The colonel stood there, thinking over Jackie's proposition. Jackie and Emiliano waited anxiously for Sanchez to make up his mind. In the meantime, whether it was from the heat or the stress, one of the prisoners passed out where he was standing and fell to the ground. The prisoner to his right went to his aid but was waved away by the sister nearest him, who threatened to stitch him full of bullet holes if he didn't get back against the wall.

Finally, the colonel took out a pad and a piece of paper and wrote something on it. When he was finished, he ripped off the sheet of paper and handed it to Emiliano. "I want five hundred thousand American dollars. This is the number for my Swiss bank account. Once I have word that the money has been wired to that account, I will release your friend here."

Jackie and Emiliano exchanged relieved glances. If the colonel was true to his word, the prisoners would be released, and so would Jackie once the money was transferred. There was something else that Jackie and Emiliano had always suspected—that this treasure hunt had been Sanchez's private operation right from the start. He had had no plans to hand over the treasure to Batista. It was going right into his pocket. As in so many of these dictatorships, corruption, like a severed hydra's head, seemed to multiply itself.

The colonel turned to Emiliano. "What are you waiting for? Take your people and get out of here."

Emiliano looked at Jackie. "I'm so sorry."

"Don't be. This is the only right thing to do. Don't worry about me. I'll be fine. The colonel will treat me with kid gloves. He knows the U.S. government won't like it if I'm returned in less than mint condition."

Emiliano went to hug Jackie, but the colonel was there to stop him. He jammed the muzzle of his machine gun into the lawyer's stomach. "Thin ice may be in short supply on this island, but that is exactly what you are treading on here. So take your people and go, before I change my mind. *Andele!*"

Emiliano walked over to the prisoners and spoke to them in a soft voice. From the relieved looks on their faces, Jackie could see how glad they were to hear news of their reprieve. Together, all the prisoners lined up behind Emiliano and followed him as he led them out of the fortress that had almost become their mass grave.

The colonel called out to Emiliano. "I will see you again, *Señor Abogado*."

Emiliano turned to the colonel and said, "I look forward to it."

Jackie looked at Emiliano, and her heart soared. He was full of a confidence that seemed so much in keeping with his quiet strength. She knew that he would make sure that the American authorities at the embassy saw to her release.

As he left the fort, Emiliano gave Jackie a searching look, which she tried to return with a brave one of her own. Last out of the fortress was Gabriela, who looked back at Jackie with an expression of eternal gratitude on her face. All Jackie could do in return was give her a small but determined nod. The last words of noble Sydney Carton facing the guillotine came immediately to mind: *"It is a far, far better thing that I do…"* although Jackie was careful to mentally edit out his final thought: *"It is a far, far better rest that I go to…"*

Now that Jackie was left alone, the ramifications of her deal fully dawned on her. She was now at the mercy of these three sadistic individuals, who had already proven their readiness to spill blood. She began to quake inwardly at the thought that they could do anything that they wanted. Maybe, in the end, blood-lust would win out over a love of money. Jackie just had to hope that she was worth more to Sanchez alive than she was dead. She would be counting the minutes until Emiliano got in touch with the American embassy and made plans for her repatriation.

In the meantime, she was alone. There was no Emiliano to come to her immediate rescue should the need arise. She had never felt so bereft in all her life. But as she usually did in moments like this, Jackie called on her religion and drew great strength from it. *"But yea, though I walk through the valley of the shadow of death, I will fear no evil. For thou art with me."* If ever the words of the Twenty-Third Psalm had meaning for her, it was here and now, in this place.

Jackie's prayer was interrupted by the sound of the driver speaking into the field telephone in the truck cab. After a brief conversation, he returned to Colonel Sanchez. Jackie heard him tell his superior that the armored train car could not reach the spur line near this fortress until morning. Colonel Sanchez looked at his watch and said, "We will spend the night here."

Addressing the driver only, he said, "Check inside and see what kind of accommodations there are." To the sisters Death and Night he ordered, "And see if there is a cell where we can keep our friend here until morning." With that, he dismissed Jackie from his sight and began climbing the stone stairs leading to the parapet, from which he would look out and survey his temporary new command.

Jackie was awakened by the sound of an explosion. She bolted upright from the rickety cot on which she had fallen asleep. The cot was located in a cell in one wall of the fortress. The walls were rough, and there were only narrow slits for windows and illumination. With little light and nothing to do, Jackie lay on the cot and fell promptly asleep, hoping that she would not have to endure the claustrophobic confines of this cell for too long.

The first explosion was followed by a second, then a third. Then came the sound of multiple machine guns being fired. More explosions. More machine-gun fire. It sounded like the fortress was under siege, and the colonel and the sisters were defending their position. Abruptly, the machine-gun fire cut off, but the explosions continued at a rate of, Jackie reckoned, one every minute or so.

Jackie went over to the locked door. There was a small barred opening set in it. She had to stand on tiptoes so her mouth was even close to the bars. She called out, "Is anybody there? Is anybody there? Help! Help me! I'm being held prisoner here."

Soon after, the explosions stopped too, and Jackie sank to the floor, fearful that she would be forgotten and left to die here. She got her second wind and was all set to commence her shouting again when a familiar voice called to her.

"Jackie?"

Jackie looked up. It was Emiliano. She couldn't believe it. She felt a wave of gratefulness wash over her like a balm. She stood up and called out to him. "Emiliano, I'm here."

Looking up through the bars, Jackie was relieved to see Emiliano's face. With a half sob, she cried out, "Emiliano, I'm—"

But he cut her off. "Jackie, listen carefully. We haven't much time. Is there a mattress in your cell?"

"Yes," Jackie said, wondering why he was asking.

"Good. Now, I want you to take the mattress, go over to the corner farthest from the door, then crouch down with the mattress entirely covering you. Do you understand me?"

"Yes."

"Do that and you'll be free momentarily."

"All right."

Dutifully, Jackie lifted the mattress off the cot and remembered thinking that it was dark when she fell asleep, so she couldn't see how stained it might be. Now she was grateful to have it. She dragged it to the corner that she judged to be farthest from the door, knelt down with her back in the corner, and placed the mattress in front of her to fully protect her body. Then, heart pounding loudly in her chest, she held her breath and waited for whatever was to happen next.

There was a semiloud explosive sound, followed by a concussive burst of air and a grating noise as something was propelled across the cell. There was also the sudden eye-watering tang of cordite in the air. Jackie had noted that smell before, after the demolition of the rock shelf above the roadway in the Escambray Mountains. Smoke began to fill the room, and all of a sudden someone was there moving the mattress aside—Emiliano. Jackie had never been so glad to see anyone in her life. She was instantly reminded of Jacques rescuing her from the top of Notre Dame. She was lucky that when danger threatened, there always seemed to be a heroic and resourceful man waiting in the wings to come to her rescue.

"Jacqueline, are you all right?"

Jackie was so overcome with emotion that all she could do was nod.

"Then let's get out of here."

Shoving away the mattress, Emiliano helped Jackie to her feet. An explosive charge had blown the heavy cell door off its hinges, and it now lay twisted on the opposite side of the cell.

Emiliano led Jackie out and said, "Good thing I still had some of those dynamite sticks you took from El Teatro de Cinema. I used the last one on the cell door."

Jackie was happy that she had had the foresight to purchase a camera bag capacious enough to hold such nonphotographic items as a reel of film and a bundle of dynamite sticks.

As they rushed outside, Jackie said, "So that's what caused those explosive sounds I heard?"

"Yes, we lobbed the other ones over the walls one at a time. Made Sanchez think that he was under attack by overwhelming forces. Must have thought it was an artillery barrage. Coward that he is, he hightailed it out of here, along with the sisters Death and Night." Jackie smiled to hear Emiliano use the same term of reference as she did for the colonel's henchwomen.

Now they were back on the parade ground. Sanchez and his agents were gone, along with their truck. But there was Gabriela, a big smile on her face, and her fellow former prisoners. They looked like an impromptu vagabond army. Jackie saw that the prisoners were all armed with cestas, the wicker baskets jai alai players used to hurl the pelota around the court. Of course, what better way to loft those dynamite sticks over the twelve-foot walls of this fortification. She once again admired Emiliano's ability to improvise a solution to a seemingly impenetrable problem.

"What did you do," Jackie asked, "hold up a jai alai fronton?"

Emiliano smiled. "Gabriela and I took off in the jeep to get help and found a closed one not too far from here. So we broke in, took the cestas, and I called your embassy and asked for help."

"I didn't know you knew how to play jai alai. Wait, let me guess. You played it semiprofessionally during college?"

Emiliano looked like a little boy caught with his proverbial hand in the cookie jar, but it was Gabriela who stepped in and said, "Who do you think it was taught me to throw the pelota?"

Jackie went over to Gabriela and took one hand in both of hers, "Thank you for saving my life again."

"For what you did, for the sacrifice you made, I will be forever grateful."

Jackie seemed suddenly confused, "But what…? How…?"

Emiliano stepped in with an explanation. "We didn't get very far when Gabriela and I decided that we couldn't leave you with the colonel. So we made plans to rescue you. I remembered we still had that dynamite back in the jeep. We were lucky that the colonel never noticed the jeep parked on the far side of the cemetery. Otherwise, none of this would have worked. Now we better hurry. I have arranged your escort back to the U.S."

"When?"

"Now."

Jackie looked incredulous. "Now?"

"Yes. And we better get started or you're going to miss the boat—literally."

While the other former prisoners remained behind in the fort, Emiliano and Gabriela walked Jackie past the cemetery and down to the pirate inlet, stopping off at the jeep first so

Jackie could retrieve her camera bag. They walked down to the beach, now bathed bright by the rising Caribbean moon, and waited for whoever was supposed to come take Jackie home.

As they stood there, Jackie noticed something reflecting in the moonlight around Gabriela's neck—a silver locket; no, a half of a silver locket. She couldn't believe it. That jagged shape was unmistakable. With an excitement she could barely contain, Jackie reached into her pocket and withdrew the other half of the silver locket from the envelope. She presented it to Gabriela and said, "This is the only piece of jewelry we found in Walker's sea chest. Does it look familiar to you?"

She held it up to Gabriela, whose mouth and eyes opened wide in amazement. "My locket," she said. She removed the half locket from around her neck and tried to mate it with the other half Jackie had given her. They made a perfect fit. The locket was now whole again.

Gabriela looked up at Jackie. "But what does this mean?" she asked with the wondering voice of a child.

Jackie worked it out in her head, knowing Gabriela's story from Emiliano. "It means that you are the great-great-great-granddaughter of William Walker and Maria Consuela. This locket was a gift from William Walker to his mistress, Maria Consuela Garcia, a former convent novitiate. She and a soldier named Metzger escaped to Cuba in 1857. She was pregnant at the time and gave birth here, in Oriente Province, to your great-great-grandmother. This locket was obviously handed down from generation to generation until your mother gave it to you. But she died before she could explain the significance of it. Here's the birth certificate we found along with it."

Jackie handed the document over to Gabriela, who looked it over with tears in her eyes.

"Yes," agreed Emiliano, equally dumbfounded by Jackie's

discovery. "The blood of liberators flows in your veins. Being a part of this revolution is a role you were destined to play."

Jackie said, "I have a diary left behind by Metzger. It will explain everything. When I return home, I will figure out a way to get it to you."

All this information was too much for Gabriela. She collapsed in the sand, as though the weight of her heritage was suddenly too much for her to bear. She looked up at Jackie and Emiliano and said, "But all I ever wanted to be was a dancer."

Emiliano looked down at her and said, "It looks like history has other plans for you."

He helped Gabriela to her feet. She still looked shaken by this unexpected revelation. She held the two halves of the locket in her hands, anxious not to let go of them. The three of them stood there in silence, none of them knowing what to say. Their tableau was suddenly illuminated by a beam of light aimed at them from the water. Instinctively, the trio hit the sand, trying to make themselves invisible on the beach.

There was the sound of twin motors as a boat entered the pirate inlet. Jackie and the others could not see if it was a Cuban patrol boat or perhaps a fishing boat that had gone astray. Finally, a familiar-sounding voice called out to them. "Emiliano, are you there?"

"It's him," Emiliano said, jumping up. To the boat, he called out, "Yes, we're here."

The boat dropped anchor in the inlet. There was a splashing sound as someone from the vessel jumped into the shallow water and waded through the surf to the shore. In the moonlight, Jackie could make out the outline of a beefy, bearded man in a long-billed fishing cap.

"Your water taxi awaits, *señorita*," Ernest Hemingway said.

XXIII

The most famous living writer in America waited nearby, visibly impatient, as Jackie said her good-byes to Emiliano and Gabriela by the shoreline. The young Cuban woman hugged Jackie, holding her so tight that Jackie felt like she might break in two—or was that just the emotion she was feeling? Tears in her eyes, Gabriela said, "I was an orphan for so long. I barely remember my parents. And now you have restored my family to me. I will be forever in your debt."

Jackie found herself too moved to speak.

After a kiss on both cheeks, Gabriela moved to one side, and Emiliano took her place. "Do you remember what you told me in the truck after we left Havana?" he asked Jackie.

She looked at him, mystified.

"You said one person is more important than a single cause. Do you recall?"

She nodded.

"I think you might have been right."

Jackie looked at him closely. "And what made you change your mind?"

"Let's just say one brave woman's act of self-sacrifice," he answered with a little smile.

Well, Jackie thought, once again Emiliano had managed to

surprise her. Maybe there was hope for this Cuban revolutionary movement after all.

Emiliano reached out with both arms and pulled her into
his warm embrace.

"I will miss you, Jacqueline Bouvier, miss you more than I
can say."

"And I you."

Emiliano leaned down and kissed Jackie full on the lips.
Jackie knew that this was the last time this would happen and
the memory of this kiss would have to last for a long time. The
kiss simultaneously seemed to go on forever and was over in
the blink of an eye. She didn't recall who broke it off first, but
suddenly, there they were, with Emiliano holding her at arm's
length. The time had come to say good-bye.

"*Mi corazón,*" whispered Emiliano tenderly. Jackie felt as
though her own *corazón* might break in two.

There was more that they wanted to say to each other, much
more. But there was not enough time to say it. So perhaps it
was better to say nothing at all and let the silence do all the
talking. They just stood there, holding each other and looking
longingly into each other's eyes until Papa barked out, "The
tide's coming in, and I'm not getting any younger. So could we
please haul anchor? *Now!*"

The mood broken, Jackie and Emiliano reluctantly let go of
each other. Then Jackie had an idea and said, "Come with us."

"What?" Emiliano asked.

"Come with us. To America. You too, Gabriela. Sanchez
knows who you are. Your lives are in jeopardy if you remain
here. So come to America, where you'll be safe."

Emiliano looked at Gabriela, who adamantly shook her
head, and turned his attention to Jackie.

"I'm sorry, but this we cannot do," he said. "Cuba is our

home. We are committed to a cause. To leave now would be an act of cowardice on both our parts. So we must stay to make things better for our people." Emiliano paused, his voice strained with emotion, then said, "Jacqueline, I hope you understand."

"I do," Jackie replied, fighting hard to keep the emotion out of her voice, knowing Emiliano would appreciate her more if she dropped the subject.

Papa gave a loud *ahem*. It was definitely time to go. Giving Emiliano one last look, trying to fix his handsome, noble face in her mind forever, Jackie abruptly broke off contact and followed Papa through the shallows and up onto the fishing well of *Pilar*. There were tears in her eyes. She wiped them away and looked back. But it was too late. Emiliano and Gabriela had melted into the shadows.

Pilar sailed through the purple Caribbean night, the moon above playing hide-and-seek through the clouds. Jackie stood beside Papa on the flying bridge of the fishing boat, watching as he adjusted the helm and throttle and navigated by the light of the compass binnacle to pilot his way around the eastern tip of the island, past Guantánamo Bay, and head northwest into the Atlantic Ocean toward Key West, the southernmost point of the United States, where Papa also kept a home.

"It's a good thing I was fishing in the vicinity when the call from the embassy came," Papa explained.

Standing alongside him, Jackie's thoughts were still with Emiliano and Gabriela. She wished them well. She knew how difficult their fight for freedom would be. Hiding in the jungle with Fidel and his men. Living off the land. Fear of betrayal at every turn. Suddenly, a memory of Jacques came unbidden to her mind, and she wondered why it was that she was always falling for men only to have them leave her for the causes that were really their true passion.

Papa's words intruded on her reverie. "So you're it, daughter? Their man in Havana. Or should I say woman? Who'da thunk it?"

Papa slapped the helm with one meaty hand, and Jackie smiled. Hemingway went to such lengths to sound more like a backwoods hunter than a famous literary lion, and having adopted the name "Papa," he felt it only right to call younger women "daughter."

"I didn't know you worked for the CIA," Jackie said. There was a strong breeze on the flying bridge, and she buttoned her shirt to the neck to ward off the cold.

"I let the CIA know they could always depend on me if I was in Cuba and they needed something," Papa said. "I did the same thing for the U.S. government during the war. I volunteered to work as a U-boat spotter. Fitted out *Pilar* with weapons and special electronics equipment and used her to hunt U-boats trolling these waters. Called us the Hooligan Navy, they did. We never found any of those Nazi U-boats, but that doesn't matter. The way I figure it, word of our antisubmarine patrol got out and kept them away."

Jackie smiled at Papa again. Obviously, he couldn't envision any outcome other than one that cast him in a heroic light. She suddenly shivered from the dropping temperature.

"If you're cold, daughter, I've got some sweaters belowdecks," Papa said. "Just take any one you like. Mary might have left one or two behind too." Jackie knew that he was making a reference to his fourth and current wife. She'd read somewhere that Mary was nine years younger than Hemingway and that he called her "daughter" too.

Papa's cabin was located right below the flying bridge. Jackie found it littered with clothes and fishing and nautical equipment, like the combined inventory of Abercrombie & Fitch and a ship chandler's had been dumped in there. The only thing she could find to wear that looked appropriate was a tattered, faded fisherman's sweater. She put it on, and it almost swallowed her up.

When she climbed the ladder to the flying bridge, she saw that Papa wore a concerned look. Before she could ask him what was the matter, he said, "See those running lights in the distance?" He pointed off to starboard and abaft *Pilar*. Jackie looked in that direction and could see the running lights of a boat coming up fast, looking like it was headed on an interception course with *Pilar*.

"I don't like it," Papa said, assessing the situation. "Going too fast for a fishing boat. Probably a Cuban patrol boat. We gave the country six of our coast guard patrol boats during the war. They're faster than *Pilar*, more powerful engines. If it is them, we just have to hope we get to the three-mile limit before they catch up with us. Once we're in international waters, there's nothing they can do to us."

"And if they do catch up with us?" Jackie asked, fearing the worst.

"Let's just hope they don't and leave it at that for now."

Papa pulled out a pair of binoculars from a nearby cupboard and put the glass to the boat that was narrowing the gap with every passing minute. He put down the binoculars and pulled a face. "Damn it to hell, it's the Cuban navy, all right."

Jackie felt a chill as she realized that the long arm of Colonel Sanchez was reaching out to pull her back. And now he had called on the Cuban navy for assistance. Heaven only knew what story he'd told them to get her back in his clutches.

Papa pushed forward on the boat's throttle and said, "C'mon, sweetheart, let's see what you can do."

Despite the danger she was in, Jackie had to smile hearing Papa refer to his boat as a woman (in fact, *Pilar* was the pet name of his second wife, Pauline). In Paris, Jackie had known a safecracker who said that opening a safe was like seducing a woman. She wondered what it was about men that constantly caused them to liken inanimate objects—safes, boats, race cars, and such—to women.

"They're gaining on us," Papa said, looking back. The three-mile limit was not far off now, but it was anyone's guess whether *Pilar* would get to it before the patrol boat got to them. Turning forward again, Papa said to Jackie, "Hey, daughter, do me a favor and take the helm for a minute."

Jackie looked surprised but immediately grabbed the wheel, which turned out to be a steering wheel from a car, good for easier handling. If she could steer an amphibious vehicle up the Seine on a wild chase to save a princess's life, she could surely keep this fishing boat on course. As she took firm hold of the wheel, Papa disappeared down the ladder, and she could hear him rummaging in the locker directly under the flying bridge. When he returned, he carried a weapon that Jackie recognized from her firearms course at the Farm as a Browning automatic rifle, more commonly referred to as a BAR. As she watched, Papa slapped a clip into the slot beneath the rifle and said, "Say hello to my little friend. Kept it as a souvenir from my sub-hunting days. Knew it would come in handy eventually."

"What do you plan on doing with it?" Jackie suspected that the Cuban patrol boat had more powerful weapons onboard.

"Maybe I'll fire off a clip or two if they get too close. Give 'em a shave and a haircut. They can keep the two bits." Papa smiled at Jackie, but she knew that although he meant well, his bravado was as inflated as his expanding gut.

"Maybe you should have just dropped me off at Guantánamo," Jackie said, dubious whether one BAR could stand up to the patrol boat's superior firepower.

"Couldn't. Under orders not to. The last thing the CIA wants to do is get the U.S. Navy involved in your assignment. Too many embarrassing questions to be answered."

Jackie couldn't help but notice that Papa sounded a lot like Harry Morgan, the smuggler hero in his novel *To Have and Have Not*.

"Mind if I take a look?" Jackie asked Papa as he took the wheel back from her.

He handed her the binoculars and Jackie put the glass on the Cuban patrol boat. It was bristling with machine guns and cannons and looked like a giant seaborne wasp with a lot of extra stingers.

Jackie returned the binoculars to Papa and said, "I think you're going to need a bigger gun."

Only several minutes had passed, but in those moments, it had become obvious that the Cuban patrol boat was going to catch up to them before they could reach the three-mile limit. You had to give Papa credit, though. He never panicked. He was the true exemplar of his own phrase "grace under pressure." Instead of looking panic-stricken, he scrunched up his features as though deep in thought.

After a minute, Jackie put her hand on his arm and said, "Papa?"

Papa shook himself out of his stupor and said, "I've got an idea, daughter. You mind the wheel till I get back."

Once again, Papa descended the ladder to the fishing well and rummaged around in the locker beneath the flying bridge. Judging from the racket he was making, that locker must have been as overstuffed as Fibber McGee's closet. A slight explosive pop from the fishing well startled her, but Jackie held on to the wheel, looking at the compass binnacle occasionally to make sure that *Pilar* remained on course.

A fog bank appeared from out of nowhere. Jackie could barely see the running lights of the patrol boat and knew that the mist had bought them a little more precious time.

Papa clattered back up the ladder, knotted an anchored piece of rope over one of the steering wheel spokes to hold it in place—a very crude form of autopilot—and told Jackie to come with him. She followed Papa down the ladder and immediately saw that the fishing well was taken up with an inflated yellow life raft. Before she could ask its purpose, Papa began to speak.

"I've thought it all out, and this is our only choice. This is a small boat. There's no place to hide. If the Cubans board us and search *Pilar*, they'll be sure to find you. And I don't think I can pass you off as my first mate. Then they'll haul you back to Cuba and throw you in the deepest, darkest prison cell you've ever seen, and you probably won't be heard from again."

"Me? What about you?"

"I'll just play dumb. A role that comes naturally to me." Papa smiled at Jackie, a token attempt to break the tension. "Say you chartered my boat for a tour of the island."

"At night?"

"I'll tell 'em you're too fair-skinned to go sightseeing during the day."

Jackie looked at Papa. Who knew that the author of *A Farewell to Arms* could be so funny?

Papa's expression suddenly changed to one of complete seriousness.

"So the only thing for you to do is take off in this life raft."

Jackie laughed, thinking that Papa was making another joke. But when she looked into his face, she could see he wasn't laughing with her.

"You can't be serious."

"As a heart attack, daughter. I am."

Jackie looked horrified and could tell that the expression on her face had registered with Papa.

"Don't worry. I've tied an eighty-pound test-fishing line to the raft and will cleat it to this davit." He pointed to a davit on the stern transom. "It'll pay out five hundred yards, so you'll be far enough away there's no chance of the patrol boat spotting you in the water. Besides, they'll be concentrating on me and *Pilar* and not what's out there." He motioned with his hand to take in the wide expanse of the Atlantic. "And this line'll be invisible to 'em. I'll just reel you out and, after they're gone, reel you back in. Easy as your mother's apple pie."

Jackie wanted to tell Papa that her mother had never made an apple pie in her life but chose instead to utter the more pertinent, "But what if something goes wrong and I end up adrift?"

"It won't happen. This is the same line I used to reel in a five-hundred-pound marlin. It'll more than hold you and the raft. But if it does break, Florida is only ninety miles away. Look at this map—it's nothing."

To prove his point, he removed a map from the life raft, unfolded it and placed his thumb over the narrow gap between Cuba and Key West.

"You don't even have to steer or paddle," Papa went on. "The Gulf Stream is right there and will take you straight to Florida. It's like a highway in the ocean. And if worse comes to worst, I'll call the coast guard as soon as the patrol boat leaves, and they'll send out a PBY to search for you and pick you up." Jackie knew that a PBY was a Catalina flying boat, used by both the navy and the coast guard for air-sea rescue operations.

She could not believe she was hearing this. Papa was going to abandon her to the elements.

He continued, "Besides, I've provisioned this life raft for just that emergency, and here's what you've got. A map of the waters between Cuba and Florida. Enough K rations to last for a week. Enough water to last for a week. One compass. One fishing hook—that's if you run out of food, which definitely won't happen. One flashlight, in a waterproof pouch. Spare flashlight batteries, also in a waterproof pouch. One flare gun, for when you spot that PBY. Some spare flares; the gun's easy to reload. And here, I'll even throw in my binoculars so you can catch sight of that PBY early."

He took the binoculars from around his neck, threw them into the life raft, and went on, "There's a blanket in case you get cold. Oars if you feel like rowing. And a canvas cover to keep the sun and spray off you. Oh, and if you get bored during the day, I've thrown in a book. It's by my late friend Scott, *This Side of Paradise*. It has the strengths and weaknesses of all first novels, but you'll still find it entertaining. Okay, I guess that's about it. Are you ready?"

Jackie looked at him. "No."

"What's the holdup?"

"This sounds like a desperate maneuver to me."

"It is. Unfortunately, it's the only one we have left in this chess match." So, Jackie noted, even in life, Papa couldn't resist a gaming or sports metaphor.

"Then I have no choice, do I?"

"Not unless you want to spend time in a Cuban jail, which

will not be anywhere near as luxuriously appointed as this life raft."

Jackie sighed. She knew that she had run out of options. It was risk either the open sea or the close confines of a Cuban jail cell. She had already been incarcerated twice during her visit to Cuba and guessed she would choose the former any day of the week.

Papa could obviously sense that she was stalling. "Okay, here's the thing," he said. "We have to get you in the water... now. You have to be far enough away by the time they get here. And that's going to be at any moment now."

In the weakest of voices, Jackie said, "Okay, let's do it."

"Great. I knew you were as game as you looked."

As Jackie watched, Papa lowered the life raft over the low stern of *Pilar* on the port side, where the fishing boat itself would mask this activity from the oncoming patrol boat.

"Okay, daughter, your turn."

He helped Jackie cross the fishing well to the stern. Before she went over the side, she stalled again. Then she drew courage from her reservoir of inner strength and started to put one leg over the low stern of the craft.

Papa held her arm to steady her and said, "In my life, I've known plenty of brave women. Young girls who fought the fascists during the Spanish Civil War. Housewives and mothers who served in the French Resistance during World War II. But I have to say, daughter, that you're the bravest woman I've ever seen."

A melancholy expression suddenly transformed Papa's usually ebullient face. It was like he was looking back to the past or peering into the future and had seen something troubling. Jackie understood that, like the currents surrounding the waters of Cuba, there was a darkness in Hemingway's psyche, and this darkness disturbed his otherwise confident demeanor.

Jackie also knew that Papa was playing a kind of trick on her. She had once read that in order to get soldiers to volunteer for a particularly dangerous artillery position, Napoléon had posted a sign that read, "This battery is manned by the bravest soldiers in the army." Apparently it worked for Napoléon, for he couldn't keep his men away from that suicidal battery.

Despite her foreknowledge, it looked like the ploy was going to work again here, because Jackie climbed over the stern of *Pilar* and into the life raft, which began to bob up and down in the water as it adjusted to her weight. Jackie quickly sat and got her bearings. As she looked up, she saw Papa holding the fishing reel whose line was attached to the life raft. He looked down at her and whispered, "Godspeed, daughter. I'll see you in a little while."

Papa stood there, looking over the stern as he paid out the fishing line from the reel, and the life raft slowly began to drift away from *Pilar*. Jackie sat in the raft and watched as the fog bank lifted and the running lights of the fishing boat could be seen receding into the distance.

They were soon joined by a second set of running lights, obviously belonging to the Cuban patrol boat. It looked like Jackie had gotten off *Pilar* in the proverbial nick of time. Now all she had to worry about was that the moon, once again ducking behind the clouds, might put in another appearance at any moment, illuminating her, and that she was not far enough away and would be spotted by the patrol boat's searchlight if it should turn in her direction.

From this vantage point, she watched breathlessly as the running lights of the Cuban patrol boat circled around the now stationary running lights of *Pilar*. Then these running lights stopped too, and Jackie knew that Papa's fishing boat was about to be boarded. She hoped he had put away that silly BAR; it could only get him hurt.

Suddenly, the searchlight from the patrol boat stabbed out through the night. Jackie instinctively ducked and peered over the edge of the life raft. But the searchlight passed harmlessly overhead as it continued its circuit of the surrounding ocean, and she felt safe once more.

The life raft continued to drift away from the two stationary boats, whose running lights grew smaller and smaller until they were no larger than the stars that dotted the night sky of the Atlantic. Jackie began to get a very bad feeling. Surely, at some point, the lights should have stopped receding and remained fixed. Something must have gone wrong. The line must have come loose from the davit. Or maybe it had been cut in two by the patrol boat's propeller. Whatever the case, she felt certain that she was no longer attached to *Pilar* and was now drifting through the Atlantic.

Jackie started to panic. She was afraid of being all alone in this ocean, afraid that Papa had miscalculated how easy it was to get back to the U.S., afraid that the life raft would slip past the PBY that was sure to come out searching for her and she would die of starvation or lack of water before she encountered land.

Her first instinct was to call out for help, but she just as quickly stifled herself; that would only bring the Cuban patrol boat to her. Her second instinct was to grab a paddle and try to row her way back to *Pilar*. But then she would surely be spotted by the patrol boat too. *Easy, Jackie,* she told herself, *you're letting your imagination get the better of you.* She talked herself into remaining calm, weighing her options and taking things one step at a time. That was the only way to stay sane in this kind of situation.

An unexpected thought came to her. Jack Kennedy was a sailor. Boy, would she have a story for him the next time they saw each other. And then she realized that this was a top secret mission. There was no way she could ever tell any of this to him, or anyone else for that matter. Too bad, because she was sure it would have impressed the hell out of Jack to know that she had once gone fishing with Papa Hemingway.

The moon continued its game of peekaboo through the clouds. When it disappeared again, Jackie was shocked at just how stygian the ocean around her was. It was an immense darkness, a crushing presence that seemed to go on forever, and Jackie shivered at the knowledge of how small her life raft was compared to the vast ocean. She hoped that Papa was correct and prayed that the Gulf Stream would transport her back to the United States as swiftly as possible.

In the meantime, she shuffled through the provisions until she found what she was looking for—the flashlight and the book. The best way to stay calm, she knew, was to distract herself. So she turned on the flashlight and opened the book and began to read about the Princeton adventures of Amory Blaine.

XXIV

Of all the places the raft could have washed ashore, Miami Beach couldn't have been more inviting. Jackie thought she was dreaming when a handsome lifeguard helped her out of the raft and, after hearing of her predicament, had a beach boy escort her to the magnificent Versailles Hotel. When she contacted Dulles, he was eager to make up for this latest mishap and once again provided her with first-class accommodations.

So now Jackie was swimming laps in the hotel's gigantic pool. When she counted twenty, she climbed out of the pool and, feeling invigorated from her swim, quick-stepped over to a nearby chaise longue, where she began to dry herself off with a beach towel. Deciding to let her hair dry naturally in the sun, she put down the towel, sat back in her chair, and picked up Papa's copy of *This Side of Paradise* (now slightly warped from seawater) and once again immersed herself in Princeton student Amory Blaine's world of "speeds" and "parlor snakes."

The book reminded her of her recent ordeal in the Atlantic, two days and nights that she didn't really want to relive or ever repeat. Unfortunately, Papa's prediction that she would be picked up by a PBY hadn't come true. Fortunately, his prediction that she would float back to Florida had come true, although she had bypassed Key West entirely and ended up in Miami Beach instead. Not only had Dulles reserved a room for her at the Versailles, but he had even arranged for a physician on the CIA payroll to see her in her hotel room. The doctor pronounced her healthy, although a little too heavily suntanned. Dulles also wired her money so she could go to the shops in Bal Harbour and buy herself some clothes to replace the ones left behind in Cuba. And now here she was in her new Jantzen swimsuit, poolside at the Versailles, recuperating nicely from her ordeal, and waiting to receive her new orders and return home to D.C. for her debriefing.

As she attempted to read, she heard a familiar-sounding voice and looked up. In the near distance, she caught sight of Arthur Phillips, wearing a crisply pressed Palm Beach suit and looking as at home here as he had in the two places in Cuba where she had bumped into him. She wondered what he was doing here, in Miami Beach, and if it was any coincidence that they were both staying at the same hotel. He was greeted by another man, and the two of them walked to a table under an awning at the far side of the swimming pool, where they ordered drinks and watched pretty young women dive into the deep end from the high board.

It was good that he hadn't noticed her. In a flash, Jackie gathered up her beach towel, Coppertone suntan lotion, and book and was back in her room. There, she called the front desk and charmed the room number for Arthur Phillips out of the desk clerk. Venturing out into the hallway, she came across a chambermaid and, taking a page from Emiliano's book, bribed the woman into lending her a spare maid's uniform and her passkey. She then used the passkey to enter Phillips's room, where she quickly spotted an open attaché case on a desk near the sliding glass door that led to his terrace. She put down the feather duster she had used to complete her disguise, then began going through the documents Phillips had left unattended in his attaché case.

Returning to her room, she quickly changed into her clothes and neatly folded the spare uniform for the chambermaid to collect. Jackie then went back to the pool area, where Phillips, his meeting over, was now seated by himself, nursing a drink. Jackie sat in the chair across from him and plunged right in.

"Hello," she said.

"Hello," Phillips said, none of his usual aplomb absent from his voice. She had to hand it to him. If he was surprised to see her, he didn't show it.

"Are you enjoying your stay here?" she asked.

"Well, I usually prefer the Kenilworth."

"But you wanted to stay here so you'd be closer to me—is that right?"

Phillips said nothing.

"You don't have to worry," Jackie assured him. "I know you work for the CIA."

When Phillips didn't answer, Jackie forged ahead. "The Thorndyke Fund is a CIA proprietary company. It's secretly owned by the agency, and you run it for them."

His face remained impassive.

"You weren't in Cuba looking for investment opportunities. The only one you really wanted was Walker's treasure. Well, I'm sorry to say, there wasn't any."

For the first time, Phillips allowed his face to show some emotion. He seemed impressed with Jackie's recitation of the facts.

"I was told you were a neophyte agent. How did you come by this information?"

"Let's just say that I have my ways and leave it at that."

"It would seem that I've underestimated you, Miss Bouvier. You're right. The Thorndyke Fund is a proprietary company. It finances off-the-book operations for the CIA. What is known in the trade as black ops."

"And does Allen Dulles know about this?"

"Let's just say that what Allen Dulles knows and what he doesn't want to know are two separate things."

Jackie shook her head. Once again she had come up against the CIA's ability to use the end to justify the means. She was in over her head, and she knew it. She should just confine herself to the little picture and leave the big picture to the experts. That way she would never end up with conflicted loyalties.

The waiter came, and Jackie ordered lemonade. She told him to put it on Phillips's tab. Phillips made no objection. Under the circumstances, it was the least that he could do.

"I'm sorry there was no treasure," said Jackie with finality.

"As am I," said Phillips. "I wonder what did happen to all that money Walker looted from the Nicaraguan treasury."

Gabriela was taking a break and sunning herself. It was siesta time, and Fidel's camp had gone somnolent in the late afternoon sun, except for some of the men who had chosen up sides for a baseball game (with Fidel pitching for one of the teams, of course). As she watched, Gabriela found, to her surprise, that this new life agreed with her. She felt part of something. What was that forgotten word? Ah, yes, family. So all right, she wouldn't be a dancer. For now. But maybe, come the revolution, she would once again have her chance to fulfill her childhood dream. If she wasn't too old by then. The thought made her laugh to herself.

She saw that Emiliano was playing shortstop on Fidel's

team, which also included his brother Raúl and Camilo Cienfuegos, one of Fidel's top lieutenants. She noted that the lawyer had lost nearly all of his pasty courtroom complexion and was now as brown as every other one of Fidel's *compañeros*. It was still only a fledging army, to be sure, but it was gaining new adherents every day, and Fidel spoke of a time, probably only a year off, when they would make their first big move against the Batista government.

In the weeks since saying farewell to Jackie at the pirate inlet, Emiliano had seemed a changed person. He often kept to himself, and he didn't seem to have a lot to say. He appeared to be on some kind of inward journey, one that had nothing to do with his new situation as a fugitive from justice. Fidel was even thinking about temporarily sending him away, for safety's sake, to Mexico. She recalled overhearing part of their conversation.

"And while you are there in Mexico City," Fidel said, "I want you to meet with a man, an Argentine doctor."

"You want me to go all the way to Mexico to recruit a doctor to treat our troops?" Emiliano asked in confusion.

"No, he is some kind of genius at guerrilla warfare. We could use his expertise here. His name is Ernesto Guevara, but he prefers to be called Che."

In the past few days, Emiliano had come out of his shell somewhat and seemed interested in spending time with her. She felt flattered by this attention and wondered if it was the beginning of something else.

Idly, Gabriela reached into her pocket and pulled out the two halves of the silver locket. Maybe one day, she would take them to a jeweler and have the two pieces soldered together so the locket was whole again. Even as incomplete as they were now, Gabriela was grateful to Jackie for figuring out the puzzle of Walker's treasure and restoring her family heritage to her. She seemed to draw a certain amount of emotional sustenance from just having the locket on her person at all times.

Now, putting the two halves of the locket together, she noticed something for the first time. The second locket half also had those indecipherable markings on the inside.

But once the two halves were joined, Gabriela was surprised to see that the markings were no longer incomprehensible. In fact, they now seemed to form something entirely comprehensible— a tiny map of an island. Not Cuba. But a smaller one off the southern coast of Cuba, in Oriente Province. There was a tiny *X* on the island. You had to squint your eyes to see it. And she was sure that she could view it better with the aid of a magnifying glass. But in the meantime, she felt sure that what she was looking at was a treasure map.

In her mind, she went over the clues Emiliano had told her about. *Leprosaria. Campo Santo. 57. AD.*

Gabriela began to laugh. She knew that the tiny island, visible from the pirate inlet below the fort, had once been called Isla de Campo Santo, a fact that few people today seemed to know. And that a leper colony had been abandoned there after having been reestablished on the southern coast. Was it possible that there had been a treasure after all, and that Metzger had buried it on the island? Metzger, the former apprentice silversmith who had meticulously etched this treasure map on the inside of Maria Consuela's silver locket, then deliberately split it in two to prevent just anyone from discovering its secret.

If this were indeed the case, then he was far more ingenious than anyone had given him credit for. Maybe this had been his convoluted way of making sure that his descendants would one day meet Maria Consuela's descendants. Too bad then that Metzger had died before getting married and having children to fulfill his dream. In the end, though, it had come true in its own fashion, reuniting Gabriela with the family ancestors she had never known.

At the thought of it, she continued to laugh. She laughed so hard and so long that she caught the attention of Emiliano, who was awaiting his turn at bat. He came over to her and asked what was so funny.

And when she told him, he began to laugh too.

XXV

Washington, D.C., May 1952

Caroline Lee Bouvier's aim was so accurate that Jackie caught her wedding bouquet without even having to reach for it. As her sister's maid of honor, Jackie received Lee's bouquet like a prized talisman and earnestly hoped that it would bring her good luck in love.

During the ceremony at Georgetown's Holy Trinity Church, Jackie's heart swelled with happiness as she watched her sister exchange marriage vows with Michael Canfield in a fairy-tale wedding. Lee looked radiant in her lovely ivory organza bridal gown and rose-point lace veil, and the tall blond groom, thankfully sober for the occasion, cut an elegant figure in his white tuxedo. Yes, Jackie was genuinely happy for the glowing bride but, at the same time, couldn't help feeling a gnawing insecurity about her own unmarried state...

Jackie woke up with a start. It took her a few moments to realize that the wedding she had visualized so precisely was only a dream. But the mixed emotions it had stirred in her were all too real. After all, Lee was her *kid* sister, almost four years younger, and was engaged to be married to Michael Canfield next year while Jackie, having broken her engagement to John Husted, had no real marital prospects in sight.

Being a CIA agent hadn't left much time for dating. First,

there was all that training at Camp Peary, and then, as soon as Jackie had returned from New Orleans, she'd been dispatched to Havana. She hadn't expected to meet the man of her dreams there, but along came breathlessly handsome, adorably shy, and passionately idealistic Emiliano, and once again, as she had in Paris, Jackie fell in love. But like her romance with Jacques, the one with Emiliano was doomed to be short-lived. That sad state of affairs seemed to be an occupational hazard for a single woman CIA agent sent to glamorous foreign locales where exciting male colleagues awaited her.

Now Jackie was back home at Merrywood with that familiar ache in her heart, and her fear of ending up the spinster headmistress at Miss Porter's, her old finishing school, nagged with a vengeance. But instead of being able to look for a beau, Jackie would have to focus on courting Jack Kennedy, not as a possible suitor, but strictly to complete the unfinished business of her assignment: to woo him to befriend the CIA.

A whole year had passed since Jackie had to break her first date with Jack to go off to New Orleans, but Charlie Bartlett had assured her that Jack was eager to see her again. "He's just so busy campaigning for the Senate that he scarcely has time for anything else," Charlie had said. *He had time for a fling with a showgirl in Havana,* Jackie thought, but she kept that observation to herself.

Jackie mulled over possible ploys she could use to get to see Jack again. She could simply call him up and ask him to Sunday dinner at Merrywood, but that seemed too forward. She could drum up some social event like a charity ball and ask him to be her escort, but again, she thought that was sticking her neck out too far. It had to be an invitation that didn't have any romantic connotations, something practical that would serve his purposes as a senatorial candidate, but what would that be? *Of course,* Jackie thought as the idea hit her. She would ask to interview him for her column as the *Times-Herald*'s Inquiring Camera Girl. She would assure him that it would be a positive piece and good publicity for his campaign. How could he refuse?

Wearing a chic Coco Chanel suit and midheel Gucci pumps that added no more height than necessary, Jackie strode down the marble lobby of the Cannon House Office Building and took the elevator to the third floor. When she came to Jack's office near the end of the long hall, she paused outside the mahogany door, stared at the words JOHN FITZGERALD KEN-NEDY, MEMBER OF CONGRESS engraved on the brass nameplate, and gathered her nerve.

Inside, she was expecting to see a receptionist at the desk in the waiting room, but no one was there. It was noontime, and Jackie assumed that the receptionist had gone out for lunch, so she walked into an inner office, thinking that the secre-tary would escort her in to see Jack. But the secretary, whose name, Jackie had learned, was Mary Barelli Gallagher, wasn't there either. Actually, having impersonated Mary in her frantic phone call at the Europa, Jackie was relieved not to have to face the real Mary in person.

Jack's office door was closed, so Jackie coughed loudly to make her presence known. Within minutes, the door opened and a young woman emerged, her hair disheveled, her lipstick smeared, and her clothes in disarray.

The woman blinked at Jackie, ran a hand through her hair, tucked her blouse back into her skirt, and quickly sat down behind the desk. "Sorry to keep you waiting," she said with a guilty smile. "Congressman Kennedy's secretary and receptionist are on their lunch breaks, and I'm filling in. May I help you?"

Jackie smiled back and tried to keep the wry amusement out of her voice. "I'm Jacqueline Bouvier from the *Times-Herald*. I have an appointment to interview Congressman Kennedy for my column."

The girl glanced at a notepad on the desk. "Oh yes, Miss Bouvier," she said, nodding. She picked up the phone, announced Jackie, waited a moment, and then pointed to the door to Jack's office. "Go right in. He's expecting you."

Jack rose from behind his desk when he saw Jackie and flashed a big, shiny grin at her. He looked thinner than she had remembered and held a hand on his back as if it pained him. Apparently, the back problem that Charlie Bartlett had told her about was a chronic one, but it did nothing to dim Jack's aura of incandescent charisma that had enthralled everyone at the dinner party the night she first met him. That allure was still in full force, and he was still dazzlingly handsome.

"So nice to see you again, Jackie," he said warmly. "You look lovely. Have a seat."

He waited for Jackie to settle into an armchair facing his desk before he sat back down again in his managerial-looking leather chair. "Why don't we pick up where we left off?" he asked, his slate blue eyes sparkling with insouciance. "Armed with a degree in French literature from George Washington University, you had just come back from a trip to Paris and had some time to kill before taking a job you'd been offered as the *Times-Herald*'s Inquiring Camera Girl. Did I get that right?"

Jackie was amazed at his retentive memory. It seemed like a magic trick. "Yes, I've been working at the newspaper since the first of the year. I'm learning a lot, and it's great fun. The veteran photographers on the paper have been teaching me the tricks of the trade. Joe Heilberger even stretched all six feet of himself out on the floor on his back and told me to take my pictures from that distance."

"That was good of him," Jack said, smiling. He gave her an inquisitive look. "But where's your camera?"

Jackie laughed. "I didn't bring it because I thought I'd sketch you instead. I'd like to do something a little more original than just take another photograph to add to the hundreds of you already out there." In truth, she was afraid that lugging an ungainly four-pound camera to his office would have spoiled the sophisticated impression she wanted to make. Knowing how important appearances were in Washington, she'd spent the whole morning in the beauty salon getting her hair cut and tinted and her fingernails polished red to cover their atrocious green color caused by exposure to developing fluid in the darkroom.

"Oh, are you an artist?" Jack asked.

"I studied art history at the Sorbonne, and I've been sketching for years."

"The Sorbonne? That's impressive." Jack glanced at the folio Jackie had brought with her. "Have you brought some samples of your column with you?"

"I have," Jackie said as she took some clippings out of her folio and handed them to him.

"Very insightful," Jack said, scanning the columns. "It's a clever concept. You ask people who have been in the news some revealing question that shows their human side and helps the public identify with them, is that it?"

"Yes, exactly. The idea is to give the readers a more personal, down-to-earth view of celebrities than they normally get," Jackie said, quickly adding, "but it's never done to embarrass the subjects in any way."

"Ah, then I won't have to plead the Fifth," Jack said, smiling. "And do you pick your own subjects or does the newspaper assign them to you?"

That was a tricky question. The truth was that Jackie could make the column about anyone or anything she wanted, but if she revealed that to Jack, he might jump to the conclusion that she had some ulterior motive in selecting him for an interview. She decided to give him a plausible answer that would flatter his ego and wouldn't arouse suspicions of any kind.

"The newspaper gives me a lot of leeway," she said, "but when all of Washington is buzzing about someone, as people are about you, I'm expected to do a column about that person, but give it a different twist."

"A different twist?" he asked with raised eyebrows. "I don't know, Jacqueline; that sounds ominous, but I'm game." He folded his arms across his abdomen, bracing himself. "Okay then, what is the question you have for me?"

Jackie hesitated, hoping that he wouldn't think it was silly, and then blurted, "With what person, living or dead, would you most like to be shipwrecked on an island?" She had dreamed that one up in fond remembrance of her idyllic interlude with Emiliano on Saetía.

Jack threw his head back and chortled out loud. "That's easy. Henry Cabot Lodge. So I could hit him over the head with a coconut, swim back to shore, and win the election by default."

Jackie laughed too, but she wished Jack would turn more serious. She didn't want to waste her precious appointment with him bantering.

But he leaned back in his chair with an amused look on his face and seemed in no hurry to get on with the interview. "And what person would you most like to be shipwrecked on an island with, Miss Inquiring Photographer Without a Camera?" he asked in a teasing tone.

"Sergei Diaghilev," Jackie replied without hesitation. She could tell from Jack's cocked eyebrow that her answer had surprised him. She wondered if he even knew who Diaghilev was. "I'm a lover of the ballet and the opera, and if I were shipwrecked on an island with Diaghilev," she went on to explain, "I could learn how to discover talents like Pavlova and Nijinsky and launch a company like the Ballets Russes. I would ask that great Russian impresario to tell me how to stage operas and orchestral works by the up-and-coming geniuses of our time the way he did with Rimsky-Korsakov and Tchaikovsky in his day. That's a secret fantasy of mine."

Jack's mouth dropped open. "That's quite an ambition for a young lady fresh out of college," he said, staring at Jackie wide-eyed. "Judging by your job with the *Times-Herald*, I would have thought that you wanted to be a reporter."

"Oh, I love writing too, and I know how challenging it is, but I'm told that I have some talent for it," Jackie said in a self-effacing tone. "Actually, I'd be happy to have a career in any of the arts." *Oh God, a career in the arts; that sounds so pretentious.* She shook her head, smiled at Jack, and said in a whispery, girlish voice, "But I'm supposed to be interviewing you, not talking about myself. You're the one everyone wants to know about. You're running for the Senate, and I'm just running around like a chicken without a head."

"A brainy, beautiful, well-bred chicken," Jack said, laughing. "Even the White House executive chef wouldn't have the foggiest idea what to do with you."

Jackie fidgeted in her chair, anxious to get back to the interview and then try to swing the conversation around to more weighty matters, like Jack's feelings about the CIA.

But Jack surprised her. He leaned toward her, pursed his lips, and said, "I was just thinking, Jacqueline, that we never did get to go dancing at the Shoreham, did we? If you like, we can have a night out and do the interview after that." His eyes twinkled at her in a teasing way that she found as cute as a dimple. "You're looking pretty healthy to me, so I don't suppose you'll be catching a virus by Saturday, will you? I'd hate for you to disappoint me again."

Jackie cringed. *That's right, Jack, rub it in. He had to bring up her lame excuse for breaking their date, didn't he?* "No, I absolutely will not be catching any viruses, even if I have to be quarantined all week," Jackie said with a red face, "and I would love to go dancing at the Shoreham Saturday night."

"Good, that's what I wanted to hear." Jack rose from his chair and held out both his hands to her. "You're a fascinating woman, Jacqueline," he said, sounding as if he meant it. "I have a feeling that after I get to know you better, the person I might want to be shipwrecked with on an island is you."

XXVI

When she walked into the Blue Room on the arm of Jack Kennedy, Jackie could feel all eyes turning in their direction. She had made sure to wear something stunning—a low-cut, form-fitting black chiffon by Oleg Cassini, a French-born American designer who was gaining fame dressing stars on Broadway and in motion pictures—but Jackie was sure that it was Jack Kennedy who was drawing all the stares. Out of the corner of her eye, she could see people nudging each other and nodding in their direction, as if to say, "Isn't he that dashing young congressman and war hero from Massachusetts?" Even if they didn't recognize Jack from his picture in newspapers and magazines, they were probably drawn to him, Jackie thought, by the same irresistible magnetism that she had witnessed at the Bartletts' party.

As soon as they were seated at their table and had ordered their drinks, Jackie sensed that they would not be alone for long as she saw a short, stocky man in his early sixties approaching them.

"Hey there, Jack, nice to see you," the man said, giving Jack a friendly tap on the shoulder. "Taking some time off from campaigning in Massachusetts, are you?" He rolled the fat cigar around in his mouth as he gave Jackie an appreciative look. "And you too, Jacqueline. You're looking lovely tonight."

"Thank you, Arthur," Jackie said, smiling sweetly at Arthur Krock, the chief Washington correspondent for the *New York Times*. He was familiar to Jackie as an esteemed member of her stepfather's social circle and a constant guest at Merrywood. Charlie Barlett had told Jackie that he owed his career to Krock and that Krock was a close friend not only of Hugh Auchincloss, but of Joe Kennedy too.

"Arthur and Joe Kennedy talk on the phone every day," Charlie had told her, "and your name has come up lately."

"My name? Why?" Jackie had asked in surprise.

"According to Arthur, Joe thinks a wife and a family will improve Jack's chances of getting elected to the Senate and eventually making it into the White House," Charlie had explained. "When Arthur described you as beautiful, brainy, classy, and Catholic, Joe said, 'Sounds like she was sent from central casting.'"

Jackie had been flattered by Arthur Krock's high opinion of her, but right now, she wished that he would leave her alone with Jack Kennedy so that she could begin to lay the groundwork for accomplishing her mission for Allen Dulles.

But Krock showed no sign of wanting to leave; nor did his wife Martha, an exquisitely dressed woman standing beside him. "Hello, you two. What a handsome couple you make," Martha said, slurring her speech and looking flushed and slightly inebriated. She gave Jackie and Jack a crooked smile. "Do I have an item here for my society column?"

Jackie was an avid reader of Martha's "These Charming People" column in the *Washington Times-Herald*, but going public so soon about dating Jack might put too much pressure on him or risk blowing her cover. She didn't know how to respond.

Jack rescued her. "This is our first date, so there's not much to say," he told Martha, adding with an impish grin, "But if I'm lucky enough to get a second one with Miss Bouvier, you'll be the first to hear about it."

Martha glanced at the bar and spotted someone she knew. "Oh, there's Stu Symington. If you'll excuse me, I must say hello."

And off she tottered, possibly in search of an item for her column or more likely to get another drink. Jackie was hoping that Arthur Krock would follow her, but instead he drew up a chair from another table and began an animated conversation with Jack, leaving Jackie to nurse her drink and stare helplessly around the room.

Every now and then she caught snatches of what Krock and Jack were talking about—"MacArthur overstepped and was just asking for Truman to dismiss him..." "Eisenhower is a shoo-in if the right wing doesn't block him..." "Kefauver is the one your father thinks the Democrats will nominate..." "Stevenson has a big following, but he's an egghead..."

Jackie would have been much happier if they were discussing the Picasso exhibit at the National Gallery of Art or George Balanchine's *Theme and Variations* with artists of the Royal Ballet at the Uline Arena or Frederick Pottle's *Boswell's London Journal* on the *New York Times* best-seller list—all subjects of interest to her and about which she had something to say. But politics numbed her brain like a sedative, and she could not fathom how Charlie Bartlett and Joe Kennedy thought that she might be the perfect wife for a round-the-clock politician like Jack Kennedy.

Finally, when she was afraid that Jack and Arthur Krock had completely forgotten that she was there, Jackie excused herself and went to the ladies' room. As she passed the Tommy Dorsey orchestra, a favorite at the Blue Room ever since the band had introduced Frank Sinatra to the world, Jackie admired how spiffy the musicians looked. They were all dressed in full tuxedoes with white jackets, black pants, dress shirts with cuff links, and black bow ties. Tommy Dorsey, known as "The Sentimental Gentleman of Swing," had just launched into "Stardust," and the seductively smooth tones of his trombone made Jackie hope that Jack would ask her to dance when she returned to their table.

But on her way back, she was shocked to see that Jack was already on the dance floor, cheek to cheek with—oh no, was this a bad dream?—the ubiquitous Loretta "Hickey" Sumers! Jackie thought that she had seen the last of Loretta clinging to Jack at the Bartletts' party a year ago before he managed to break free of her clutches. The woman was as persistent as a stuck car horn.

Jackie wasn't sure what possessed her other than sheer frustration mixed with a streak of feline rivalry, but she marched right up to Jack, tapped him on the shoulder, and asked, "May I have this dance?"

When Loretta looked to see who was cutting in, Jackie flashed a false smile at her that was meant to convey thinly veiled displeasure. "Hi, Loretta, nice to see you again," she said coolly, "but if you don't mind, I'd like my date back now."

"Of course, Jackie," Loretta trilled. She gave Jack a peck on the cheek. "Thanks for the dance, Jack. Bye now, you two. Have a great evening."

As Loretta disappeared into the crowd, Jack turned to Jackie with an apologetic look on his face. "She came up to me when I was with Arthur Krock and whisked me onto the dance floor. At least Arthur took the hint and left." Jack's eyes crinkled in a mischievous smile. "I was about to send for the National Guard to have him removed."

Jackie couldn't help laughing. It seemed impossible to stay angry at Jack for long.

When the orchestra began to play "All or Nothing at All," Jackie's favorite Sinatra record, she slipped into Jack's arms and began dancing with him. She was surprised to find that for a man who had impressed her as unusually graceful when she first met him, Jack was not a good dancer. But by using subtle cues, Jackie was able to impart her sense of rhythm to him, and soon he was moving in time to the beat and humming in tune with the mellifluous sound of Tommy Dorsey's trombone.

Jackie closed her eyes dreamily, and a flurry of excitement rippled through her when Jack pressed his face close to hers and whispered in her ear, "You're a wonderful dancer, Jackie. I like the way you feel in my arms." He had probably used that line with countless women before her, Jackie thought, but the effect it had on her was remarkably potent nonetheless. She was sorry that the song had to end.

When they went back to their table, the waiter was already approaching with their supper orders—an open-face steak sandwich for Jack and seafood crêpes for Jackie. He set the dishes down and poured them each a fresh glass of wine.

"Dig in," Jack said, but their meal was constantly interrupted by a procession of people stopping by to say hello to Jack: a campaign worker from Massachusetts, a business associate of his father's, friends from Palm Beach, another congressman, and on and on.

When the waiter came to clear away their plates and asked if they wanted anything else, Jackie quipped, "Some privacy would be nice."

"I couldn't agree more," Jack said, laughing. He motioned to the waiter to bring the check, then leaned toward Jackie. "I'd love for us to have a chance to talk and do that interview I promised you. Why don't we go back to my place for a night-cap?"

Uh-oh, I can just imagine the "nightcap" that you have in mind. Jackie thought that it would be prudent to decline. On the other hand, it was probably her only chance to garner Jack's support for the CIA before he became so busy with his senatorial campaign that she never saw him again. She pursed her lips, debating what she should say.

Jack smiled at her reassuringly. "I promise you, Jackie, I'll be on my best behavior. I haven't paid you the kind of attention that you deserve. You're an intriguing woman, and I want to get to know more about you. Just some quiet conversation. There's no harm in that, is there?"

No, and Jackie would see to it that it ended there. After all, if she had been able to escape being eaten alive by crocodiles in Havana—with Gabriela's help, but still—and repeatedly defied death, couldn't she rely on her bag of tricks to keep her out of Jack Kennedy's bed?

"Okay, a nightcap and some conversation with just the two of us sounds fine," she said.

The three-story brick house that Jack was renting on Thirty-First Street in Georgetown was close by the Bartletts' home and looked almost exactly the same from the outside. Inside, the décor was fussier than the Bartletts' but still homey.

"How about some Grand Marnier?" Jack asked.

"That would be lovely," Jackie said. "Actually, it's a favorite of mine, Francophile that I am."

"You and my mother," Jack said, bringing their drinks over and sitting down next to Jackie, but at a respectable distance, on the Chippendale sofa. Jackie almost giggled at how out of place Jack looked among the pink, magenta, and white cabbage roses of the sofa's fabric, but she quietly sipped her drink as Jack went on, "Ever since I can remember, my mother was flying off to Paris two or three times a year for some haute couture fashion show."

I hope she wasn't at the House of Dior show last May, Jackie thought, remembering how she had created a ruckus so she could escape from an assassin by pretending that some snooty count stole her diamond bracelet. "Well, at least she has good taste," Jackie said.

"And so do you," Jack said, looking at her with frank admiration. "That's a beautiful dress you have on. Is it by a French designer?"

"He's French-born, but he lives here now. I do have a Givenchy and a Dior dress that I brought back from Paris, though." Jackie took a sip of her Grand Marnier, savored the tart orange taste, and plunged into the more substantive topic on her mind. "I love Paris so much that I was tempted to accept a six-month position there that *Vogue* magazine offered me, but my stepfather's friend, Allen Dulles, talked me out of it. Do you know Mr. Dulles?"

"I do know him," Jack said. "He did a brilliant job in the war gathering anti-Nazi intelligence that led to the surrender of German troops in Italy. After the war, he helped create the National Security Act of 1947 that set up the U.S. Central Intelligence Agency—you know, the CIA. In 1948, he and two other people appointed by President Truman gave the president some excellent recommendations to reform the CIA, and now Allen Dulles is deputy director of the agency."

As he had at the Bartletts' dinner party, Jack once again displayed a near encyclopedic knowledge of people that Jackie found impressive. She took another sip of her drink and asked offhandedly, "So you think highly of Mr. Dulles, then?"

"I don't know him that well personally, but he's a master at setting up intelligence networks. With Allen Dulles at the helm, I have no doubt that the CIA will play an indispensable role in stopping the spread of Soviet Communism in Eastern Europe and other Communist movements worldwide." Jack smiled and shook his head. "I'm afraid I'm starting to sound like Arthur Krock. All I need is a cigar in my mouth. I'm not boring you, am I?"

Are you kidding? You've told me exactly what I wanted to hear. "No, not at all," Jackie said. "This spy stuff is actually very interesting. In fact, I think I might try to interview Allen Dulles for my *Times-Herald* column, maybe ask him who his favorite author of spy novels is."

"I like that idea," Jack said. "A kind of busman's-holiday angle."

"Yes, but first I have to find out who Jack Kennedy would most like to be shipwrecked on an island with other than me," Jackie said, smiling. "Have you thought about that?"

Jack nodded. "Knowing my political aspirations, most people would probably expect me to pick one of our country's Founding Fathers, like George Washington or Thomas Jefferson, but I'd probably choose an author. I've always admired writers enormously. My very favorite book is *Pilgrim's Way*, the autobiography of the Scottish novelist John Buchan. I loved his tribute to friends of his who died young: 'They march on into life with a boyish grace, and their high noon keeps all the freshness of the morning.'"

"That's beautiful," Jackie said, moved that Jack was willing to display this serious, sensitive side of himself on their first date. "Writing is a passion of mine too, and I'm grateful to have this newspaper job to get a chance to develop my craft. I'm hoping it will lead to bigger things."

Jack nodded. "You know, my younger sister Kathleen—we always called her 'Kick'—was a reporter for the *Times-Herald*."

"Really? What a coincidence."

Jack studied her. "No, maybe it's not such a coincidence. You remind me of Kick. She was beautiful and high-spirited like you. She had that same spark, that flair that set her apart from other girls. She was my favorite sister. I always had the time of my life when I was with her, and she died so young—at twenty-eight—in an airplane crash in France. It was heartbreaking." A remorseful note crept into his voice. "My father was the only member of the Kennedy family at her funeral. My mother talked the rest of us out of going because my sister had married out of the Catholic Church." Jackie could see the pain clouding his eyes as he said, "I'll never forgive myself for that."

He looked so sad that Jackie put down her wineglass and stroked his cheek, not knowing what to say to comfort him. Their eyes locked, and before she knew it, he was kissing her with his mouth fully on hers. It was a deep, penetrating kiss that made Jackie's head spin and her whole body go slack. For a moment, she was back in Havana, kissing Emiliano for the first time. But then she stopped thinking about Havana, stopped thinking about anything, as Jack put his arms around her and drew her close.

Click...click...click. Jackie heard the sound of a key turning in a lock. She looked at the front door and was aghast when it opened and she saw a woman standing in the entryway, staring at them.

Jackie pushed Jack away and jumped up from the sofa, furious. *The nerve of Jack Kennedy!* He invited her back to his place just to talk, and then worked on her sympathies to soften her up for a lot more—and all the time he was living with another woman. How could he have been this low?

Jack rose from the sofa, wiped the lipstick off his face with the back of his hand, and said to the woman, "Hi. I wasn't expecting you until tomorrow."

Jackie glowered at him, steaming. Did Jack really think that he would get her to sleep with him tonight and push her out the door the next morning before his live-in lady friend got there? *He doesn't know Jacqueline Lee Bouvier. I'd have been out of here after that first kiss.*

The tall, thin, thirtyish woman, with an angular face, a full head of auburn hair, and imperious gray-blue eyes said to Jack in a Boston Brahman accent, "I would have called you from the train station, but I didn't get a chance." She looked at Jackie as if she was seeing clear through her. "Jack, why don't you introduce me to your friend?"

Nodding at Jackie, Jack said to the woman, "This is Jacqueline Bouvier." And to Jackie, with a nod toward the woman, he said, "Jackie, I'd like you to meet my sister Eunice. We're renting this place together."

His *sister*! *Oh, for heaven's sake,* Jackie thought. *I should have known—the hair, the eyes, the accent.* Jackie smiled at Eunice, trying to forget that she had just been discovered smooching with this woman's brother, and said, "So nice to meet you, Eunice." She glanced at the door. "Actually, it's getting rather late, and I need to be going."

The look of dismay on Jack's face was almost comical as Jackie said, "Good night, Congressman, and thank you for a lovely evening." She said the "congressman" for his sister's sake, trying to restore a semblance of propriety, and made it to the door without so much as a backward glance.

Jack didn't have a car in Washington, but the ride that he had arranged for the evening was waiting outside for Jackie. On the drive back to Merrywood, cushioned in the soft, leather backseat, she shut her eyes, pictured that kiss with Jack, and relived the deep, visceral thrill that it had evoked in her.

She wondered when—or if—he'd be kissing her like that again. But no matter what the future brought, one thing was certain. She would always savor the memory of that kiss like a keepsake. The attraction she felt for Jack was deeper than physical. She sensed that they were indeed the kindred spirits she thought they might be. They were both a study in contrasts. Hidden beneath his gregarious exterior, he had the same spirit of independence and stubborn streak of individuality that she concealed under her debutante manners. And they each wrestled with the same tension between a desire to be the center of attention and a need to distance themselves from others. She toyed with the idea that it could be liberating for both of them if they ever became really close. Drawn to the unconventional, they would feel free to express parts of themselves that conformity to their parents' and society's expectations had made them keep under wraps. It was something to think about.

Tomorrow, though, her first order of business would be to report to Allen Dulles and tell him that she had fully accomplished her mission. *Good work, Jacqueline,* she could hear him saying when he heard that she had solved the mystery of the missing treasure map, determined the seriousness of the threat posed by Fidel Castro's anti-imperialist zeal, and verified Jack Kennedy's high regard for the CIA.

Oh yes, and there was something else she needed to do. She wouldn't let another day go by without returning an antiquated book ironically titled *A Recent History of Cuba* to the Washington and Lee University library. It was only ninety years overdue.

XXVII

CUBAN NUN DECLARES "A MIRACLE"

HAVANA (AP)—Sister Evelina has long believed in miracles, but she never expected to experience one. As the director of the Home for Children Without Parents and Family in Oriente Province, Cuba, the nun has feared in recent years that without additional funds she would be forced to close the facility, which is home to one hundred children. "But then, what would the children do?" she would ask herself.

As Sister Evelina left the building for her morning walk yesterday, she found a briefcase on the orphanage's front doorstep. Thinking the briefcase had been left by accident, Sister Evelina brought it inside and opened it to see if she could find the identity of its owner. But to her surprise, the briefcase contained stacks of United States hundred dollar bills, adding up to $100,000. A note found with the money said simply, "For the children."

Sister Evelina contacted the Archdiocese of Santiago de Cuba, local authorities, and several newspapers in hope of discovering the identity of the benefactor. She wonders if the donor could be someone raised at the orphanage. All the nun knows for certain is that the orphanage now can be kept open indefinitely.

"It is a true miracle," she says...

EPILOGUE

"Seven Minutes to Midnight",
Monday, October 22, 1962

Jackie was suddenly awake.

She looked at the clock on the nightstand. It was seven minutes to midnight. She turned over and saw that the other side of the bed was empty. Jack was once again working late. She needed him, among other places, here in bed with her. They had been trying to make another baby and his current schedule wasn't making things any easier.

She got out of bed, put on a robe, slipped on a battered pair of tennies, and then walked down the hall to the children's bedrooms. She looked in on them, Caroline and John-John; they were both sleeping. How lovely to be a child and to be oblivious to all the frightening news that was being broadcast night and day, announcing that the U.S. and U.S.S.R. were teetering on the edge of nuclear war. She envied them their unencumbered slumber and wished that she could enjoy it as well.

Still unable to sleep, Jackie went down to the White House kitchen, which was empty at this hour. It had recently been remodeled, and its stainless-steel counters and appliances and hanging copper pots and pans gleamed even in the partial light. As she made herself a cup of coffee, she thought about the latest terrifying news.

Several hours ago, Jack had gone on TV to tell the nation that the Russians had placed offensive nuclear missiles in Cuba and that a naval blockade was now under way to prevent the Soviets from shipping any more offensive military weapons there. What happened when the Soviet ships already en route to Cuba would meet that blockade line in several days was anyone's guess at this point. Would they turn back or would they attempt to break through the blockade and quite possibly precipitate World War III?

There was a clattering from the hall and suddenly there he was in the kitchen with her. The Executive Committee meeting in the Cabinet Room must have just broken up. "Oh," Jack said in surprise. "I was hoping one of the cooks was here."

"Hungry?" Jackie asked.

"Starving," said Jack, rubbing the palms of his hands together to indicate just how much. "I sure could go for a club sandwich."

"I'll make you one," Jackie volunteered, happy that there was something concrete she could do for him.

She went over to the restaurant-sized refrigerator and began pulling out the makings for a sandwich: leftover turkey, bacon, tomatoes, mayonnaise, and bread. She took the bacon over to the stovetop, threw some pieces into a pan, and began frying them. As she did so, she turned to Jack, who was simultaneously leaning against the freestanding stainless-steel counter opposite the range and massaging his back, which suffered from a chronic condition exacerbated when his torpedo boat, PT-109, had been rammed by a Japanese destroyer during World War II. The injury could become further exacerbated by stress, so Jackie could imagine that her husband's back must have been radiating constant pain since day one of the crisis.

"So how are things going?" she asked him.

He paused before answering. "It's still touch and go. That Khrushchev is one stubborn son of a bitch. And you can say the same for his own personal Charlie McCarthy, Fidel Castro."

Jackie had a difficult time keeping a poker face. She knew that ever since the Bay of Pigs disaster in April 1961, Jack had been looking for any chance to give the Cuban dictator a pasting. She had never told him about her secret mission to Cuba for the CIA, exactly ten years ago. Even though she was long retired from the agency, that assignment was still classified top secret by Langley.

She remembered that meeting with a beardless Castro. Everybody knew what he was doing today, Fidel having overthrown Batista on New Year's Day 1959 to become the new leader of Cuba. An acceptance of Communist principles soon followed. But what about Emiliano and Gabriela? Were they still a part of the people's revolution? She had lost track of them, and they only ever came to mind once in a while. The past ten years had been a whirlwind of activity for her, taking on one covert CIA assignment after another, then being in a high-profile marriage to a U.S. senator, and ultimately assuming the role of first lady of the country. Add two children to the mix and Jackie hadn't been left with much time for looking back.

Once, though, she had seen a wire-service picture of Castro and thought she recognized Emiliano standing behind him, but the figure was kind of blurry and it was impossible to tell for certain if it truly was him. There had also been a photograph of marching women in militia uniforms. One of them seemed to resemble Gabriela, but it was hard to tell for certain behind the aviator sunglasses hiding the woman's eyes.

But now, because of the events of the past several days, her memories of those brave Cubans and the way they had stood up to Batista were constantly with her.

As the bacon was frying, Jackie went over to the counter and began to prep the rest of the sandwich: putting bread in the toaster, cutting tomato slices, and picking out choice pieces of turkey. Jack stood next to Jackie and cleared his throat. She looked up at him, knowing that he was about to say something important.

"Jackie," he said, "I want you and the children to leave Washington."

Jackie looked at him with incredulity and said, "What?"

"If this goes bad, Washington will be a prime target for Russian nuclear ICBMs. I don't want to take any chances. If the worst does happen, I want you and the children as far from D.C. as possible."

The toast popped. Jackie covered one side of all three pieces with mayo, then began layering the tomatoes, turkey and bacon among the three slices of bread. She needed this time in order to gather her thoughts.

When the sandwich was finished, she put it on a plate, pushed it in front of her husband, now seated, brought him a bottle of Heineken—his favorite beer—from the refrigerator, and said simply, "No."

Now it was Jack's turn to look incredulous. "What?"

"You heard me—no."

"Jackie, you can't be serious. Do you know how dangerous things could get?"

"Yes, but that doesn't change anything. My place is here with you."

"This is totally unprecedented—"

"No, it's not," Jackie interrupted. "During the Blitz, King George the Sixth made sure that he and the royal family remained at Buckingham Palace, to set a good example for the people of London and provide moral support to the nation."

"But no one's going to know whether you're here or not. We'll keep that a secret."

"*I'll* know," Jackie said simply.

Jack looked at Jackie and gave her a rueful smile. He sighed and took a bite of his sandwich.

"Delicious," he pronounced between mouthfuls. "Thank you."

"For the sandwich," Jackie said, seating herself next to him, "it was nothing."

"Not for the sandwich," Jack said, and paused. "For—"

He looked at Jackie. She knew a million thoughts were racing around in that complicated mind of his, a million possible ways to finish that remark. She waited to hear what he would come up with.

"For being my rock." He took her hand and squeezed it as hard as he could.

"Ouch," Jackie said. She extricated her trapped hand and caressed it with exaggerated motions, pretending that he had really hurt her.

That caused him to laugh, something he must have done little of in the past week, despite his fabled sense of humor. She joined in with him. There they were, Jackie thought, an ordinary husband and wife, sitting in their kitchen in the middle of the night, picking at leftovers, holding hands and sharing a laugh. But they weren't an ordinary couple. They were the president and his first lady. And their kitchen wasn't located in Brookline or Riverdale or Bethesda; it was in the White House. Like any other married couple, they had had their ups and downs, but, despite all the big and little upheavals, they were still together.

In a little while, Jackie knew, Jack would have to return to his Ex Comm meeting, and she would return to bed, where, she felt sure now, sleep would come. She had faith that her husband would commit to whatever course necessary to ensure the safety of the country, to turn the world away from the brink of nuclear destruction. And no matter what happened, and no matter how things turned out, Jackie affirmed to herself that she would be there, right where she had always belonged, by Jack's side.

Acknowledgments

It's been a long and circuitous road since I first came up with the concept for a series of novels about young Jacqueline Bouvier working as a spy for the CIA. And these are the people I would like to mention for providing me with assistance on this leg of the journey. With thanks and gratitude—

To our editor, Alex Logan, for having the patience of Job, the wisdom of Solomon, and the diplomatic skills of Dean Acheson.

To Beth de Guzman and the entire dedicated team at Grand Central Publishing, including our intrepid publicists, Jillian Sanders and Brianne Beers.

To our wonderful agent, Melissa Chinchillo at Fletcher & Company, for service above and beyond the call of duty.

To our movie agent, Rich Green at CAA, for displaying such early faith in the project.

To the baristas at Bourbon Coffee, where much of this book was written, for keepin' the iced tea comin'.

To Vince Cosgrove, for lending an old newsman's practiced eye to chapter 27.

To Hope Tarr and the good people at Lady Jane's Salon in NYC for making a newbie author feel right at home.

To novelist Caroline Leavitt for her generosity of spirit toward her fellow writers.

To Terry Mort, whose *The Hemingway Patrols* (Scribner, 2009) helped place me on the flying bridge of *Pilar* alongside Papa.

To T. J. English, whose *Havana Nocturne* (Morrow, 2008) transported me back to Cuba in the days leading up to Castro's revolution.

To Richard D. Mahoney, whose *Sons and Brothers: The Days of Jack and Bobby Kennedy* (Arcade, 1999) took me behind the scenes at the White House during the Cuban Missile Crisis in October 1962.

To David J. Skal, whose *The Horror Show* (Penguin Books, 1994) first introduced me to the "Mexican Dracula."

To Henri-Georges Clouzot, Sir Carol Reed, Francis Ford Coppola, Richard Lester, Sydney Pollack, Julian Schnabel, and Andy Garcia for their visual cues.

To Tito Puente, Celia Cruz, Arturo Sandoval, Perez Prado, and the Buena Vista Social Club for providing the soundtrack to which this novel was written.

And above all, to Marilyn and Rachel, for the constancy and amplitude of their love and support.

—Ken Salikof

Acknowledgments

My career as a writer has had many midwives. None of the books I've written or co-authored over the years would have seen the light of day had it not been for some wonderful agents who have represented my work, including Meredith Bernstein, Mary Tahan, and, currently, Melissa Chinchillo of Fletcher & Company. Thanks to Melissa for getting this book and its predecessor, *Paris to Die For*, to Grand Central Publishing and to Alex Logan, who assiduously edited both books and has been unflagging in her support. Beth de Guzman and the incredibly hardworking staff at Grand Central have provided an ideal home for the two novels.

I'm very grateful to the friends and family who enthusiastically embraced the concept of Jacqueline Bouvier as a CIA agent. Some early and particularly vocal supporters who deserve special thanks are Klaus Braemer, Tom King, Ellen Gordesky, Ibi Nathans, Seth Barsky, Dr. David Mitnick, Lisa Mitnick, and the rest of the Mitnick clan (you know who you are). I'm also especially grateful for the kindness I received from Monica Cataluna-Shand, Teanna McDonald, and Sally Grant of the National Association of Women Business Owners and from Evelyn Benson, Gonny Van Den Broek, Jonathan Rose, Lynn MacKinnon, Norma Chew, and Dorothy White of the South

Florida Writers Association. NBC Miami's Trina Robinson has to be the best television host *ever* when it comes to promoting an author's work.

Edward Klein's *All Too Human* and William H.A. Carr's *Those Fabulous Kennedy Women* were valuable resources for the budding romance between Jacqueline Bouvier and Jack Kennedy. I'm also grateful for a wealth of information on Fidel Castro and Fulgencio Batista provided by T. J. English's *Havana Nocturne*.

As a Floridian, I want to thank Little Havana in Miami for giving me a taste of life in its namesake city, particularly the best mojitos this side of Cuba at the landmark Versailles restaurant.

For three decades now, my husband, Larry Mitnick, has offered love and encouragement unstintingly, including footing the bill for the debut novel's gala launch party (no greater love hath any lady author's husband). My heart and thanks go out to my daughters, Ilene Schnall and Rona Schnall, who suffered with me through the early years of my journey and have been so supportive throughout. I love you more than I can say.

—Maxine Schnall

Jackie's first mission in the City
of Lights will test her strength,
her smarts, *and* her heart.

PARIS TO DIE FOR

Please turn this page for an excerpt.

1

Paris, May 8, 1951

Jacqueline Lee Bouvier wasn't exactly dressed for discovering a corpse. A black Givenchy evening ensemble was no substitute for a white lab coat or whatever those people who examined dead bodies were supposed to wear. Nor was she dressed appropriately for this place—a cramped garret in a rundown apartment building in one of Paris's less fashionable arrondissements.

Jackie found to her surprise that she could handle stumbling over the dead man on the floor of the garret, even though this was the very first corpse she had ever encountered.

She could handle it when she saw the obscenely gaping wound in his chest with the blood still dripping down, although the sight of blood, even in films, usually made her sick.

She could even handle it when she watched as a scrawny rat scurried across the scarred wooden floor and tentatively began to taste the blood that had pooled beside the corpse's torso.

What she couldn't handle was the "dead" man reaching out with his hand to grab her by the ankle.

Jackie jerked her knee up—a knee-jerk reaction if ever there was one—to get away from the apparently not-so-lifeless hand, trying to stifle the scream that was fast rising up in her throat, and asked herself what she, *une fille américaine*, was doing here. Born to wealth and privilege, crowned Queen Deb of the Year when she was presented to society at eighteen, schooled at Vassar and the Sorbonne, and recently graduated from George Washington University with a degree in French literature, how on earth had she wound up in this improbable apartment, babysitting a corpse?

Why, just twenty-four hours ago, she had been dining with this same dead man, the Russian, Petrov, at Maxim's. Of course, he hadn't been dead at the time.

And just twelve hours before that, she had been cocooned in the plush belly of a four-propeller Lockheed Constellation, curled up with a good book while flying across the Atlantic from National Airport to Le Bourget in Paris on her way to meet the Russian.

And just twelve hours before that, she had been at a party at her parents' estate in a suburb of Washington, D.C., where a chance encounter with a family friend, Allen Dulles, had set these events in motion like a rogue gene or a wayward train barreling toward an unforeseeable destination. But Jackie was forced to put all thoughts of this surreal chain of circumstances out of her head as she jumped back several steps to avoid the dead man's hand.

The Russian convulsed on the floor, and his hand opened spasmodically. Something fell out and floated across the floor to her. She leaned down to pick it up, mindful to keep a safe distance.

She looked fleetingly at what she had retrieved. It was a single ticket for the opera. She stuffed the ticket in her evening bag, then looked once more at the Russian. This time, he appeared to be well and truly dead, lifeless as the end of time. The convulsions had stopped, and he lay still. She could detect no rising and falling of his chest. She knew that she should do something. Listen for a pulse. Hold a mirror over his mouth and check it for condensation. But somehow, she couldn't bring herself to do any of those things. The fey thought nibbled at the edges of her mind that Death might be something contagious, and if she weren't careful, she could catch it too.

Incongruously, an old line from Oscar Wilde came to her: "Dying in Paris is a terribly expensive business for a foreigner."

For the first time, Jackie became aware of her surroundings. She had discovered the corpse almost as soon as she entered the garret. Now, looking around, she took in the room's few furnishings. A bed with an iron bedstead and a sagging mattress. A threadbare Algerian rug on the floor, its rucked-up condition showing that a struggle had definitely taken place here. A wooden chair and desk, both heavily pockmarked and worn with age. In the two open windows overlooking a cityscape of low rooftops, twin moth-eaten curtains fluttered in the breeze. From outside, a recording of Edith Piaf singing "La Vie en Rose" wafted through the steamy air of a Parisian summer night. The poignant music and the sultry night air created an alluring mood. And if it hadn't been for the corpse on the floor, Jackie could have seen the romantic possibilities of even such an impoverished garret. She could imagine Rodolfo and Mimi and their bohemian friends feeling right at home in this seedily seductive attic setting.

The room was illuminated by a single bare lightbulb set in an uncovered fixture in the low-hanging ceiling. The light from the lone bulb was dim, but not so dim that she couldn't see it shining off the tips of a pair of men's shoes peeking out from the bottom of the hanging sheet that served as a closet. And when one of those shoes moved ever so slightly, she knew, with a chill that froze her breath, that she was not alone in the garret.

Suddenly, the shock-induced aplomb that had carried her along like a robot until now shattered, and her numbed senses jangled alive. Every nerve in Jackie's body screamed for her feet to make for the exit. But that closet stood between Jackie and the door leading to the hallway. She was afraid of being seized as soon as she attempted to move past it. There was no other way out of the garret except through the window. But she was saving that as a last resort.

The only thing left was to stay and defend herself against an almost certain assault. But she wasn't armed. Dulles hadn't allowed for that eventuality. So Jackie looked around the room and inventoried it as quickly as possible. She saw nothing obvious that she could use as a weapon. No lamp. No heavy ashtray. Even the modest kitchenette looked bare of utensils. Where was a steak knife or a meat cleaver when you really needed one? Not that she had any expectation she could ever use one to defend herself. That kind of self-defense had not been part of her finishing-school education.

And then a lightning flash of inspiration struck, divinely, and she realized there was something in her evening bag that she could use as a weapon. Not for killing certainly, but for causing a distraction. She flicked open the clip on her beaded evening bag with her French-manicured thumbnail and fumbled around until she found what she was searching for.

With one hand in her bag and the other left free, palms sweating and her heart thumping insanely in her chest, Jackie approached the sheet-covered closet. It was only a few steps, but it felt like the longest journey of her life. With the warped floorboards creaking shrilly with each movement of her feet, there was no chance of her sneaking up on whoever was hiding in the closet. But Jackie came from a long line of storied military heroes—it was well-known among her relatives that twenty-four of her ancestors came over to America from France to fight in the Revolutionary War. As a young girl growing up in a household with a proud history, she listened in on many fascinating accounts of relatives' exploits on the battlefield. And she knew that a good general didn't wait to be attacked, but always took the attack to the enemy.

Arriving at the closet, Jackie took a deep, deep breath and flung back the sheet. A beefy, sinister-looking man was standing there inside the empty closet, and it was difficult to judge which of them was more surprised. The man recovered first and abruptly brought up a wicked-looking knife. It gave off a deadly gleam, even in this dim light.

As the knife began its swift downward plunge toward Jackie's chest, she grasped the object of her search in her handbag and held it up in front of him. She dropped her purse so she could squeeze the bulb, and the atomizer jetted a pungent spray of Chanel No. 5 smack into his face. The man screamed, pawing at his burning eyeballs, and was forced to drop the knife.

Jackie kicked the weapon across the room—it skidded under the bed—and tried to make it to the door. But the man reached out blindly, caught her by the arm, and flung her back across the cramped room. Fortunately, Jackie landed on the sagging mattress, and it broke her fall. With no other way out, she knew she had no choice but to go with the dead Russian's original plan.

She levered herself off the bed, then quick-stepped over to the nearest window and went through it, first one leg over the sill, then the other, cursing Givenchy for making this season's skirts so tight. Holding on to the windowsill with both hands, she felt around below until her feet came in contact with the narrow ledge that, according to the Russian, would be there. Jackie looked down and saw that it was six dizzying stories to the courtyard below. The Russian said to follow the ledge around the building and escape to the roof of a neighboring building in the next *rue*. As forbidding as it looked, she would take this dangerous route to avoid the killer, who looked much too big to follow her onto the ledge. Before moving any farther, she kicked off her shoes—there was no way she could negotiate this narrow ledge in black satin peep-toe stiletto heels—and heard them land with a clatter in the courtyard below.

Just then, the ledge beneath her feet crumbled away, and she lost her grip on the windowsill. So much for the Russian's plan. Jackie could feel herself falling and closed her eyes, her panic mercifully turning into stoicism. She braced herself, hoping that the impact wouldn't hurt too much or make a grisly mess in the courtyard.

Something unexpectedly arrested her fall. She opened her eyes, looked up, and saw that the man, blinking rapidly from the sting of the perfume spray, was gripping her by her right hand. He had the iron clasp of a catcher in a trapeze act, and it was this steadfast grip that had saved her life. Jackie's body swung like a pendulum from her one outstretched arm. But she was wearing silk evening gloves. Her hand began to slip ever so slowly but inexorably out of its glove, and she knew that her salvation was only temporary. *This is what happens when you're a slave to fashion,* she told herself as she felt her hand slip even farther.

As she dangled six stories above the courtyard, alone except for a dead body in the room above her and a killer providing a lifeline just so he could do her in himself, Jacqueline Lee Bouvier asked herself, *For God's sake, how did I get into this mess?*